THE
BABY-SITTERS CLUB

LOGAN LIKES MARY ANNE!

DON'T MISS THE OTHER
BABY-SITTERS CLUB GRAPHIC NOVELS!

KRISTY'S GREAT IDEA

THE TRUTH ABOUT STACEY

MARY ANNE SAVES THE DAY

CLAUDIA AND MEAN JANINE

DAWN AND THE IMPOSSIBLE THREE

KRISTY'S BIG DAY

BOY-CRAZY STACEY

ANN M. MARTIN

THE BABY-SITTERS CLUB

LOGAN LIKES MARY ANNE!

A GRAPHIC NOVEL BY

GALE GALLIGAN

WITH COLOR BY BRADEN LAMB

An Imprint of
■SCHOLASTIC

Library of Congress Control Number: 2019950319

ISBN 978-1-338-30455-8 (hardcover)
ISBN 978-1-338-30454-1 (paperback)

10 9 8 7 6 5 4 3 2 1   20 21 22 23 24

Printed in the U.S.A.   40
First edition, September 2020

Color assistants: Shelli Paroline, Sam Bennett,
Alenna Smith Boeker, and Jase Dale Boeker.

Edited by Cassandra Pelham Fulton and David Levithan
Book design by Phil Falco
Publisher: David Saylor

This book is for my old
baby-sitters, Maura and Peggy
A. M. M.

For Patrick, and the full minute we spent
laughing at a weird face Dipper made.

And for you! I'm so glad we got
to spend this time together.
G. G.

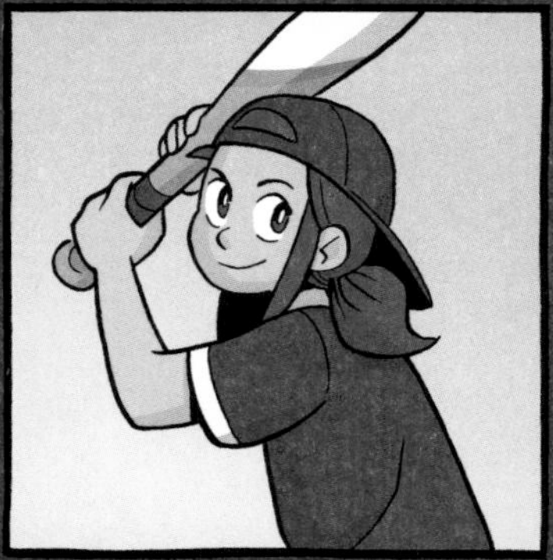

KRISTY THOMAS
PRESIDENT

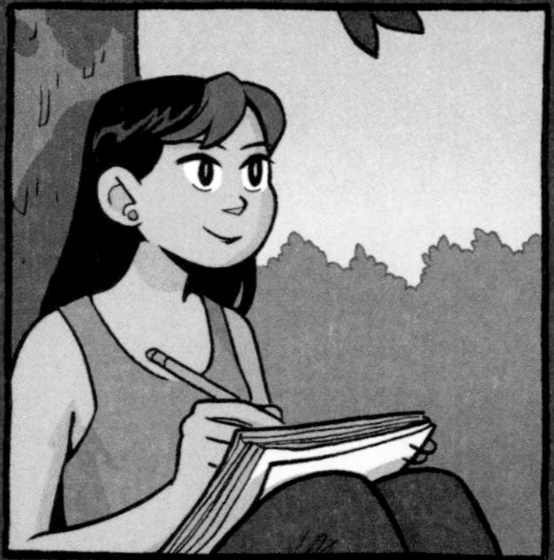

CLAUDIA KISHI
VICE PRESIDENT

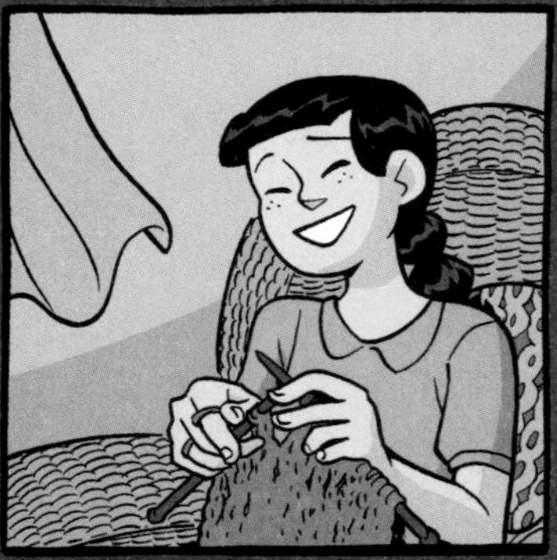

MARY ANNE SPIER
SECRETARY

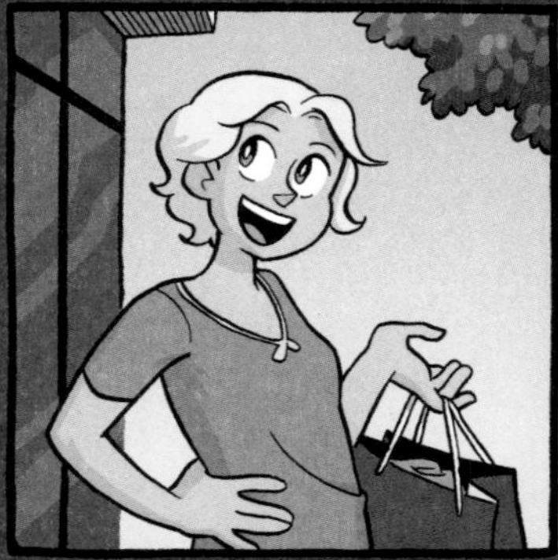

STACEY MCGILL
TREASURER

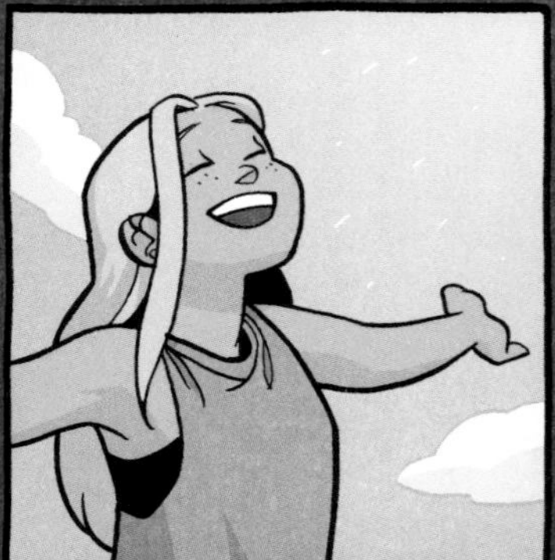

DAWN SCHAFER
ALTERNATE OFFICER

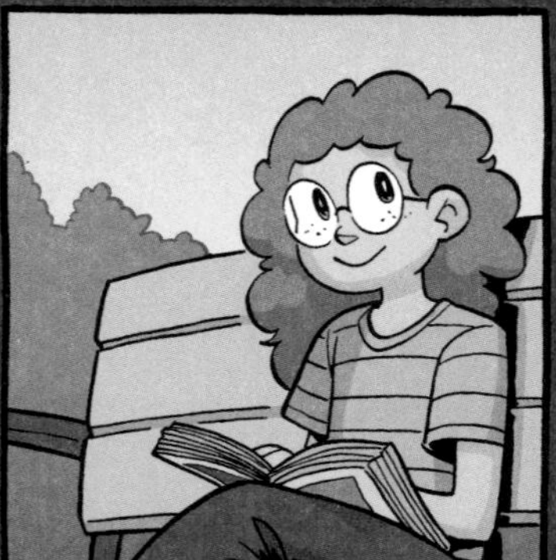

MALLORY PIKE
JUNIOR OFFICER

CHAPTER 1

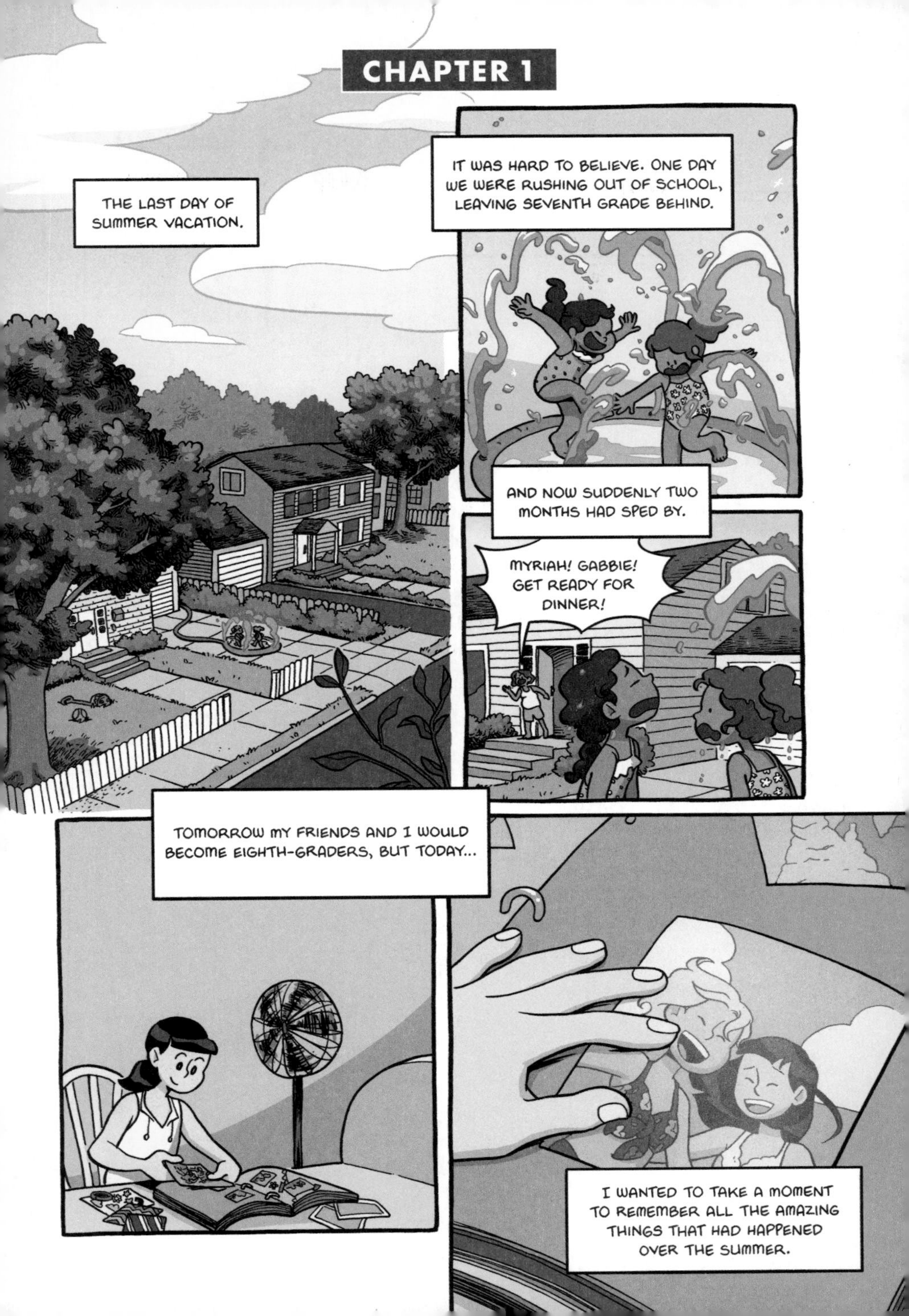
THE LAST DAY OF SUMMER VACATION.
IT WAS HARD TO BELIEVE. ONE DAY WE WERE RUSHING OUT OF SCHOOL, LEAVING SEVENTH GRADE BEHIND.
AND NOW SUDDENLY TWO MONTHS HAD SPED BY.
MYRIAH! GABBIE! GET READY FOR DINNER!
TOMORROW MY FRIENDS AND I WOULD BECOME EIGHTH-GRADERS, BUT TODAY...
I WANTED TO TAKE A MOMENT TO REMEMBER ALL THE AMAZING THINGS THAT HAD HAPPENED OVER THE SUMMER.

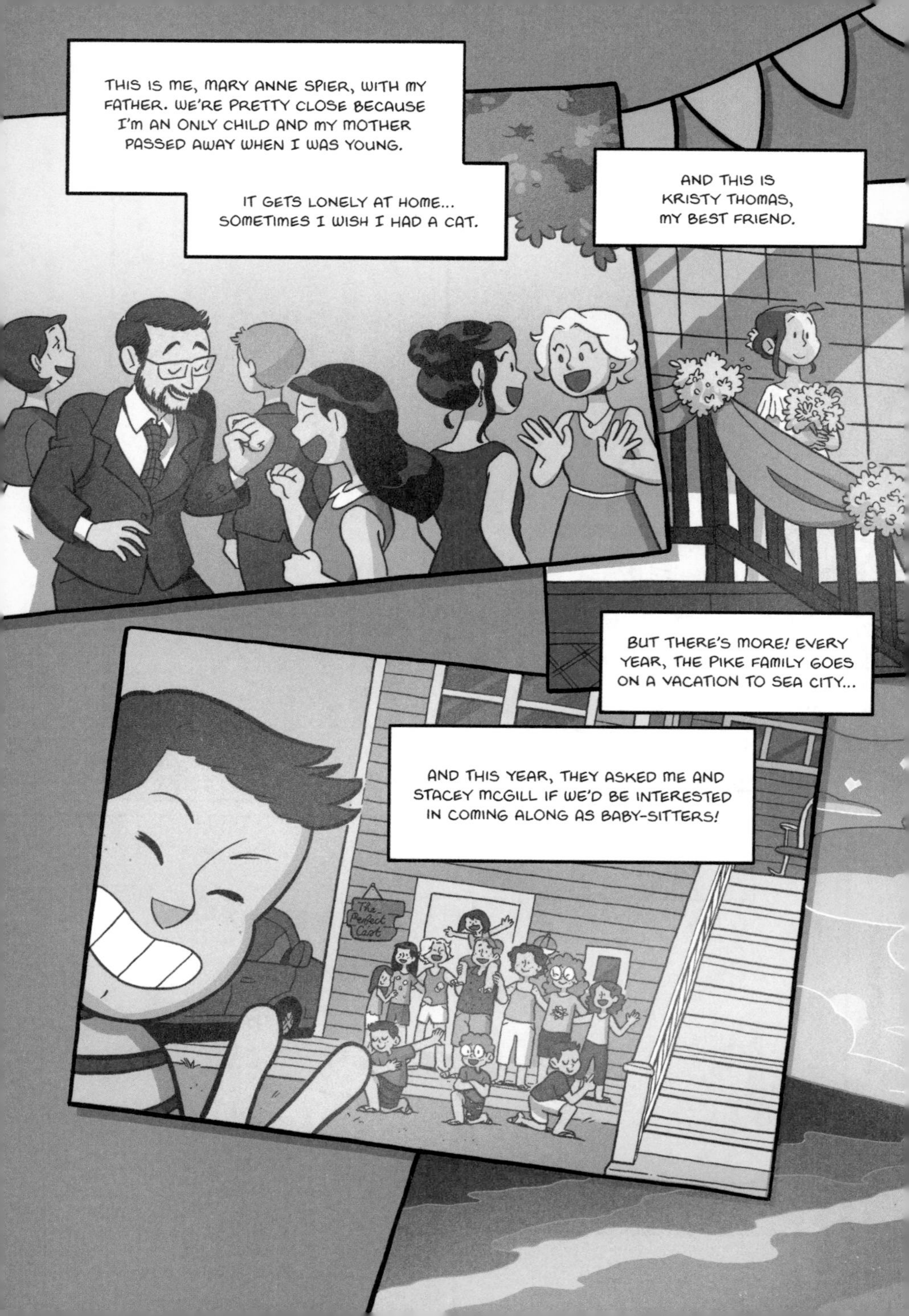
THIS IS ME, MARY ANNE SPIER, WITH MY FATHER. WE'RE PRETTY CLOSE BECAUSE I'M AN ONLY CHILD AND MY MOTHER PASSED AWAY WHEN I WAS YOUNG.
IT GETS LONELY AT HOME... SOMETIMES I WISH I HAD A CAT.
AND THIS IS KRISTY THOMAS, MY BEST FRIEND.
BUT THERE'S MORE! EVERY YEAR, THE PIKE FAMILY GOES ON A VACATION TO SEA CITY...
AND THIS YEAR, THEY ASKED ME AND STACEY MCGILL IF WE'D BE INTERESTED IN COMING ALONG AS BABY-SITTERS!
The Perfect Cast

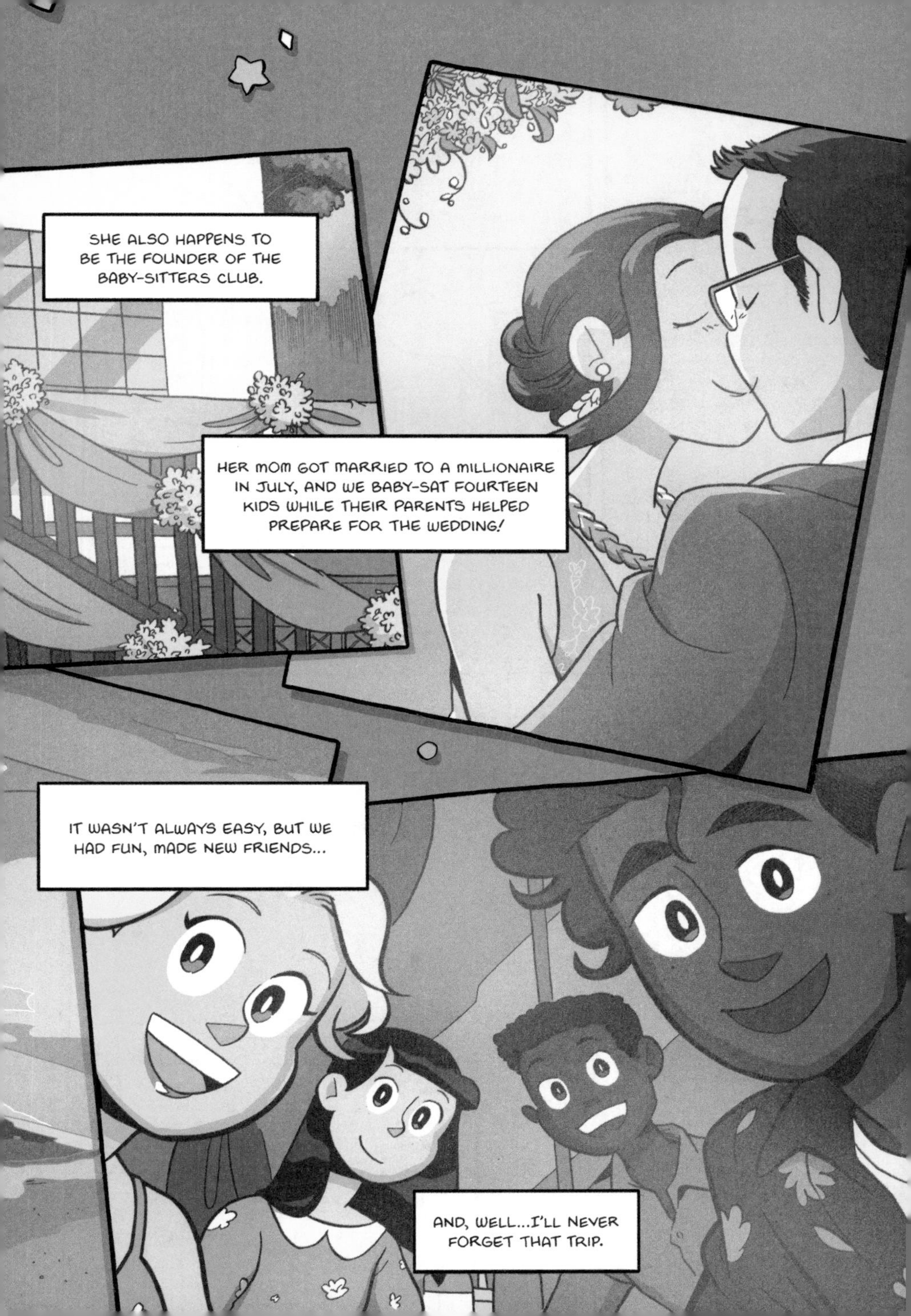
SHE ALSO HAPPENS TO BE THE FOUNDER OF THE BABY-SITTERS CLUB.
HER MOM GOT MARRIED TO A MILLIONAIRE IN JULY, AND WE BABY-SAT FOURTEEN KIDS WHILE THEIR PARENTS HELPED PREPARE FOR THE WEDDING!
IT WASN'T ALWAYS EASY, BUT WE HAD FUN, MADE NEW FRIENDS...
AND, WELL...I'LL NEVER FORGET THAT TRIP.

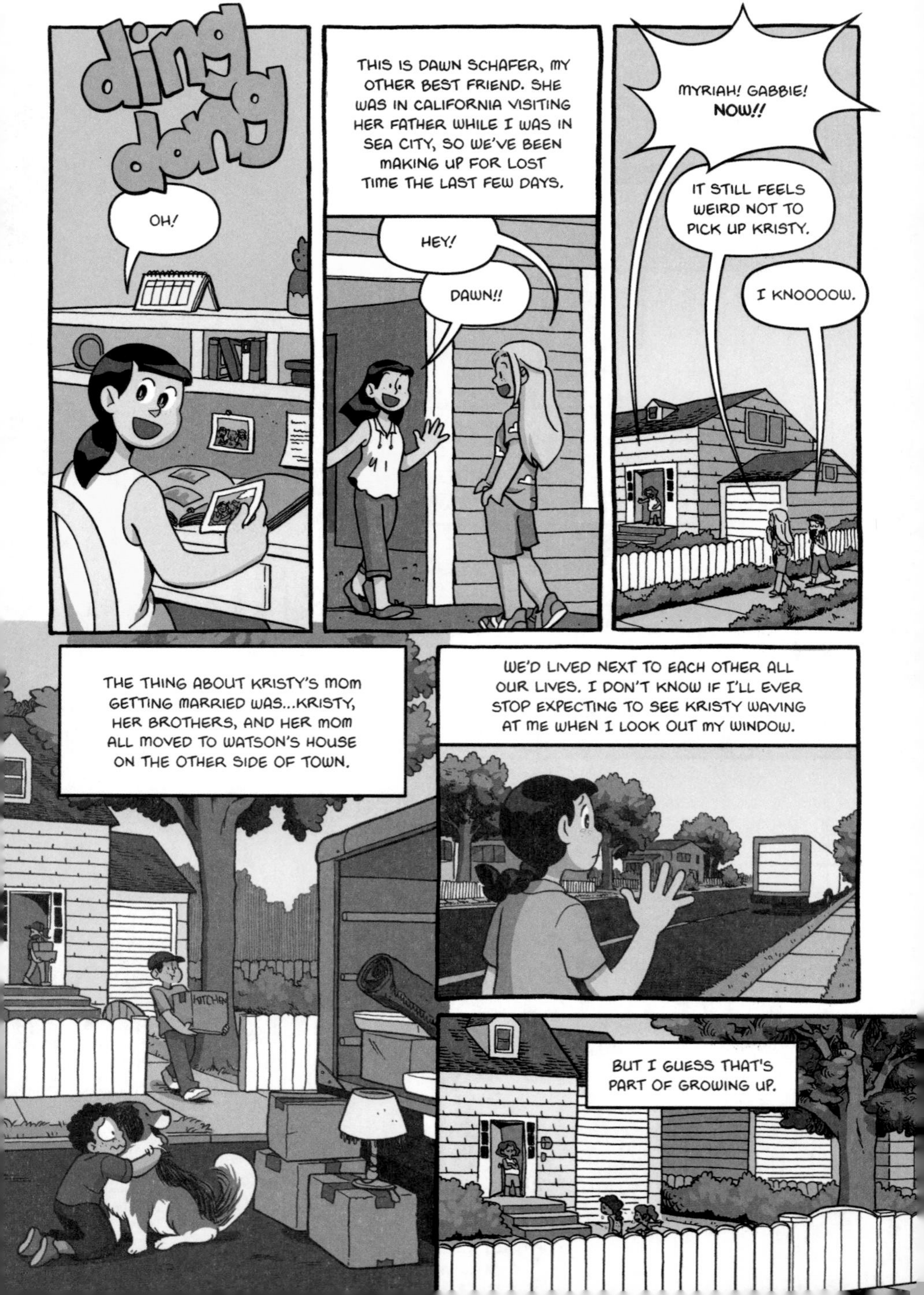
ding dong
OH!
THIS IS DAWN SCHAFER, MY OTHER BEST FRIEND. SHE WAS IN CALIFORNIA VISITING HER FATHER WHILE I WAS IN SEA CITY, SO WE'VE BEEN MAKING UP FOR LOST TIME THE LAST FEW DAYS.
HEY!
DAWN!!
MYRIAH! GABBIE! **NOW!!**
IT STILL FEELS WEIRD NOT TO PICK UP KRISTY.
I KNOOOOW.
THE THING ABOUT KRISTY'S MOM GETTING MARRIED WAS...KRISTY, HER BROTHERS, AND HER MOM ALL MOVED TO WATSON'S HOUSE ON THE OTHER SIDE OF TOWN.
KITCHEN
WE'D LIVED NEXT TO EACH OTHER ALL OUR LIVES. I DON'T KNOW IF I'LL EVER STOP EXPECTING TO SEE KRISTY WAVING AT ME WHEN I LOOK OUT MY WINDOW.
BUT I GUESS THAT'S PART OF GROWING UP.

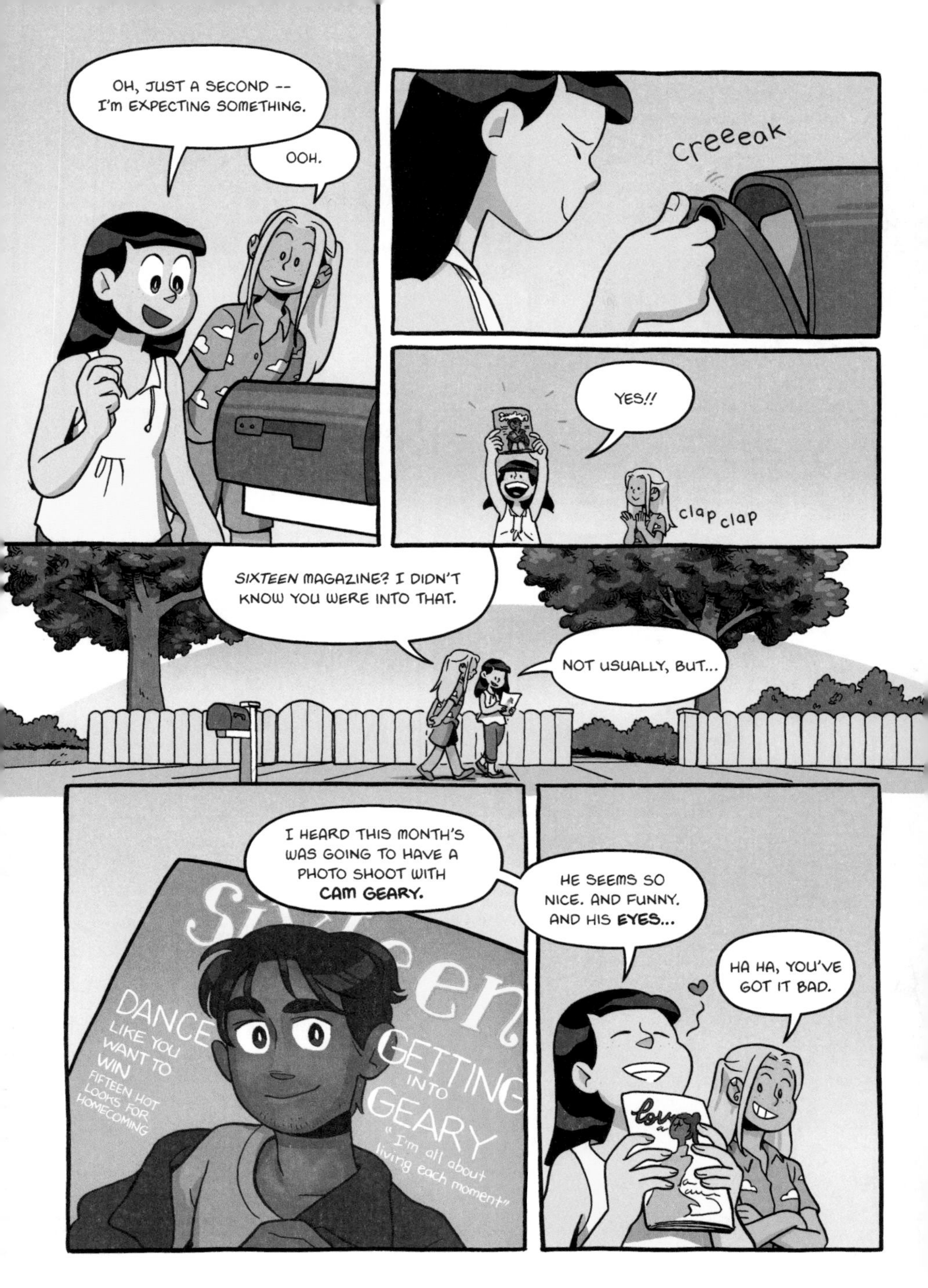

OH, JUST A SECOND -- I'M EXPECTING SOMETHING.
OOH.
creeeak
YES!!
clap clap
SIXTEEN MAGAZINE? I DIDN'T KNOW YOU WERE INTO THAT.
NOT USUALLY, BUT...
I HEARD THIS MONTH'S WAS GOING TO HAVE A PHOTO SHOOT WITH **CAM GEARY.**
DANCE LIKE YOU WANT TO WIN
FIFTEEN HOT LOOKS FOR HOMECOMING
GETTING INTO GEARY
"I'm all about living each moment"
HE SEEMS SO NICE. AND FUNNY. AND HIS **EYES...**
HA HA, YOU'VE GOT IT BAD.

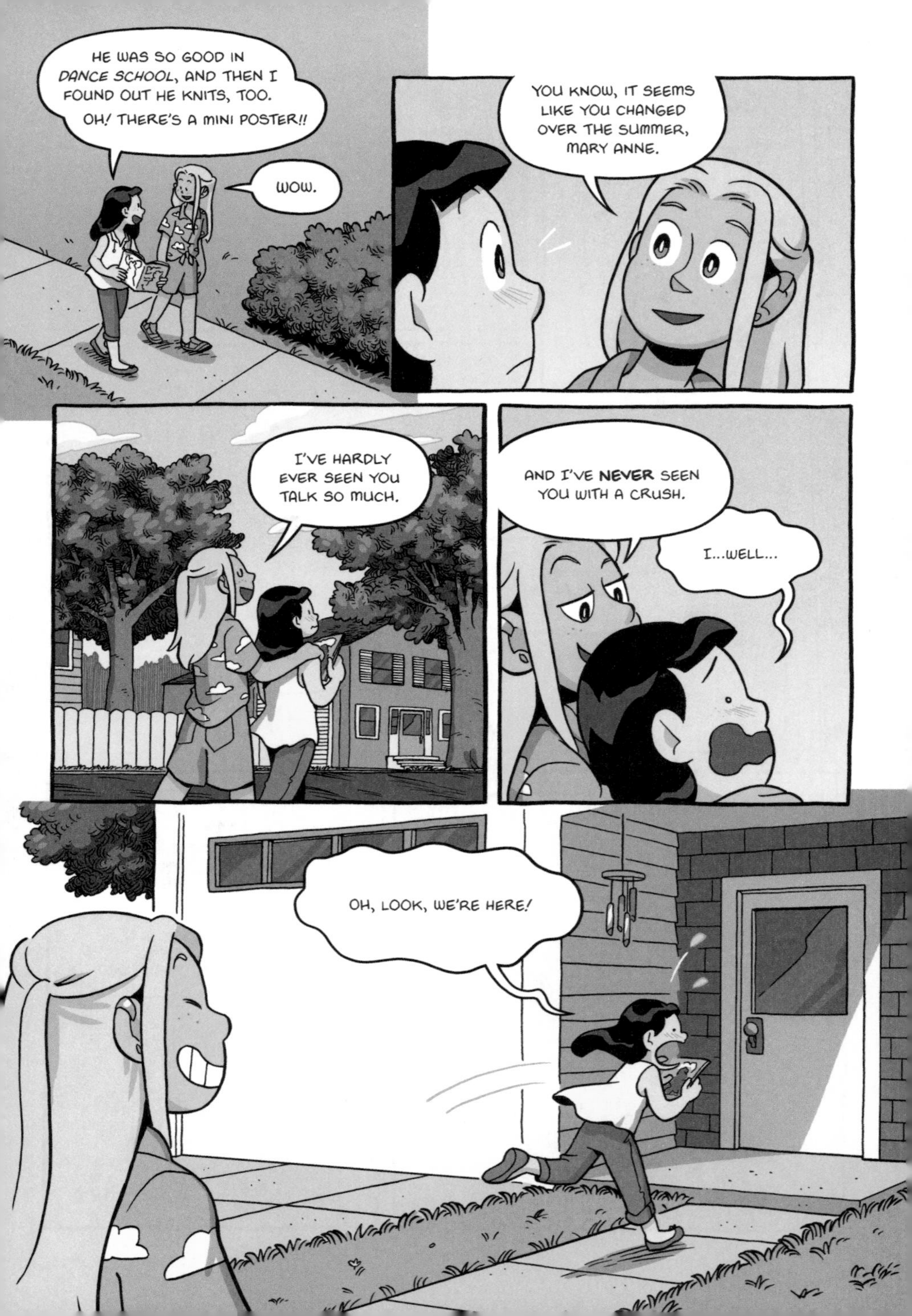
HE WAS SO GOOD IN *DANCE SCHOOL*, AND THEN I FOUND OUT HE KNITS, TOO.
OH! THERE'S A MINI POSTER!!
WOW.
YOU KNOW, IT SEEMS LIKE YOU CHANGED OVER THE SUMMER, MARY ANNE.
I'VE HARDLY EVER SEEN YOU TALK SO MUCH.
AND I'VE **NEVER** SEEN YOU WITH A CRUSH.
I...WELL...
OH, LOOK, WE'RE HERE!

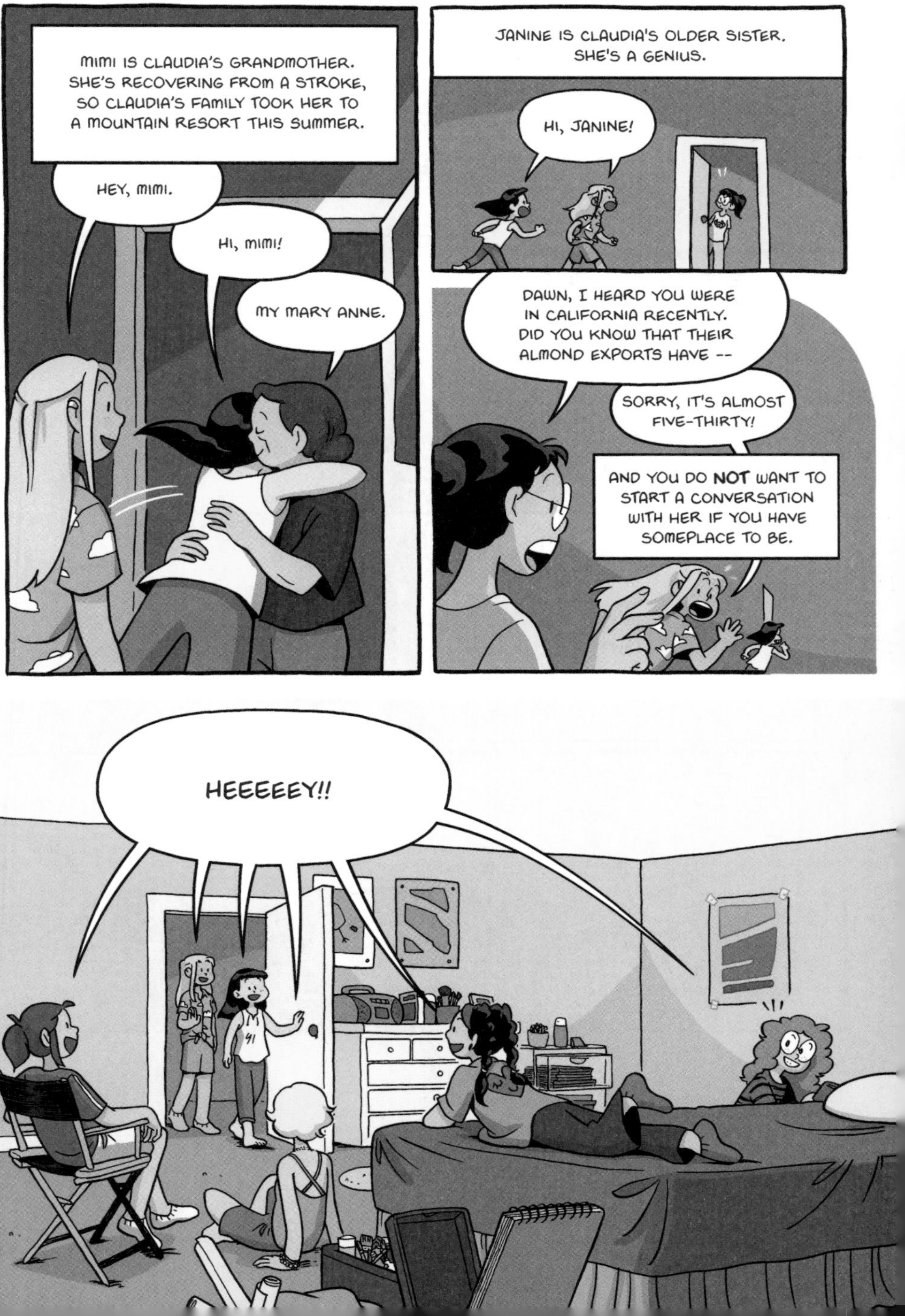
MIMI IS CLAUDIA'S GRANDMOTHER. SHE'S RECOVERING FROM A STROKE, SO CLAUDIA'S FAMILY TOOK HER TO A MOUNTAIN RESORT THIS SUMMER.
HEY, MIMI.
HI, MIMI!
MY MARY ANNE.
JANINE IS CLAUDIA'S OLDER SISTER. SHE'S A GENIUS.
HI, JANINE!
DAWN, I HEARD YOU WERE IN CALIFORNIA RECENTLY. DID YOU KNOW THAT THEIR ALMOND EXPORTS HAVE --
SORRY, IT'S ALMOST FIVE-THIRTY!
AND YOU DO **NOT** WANT TO START A CONVERSATION WITH HER IF YOU HAVE SOMEPLACE TO BE.
HEEEEEY!!

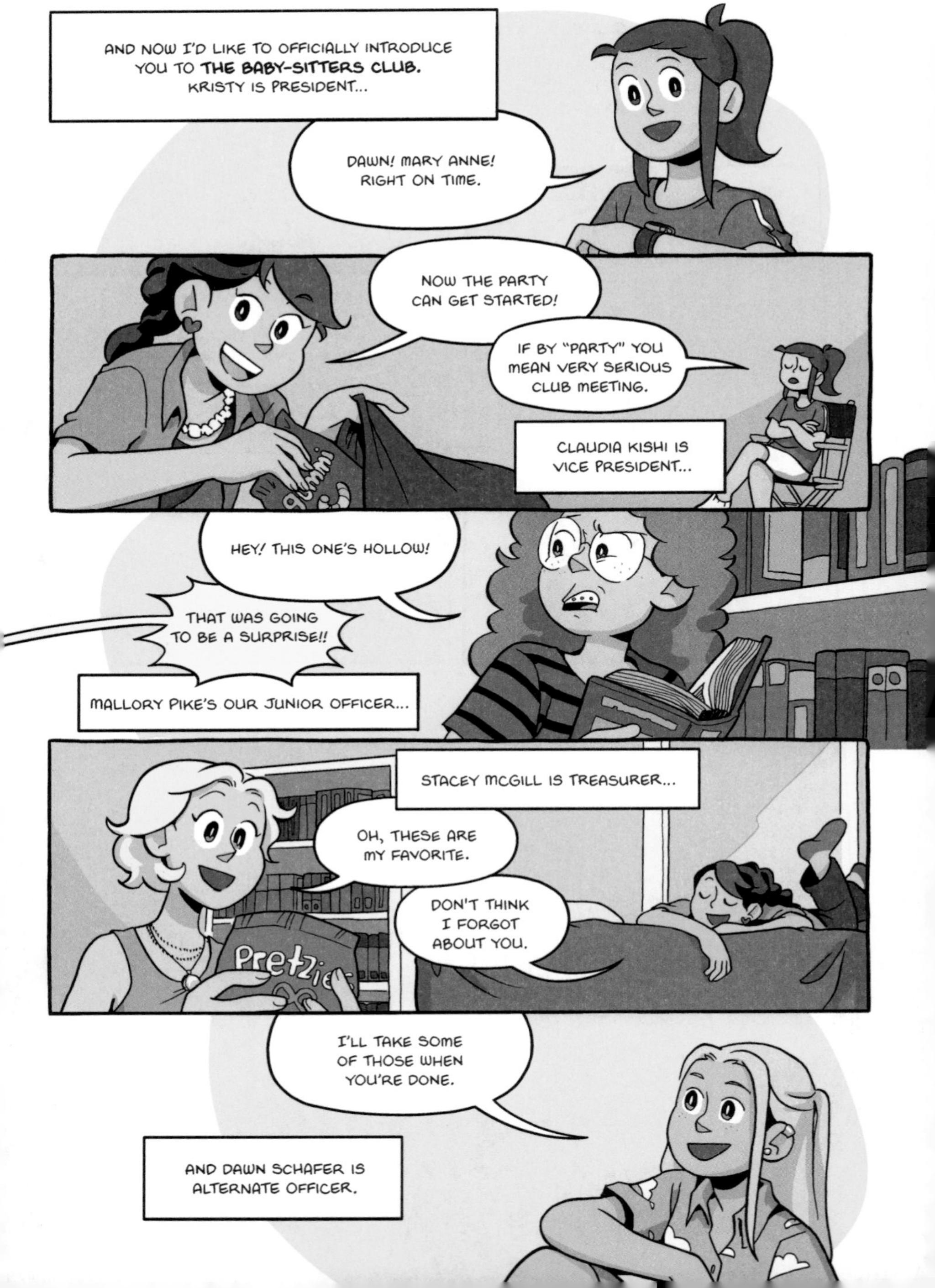
AND NOW I'D LIKE TO OFFICIALLY INTRODUCE YOU TO **THE BABY-SITTERS CLUB.** KRISTY IS PRESIDENT...
DAWN! MARY ANNE! RIGHT ON TIME.
NOW THE PARTY CAN GET STARTED!
IF BY "PARTY" YOU MEAN VERY SERIOUS CLUB MEETING.
CLAUDIA KISHI IS VICE PRESIDENT...
gummi
HEY! THIS ONE'S HOLLOW!
THAT WAS GOING TO BE A SURPRISE!!
MALLORY PIKE'S OUR JUNIOR OFFICER...
STACEY MCGILL IS TREASURER...
OH, THESE ARE MY FAVORITE.
Pretzie
DON'T THINK I FORGOT ABOUT YOU.
I'LL TAKE SOME OF THOSE WHEN YOU'RE DONE.
AND DAWN SCHAFER IS ALTERNATE OFFICER.

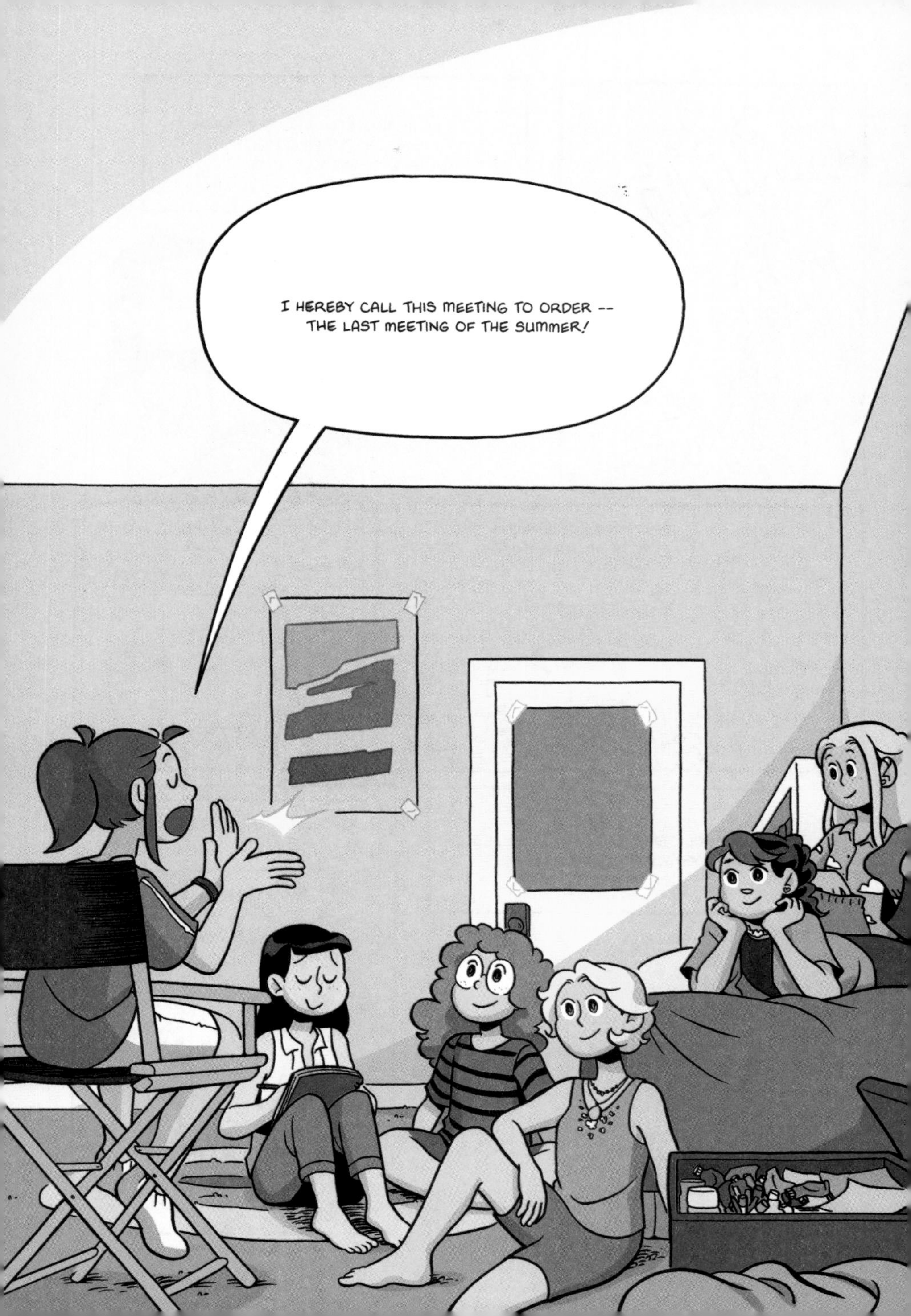
I HEREBY CALL THIS MEETING TO ORDER -- THE LAST MEETING OF THE SUMMER!

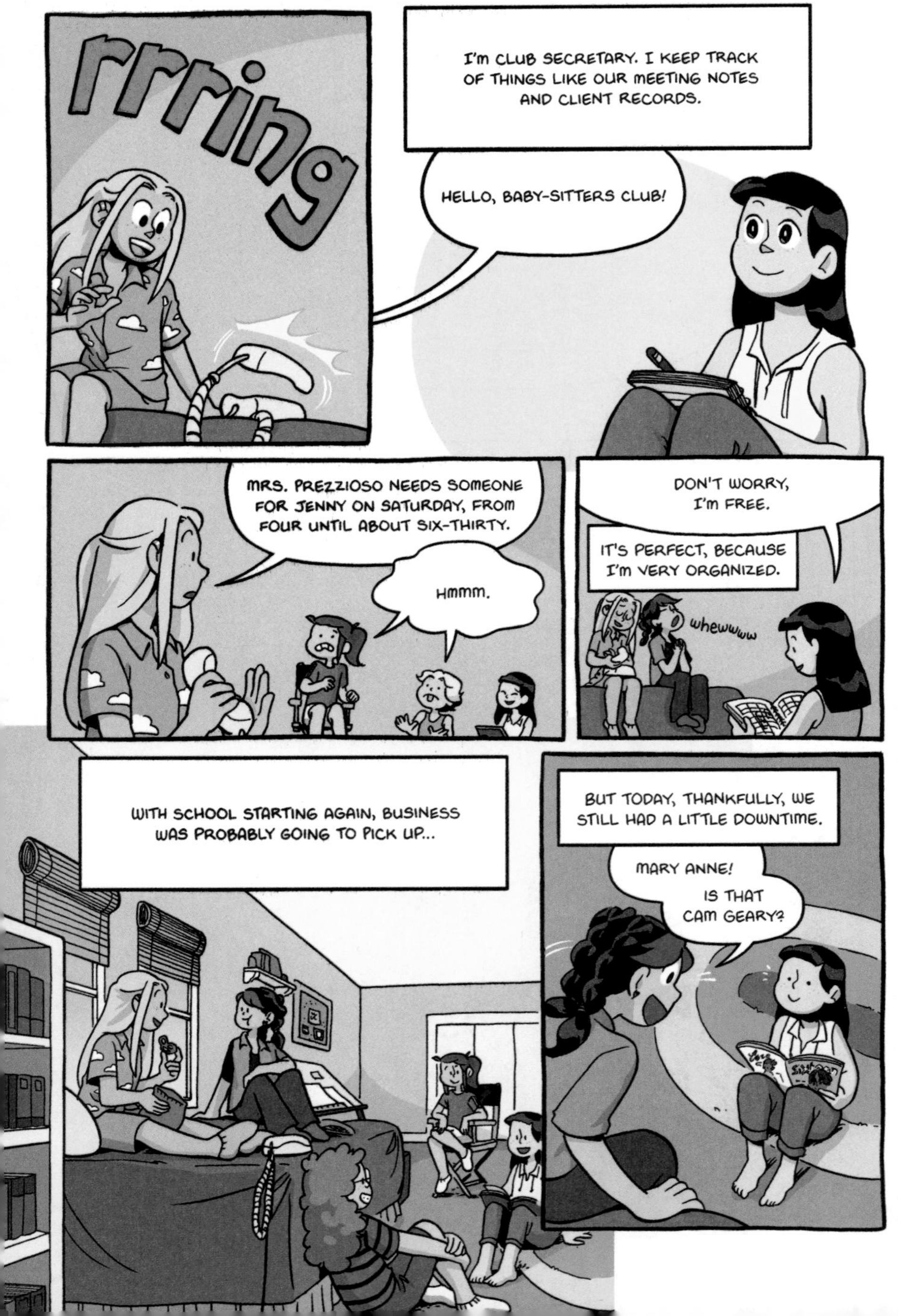
rrring
I'M CLUB SECRETARY. I KEEP TRACK OF THINGS LIKE OUR MEETING NOTES AND CLIENT RECORDS.
HELLO, BABY-SITTERS CLUB!
MRS. PREZZIOSO NEEDS SOMEONE FOR JENNY ON SATURDAY, FROM FOUR UNTIL ABOUT SIX-THIRTY.
Hmmm.
DON'T WORRY, I'M FREE.
IT'S PERFECT, BECAUSE I'M VERY ORGANIZED.
whewwww
WITH SCHOOL STARTING AGAIN, BUSINESS WAS PROBABLY GOING TO PICK UP...
BUT TODAY, THANKFULLY, WE STILL HAD A LITTLE DOWNTIME.
MARY ANNE!
IS THAT CAM GEARY?

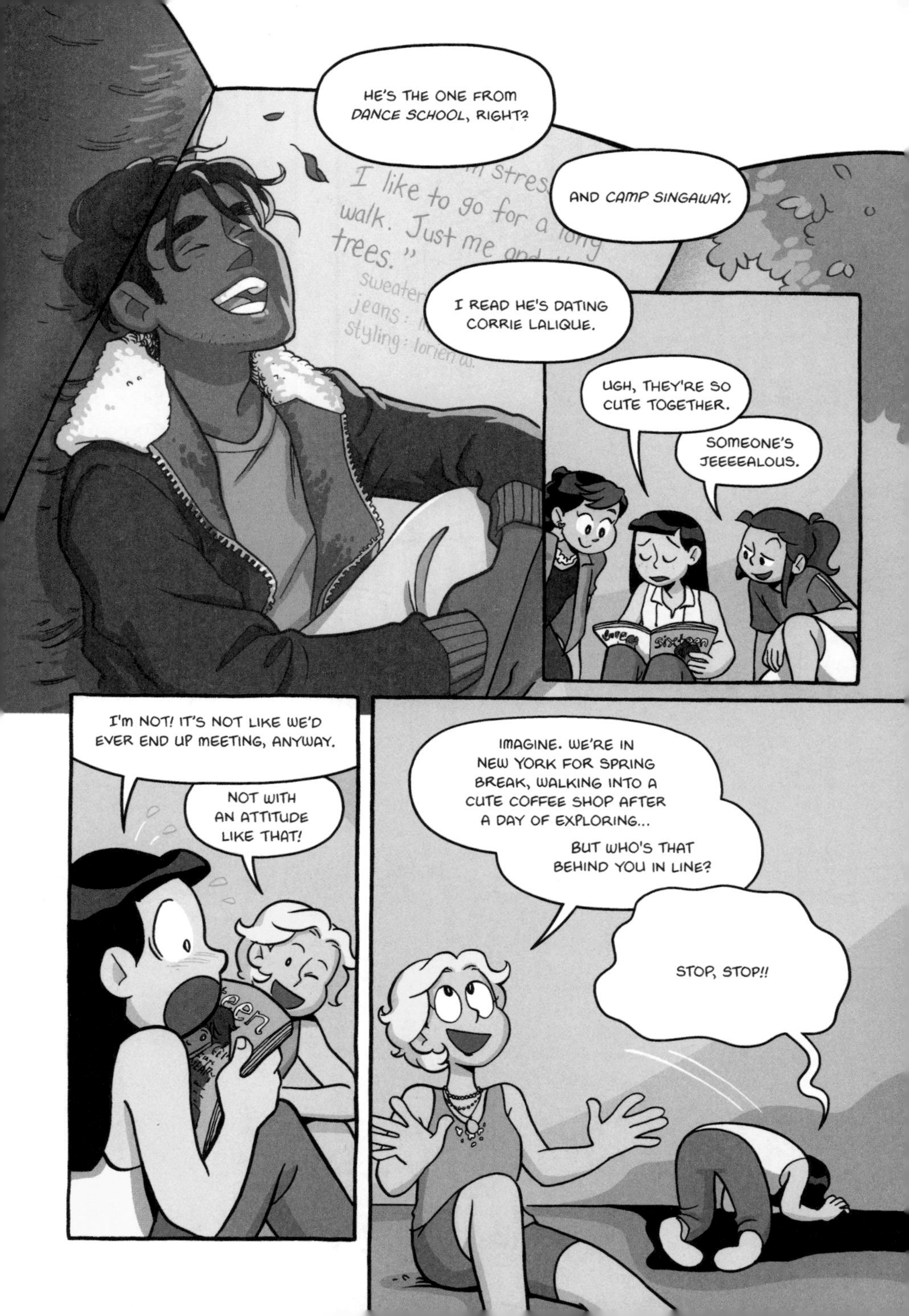

HE'S THE ONE FROM DANCE SCHOOL, RIGHT?
AND CAMP SINGAWAY.
I READ HE'S DATING CORRIE LALIQUE.
UGH, THEY'RE SO CUTE TOGETHER.
SOMEONE'S JEEEEALOUS.
I'M NOT! IT'S NOT LIKE WE'D EVER END UP MEETING, ANYWAY.
NOT WITH AN ATTITUDE LIKE THAT!
IMAGINE. WE'RE IN NEW YORK FOR SPRING BREAK, WALKING INTO A CUTE COFFEE SHOP AFTER A DAY OF EXPLORING...
BUT WHO'S THAT BEHIND YOU IN LINE?
STOP, STOP!!

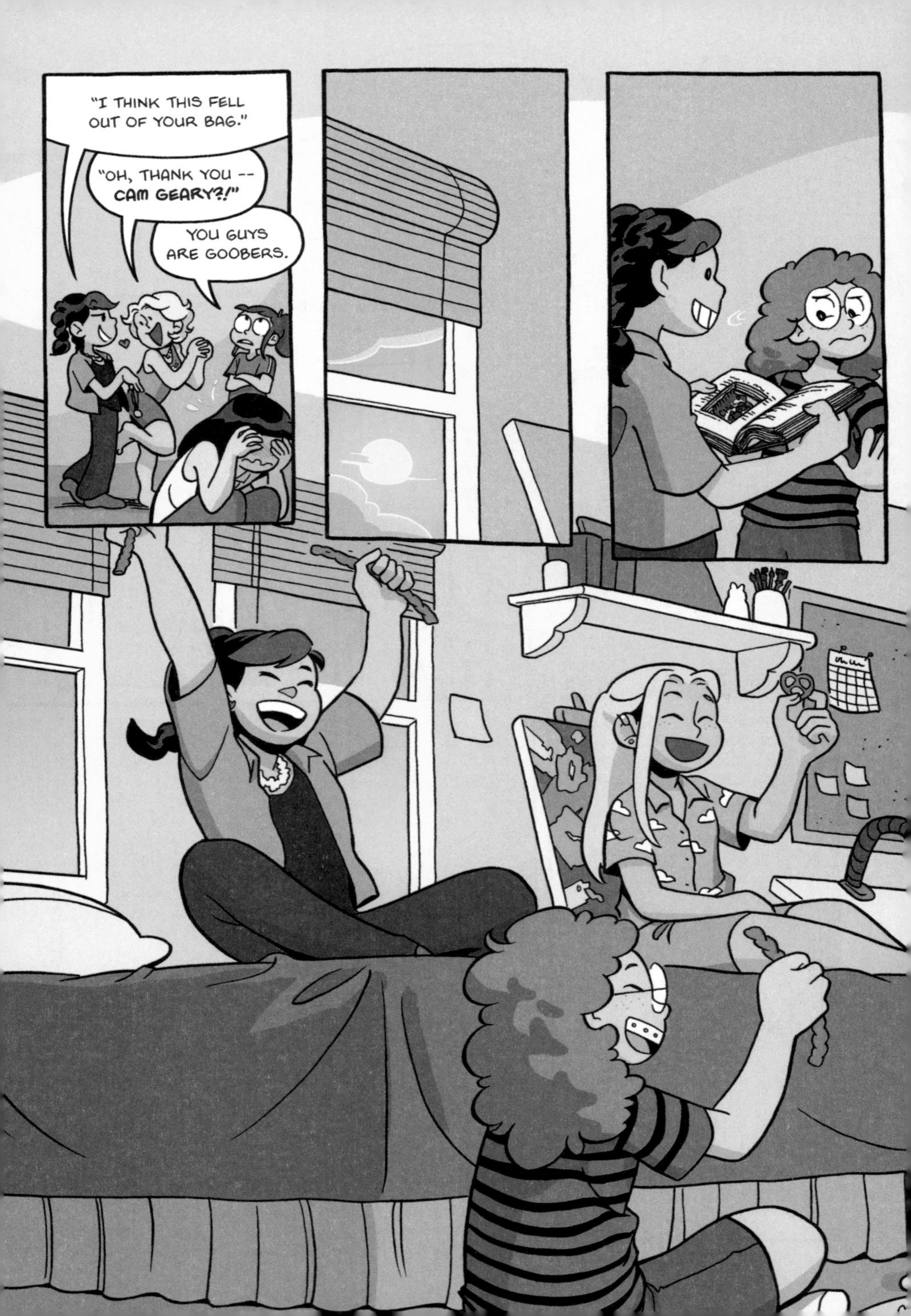
"I THINK THIS FELL OUT OF YOUR BAG."
"OH, THANK YOU -- **CAM GEARY?!**"
YOU GUYS ARE GOOBERS.

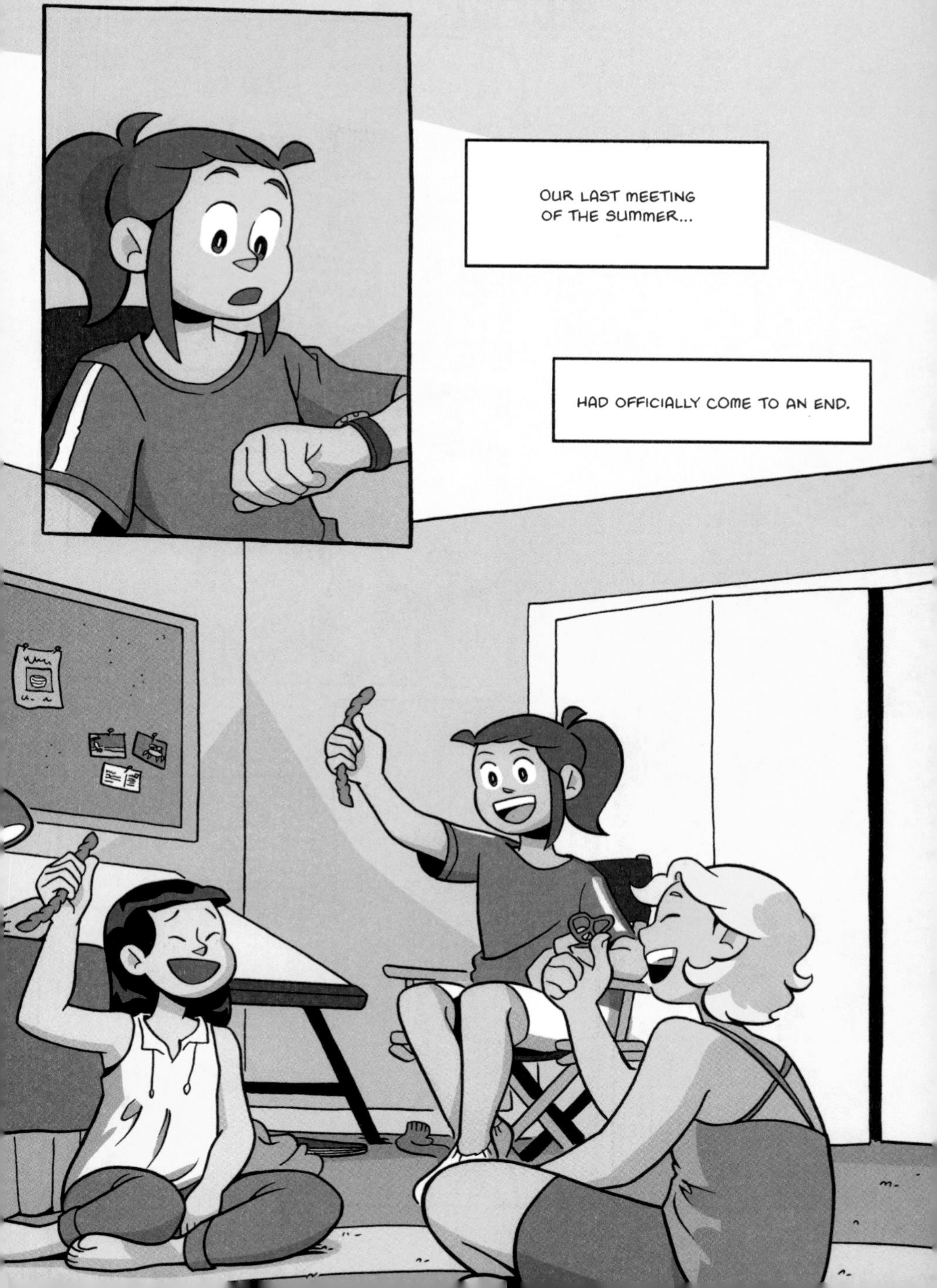
OUR LAST MEETING OF THE SUMMER...
HAD OFFICIALLY COME TO AN END.

CHAPTER 2

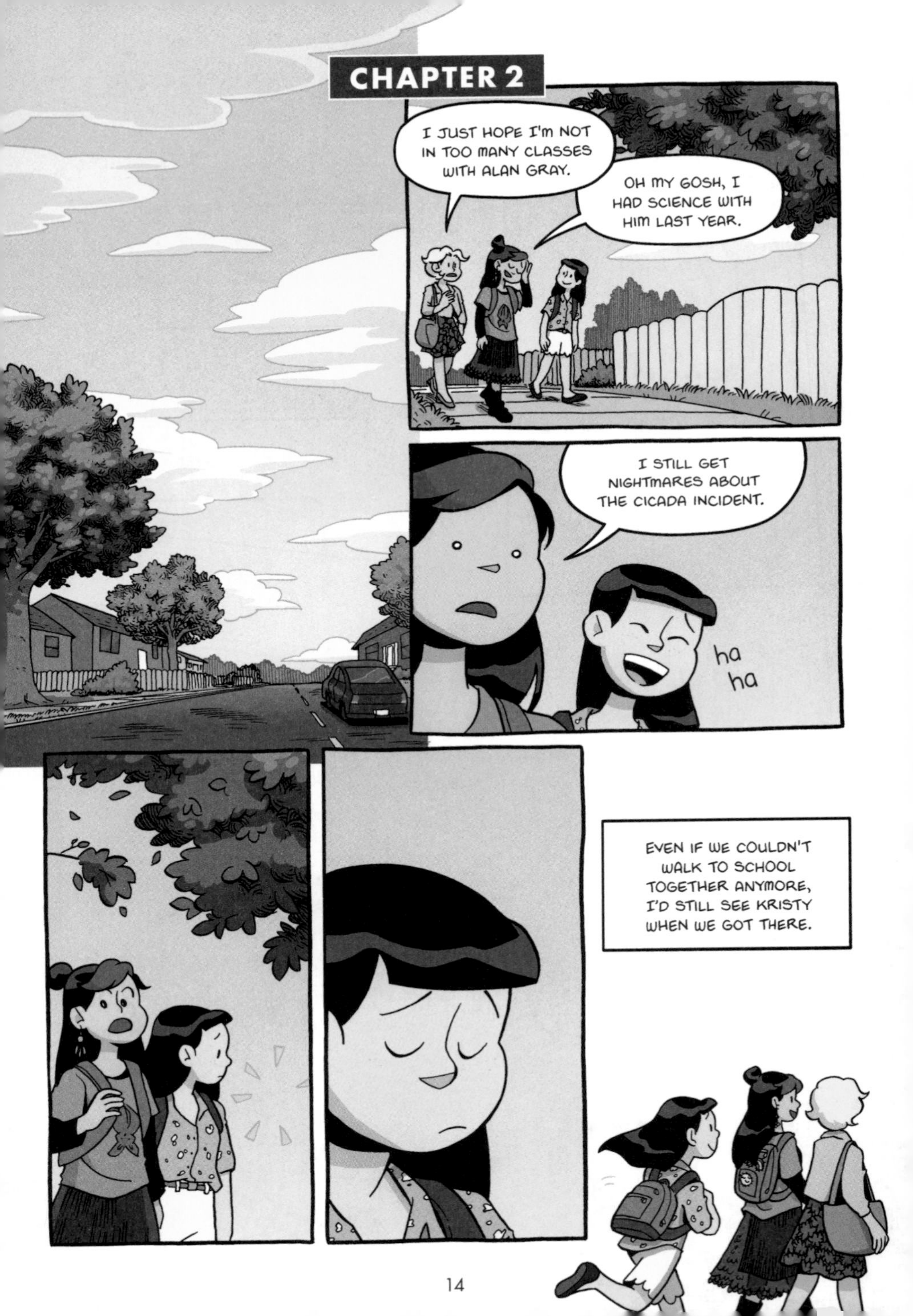
I JUST HOPE I'm NOT IN TOO MANY CLASSES WITH ALAN GRAY.
OH MY GOSH, I HAD SCIENCE WITH HIM LAST YEAR.
I STILL GET NIGHTMARES ABOUT THE CICADA INCIDENT.
ha ha
EVEN IF WE COULDN'T WALK TO SCHOOL TOGETHER ANYMORE, I'D STILL SEE KRISTY WHEN WE GOT THERE.

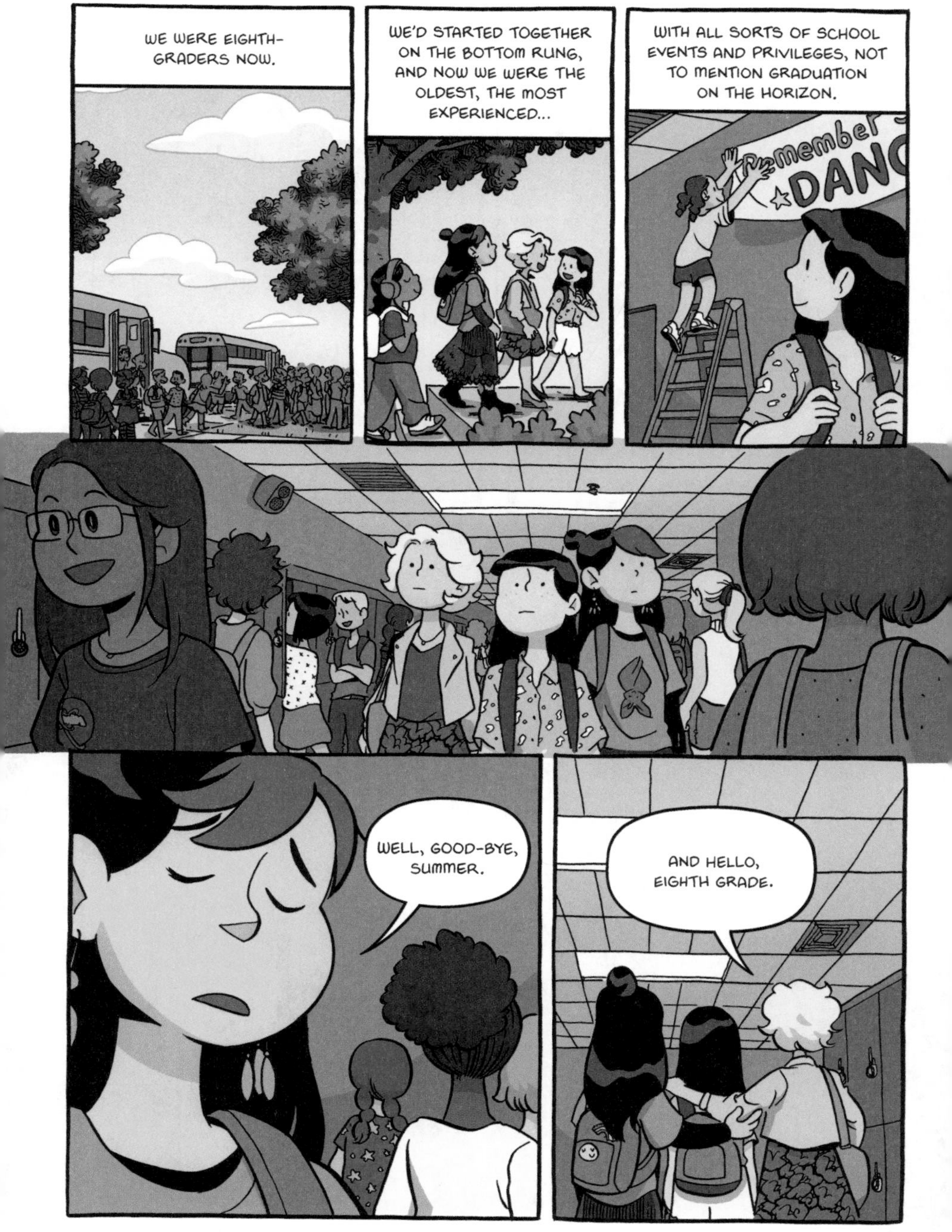
WE WERE EIGHTH-GRADERS NOW.
WE'D STARTED TOGETHER ON THE BOTTOM RUNG, AND NOW WE WERE THE OLDEST, THE MOST EXPERIENCED...
WITH ALL SORTS OF SCHOOL EVENTS AND PRIVILEGES, NOT TO MENTION GRADUATION ON THE HORIZON.
WELL, GOOD-BYE, SUMMER.
AND HELLO, EIGHTH GRADE.

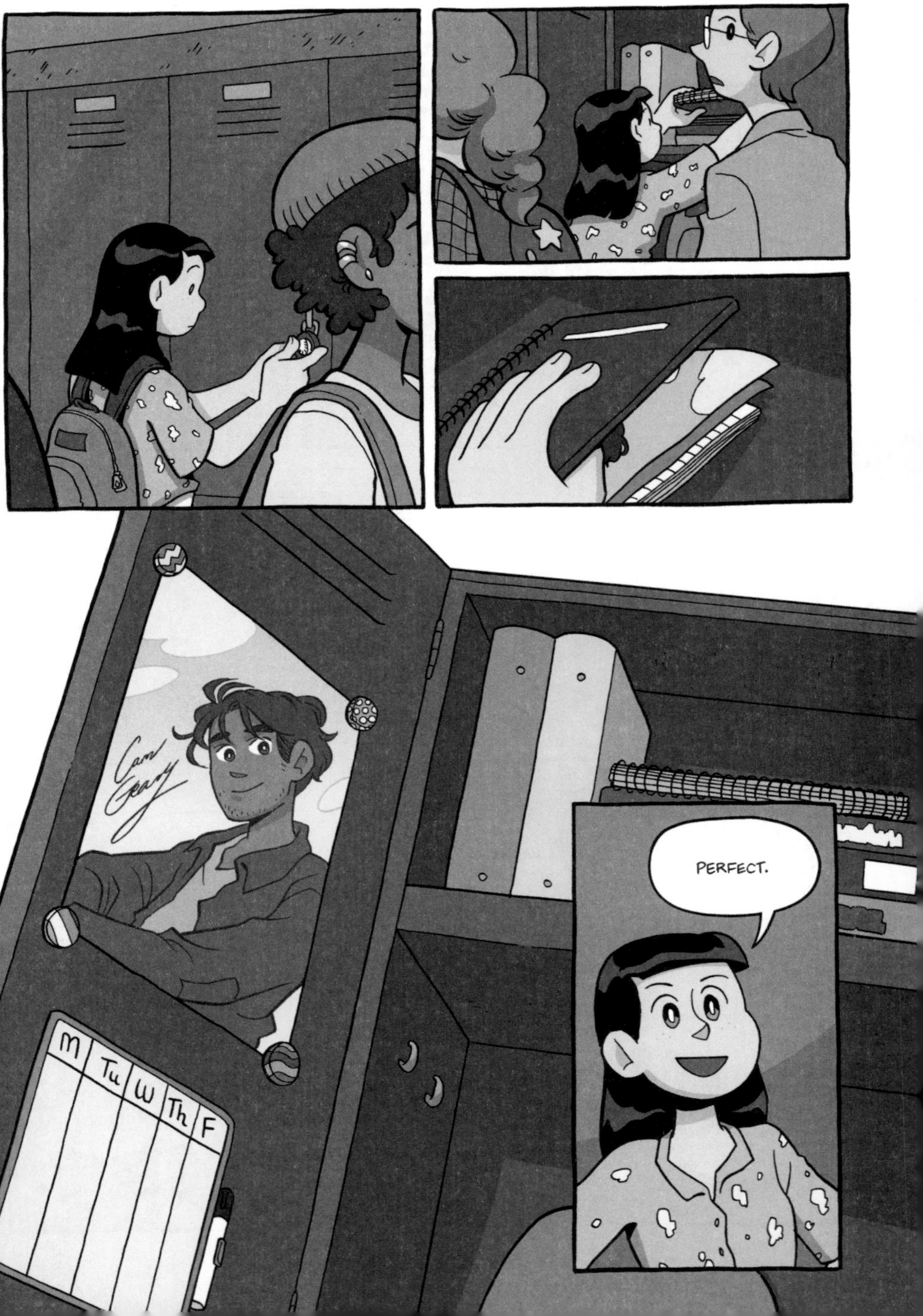
PERFECT.
M
Tu
W
Th
F

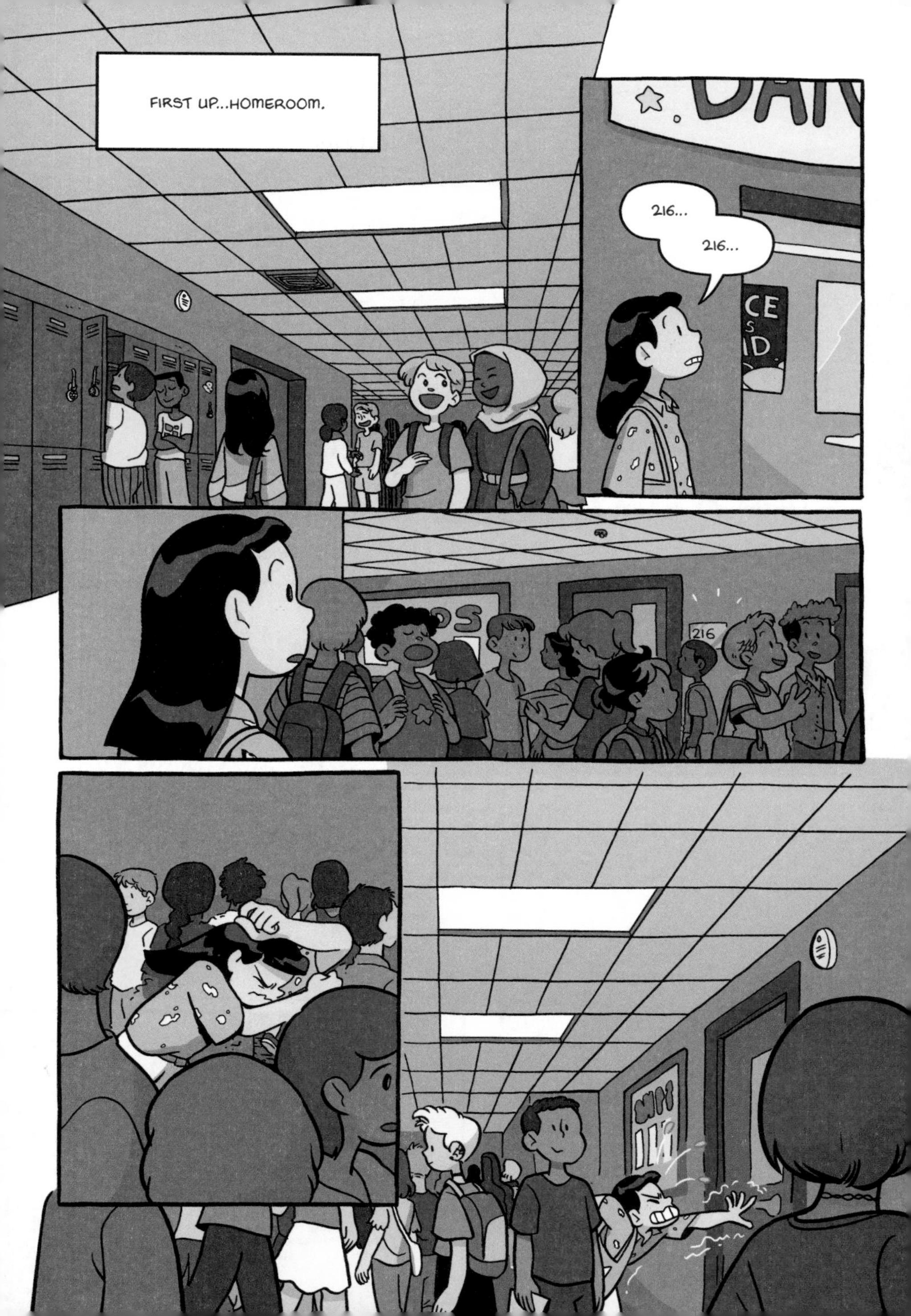
FIRST UP...HOMEROOM.
216...
216...
216

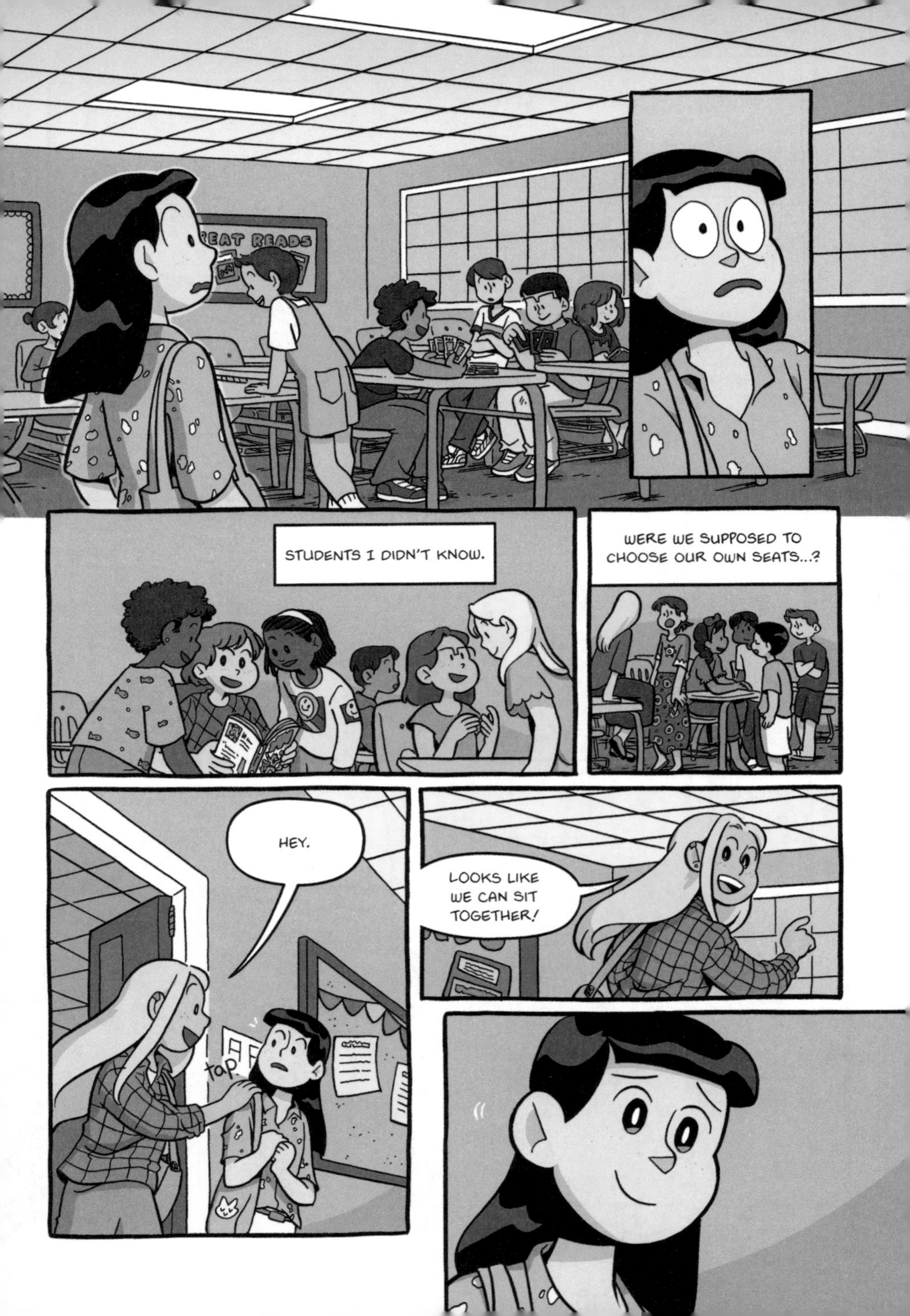
GREAT READS
STUDENTS I DIDN'T KNOW.
WERE WE SUPPOSED TO CHOOSE OUR OWN SEATS...?
HEY.
TAP
LOOKS LIKE WE CAN SIT TOGETHER!

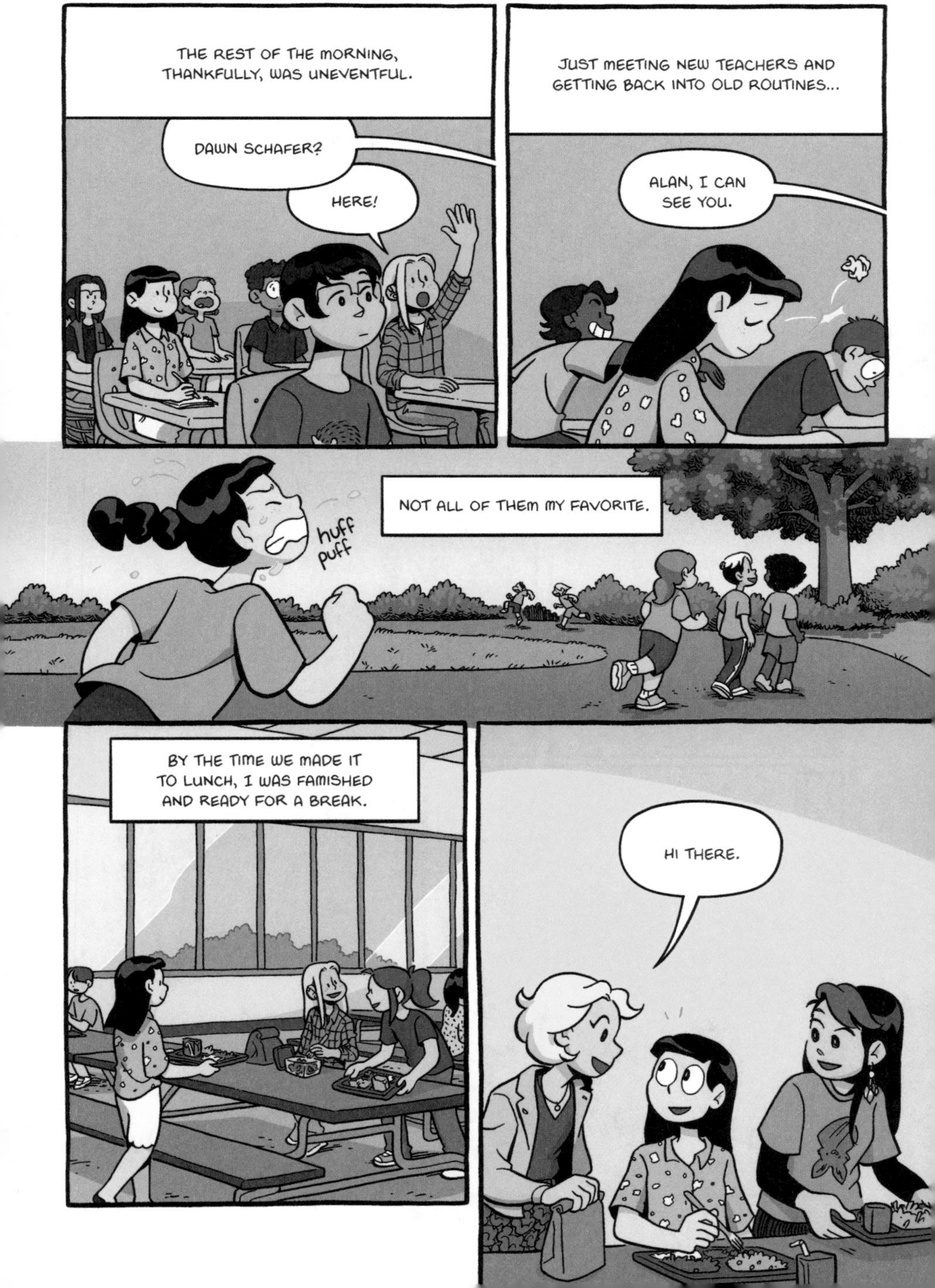
THE REST OF THE MORNING, THANKFULLY, WAS UNEVENTFUL.
DAWN SCHAFER?
HERE!
JUST MEETING NEW TEACHERS AND GETTING BACK INTO OLD ROUTINES...
ALAN, I CAN SEE YOU.
NOT ALL OF THEM MY FAVORITE.
huff puff
BY THE TIME WE MADE IT TO LUNCH, I WAS FAMISHED AND READY FOR A BREAK.
HI THERE.

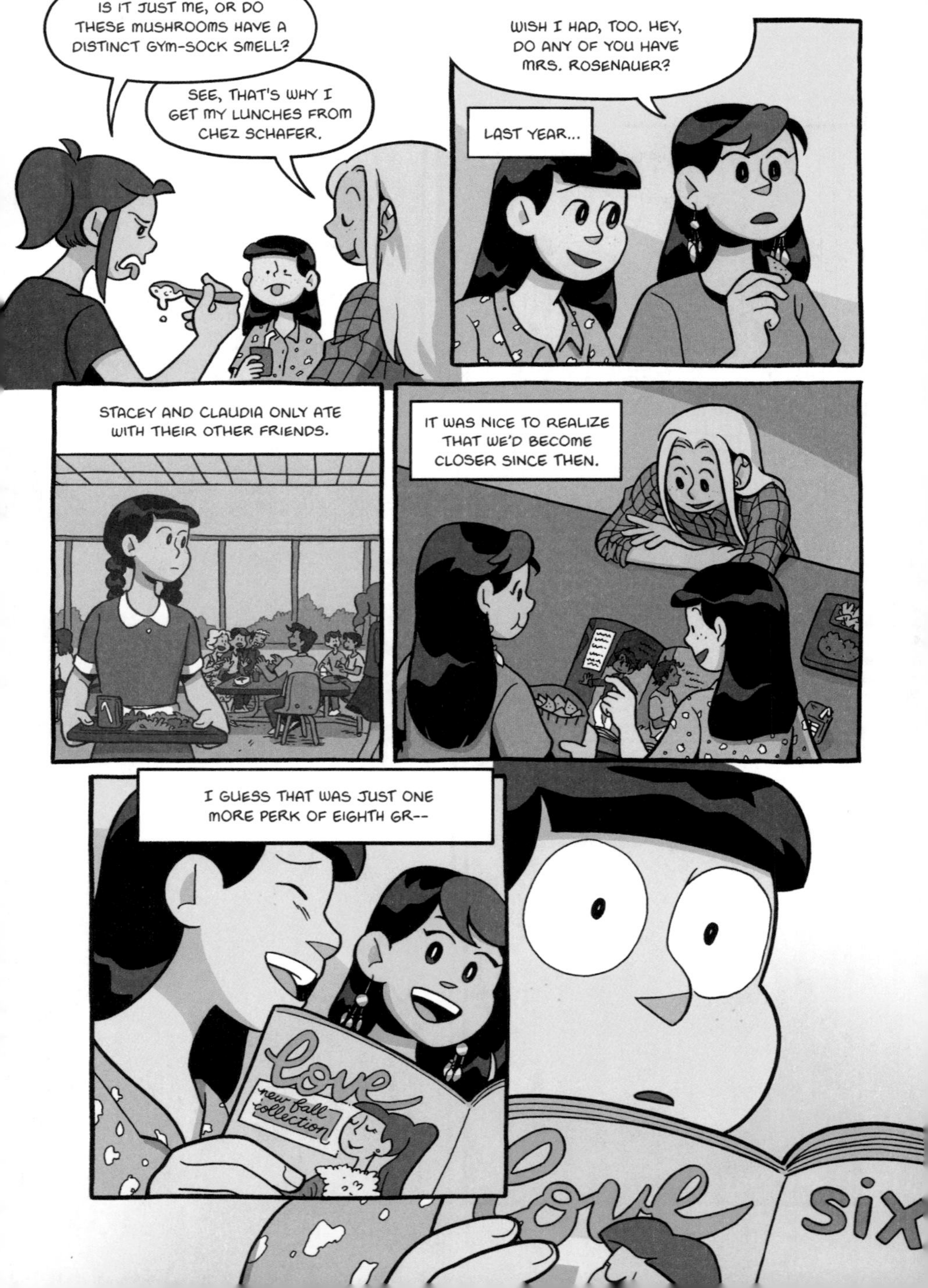
IS IT JUST ME, OR DO THESE MUSHROOMS HAVE A DISTINCT GYM-SOCK SMELL?
SEE, THAT'S WHY I GET MY LUNCHES FROM CHEZ SCHAFER.
WISH I HAD, TOO. HEY, DO ANY OF YOU HAVE MRS. ROSENAUER?
LAST YEAR...
STACEY AND CLAUDIA ONLY ATE WITH THEIR OTHER FRIENDS.
IT WAS NICE TO REALIZE THAT WE'D BECOME CLOSER SINCE THEN.
I GUESS THAT WAS JUST ONE MORE PERK OF EIGHTH GR--
love
new fall collection
love
six

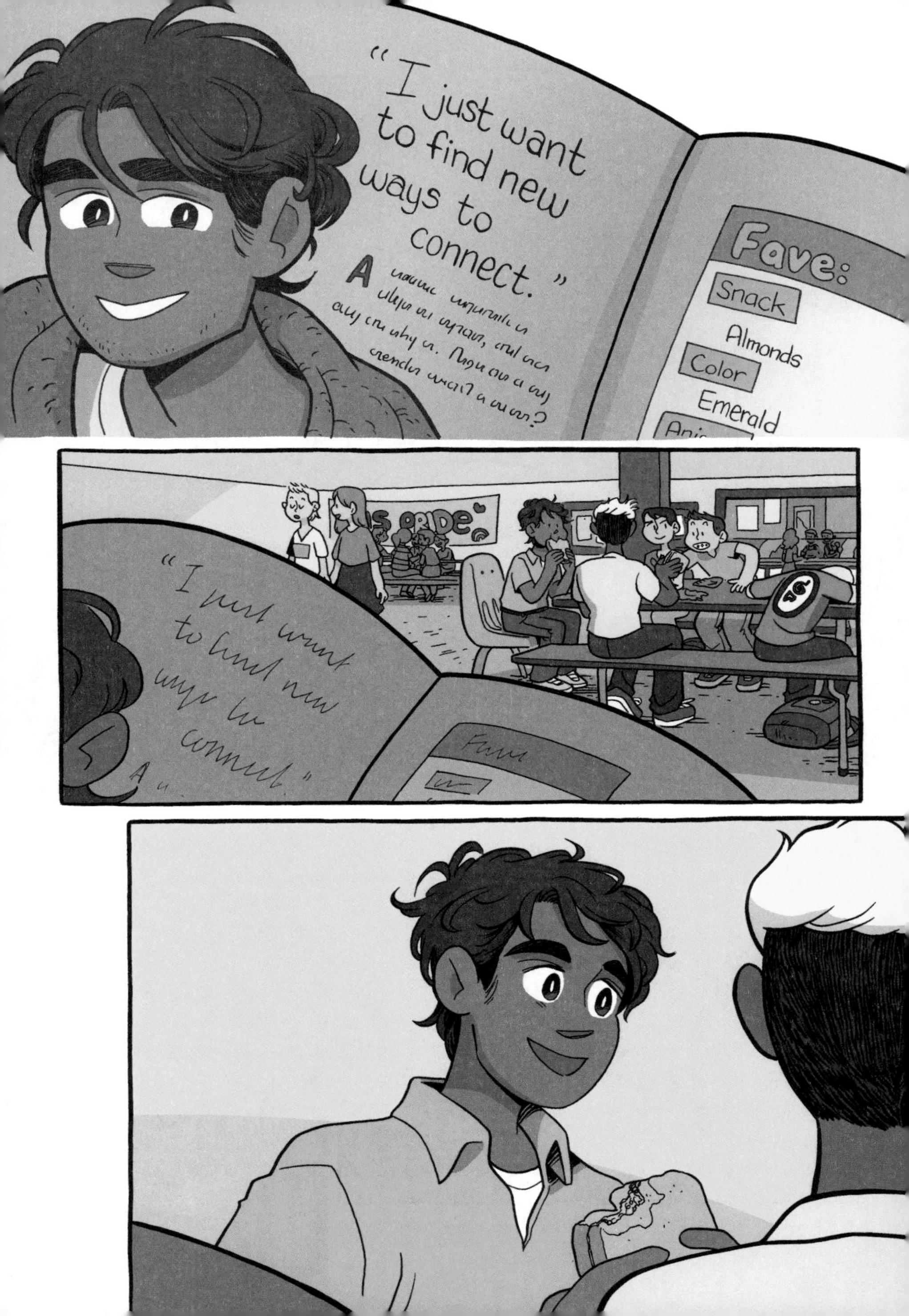
"I just want to find new ways to connect."
A
Fave:
Snack
Almonds
Color
Emerald
S PRIDE

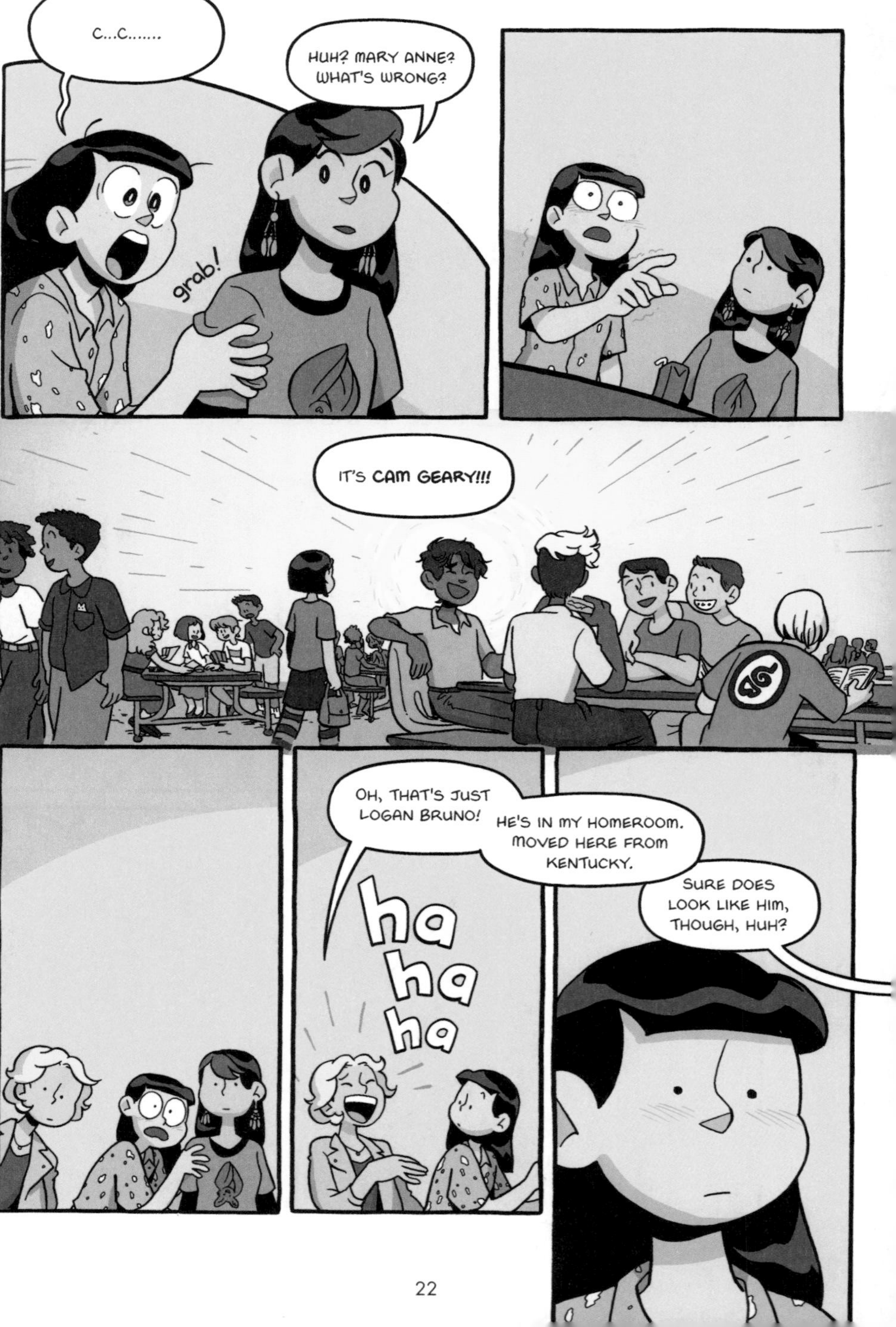
C...C.......
HUH? MARY ANNE? WHAT'S WRONG?
grab!
IT'S **CAM GEARY!!!**
OH, THAT'S JUST LOGAN BRUNO!
HE'S IN MY HOMEROOM. MOVED HERE FROM KENTUCKY.
ha ha ha
SURE DOES LOOK LIKE HIM, THOUGH, HUH?

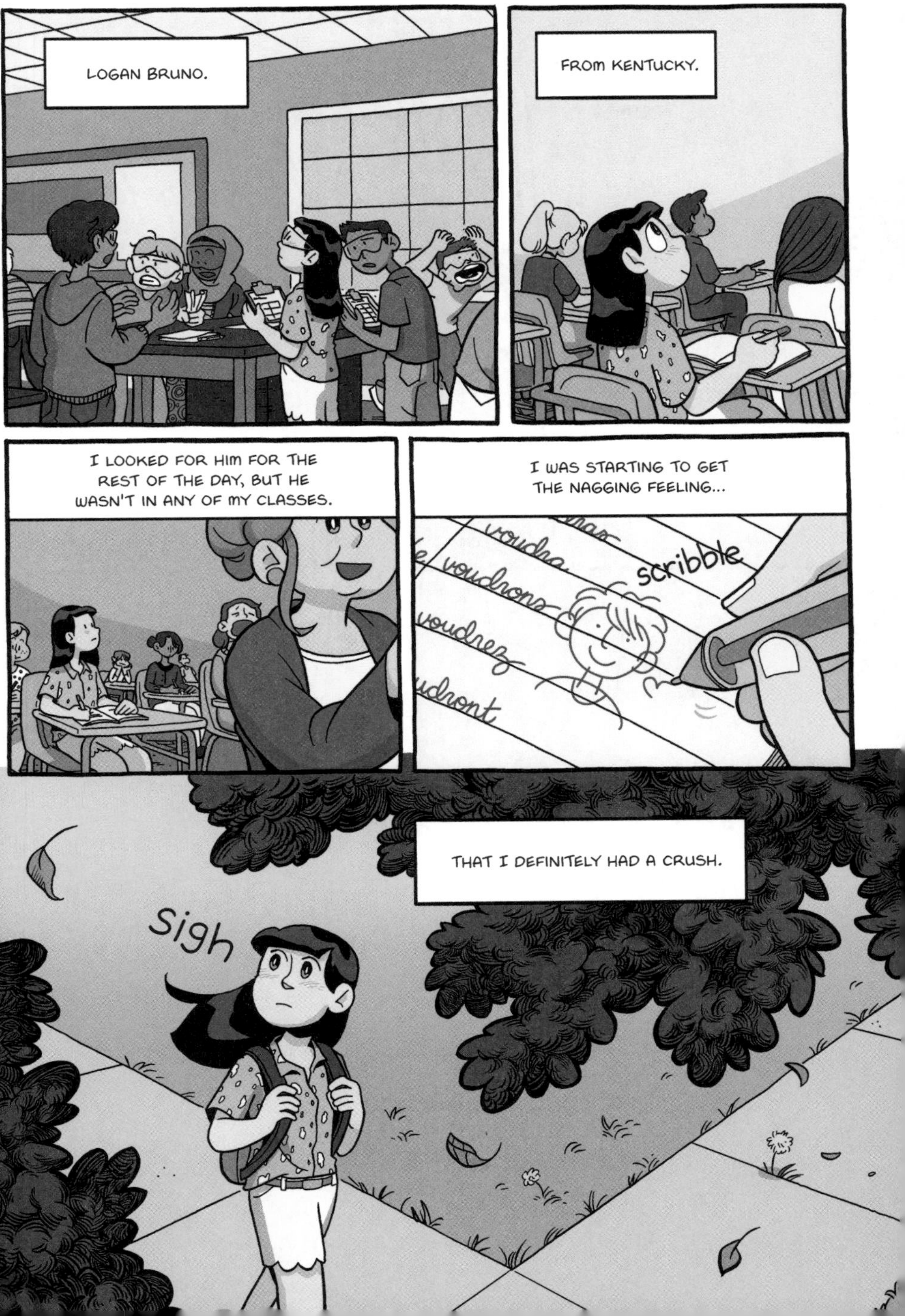
LOGAN BRUNO.
FROM KENTUCKY.
I LOOKED FOR HIM FOR THE REST OF THE DAY, BUT HE WASN'T IN ANY OF MY CLASSES.
I WAS STARTING TO GET THE NAGGING FEELING...
voudra
voudrons
voudrez
scribble
THAT I DEFINITELY HAD A CRUSH.
Sigh

CHAPTER 3

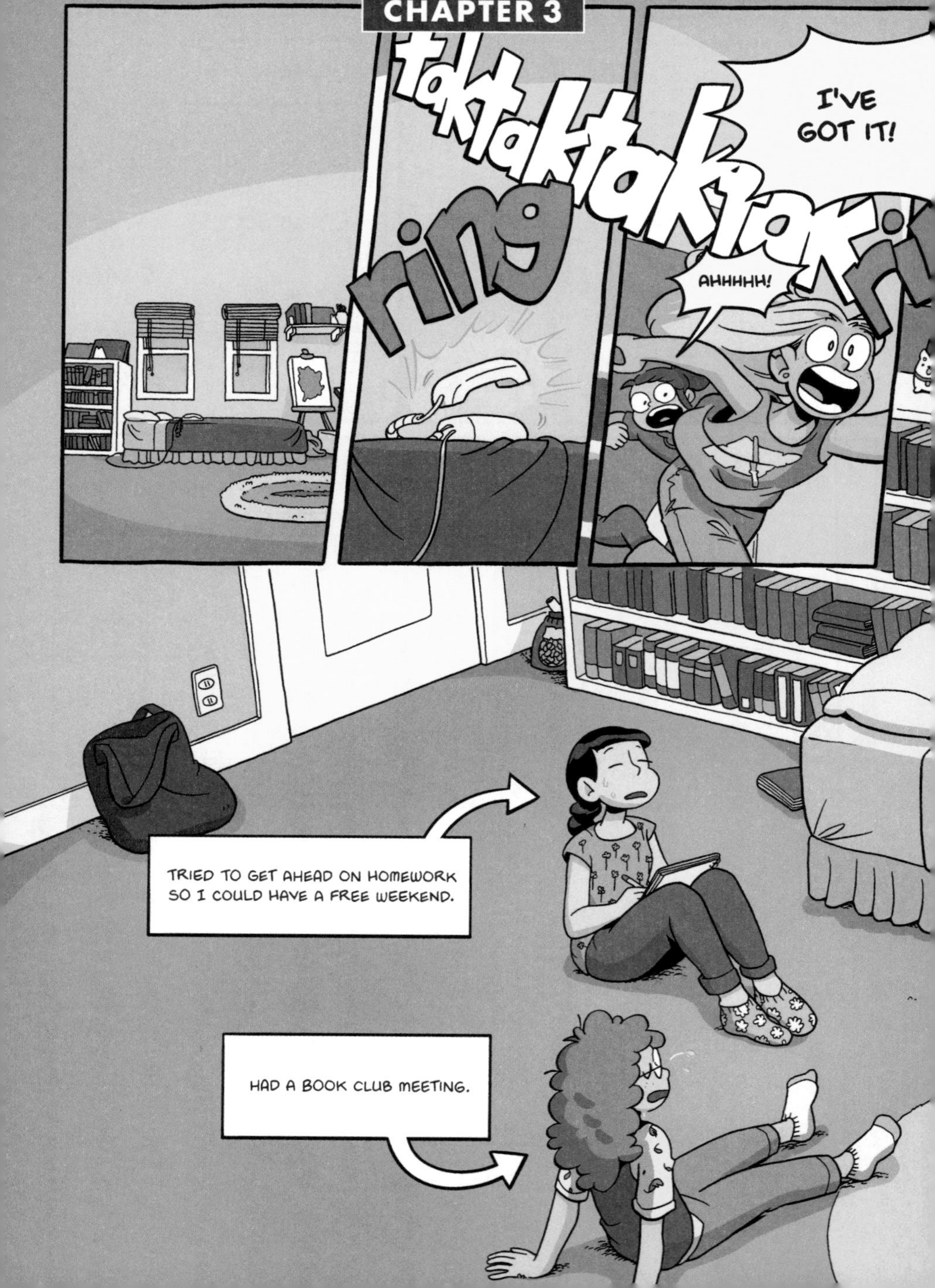
taktaktaktak
ring
I'VE GOT IT!
AHHHHH!
TRIED TO GET AHEAD ON HOMEWORK SO I COULD HAVE A FREE WEEKEND.
HAD A BOOK CLUB MEETING.

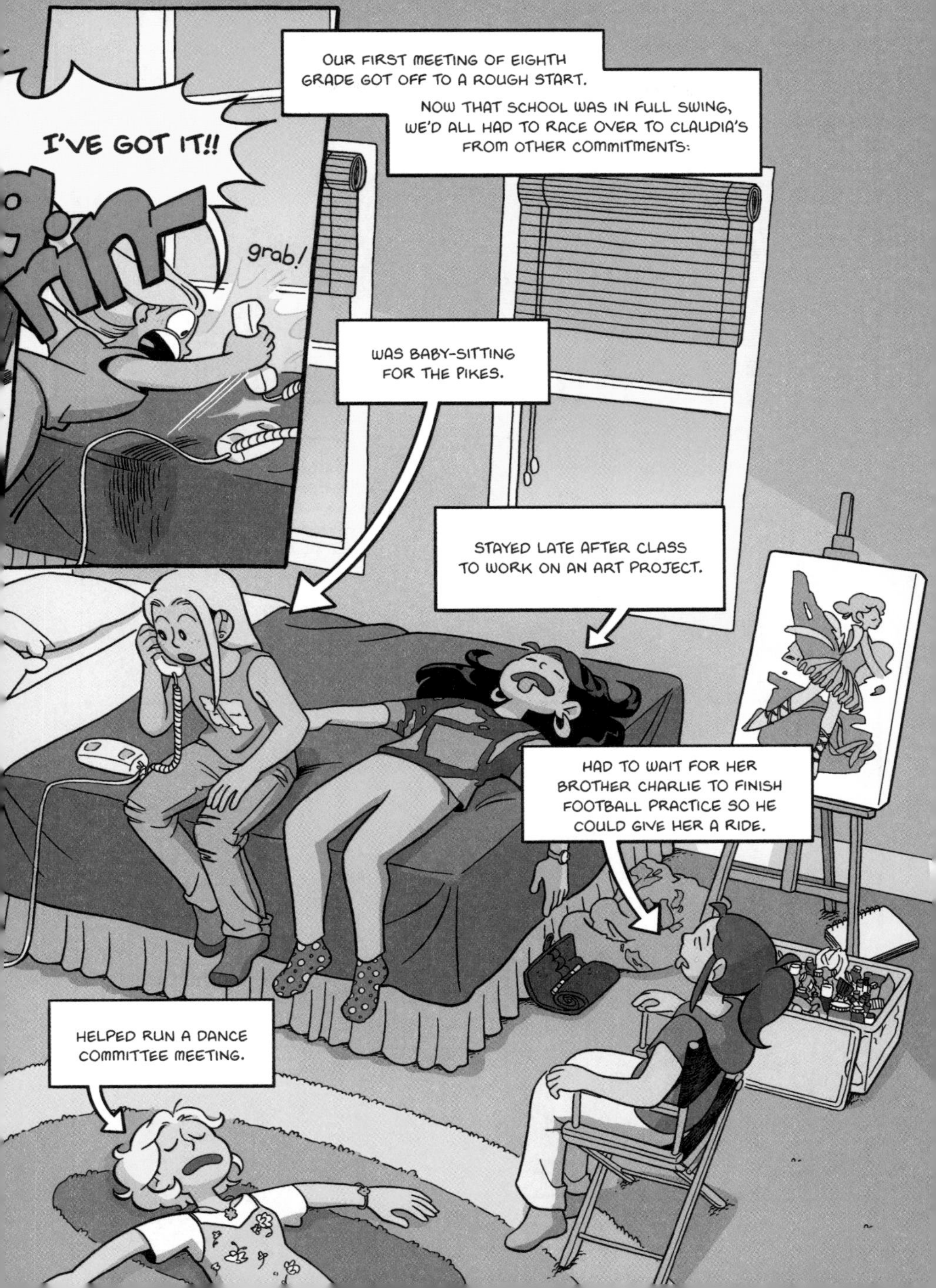
I'VE GOT IT!!
grab!
OUR FIRST MEETING OF EIGHTH GRADE GOT OFF TO A ROUGH START.
NOW THAT SCHOOL WAS IN FULL SWING, WE'D ALL HAD TO RACE OVER TO CLAUDIA'S FROM OTHER COMMITMENTS:
WAS BABY-SITTING FOR THE PIKES.
STAYED LATE AFTER CLASS TO WORK ON AN ART PROJECT.
HAD TO WAIT FOR HER BROTHER CHARLIE TO FINISH FOOTBALL PRACTICE SO HE COULD GIVE HER A RIDE.
HELPED RUN A DANCE COMMITTEE MEETING.

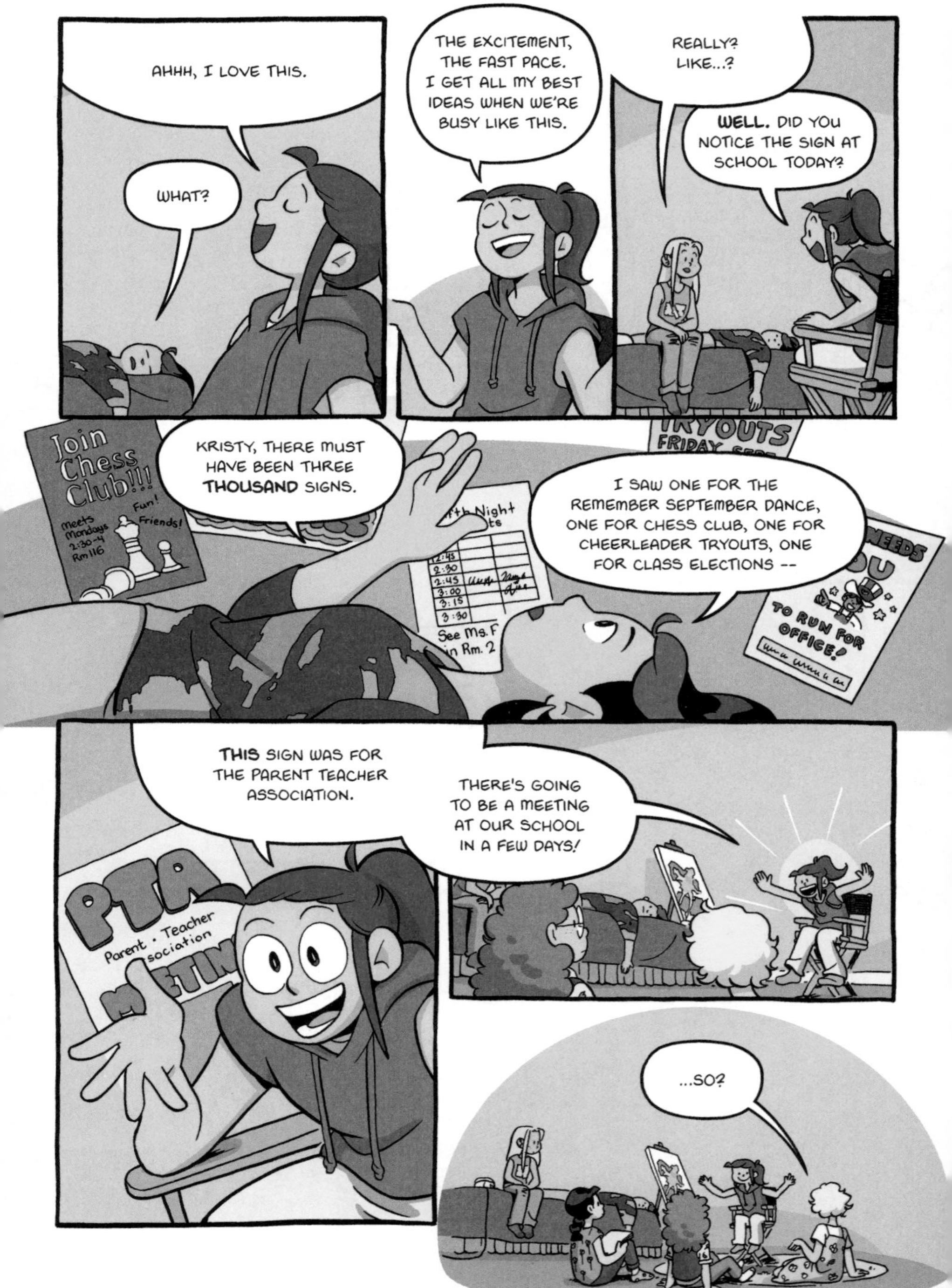
AHHH, I LOVE THIS.
WHAT?
THE EXCITEMENT, THE FAST PACE. I GET ALL MY BEST IDEAS WHEN WE'RE BUSY LIKE THIS.
REALLY? LIKE...?
WELL. DID YOU NOTICE THE SIGN AT SCHOOL TODAY?
Join Chess Club!!! Fun! Friends! meets Mondays 2:30-4 Rm 116
TRYOUTS FRIDAY
KRISTY, THERE MUST HAVE BEEN THREE THOUSAND SIGNS.
I SAW ONE FOR THE REMEMBER SEPTEMBER DANCE, ONE FOR CHESS CLUB, ONE FOR CHEERLEADER TRYOUTS, ONE FOR CLASS ELECTIONS --
TO RUN FOR OFFICE!
THIS SIGN WAS FOR THE PARENT TEACHER ASSOCIATION.
PTA Parent • Teacher Association
THERE'S GOING TO BE A MEETING AT OUR SCHOOL IN A FEW DAYS!
...SO?

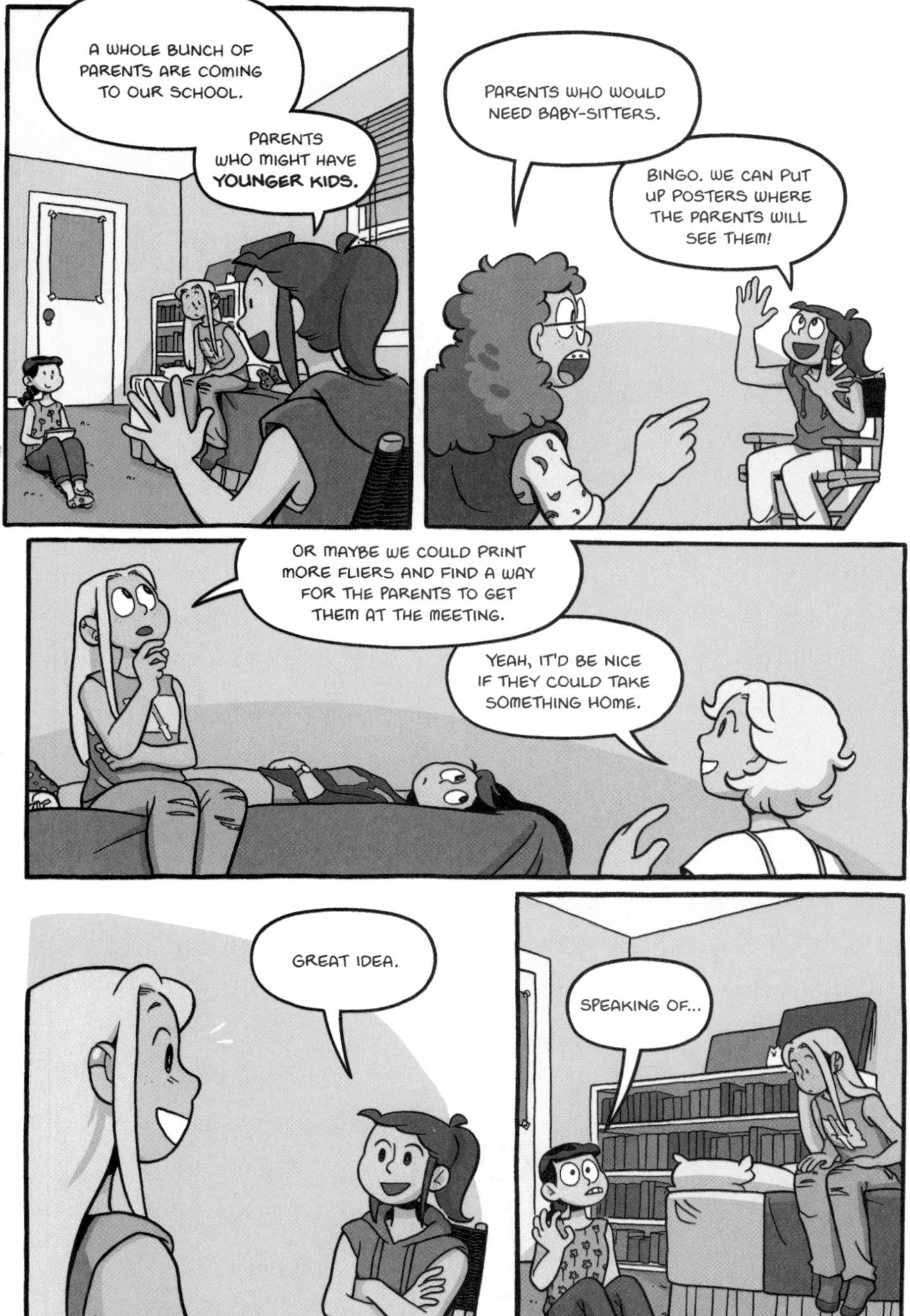
A WHOLE BUNCH OF PARENTS ARE COMING TO OUR SCHOOL.
PARENTS WHO MIGHT HAVE **YOUNGER KIDS.**
PARENTS WHO WOULD NEED BABY-SITTERS.
BINGO. WE CAN PUT UP POSTERS WHERE THE PARENTS WILL SEE THEM!
OR MAYBE WE COULD PRINT MORE FLIERS AND FIND A WAY FOR THE PARENTS TO GET THEM AT THE MEETING.
YEAH, IT'D BE NICE IF THEY COULD TAKE SOMETHING HOME.
GREAT IDEA.
SPEAKING OF...

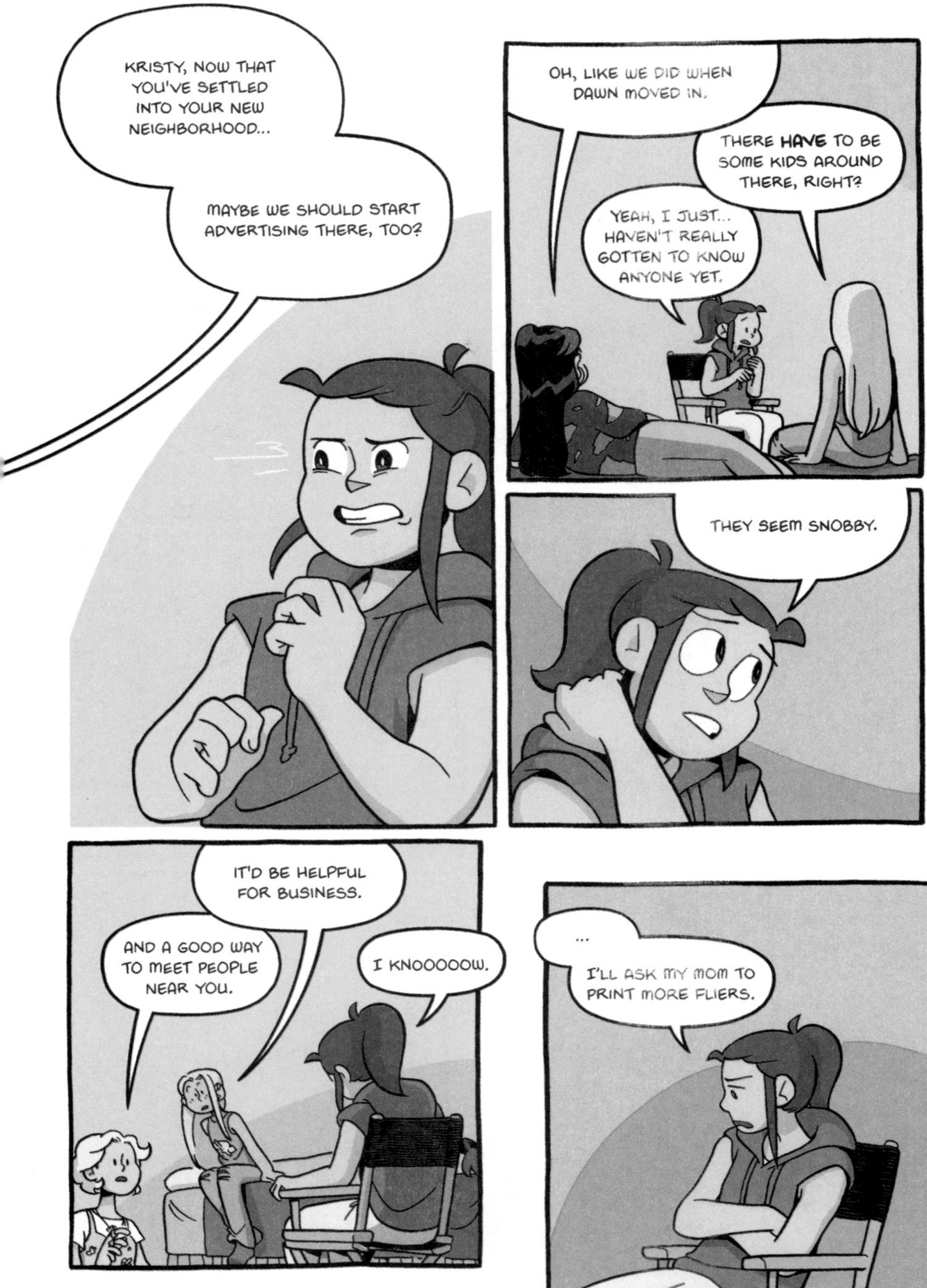
KRISTY, NOW THAT YOU'VE SETTLED INTO YOUR NEW NEIGHBORHOOD...
MAYBE WE SHOULD START ADVERTISING THERE, TOO?
OH, LIKE WE DID WHEN DAWN MOVED IN.
THERE **HAVE** TO BE SOME KIDS AROUND THERE, RIGHT?
YEAH, I JUST... HAVEN'T REALLY GOTTEN TO KNOW ANYONE YET.
THEY SEEM SNOBBY.
IT'D BE HELPFUL FOR BUSINESS.
AND A GOOD WAY TO MEET PEOPLE NEAR YOU.
I KNOOOOOW.
...
I'LL ASK MY MOM TO PRINT MORE FLIERS.

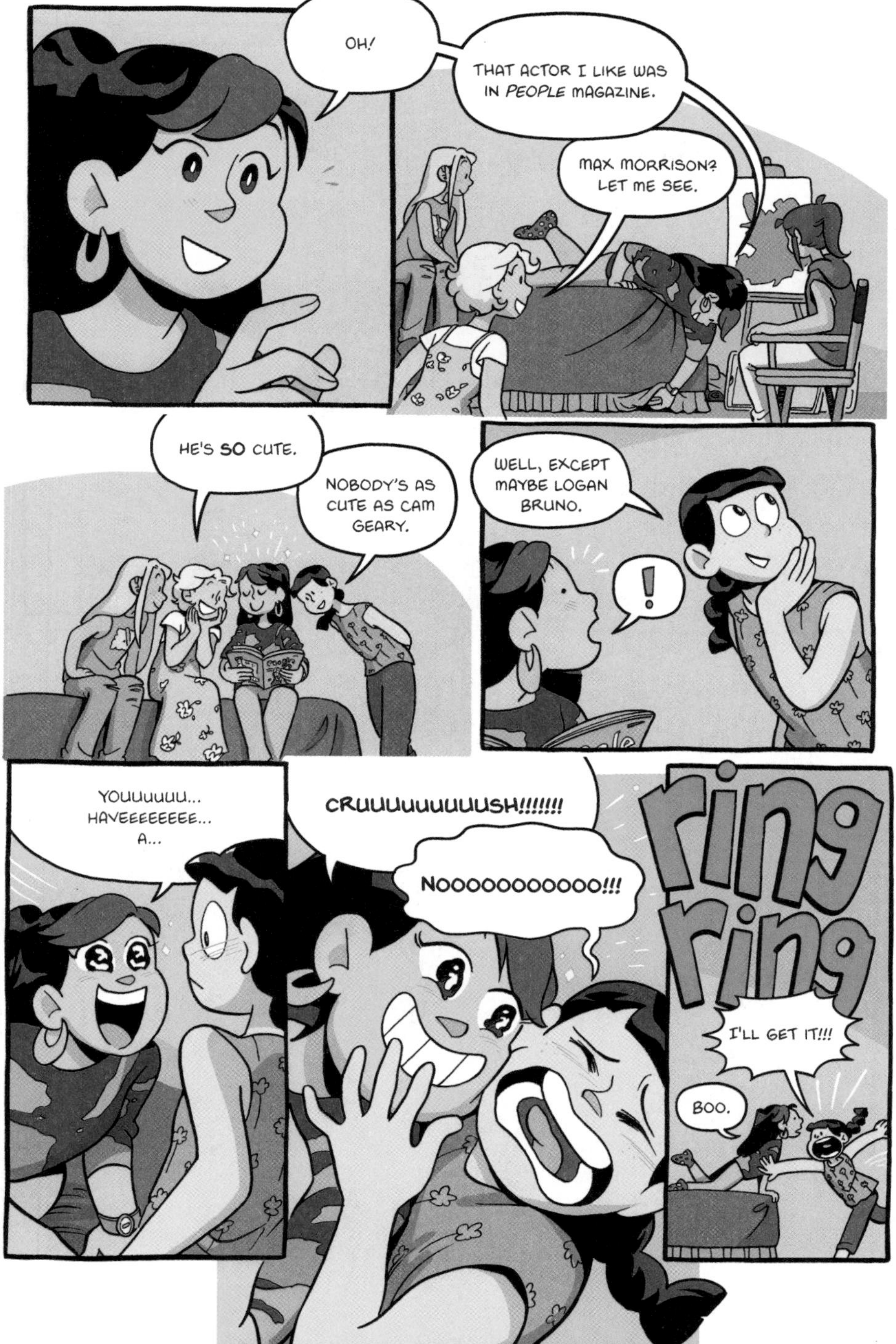
OH!
THAT ACTOR I LIKE WAS IN *PEOPLE* MAGAZINE.
MAX MORRISON? LET ME SEE.
HE'S **SO** CUTE.
NOBODY'S AS CUTE AS CAM GEARY.
WELL, EXCEPT MAYBE LOGAN BRUNO.
!
YOUUUUUU... HAVEEEEEEEE... A...
CRUUUUUUUUUSH!!!!!!!
NOOOOOOOOOOO!!!
ring ring
I'LL GET IT!!!
BOO.

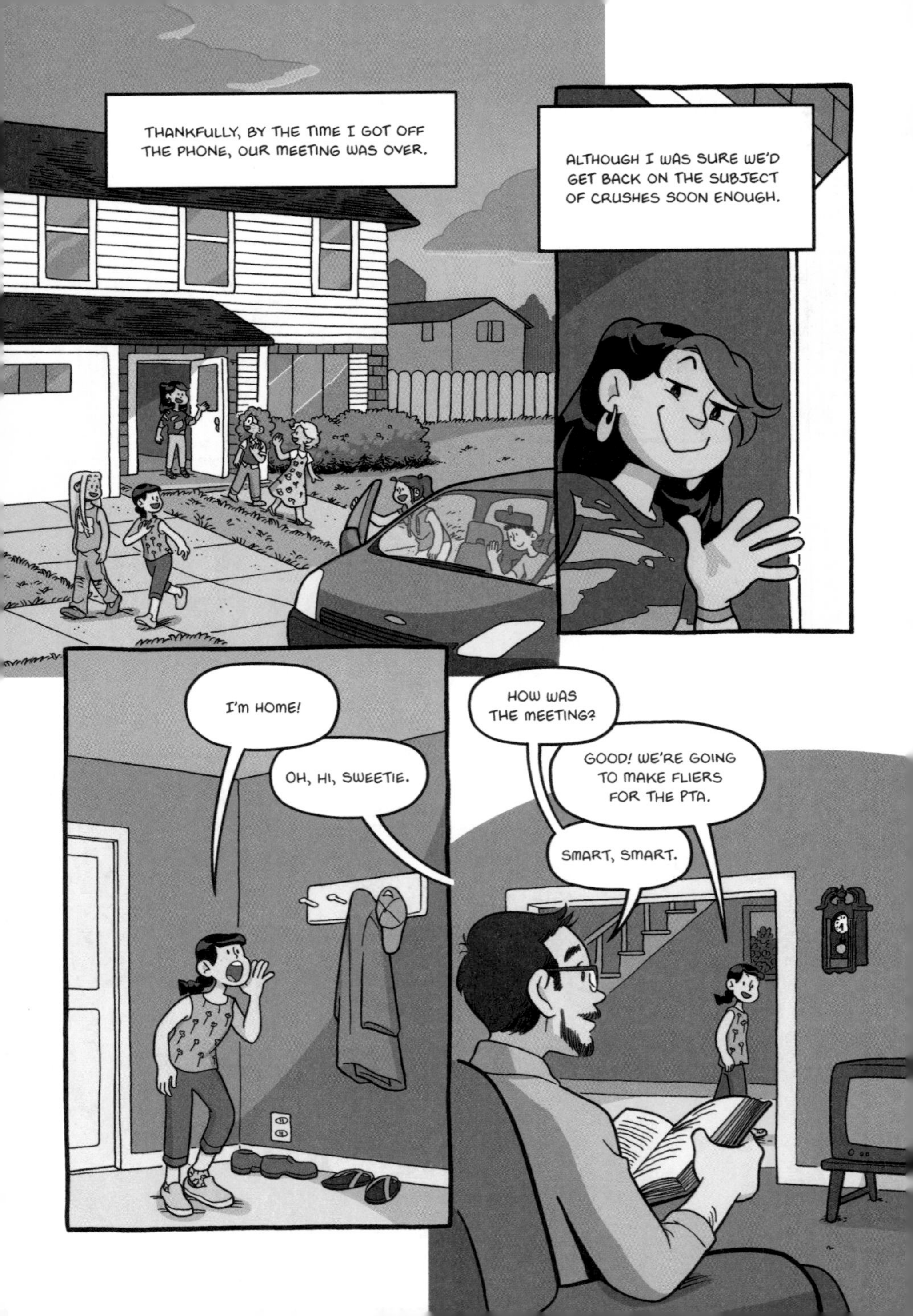
THANKFULLY, BY THE TIME I GOT OFF THE PHONE, OUR MEETING WAS OVER.
ALTHOUGH I WAS SURE WE'D GET BACK ON THE SUBJECT OF CRUSHES SOON ENOUGH.
I'M HOME!
OH, HI, SWEETIE.
HOW WAS THE MEETING?
GOOD! WE'RE GOING TO MAKE FLIERS FOR THE PTA.
SMART, SMART.

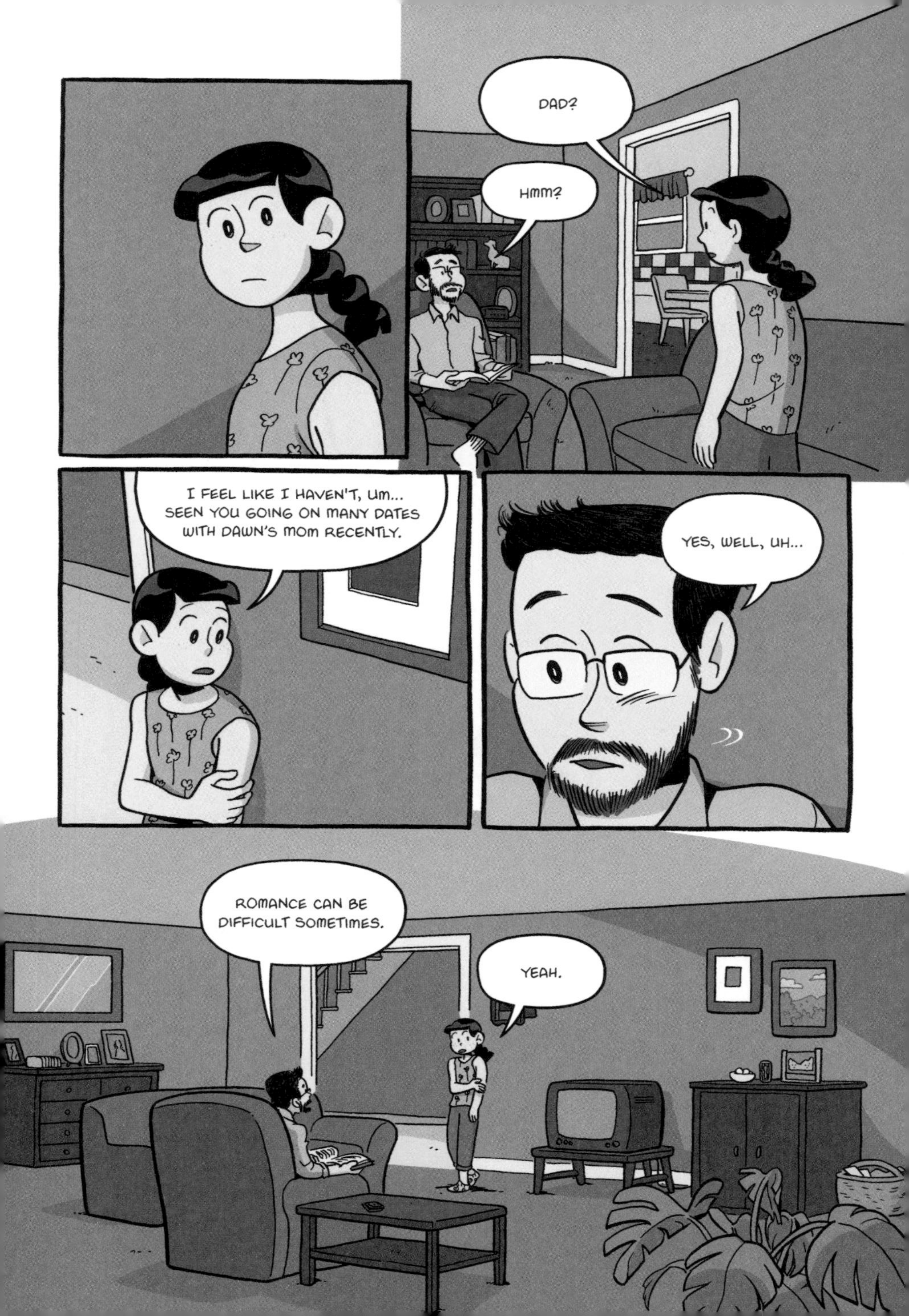
DAD?
HMM?
I FEEL LIKE I HAVEN'T, UM... SEEN YOU GOING ON MANY DATES WITH DAWN'S MOM RECENTLY.
YES, WELL, UH...
ROMANCE CAN BE DIFFICULT SOMETIMES.
YEAH.

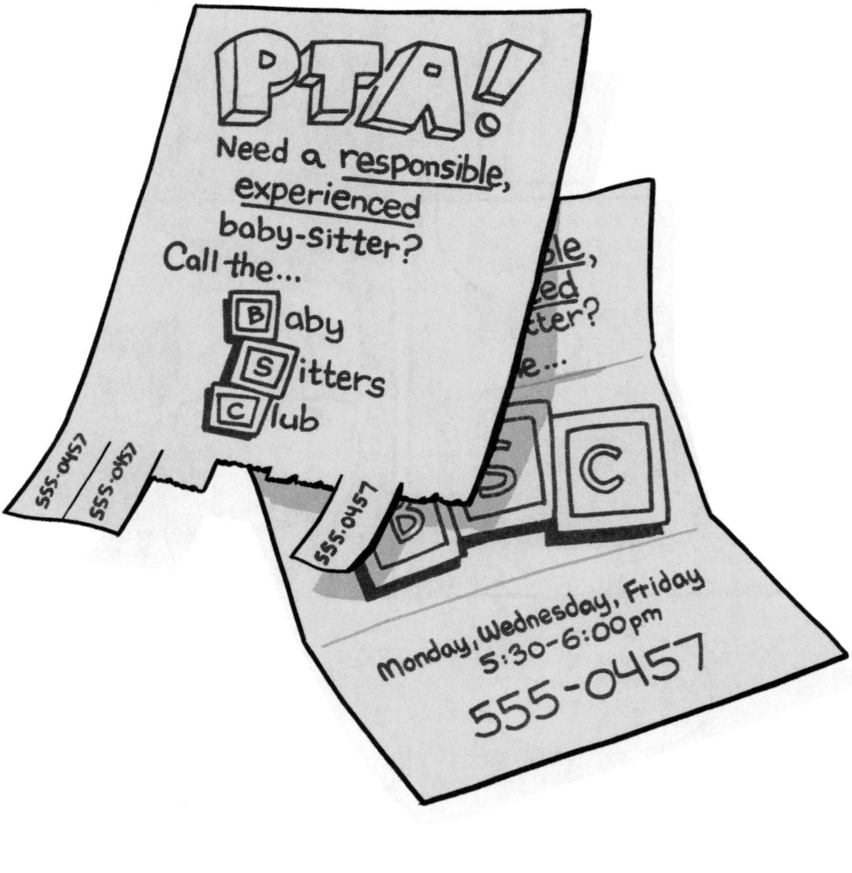
PTA!
Need a responsible, experienced baby-sitter?
Call the...
Baby
Sitters
Club
555-0457
555-0457
555-0457
Monday, Wednesday, Friday
5:30-6:00 pm
555-0457

CHAPTER 4

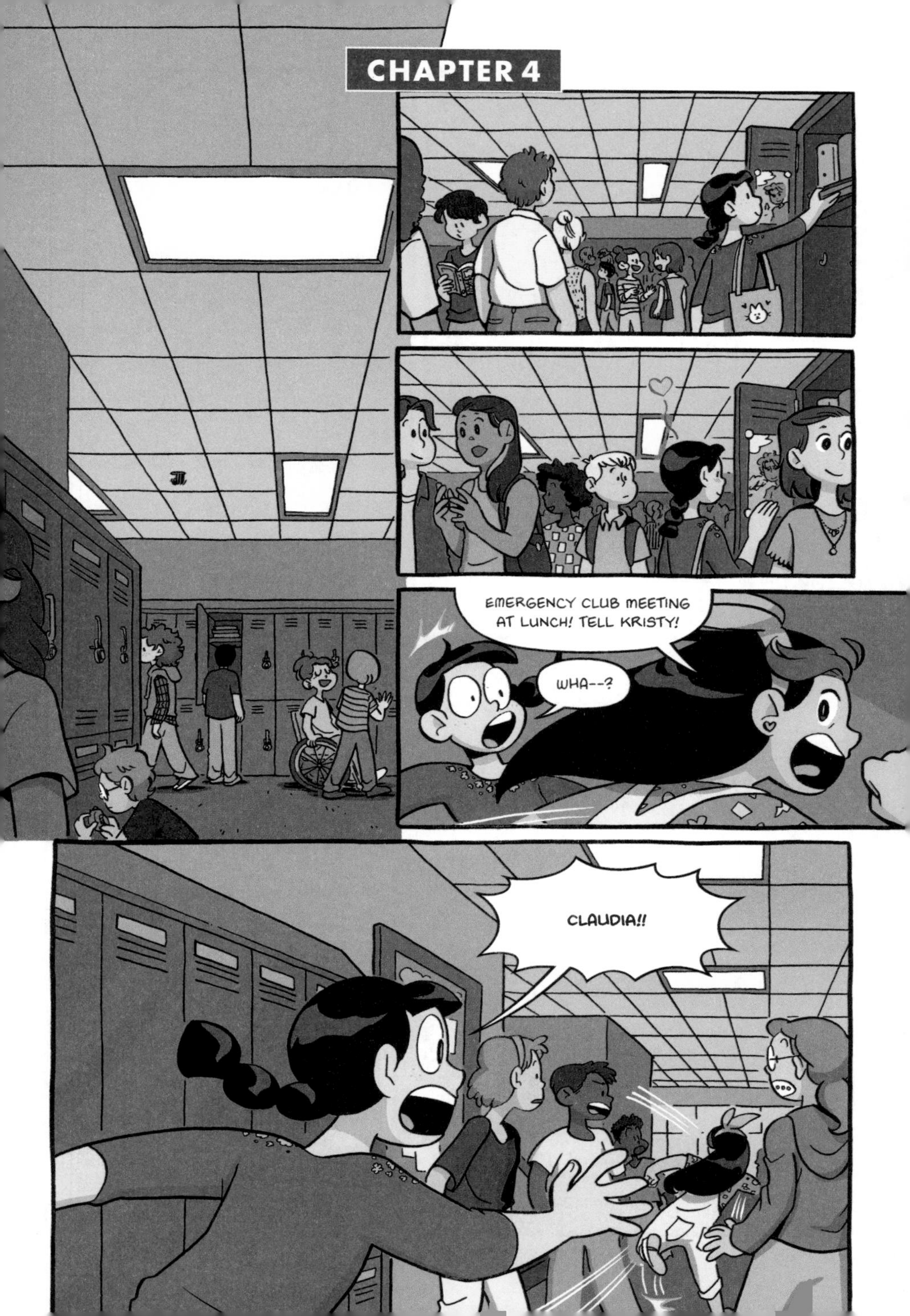

EMERGENCY CLUB MEETING AT LUNCH! TELL KRISTY!
WHA--?
CLAUDIA!!

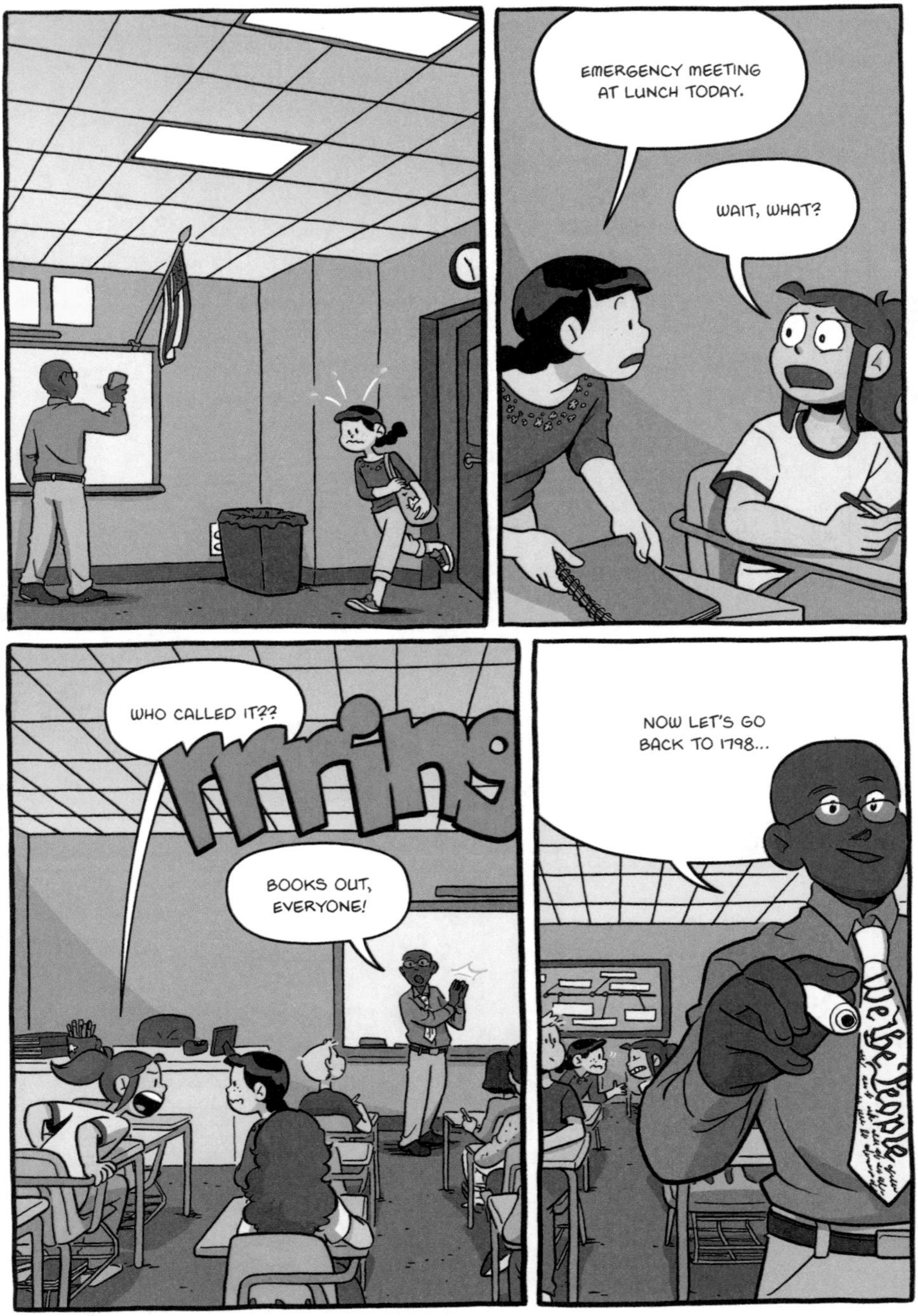
EMERGENCY MEETING AT LUNCH TODAY.
WAIT, WHAT?
WHO CALLED IT??
rrring
BOOKS OUT, EVERYONE!
NOW LET'S GO BACK TO 1798...
We the People

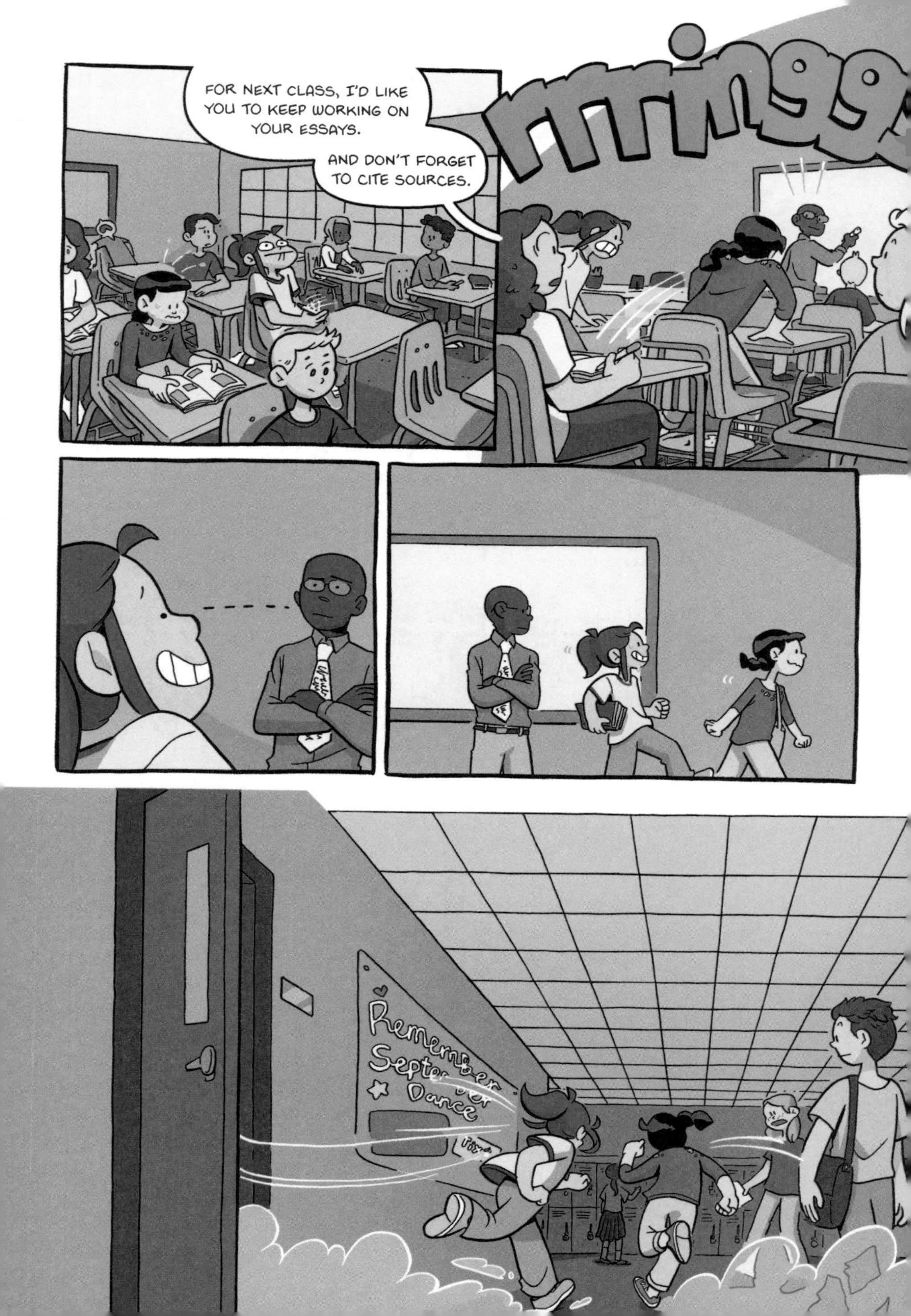
FOR NEXT CLASS, I'D LIKE YOU TO KEEP WORKING ON YOUR ESSAYS.
AND DON'T FORGET TO CITE SOURCES.

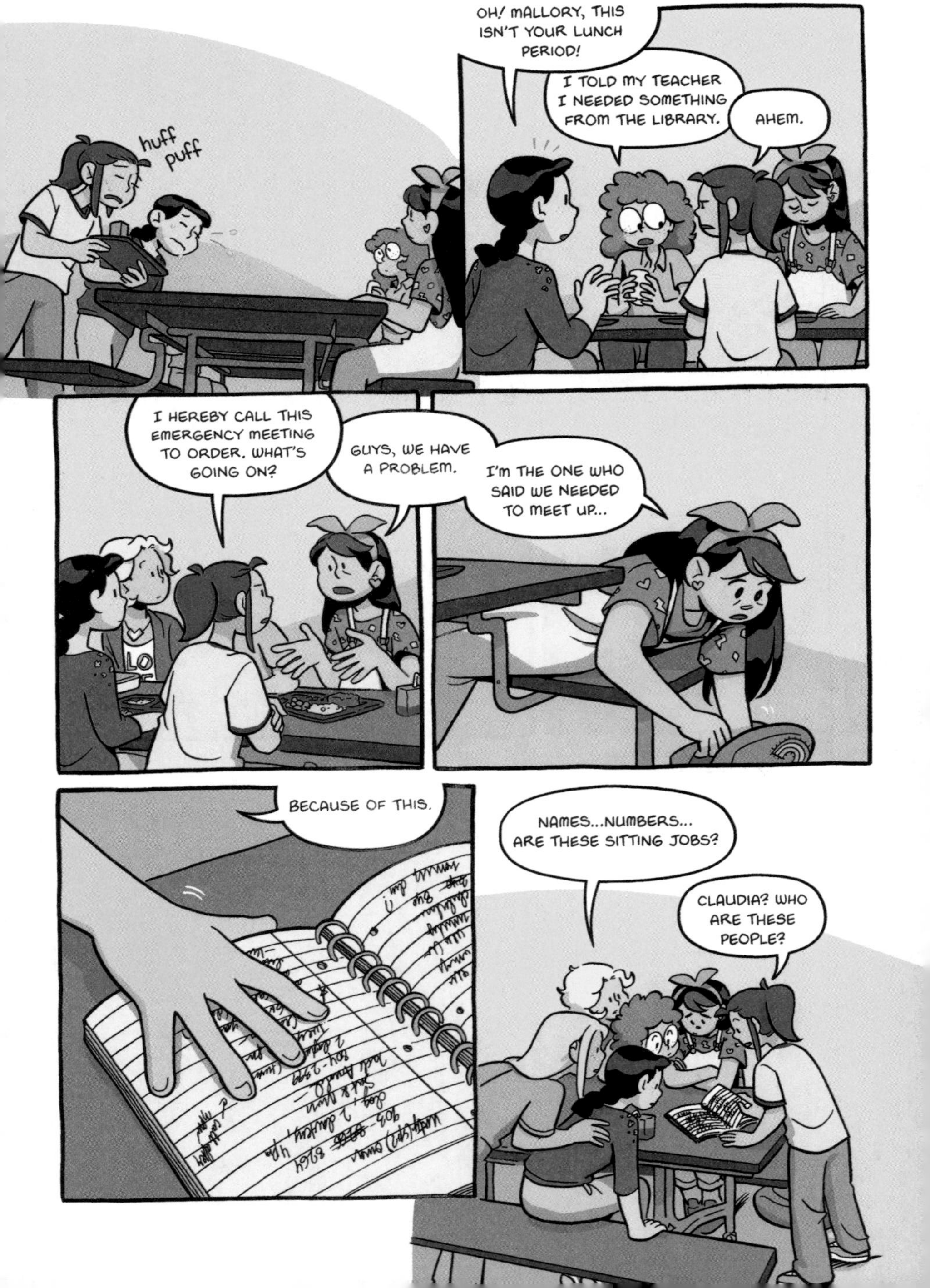
huff puff
OH! MALLORY, THIS ISN'T YOUR LUNCH PERIOD!
I TOLD MY TEACHER I NEEDED SOMETHING FROM THE LIBRARY.
AHEM.
I HEREBY CALL THIS EMERGENCY MEETING TO ORDER. WHAT'S GOING ON?
GUYS, WE HAVE A PROBLEM.
I'M THE ONE WHO SAID WE NEEDED TO MEET UP...
BECAUSE OF THIS.
NAMES...NUMBERS... ARE THESE SITTING JOBS?
CLAUDIA? WHO ARE THESE PEOPLE?

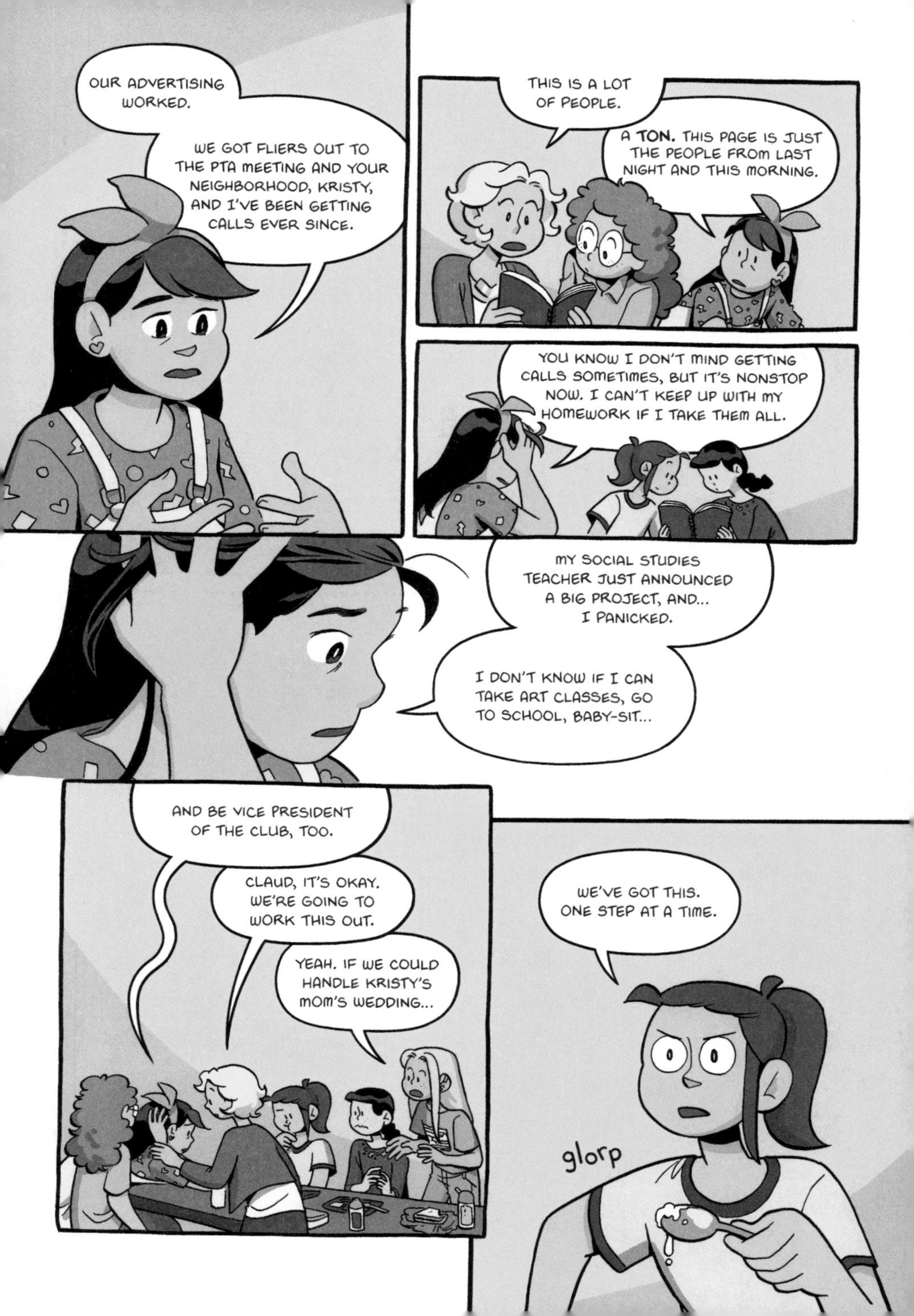
OUR ADVERTISING WORKED.
WE GOT FLIERS OUT TO THE PTA MEETING AND YOUR NEIGHBORHOOD, KRISTY, AND I'VE BEEN GETTING CALLS EVER SINCE.
THIS IS A LOT OF PEOPLE.
A **TON.** THIS PAGE IS JUST THE PEOPLE FROM LAST NIGHT AND THIS MORNING.
YOU KNOW I DON'T MIND GETTING CALLS SOMETIMES, BUT IT'S NONSTOP NOW. I CAN'T KEEP UP WITH MY HOMEWORK IF I TAKE THEM ALL.
MY SOCIAL STUDIES TEACHER JUST ANNOUNCED A BIG PROJECT, AND... I PANICKED.
I DON'T KNOW IF I CAN TAKE ART CLASSES, GO TO SCHOOL, BABY-SIT...
AND BE VICE PRESIDENT OF THE CLUB, TOO.
CLAUD, IT'S OKAY. WE'RE GOING TO WORK THIS OUT.
YEAH. IF WE COULD HANDLE KRISTY'S MOM'S WEDDING...
WE'VE GOT THIS. ONE STEP AT A TIME.
glorp

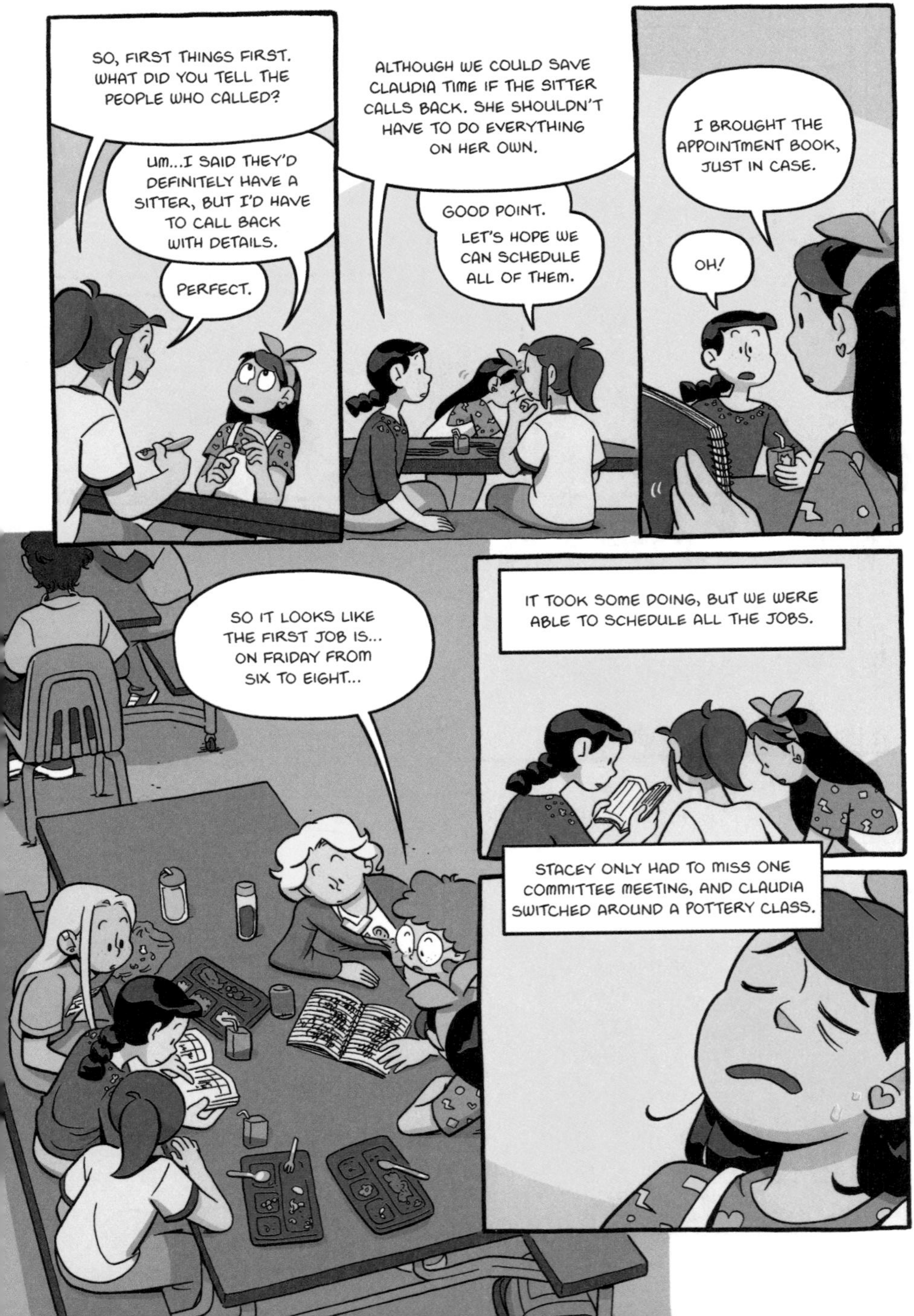

SO, FIRST THINGS FIRST. WHAT DID YOU TELL THE PEOPLE WHO CALLED?
UM...I SAID THEY'D DEFINITELY HAVE A SITTER, BUT I'D HAVE TO CALL BACK WITH DETAILS.
PERFECT.
ALTHOUGH WE COULD SAVE CLAUDIA TIME IF THE SITTER CALLS BACK. SHE SHOULDN'T HAVE TO DO EVERYTHING ON HER OWN.
GOOD POINT.
LET'S HOPE WE CAN SCHEDULE ALL OF THEM.
I BROUGHT THE APPOINTMENT BOOK, JUST IN CASE.
OH!
SO IT LOOKS LIKE THE FIRST JOB IS... ON FRIDAY FROM SIX TO EIGHT...
IT TOOK SOME DOING, BUT WE WERE ABLE TO SCHEDULE ALL THE JOBS.
STACEY ONLY HAD TO MISS ONE COMMITTEE MEETING, AND CLAUDIA SWITCHED AROUND A POTTERY CLASS.

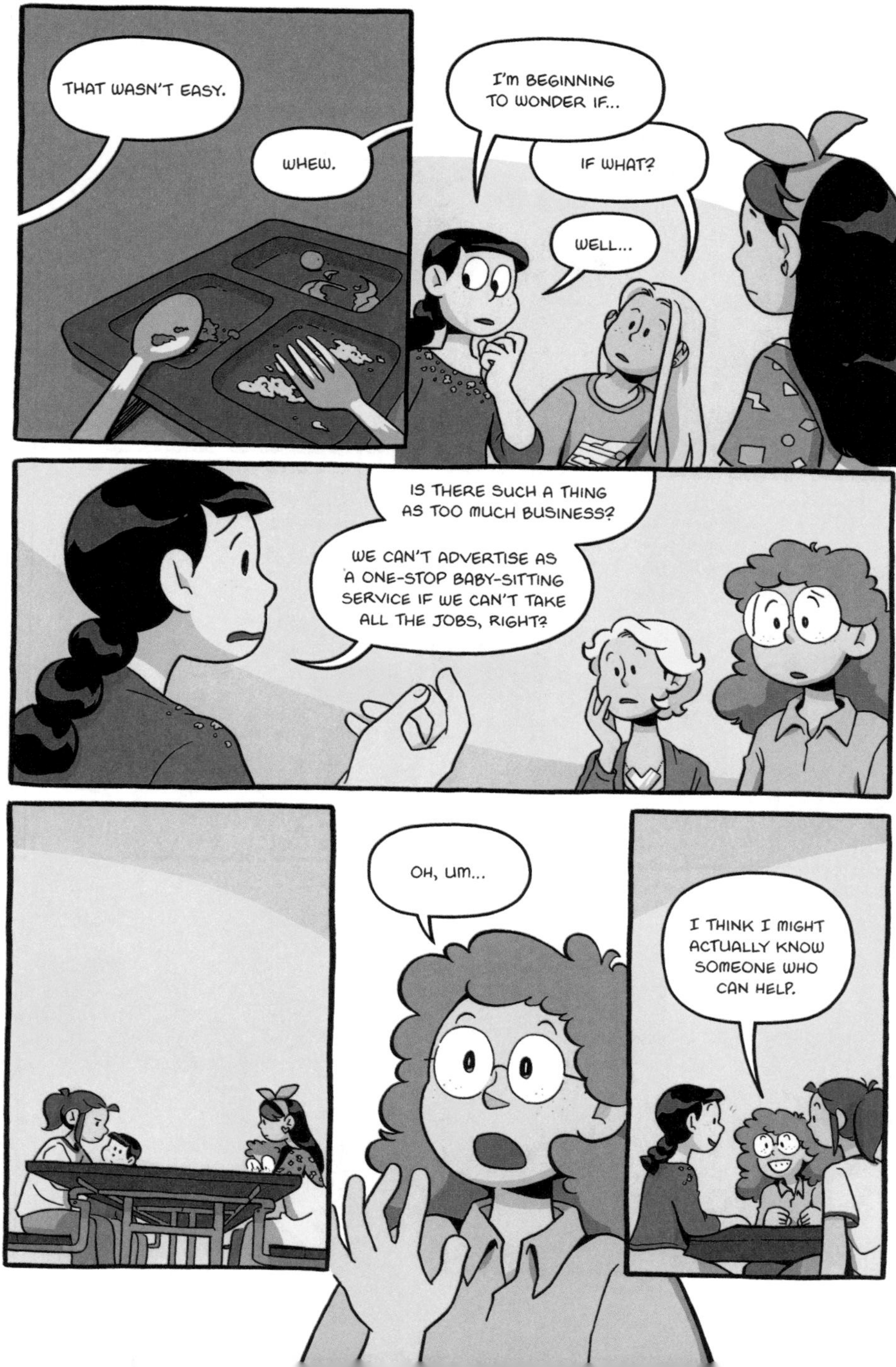
THAT WASN'T EASY.
WHEW.
I'M BEGINNING TO WONDER IF...
IF WHAT?
WELL...
IS THERE SUCH A THING AS TOO MUCH BUSINESS?
WE CAN'T ADVERTISE AS A ONE-STOP BABY-SITTING SERVICE IF WE CAN'T TAKE ALL THE JOBS, RIGHT?
OH, UM...
I THINK I MIGHT ACTUALLY KNOW SOMEONE WHO CAN HELP.

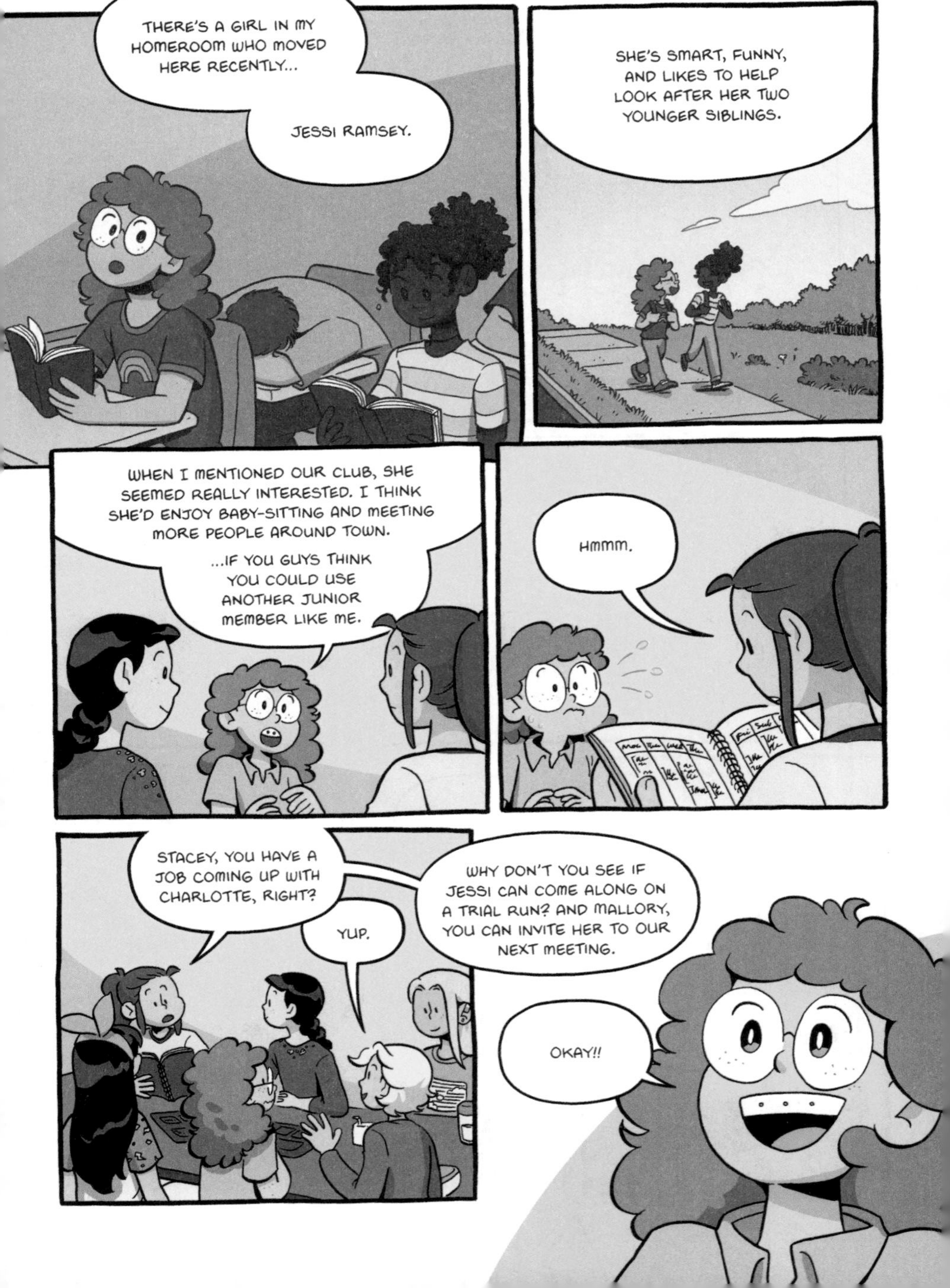
THERE'S A GIRL IN MY HOMEROOM WHO MOVED HERE RECENTLY...
JESSI RAMSEY.
SHE'S SMART, FUNNY, AND LIKES TO HELP LOOK AFTER HER TWO YOUNGER SIBLINGS.
WHEN I MENTIONED OUR CLUB, SHE SEEMED REALLY INTERESTED. I THINK SHE'D ENJOY BABY-SITTING AND MEETING MORE PEOPLE AROUND TOWN.
...IF YOU GUYS THINK YOU COULD USE ANOTHER JUNIOR MEMBER LIKE ME.
HMMM.
STACEY, YOU HAVE A JOB COMING UP WITH CHARLOTTE, RIGHT?
YUP.
WHY DON'T YOU SEE IF JESSI CAN COME ALONG ON A TRIAL RUN? AND MALLORY, YOU CAN INVITE HER TO OUR NEXT MEETING.
OKAY!!

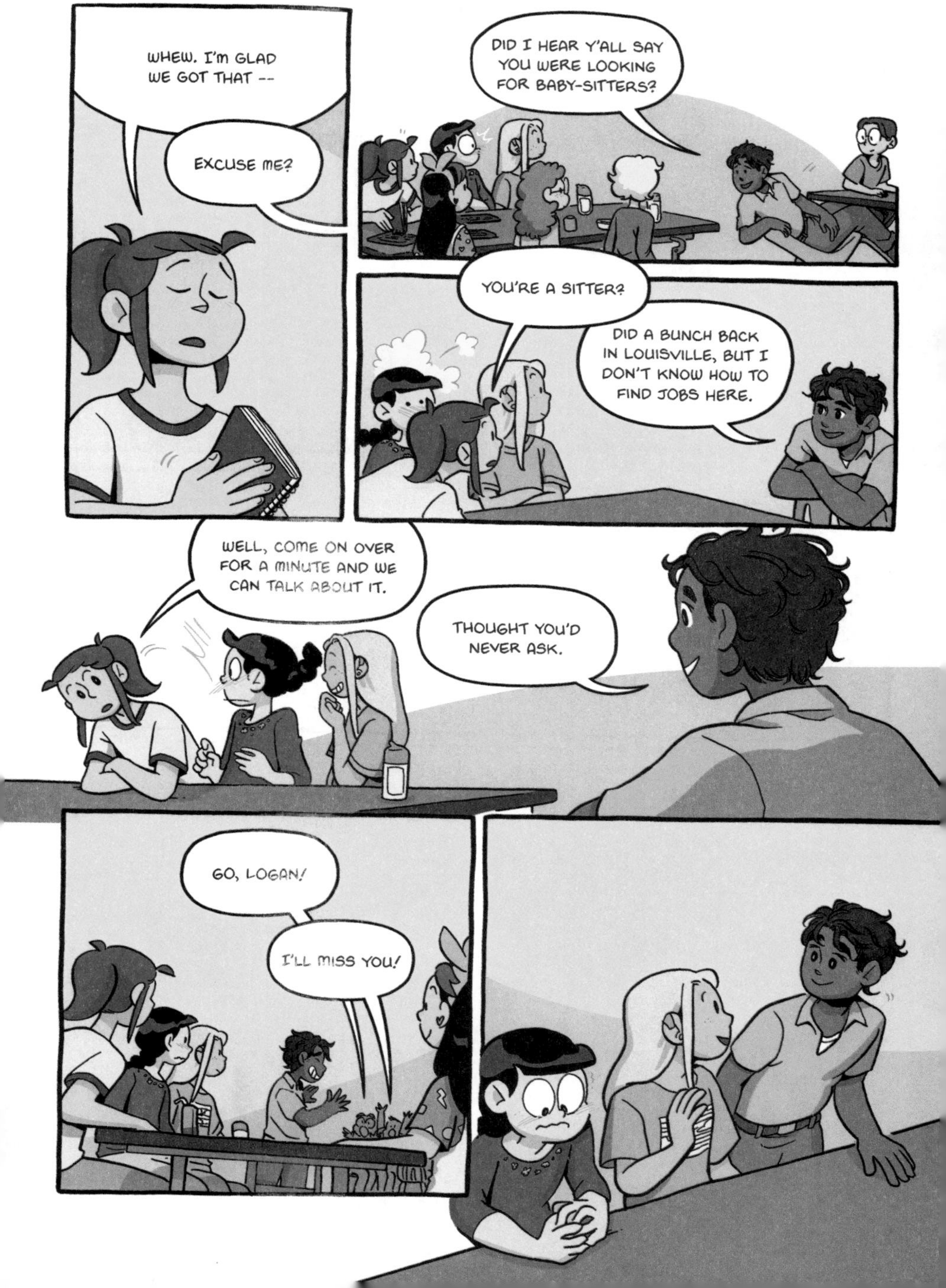
WHEW. I'M GLAD WE GOT THAT --
EXCUSE ME?
DID I HEAR Y'ALL SAY YOU WERE LOOKING FOR BABY-SITTERS?
YOU'RE A SITTER?
DID A BUNCH BACK IN LOUISVILLE, BUT I DON'T KNOW HOW TO FIND JOBS HERE.
WELL, COME ON OVER FOR A MINUTE AND WE CAN TALK ABOUT IT.
THOUGHT YOU'D NEVER ASK.
GO, LOGAN!
I'LL MISS YOU!

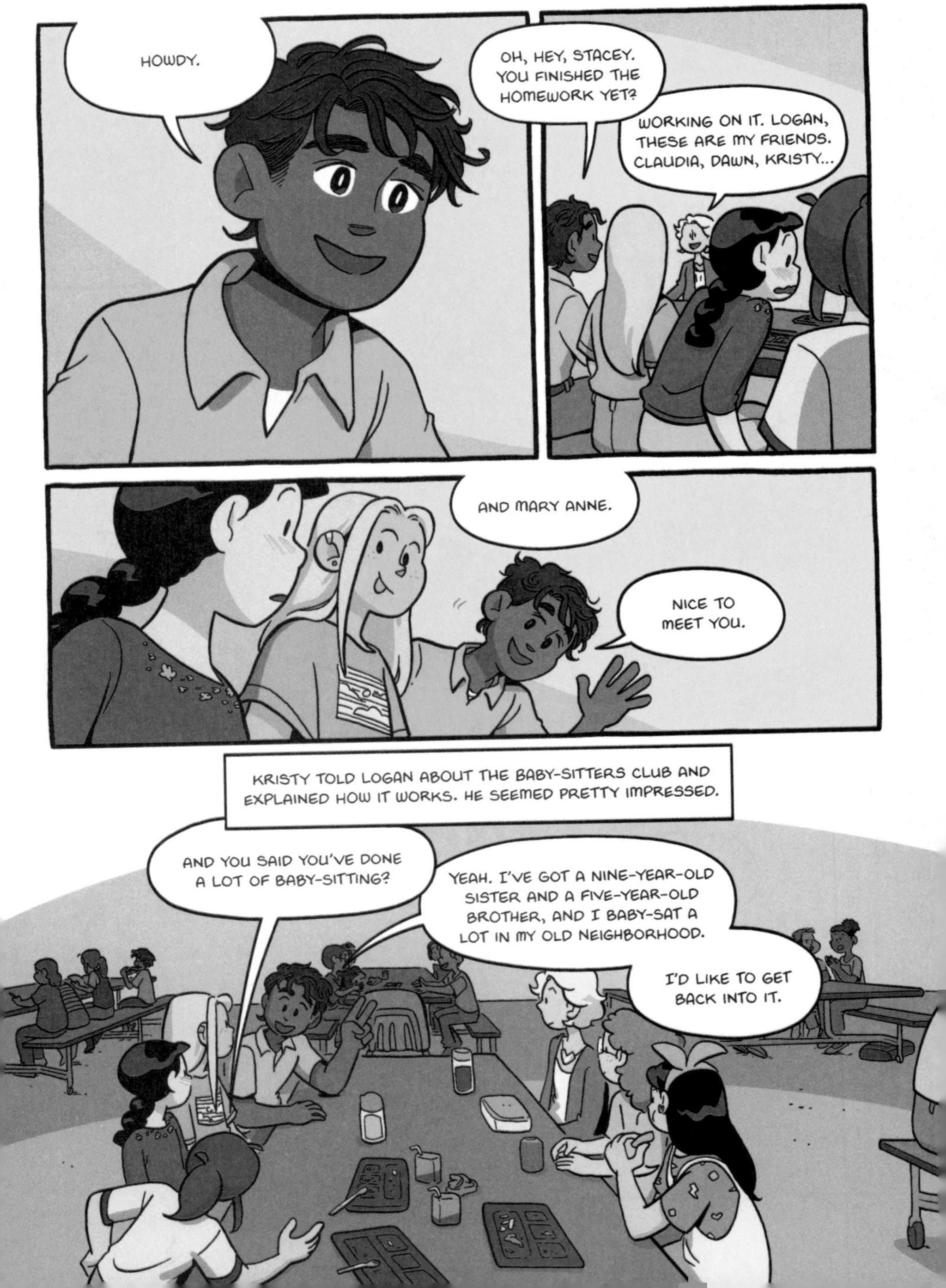
HOWDY.
OH, HEY, STACEY. YOU FINISHED THE HOMEWORK YET?
WORKING ON IT. LOGAN, THESE ARE MY FRIENDS. CLAUDIA, DAWN, KRISTY...
AND MARY ANNE.
NICE TO MEET YOU.
KRISTY TOLD LOGAN ABOUT THE BABY-SITTERS CLUB AND EXPLAINED HOW IT WORKS. HE SEEMED PRETTY IMPRESSED.
AND YOU SAID YOU'VE DONE A LOT OF BABY-SITTING?
YEAH. I'VE GOT A NINE-YEAR-OLD SISTER AND A FIVE-YEAR-OLD BROTHER, AND I BABY-SAT A LOT IN MY OLD NEIGHBORHOOD.
I'D LIKE TO GET BACK INTO IT.

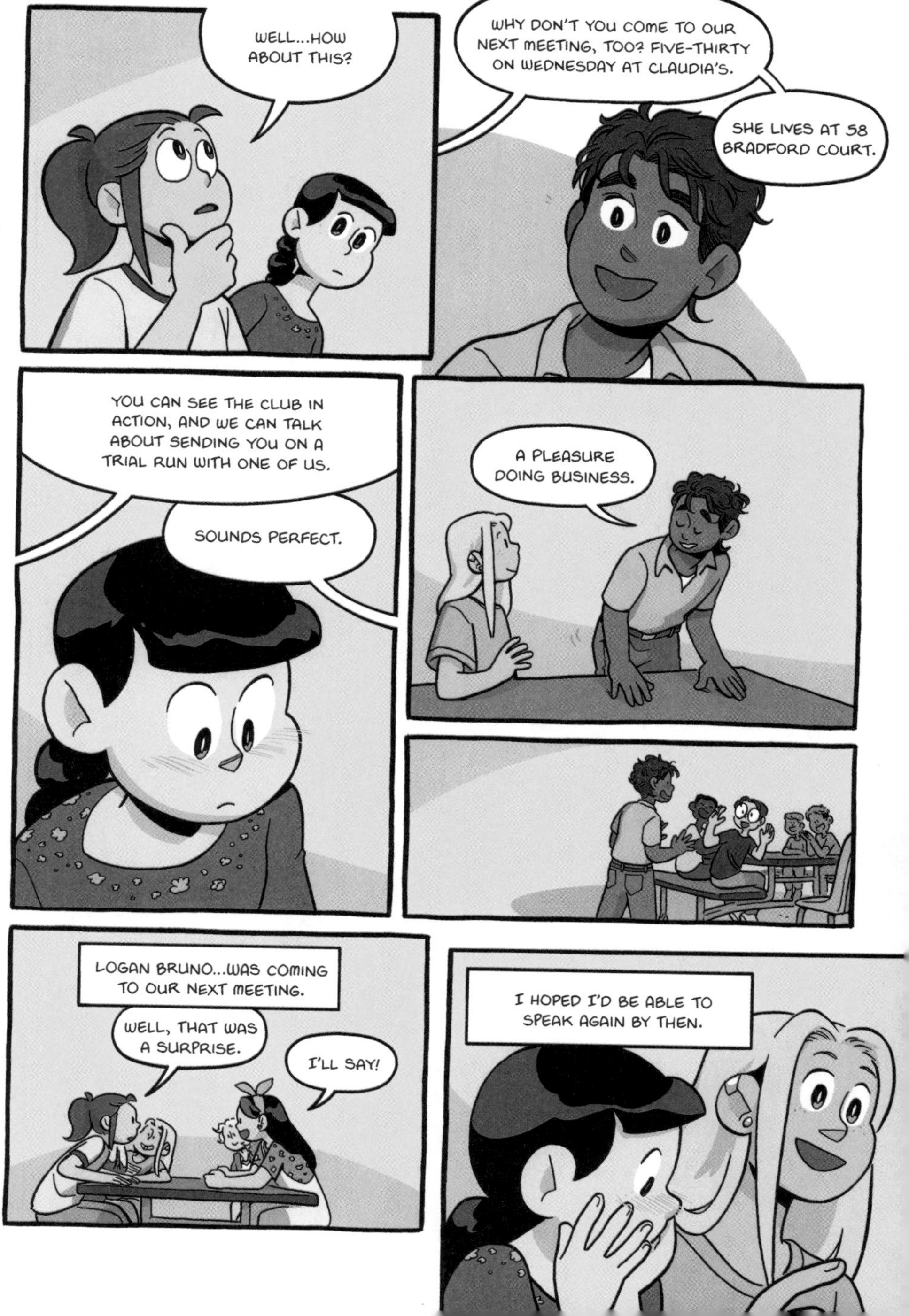
WELL...HOW ABOUT THIS?
WHY DON'T YOU COME TO OUR NEXT MEETING, TOO? FIVE-THIRTY ON WEDNESDAY AT CLAUDIA'S.
SHE LIVES AT 58 BRADFORD COURT.
YOU CAN SEE THE CLUB IN ACTION, AND WE CAN TALK ABOUT SENDING YOU ON A TRIAL RUN WITH ONE OF US.
SOUNDS PERFECT.
A PLEASURE DOING BUSINESS.
LOGAN BRUNO...WAS COMING TO OUR NEXT MEETING.
WELL, THAT WAS A SURPRISE.
I'LL SAY!
I HOPED I'D BE ABLE TO SPEAK AGAIN BY THEN.

CHAPTER 5

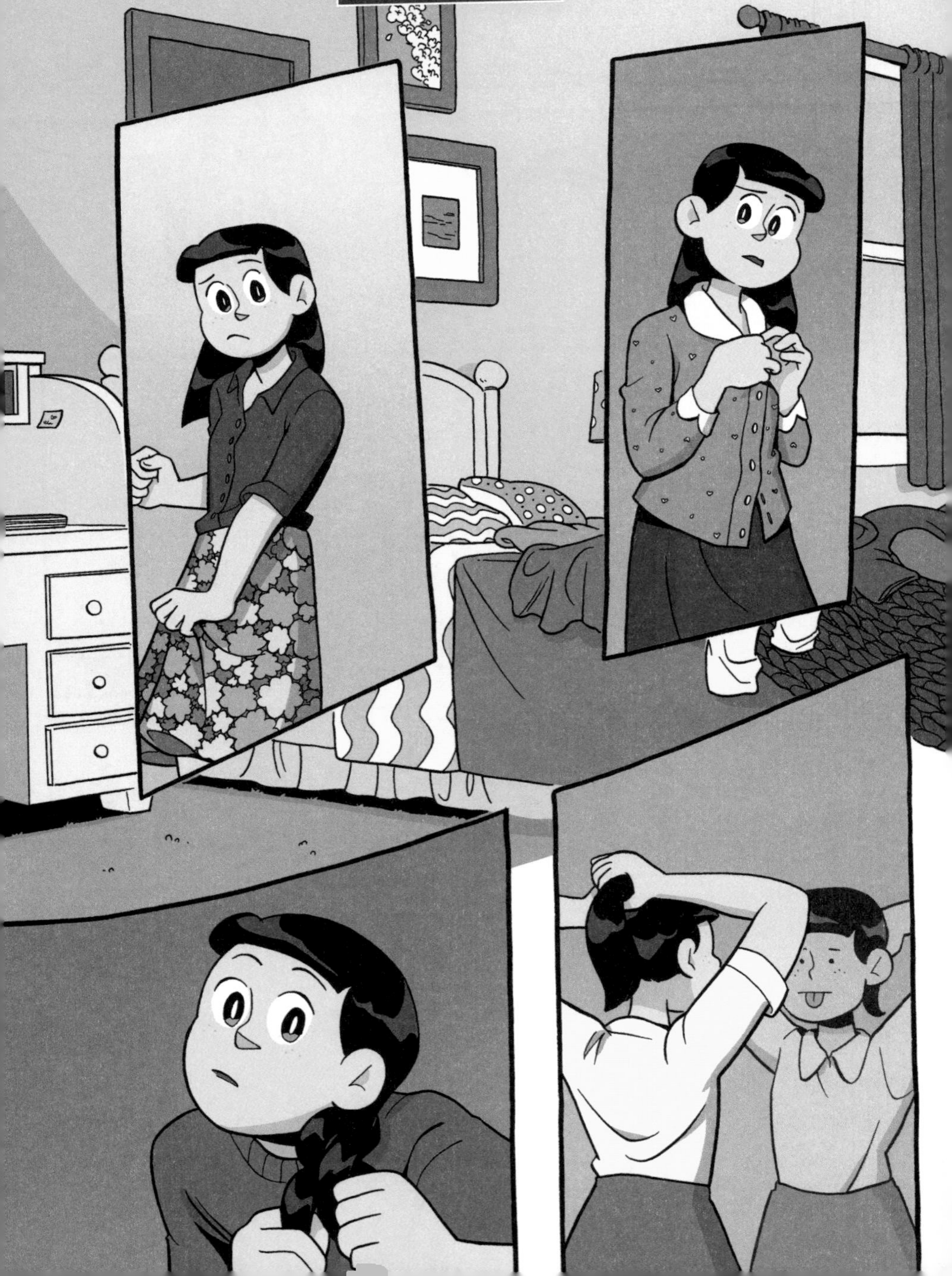

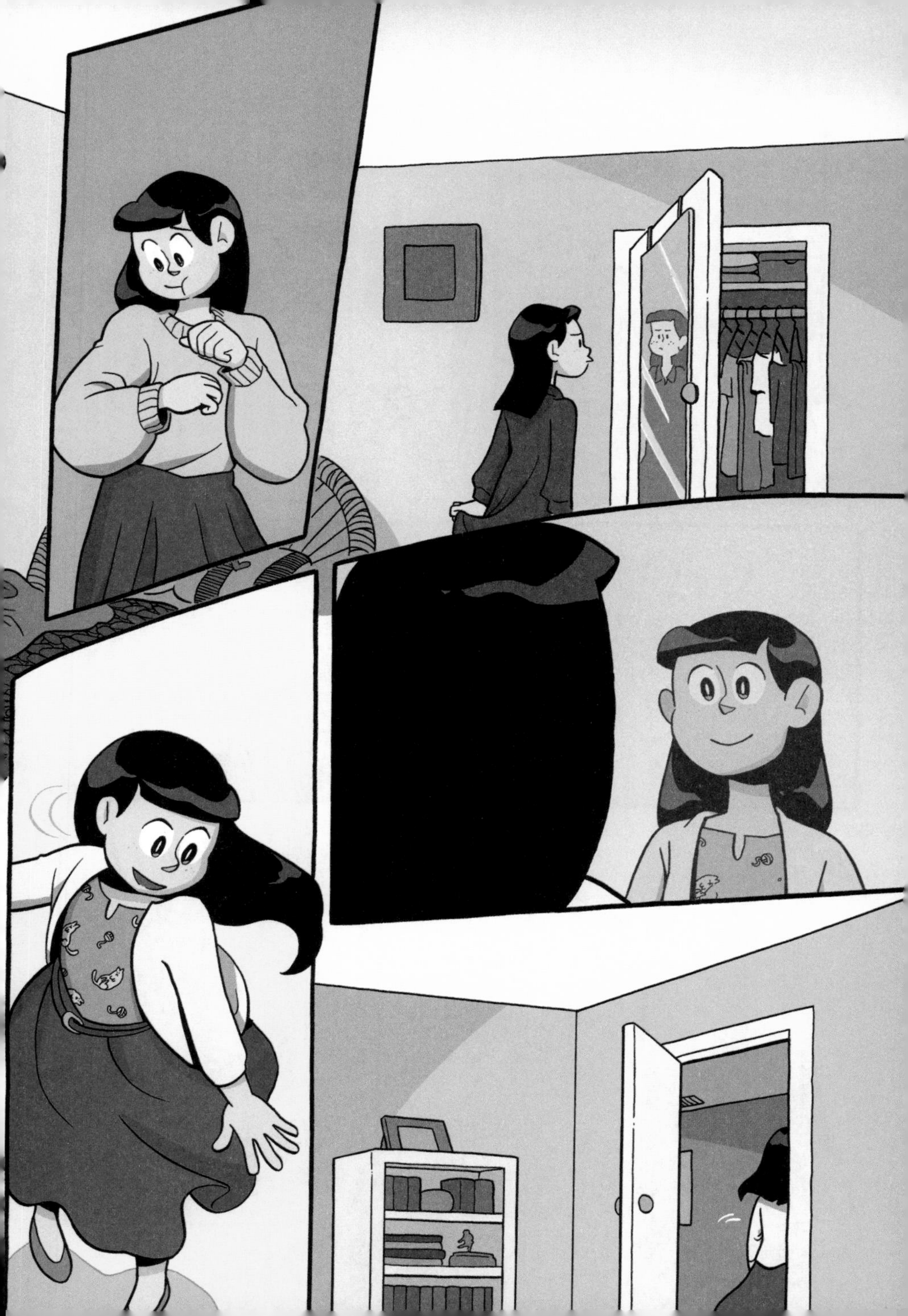

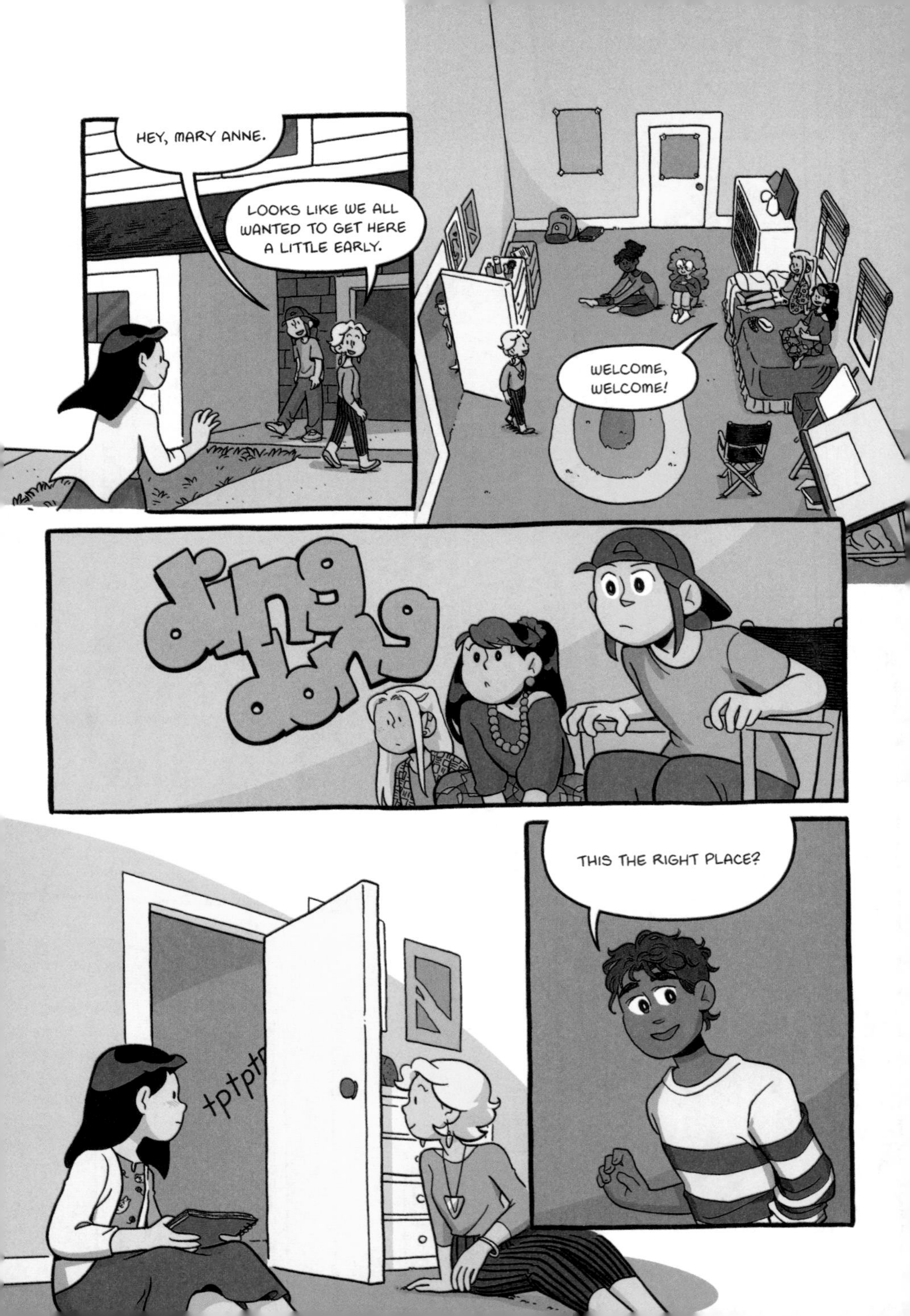
HEY, MARY ANNE.
LOOKS LIKE WE ALL WANTED TO GET HERE A LITTLE EARLY.
WELCOME, WELCOME!
ding dong
tptptp
THIS THE RIGHT PLACE?

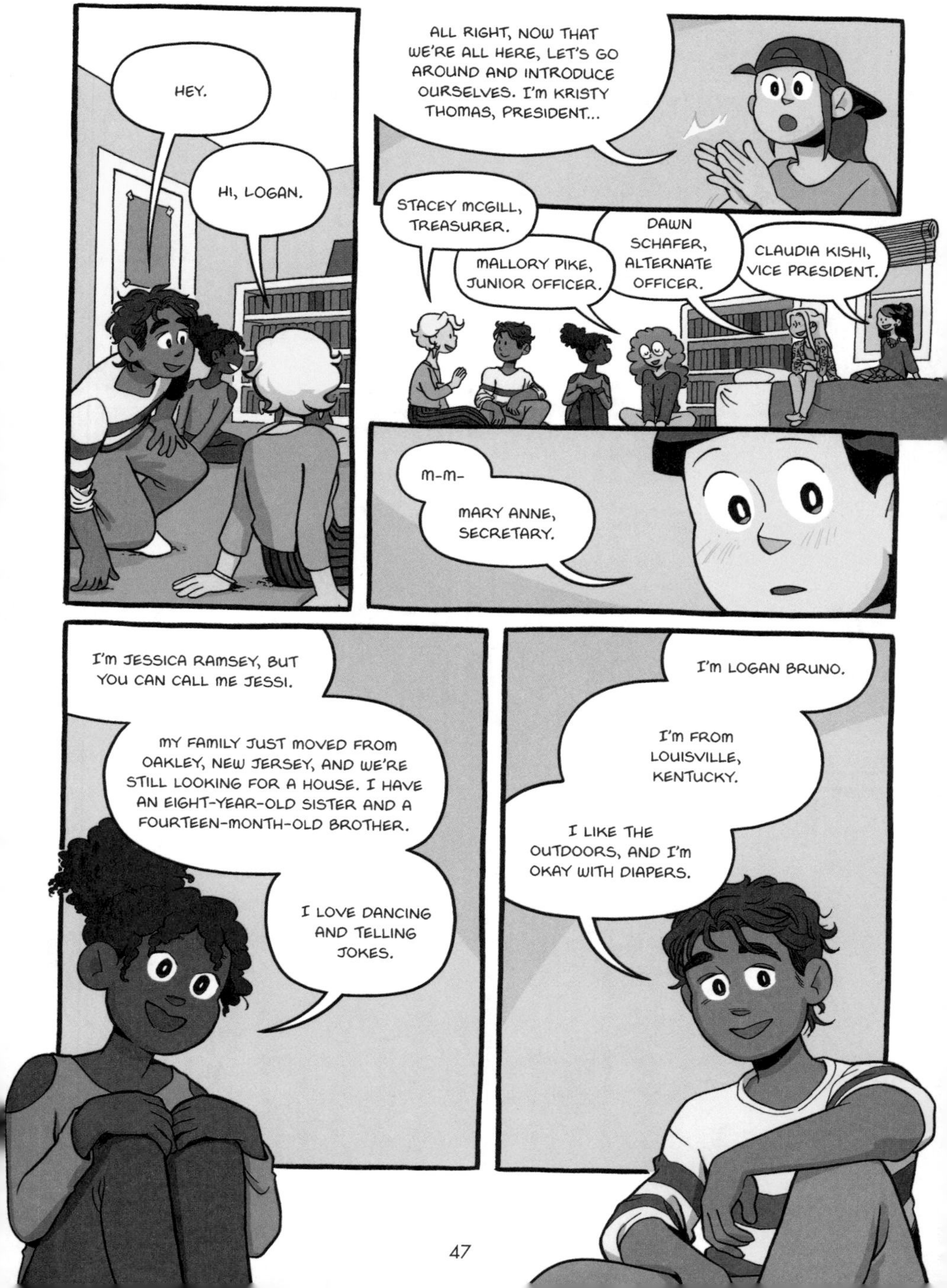
HEY.
HI, LOGAN.
ALL RIGHT, NOW THAT WE'RE ALL HERE, LET'S GO AROUND AND INTRODUCE OURSELVES. I'M KRISTY THOMAS, PRESIDENT...
STACEY MCGILL, TREASURER.
MALLORY PIKE, JUNIOR OFFICER.
DAWN SCHAFER, ALTERNATE OFFICER.
CLAUDIA KISHI, VICE PRESIDENT.
M-M-
MARY ANNE, SECRETARY.
I'M JESSICA RAMSEY, BUT YOU CAN CALL ME JESSI.
MY FAMILY JUST MOVED FROM OAKLEY, NEW JERSEY, AND WE'RE STILL LOOKING FOR A HOUSE. I HAVE AN EIGHT-YEAR-OLD SISTER AND A FOURTEEN-MONTH-OLD BROTHER.
I LOVE DANCING AND TELLING JOKES.
I'M LOGAN BRUNO.
I'M FROM LOUISVILLE, KENTUCKY.
I LIKE THE OUTDOORS, AND I'M OKAY WITH DIAPERS.

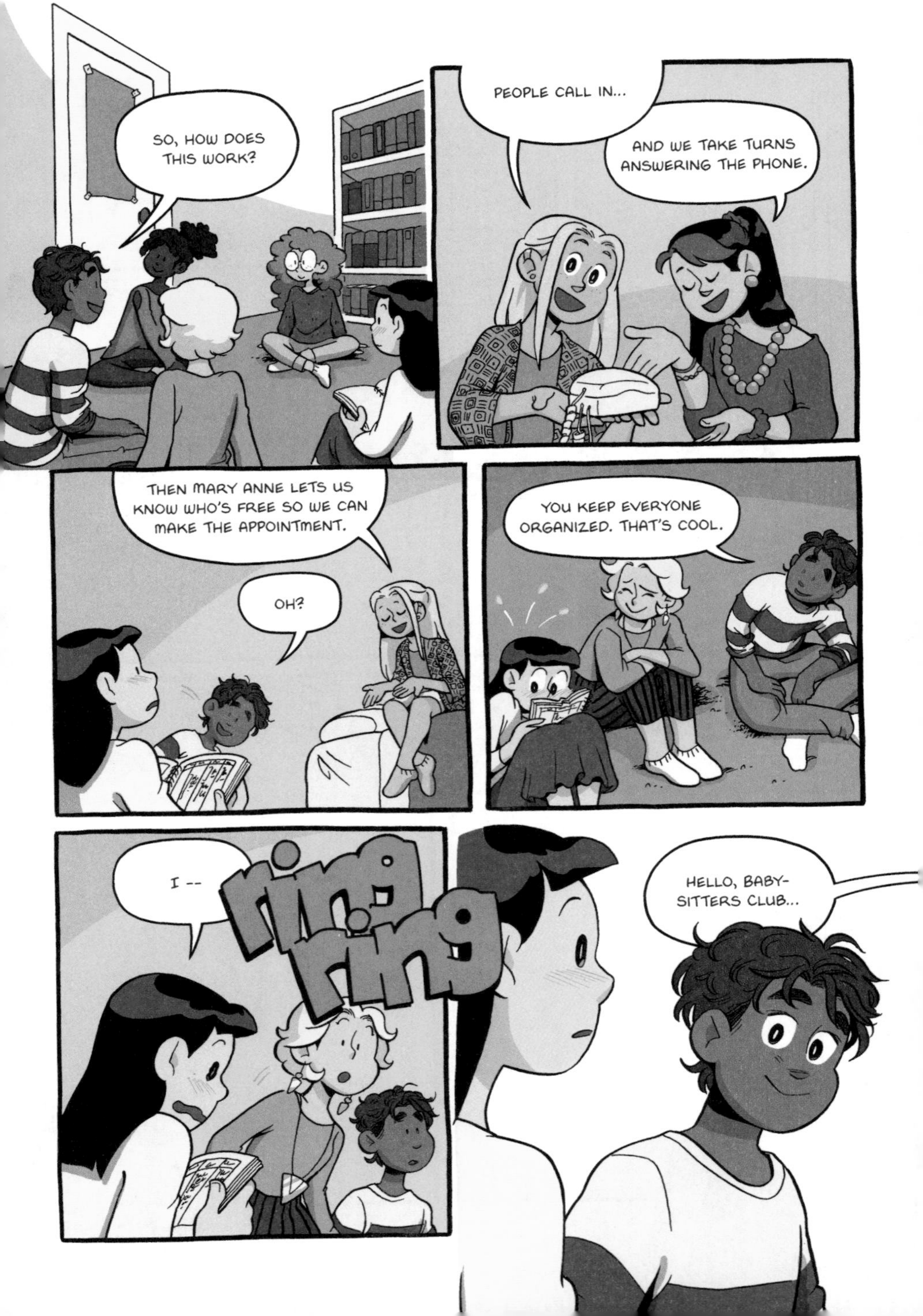
SO, HOW DOES THIS WORK?
PEOPLE CALL IN...
AND WE TAKE TURNS ANSWERING THE PHONE.
THEN MARY ANNE LETS US KNOW WHO'S FREE SO WE CAN MAKE THE APPOINTMENT.
OH?
YOU KEEP EVERYONE ORGANIZED. THAT'S COOL.
I --
RING RING
HELLO, BABY-SITTERS CLUB...

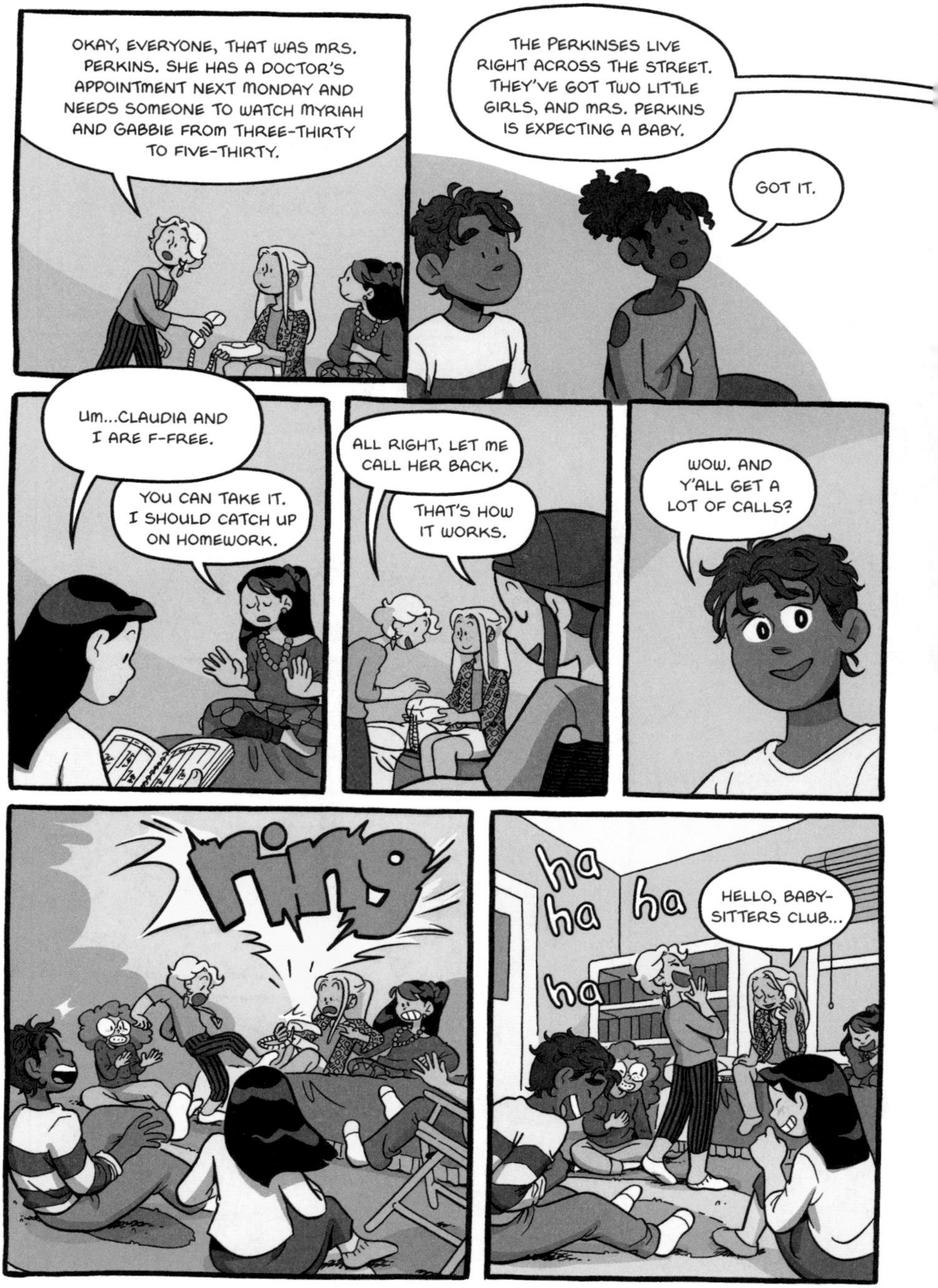
OKAY, EVERYONE, THAT WAS MRS. PERKINS. SHE HAS A DOCTOR'S APPOINTMENT NEXT MONDAY AND NEEDS SOMEONE TO WATCH MYRIAH AND GABBIE FROM THREE-THIRTY TO FIVE-THIRTY.
THE PERKINSES LIVE RIGHT ACROSS THE STREET. THEY'VE GOT TWO LITTLE GIRLS, AND MRS. PERKINS IS EXPECTING A BABY.
GOT IT.
UM...CLAUDIA AND I ARE F-FREE.
YOU CAN TAKE IT. I SHOULD CATCH UP ON HOMEWORK.
ALL RIGHT, LET ME CALL HER BACK.
THAT'S HOW IT WORKS.
WOW. AND Y'ALL GET A LOT OF CALLS?
ring
ha ha ha ha
HELLO, BABY-SITTERS CLUB...

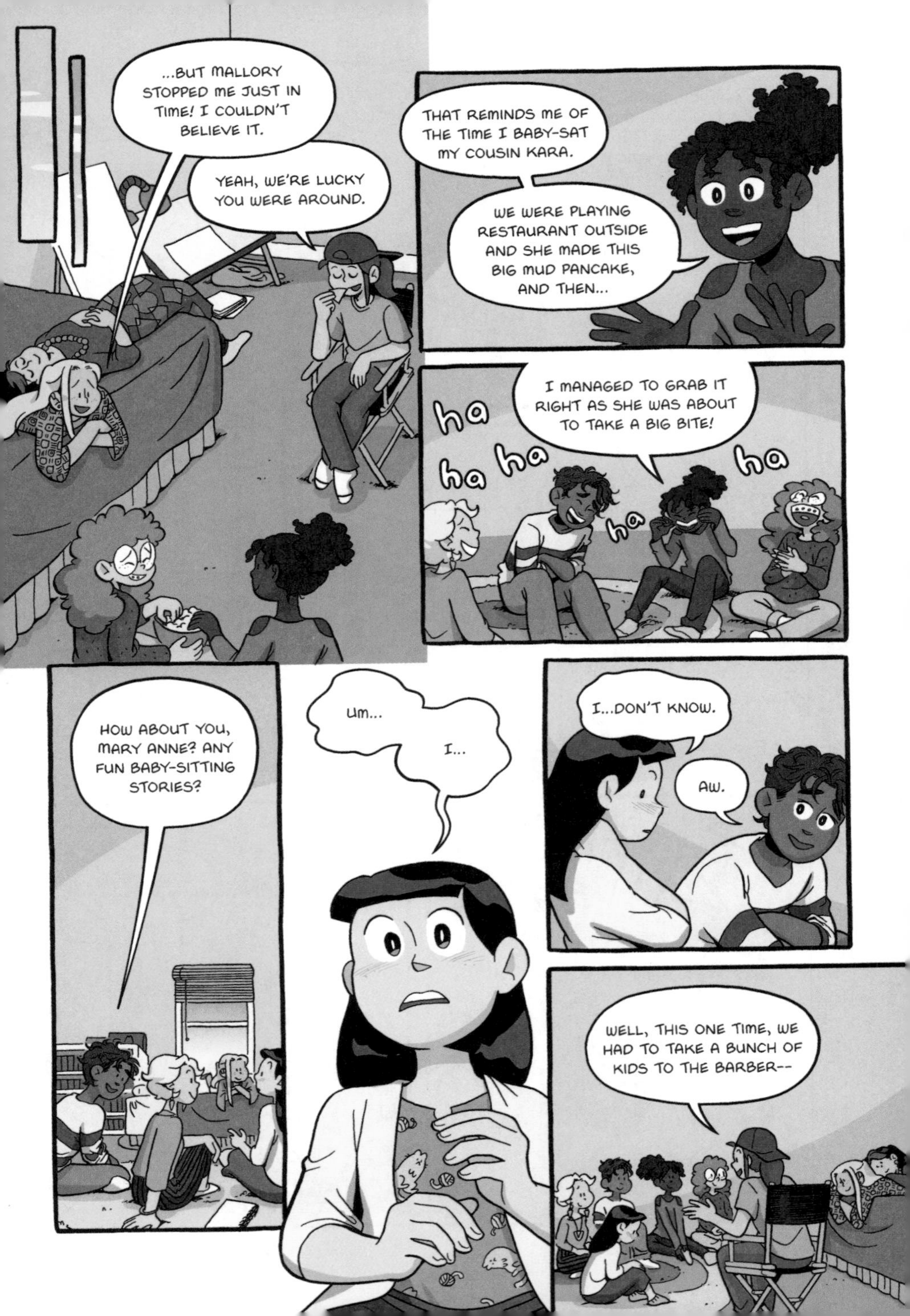
...BUT MALLORY STOPPED ME JUST IN TIME! I COULDN'T BELIEVE IT.
YEAH, WE'RE LUCKY YOU WERE AROUND.
THAT REMINDS ME OF THE TIME I BABY-SAT MY COUSIN KARA.
WE WERE PLAYING RESTAURANT OUTSIDE AND SHE MADE THIS BIG MUD PANCAKE, AND THEN...
ha
ha ha
I MANAGED TO GRAB IT RIGHT AS SHE WAS ABOUT TO TAKE A BIG BITE!
ha
ha
HOW ABOUT YOU, MARY ANNE? ANY FUN BABY-SITTING STORIES?
um...
I...
I...DON'T KNOW.
AW.
WELL, THIS ONE TIME, WE HAD TO TAKE A BUNCH OF KIDS TO THE BARBER--

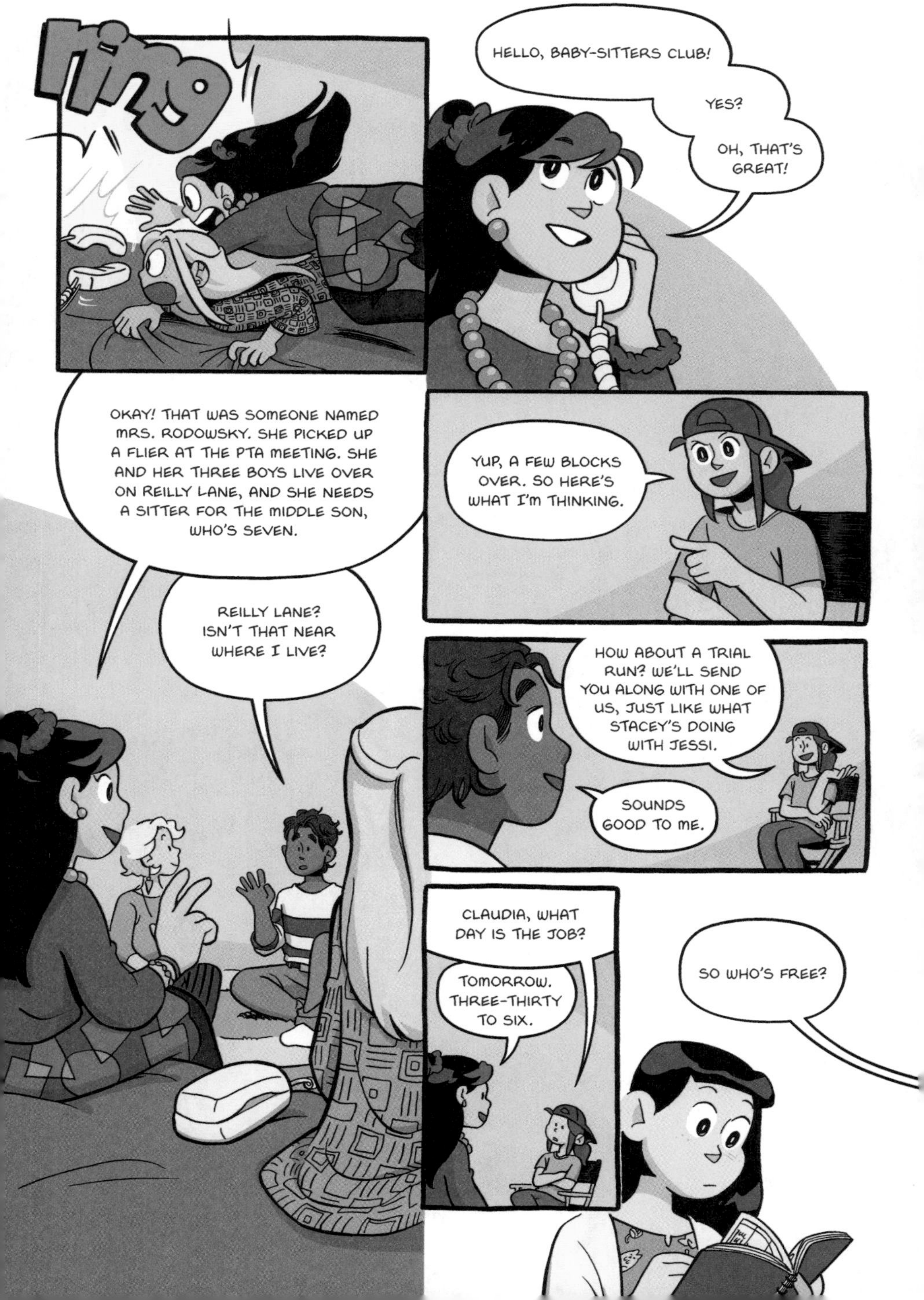

ring
HELLO, BABY-SITTERS CLUB!
YES?
OH, THAT'S GREAT!
OKAY! THAT WAS SOMEONE NAMED MRS. RODOWSKY. SHE PICKED UP A FLIER AT THE PTA MEETING. SHE AND HER THREE BOYS LIVE OVER ON REILLY LANE, AND SHE NEEDS A SITTER FOR THE MIDDLE SON, WHO'S SEVEN.
REILLY LANE? ISN'T THAT NEAR WHERE I LIVE?
YUP, A FEW BLOCKS OVER. SO HERE'S WHAT I'M THINKING.
HOW ABOUT A TRIAL RUN? WE'LL SEND YOU ALONG WITH ONE OF US, JUST LIKE WHAT STACEY'S DOING WITH JESSI.
SOUNDS GOOD TO ME.
CLAUDIA, WHAT DAY IS THE JOB?
TOMORROW. THREE-THIRTY TO SIX.
SO WHO'S FREE?

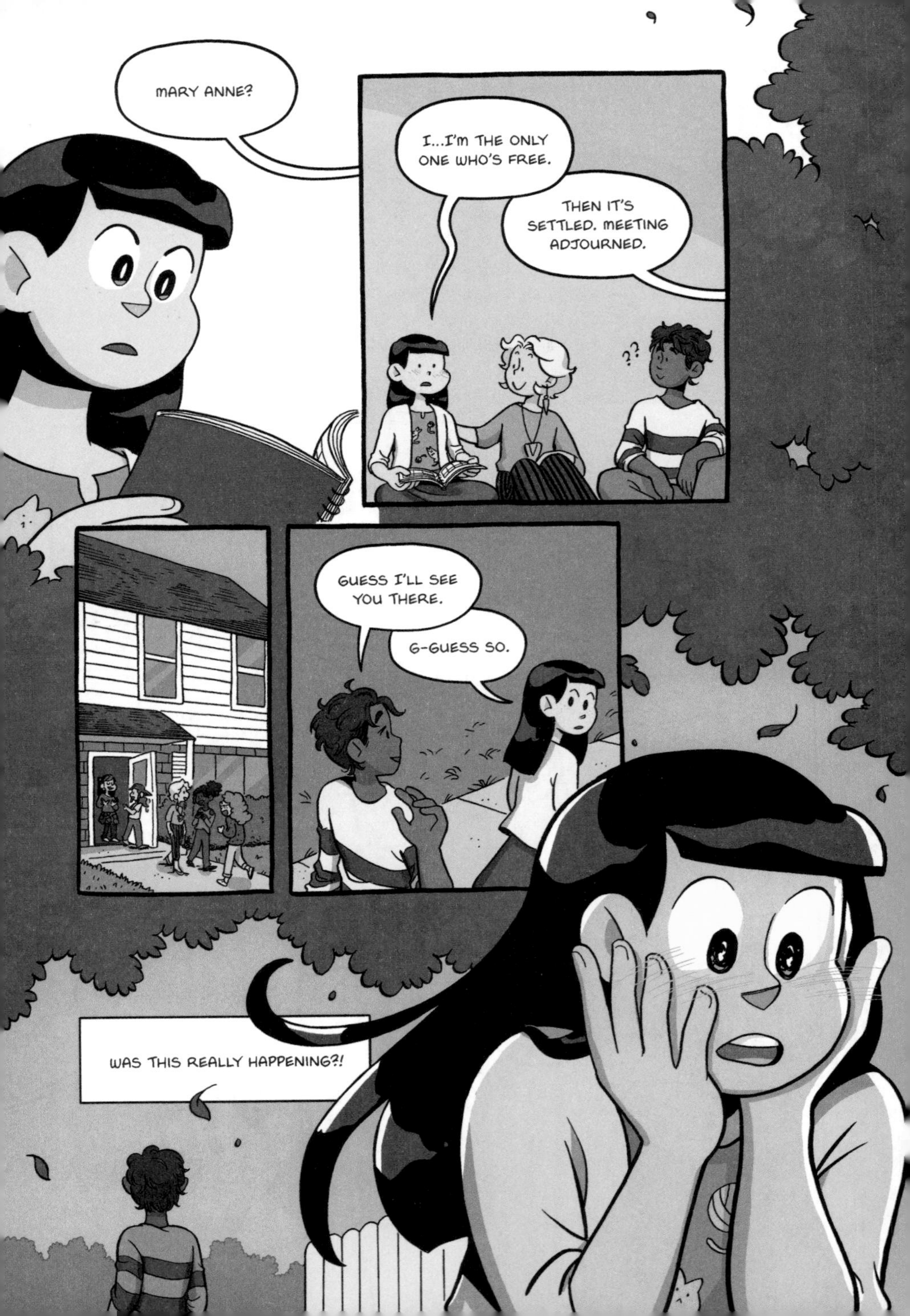
MARY ANNE?
I...I'M THE ONLY ONE WHO'S FREE.
THEN IT'S SETTLED. MEETING ADJOURNED.
??
GUESS I'LL SEE YOU THERE.
G-GUESS SO.
WAS THIS REALLY HAPPENING?!

CHAPTER 6

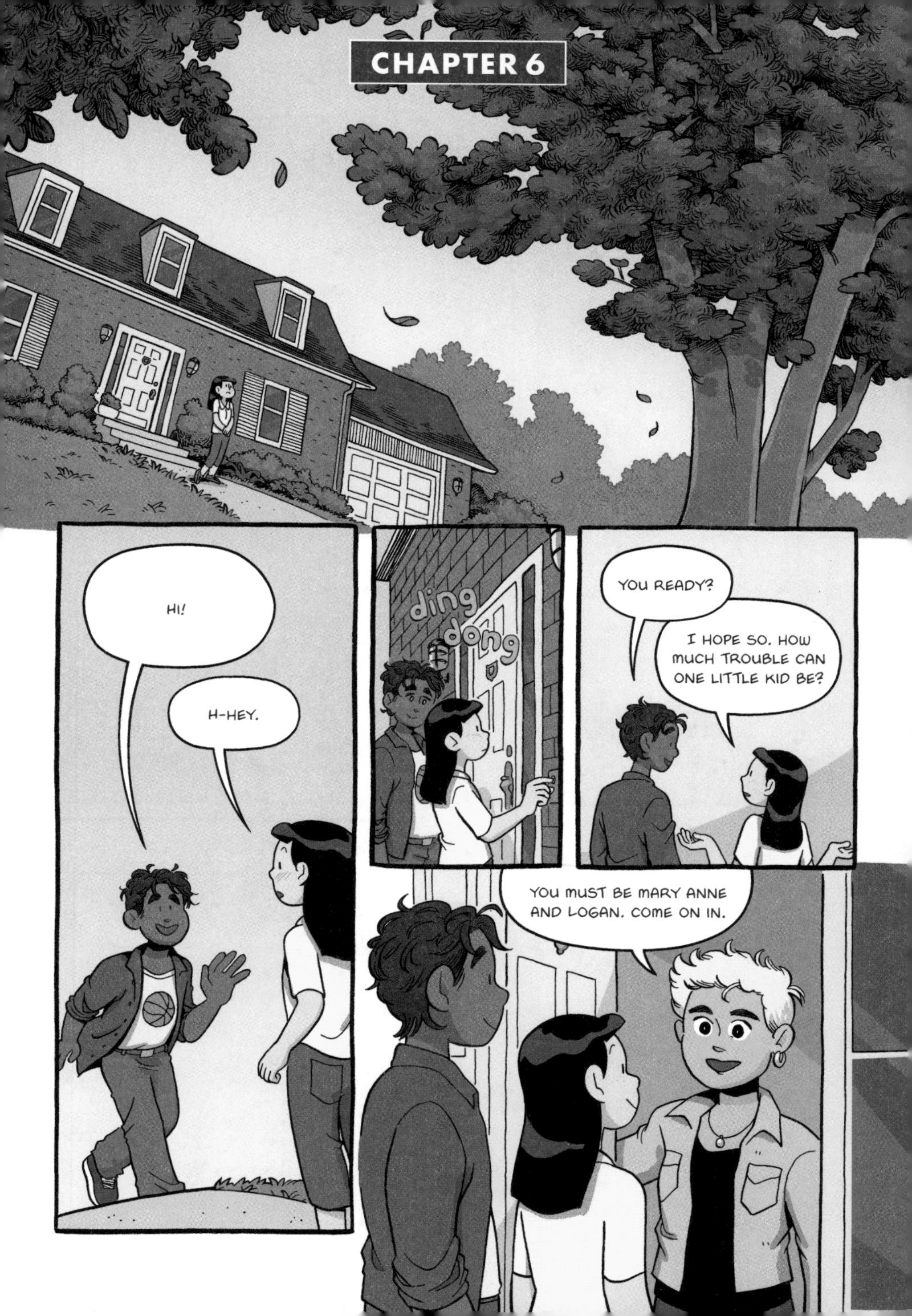
HI!
H-HEY.
ding dong
YOU READY?
I HOPE SO. HOW MUCH TROUBLE CAN ONE LITTLE KID BE?
YOU MUST BE MARY ANNE AND LOGAN. COME ON IN.

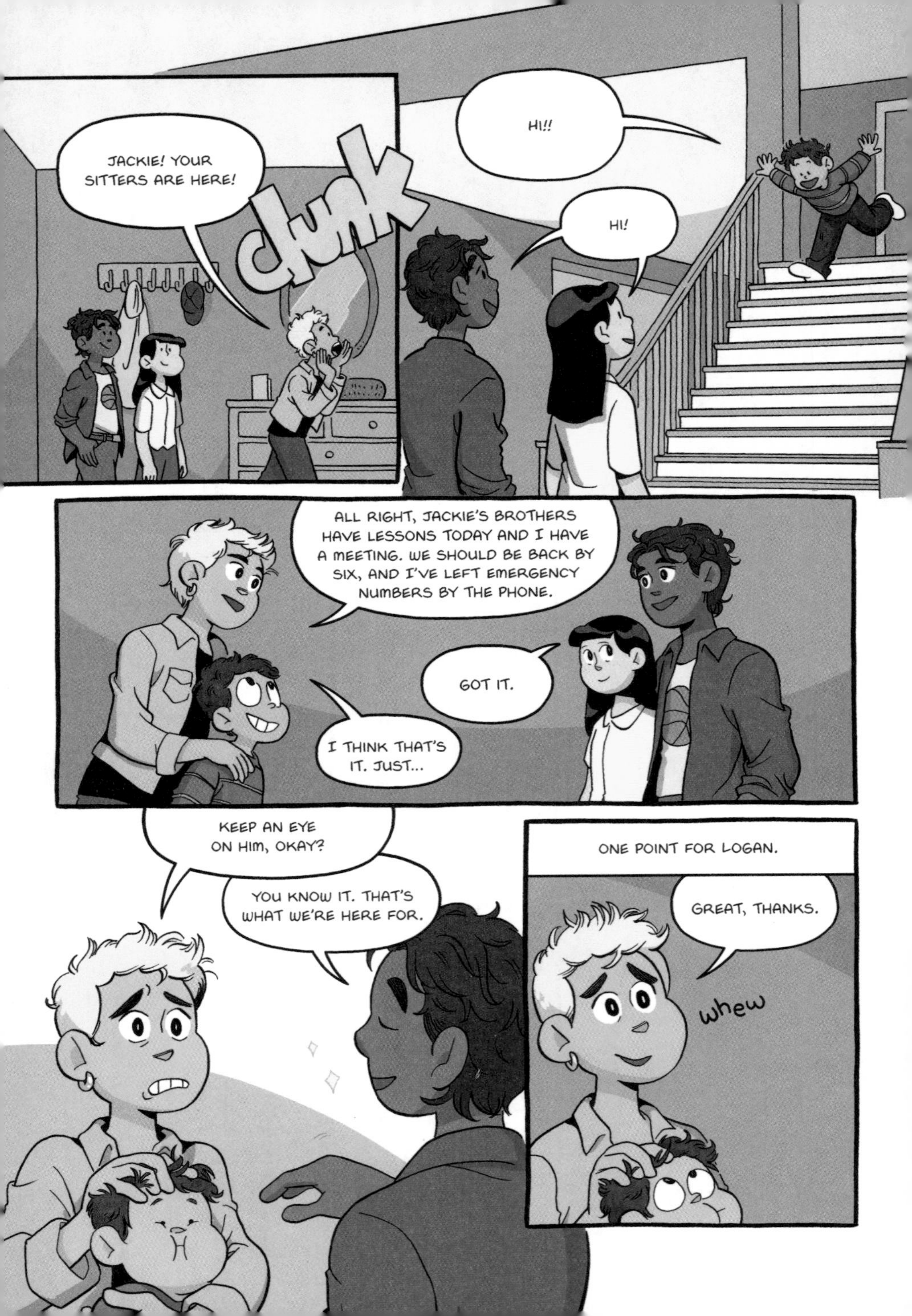
JACKIE! YOUR SITTERS ARE HERE!
clunk
HI!!
HI!
ALL RIGHT, JACKIE'S BROTHERS HAVE LESSONS TODAY AND I HAVE A MEETING. WE SHOULD BE BACK BY SIX, AND I'VE LEFT EMERGENCY NUMBERS BY THE PHONE.
GOT IT.
I THINK THAT'S IT. JUST...
KEEP AN EYE ON HIM, OKAY?
YOU KNOW IT. THAT'S WHAT WE'RE HERE FOR.
ONE POINT FOR LOGAN.
GREAT, THANKS.
whew

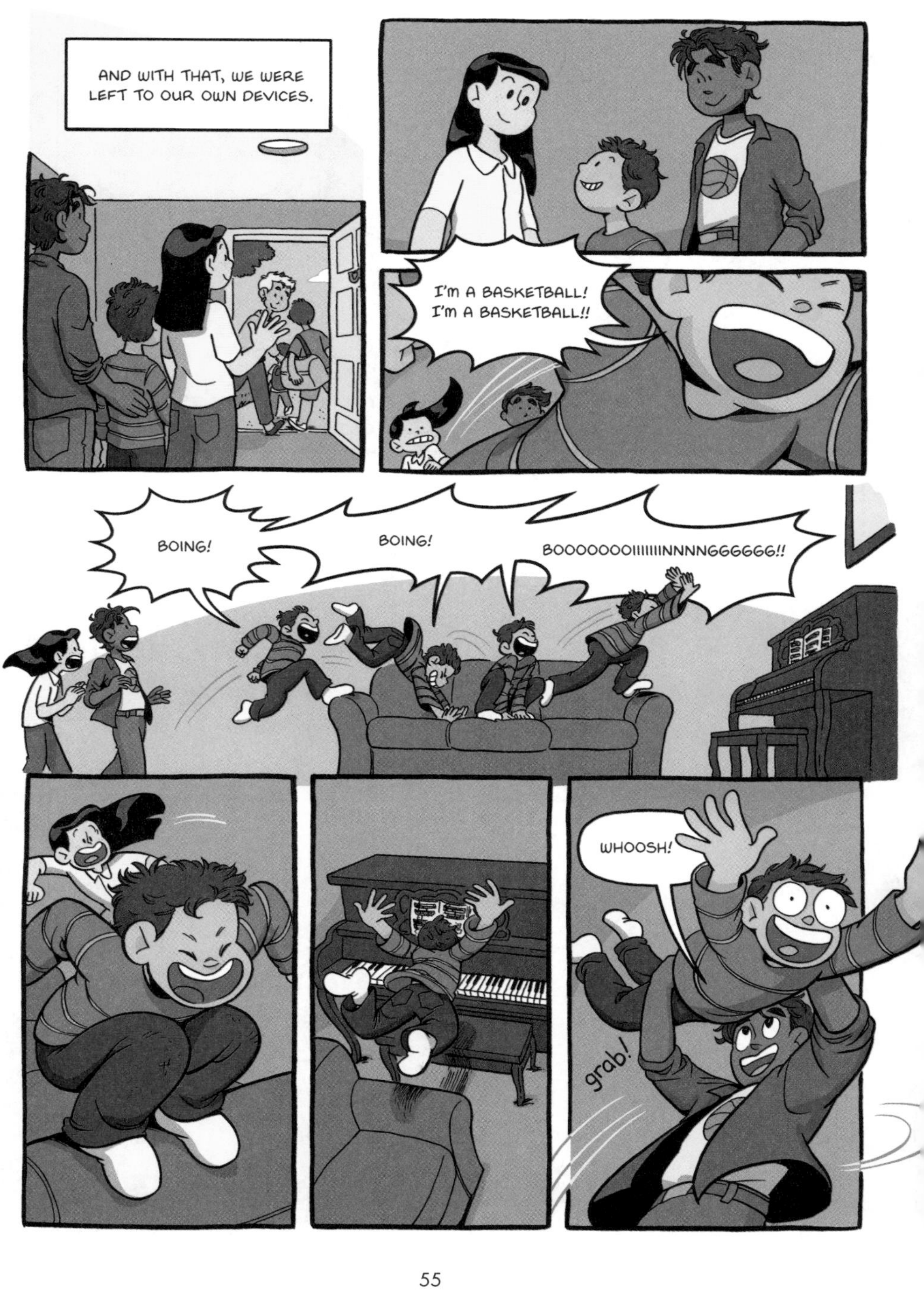
AND WITH THAT, WE WERE LEFT TO OUR OWN DEVICES.
I'M A BASKETBALL! I'M A BASKETBALL!!
BOING!
BOING!
BOOOOOOOIIIIIIINNNNGGGGGG!!
WHOOSH!
grab!

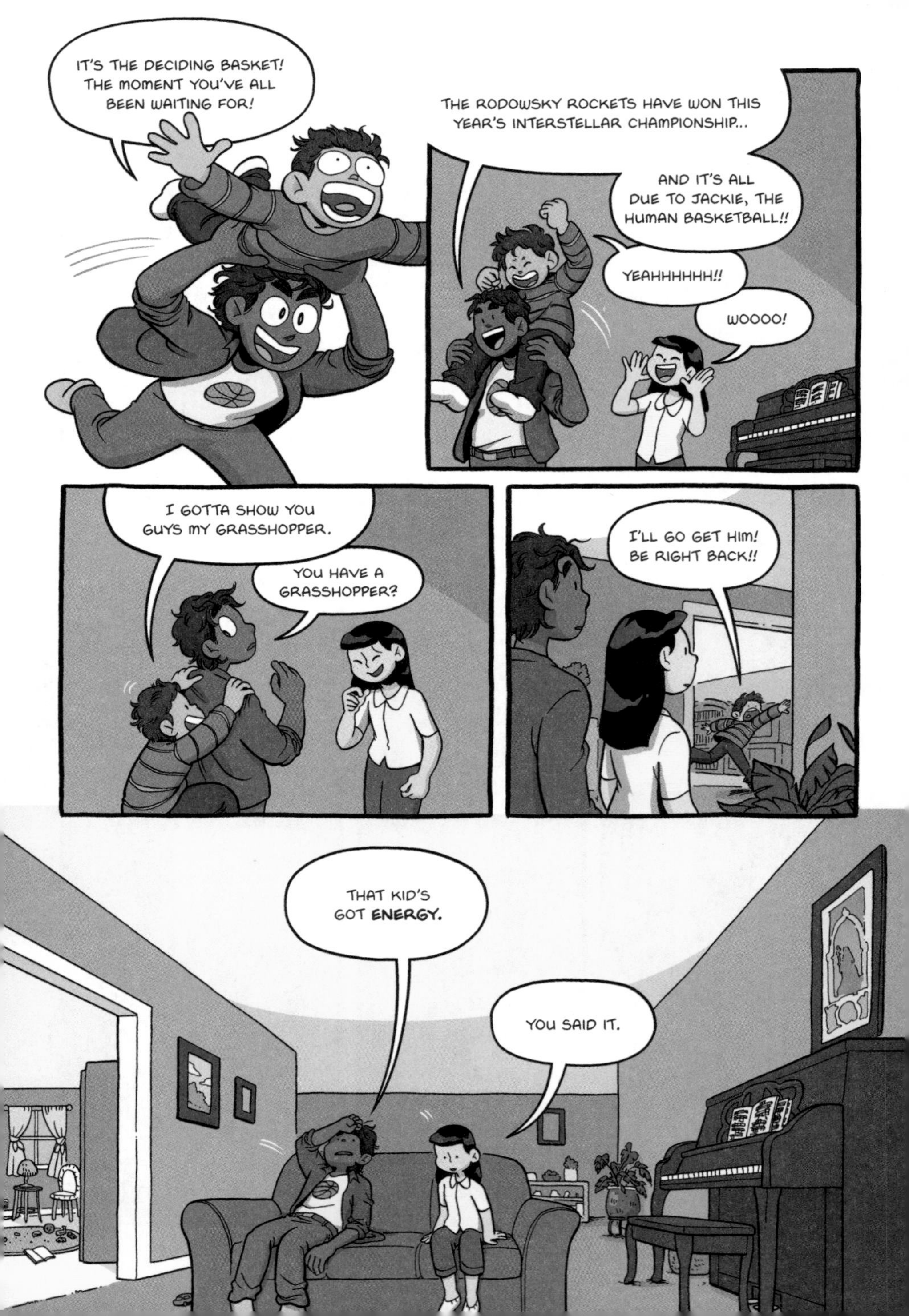
IT'S THE DECIDING BASKET! THE MOMENT YOU'VE ALL BEEN WAITING FOR!
THE RODOWSKY ROCKETS HAVE WON THIS YEAR'S INTERSTELLAR CHAMPIONSHIP...
AND IT'S ALL DUE TO JACKIE, THE HUMAN BASKETBALL!!
YEAHHHHHHH!!
WOOOO!
I GOTTA SHOW YOU GUYS MY GRASSHOPPER.
YOU HAVE A GRASSHOPPER?
I'LL GO GET HIM! BE RIGHT BACK!!
THAT KID'S GOT **ENERGY.**
YOU SAID IT.

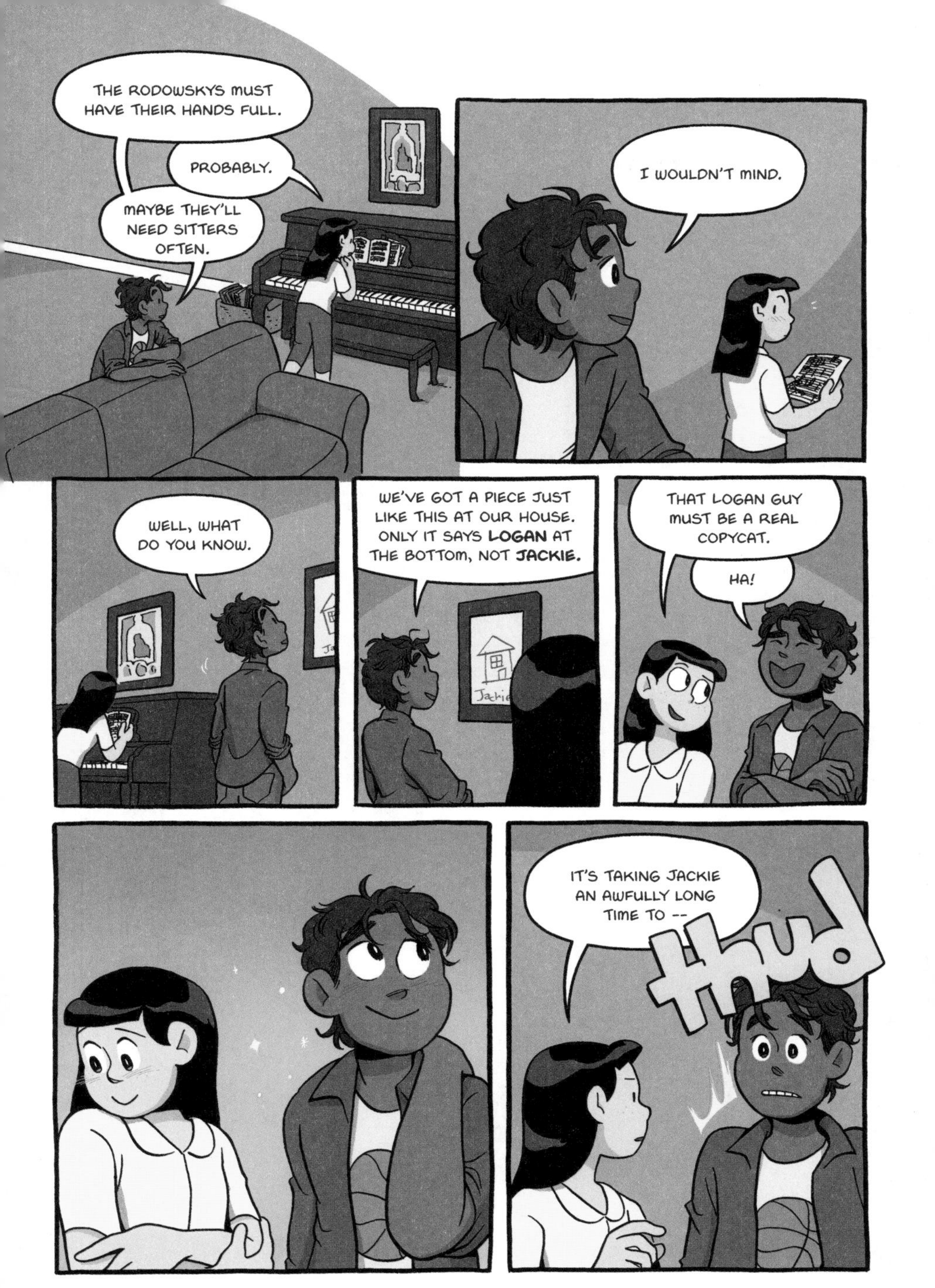
THE RODOWSKYS MUST HAVE THEIR HANDS FULL.
PROBABLY.
MAYBE THEY'LL NEED SITTERS OFTEN.
I WOULDN'T MIND.
WELL, WHAT DO YOU KNOW.
WE'VE GOT A PIECE JUST LIKE THIS AT OUR HOUSE. ONLY IT SAYS LOGAN AT THE BOTTOM, NOT JACKIE.
Jackie
THAT LOGAN GUY MUST BE A REAL COPYCAT.
HA!
IT'S TAKING JACKIE AN AWFULLY LONG TIME TO --
thud

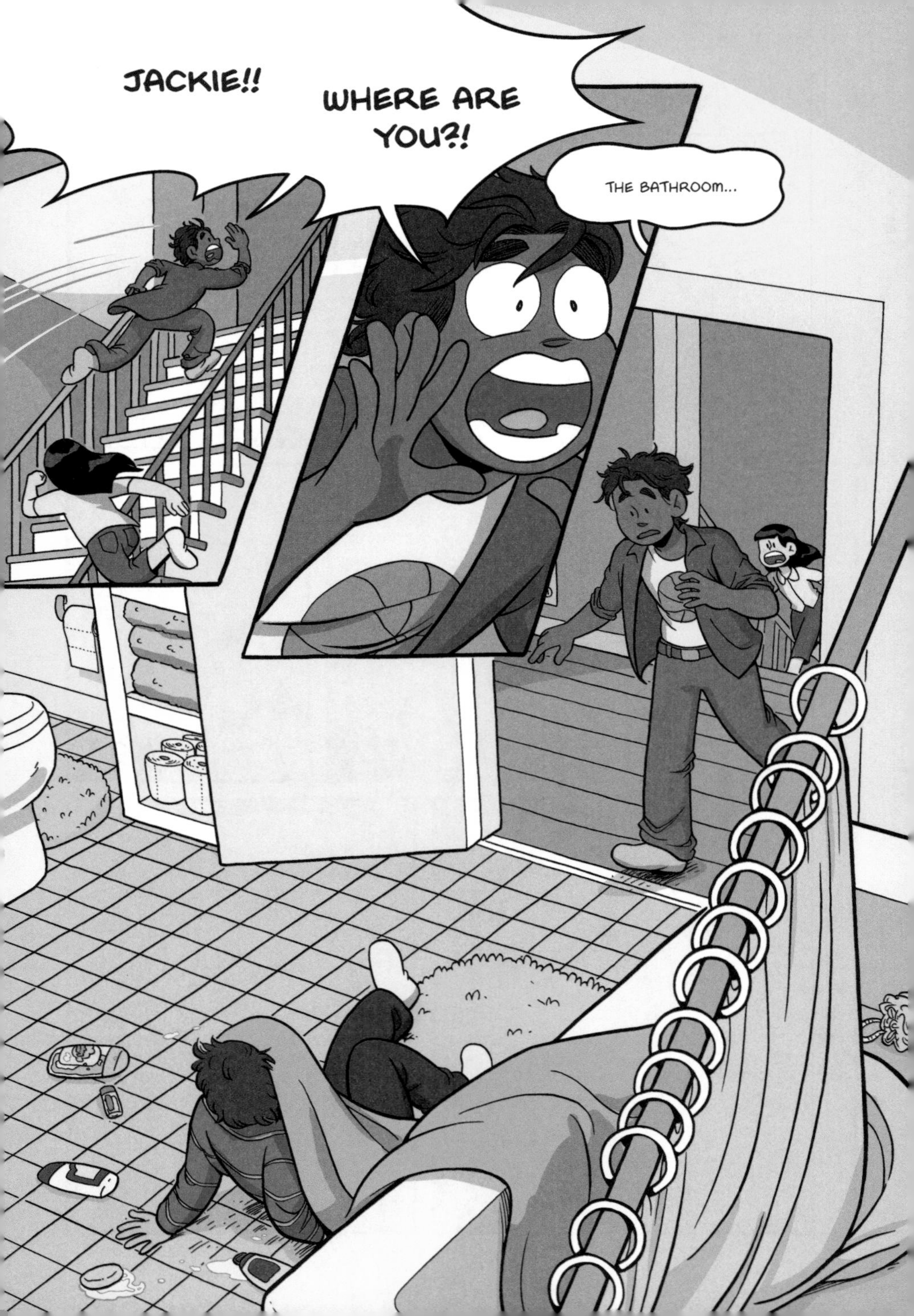
JACKIE!!
WHERE ARE YOU?!
THE BATHROOM...

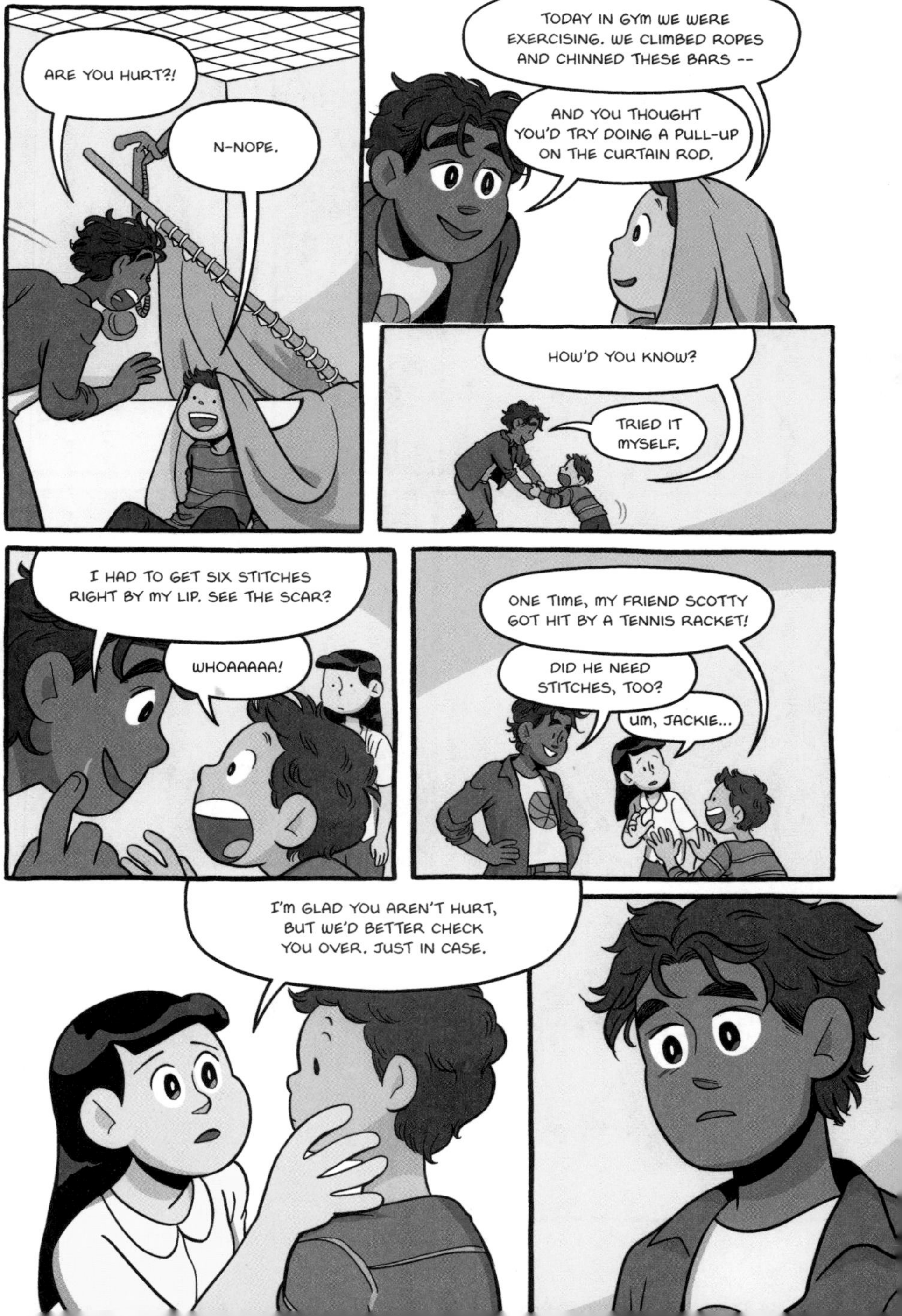
ARE YOU HURT?!
N-NOPE.
TODAY IN GYM WE WERE EXERCISING. WE CLIMBED ROPES AND CHINNED THESE BARS --
AND YOU THOUGHT YOU'D TRY DOING A PULL-UP ON THE CURTAIN ROD.
HOW'D YOU KNOW?
TRIED IT MYSELF.
I HAD TO GET SIX STITCHES RIGHT BY MY LIP. SEE THE SCAR?
WHOAAAAA!
ONE TIME, MY FRIEND SCOTTY GOT HIT BY A TENNIS RACKET!
DID HE NEED STITCHES, TOO?
UM, JACKIE...
I'M GLAD YOU AREN'T HURT, BUT WE'D BETTER CHECK YOU OVER. JUST IN CASE.

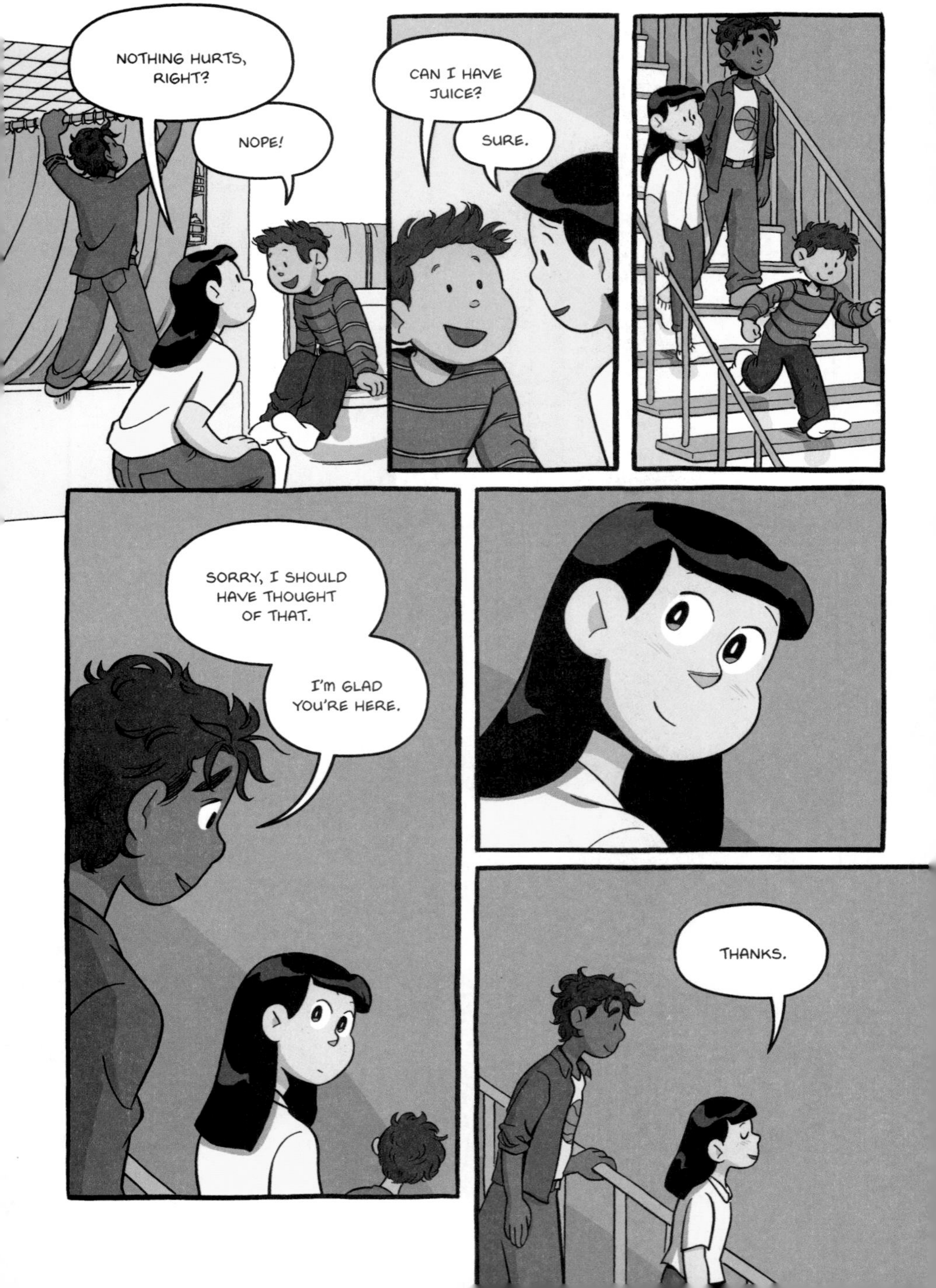
NOTHING HURTS, RIGHT?
NOPE!
CAN I HAVE JUICE?
SURE.
SORRY, I SHOULD HAVE THOUGHT OF THAT.
I'M GLAD YOU'RE HERE.
THANKS.

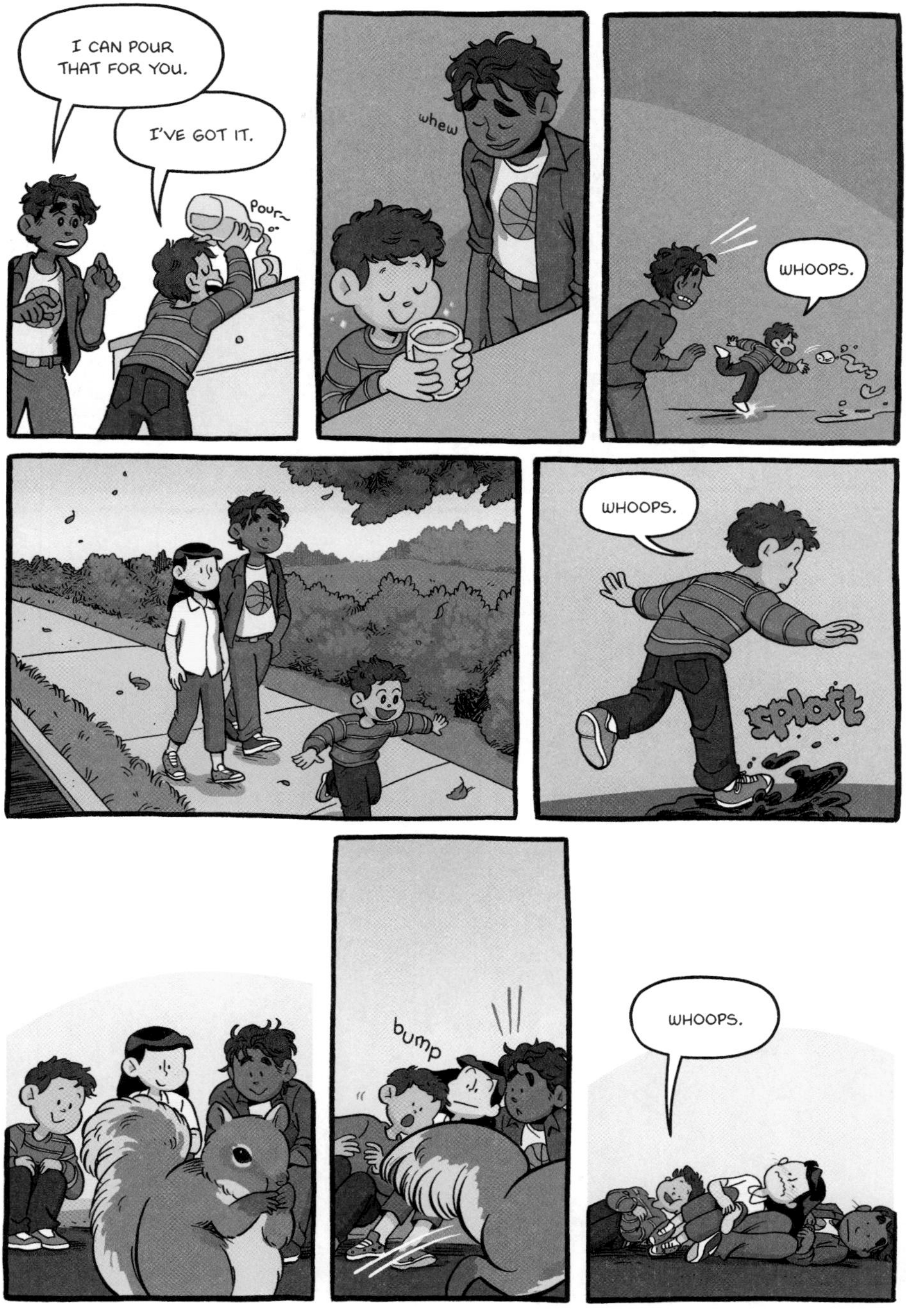
I CAN POUR THAT FOR YOU.
I'VE GOT IT.
Pour~
whew
WHOOPS.
WHOOPS.
splort
bump
WHOOPS.

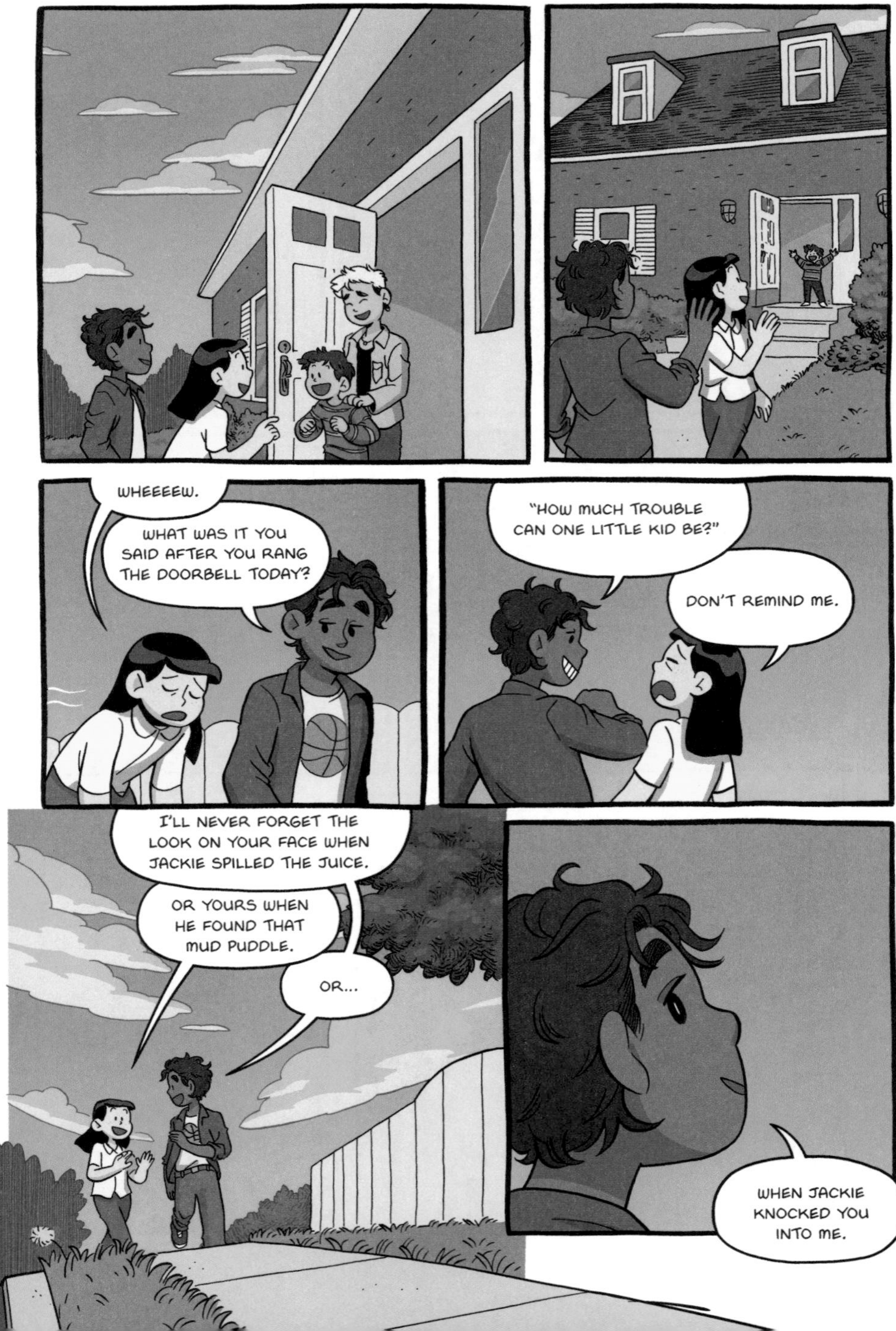
WHEEEEW.
WHAT WAS IT YOU SAID AFTER YOU RANG THE DOORBELL TODAY?
"HOW MUCH TROUBLE CAN ONE LITTLE KID BE?"
DON'T REMIND ME.
I'LL NEVER FORGET THE LOOK ON YOUR FACE WHEN JACKIE SPILLED THE JUICE.
OR YOURS WHEN HE FOUND THAT MUD PUDDLE.
OR...
WHEN JACKIE KNOCKED YOU INTO ME.

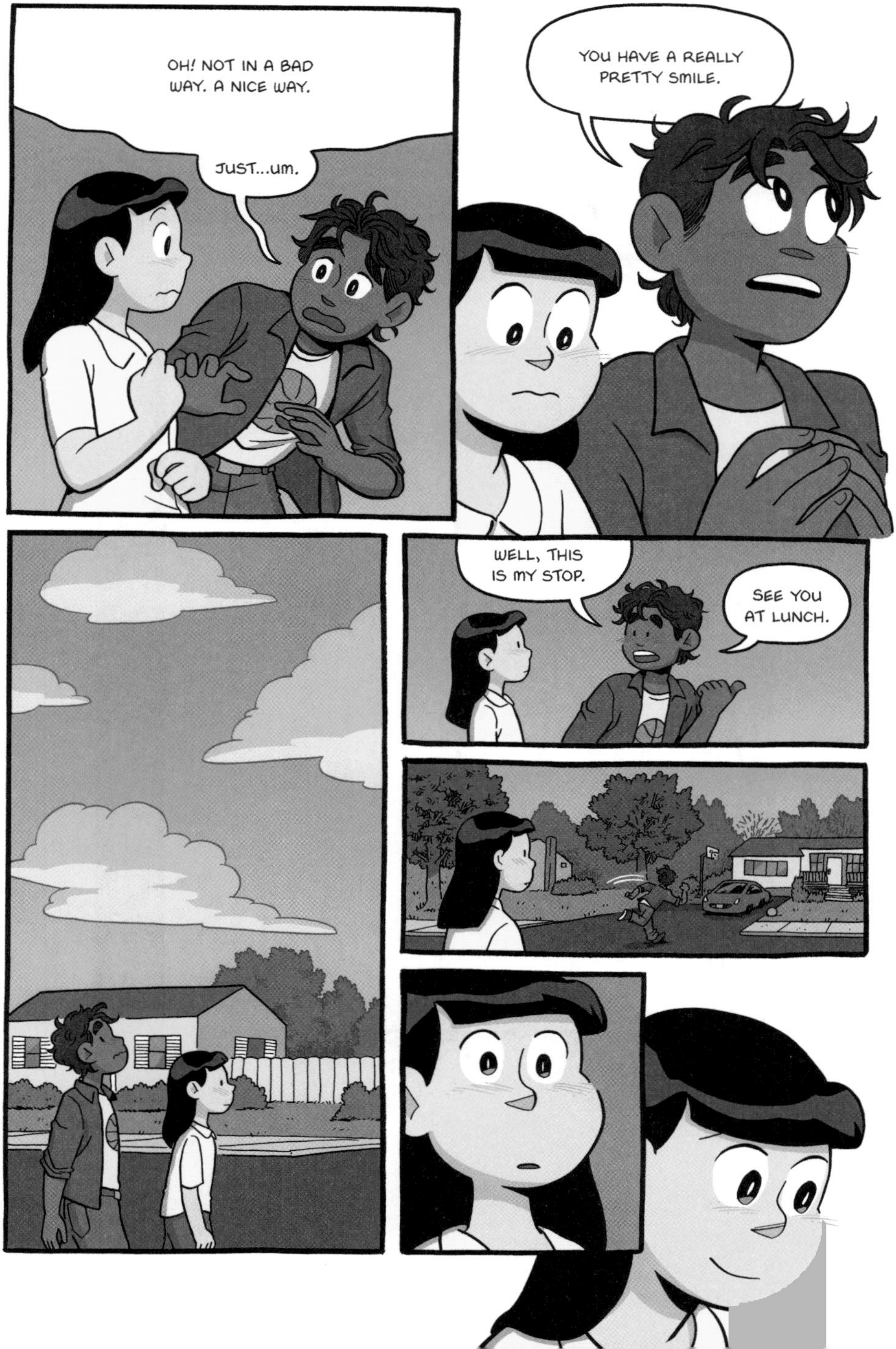
OH! NOT IN A BAD WAY. A NICE WAY.
JUST...um.
YOU HAVE A REALLY PRETTY SMILE.
WELL, THIS IS MY STOP.
SEE YOU AT LUNCH.

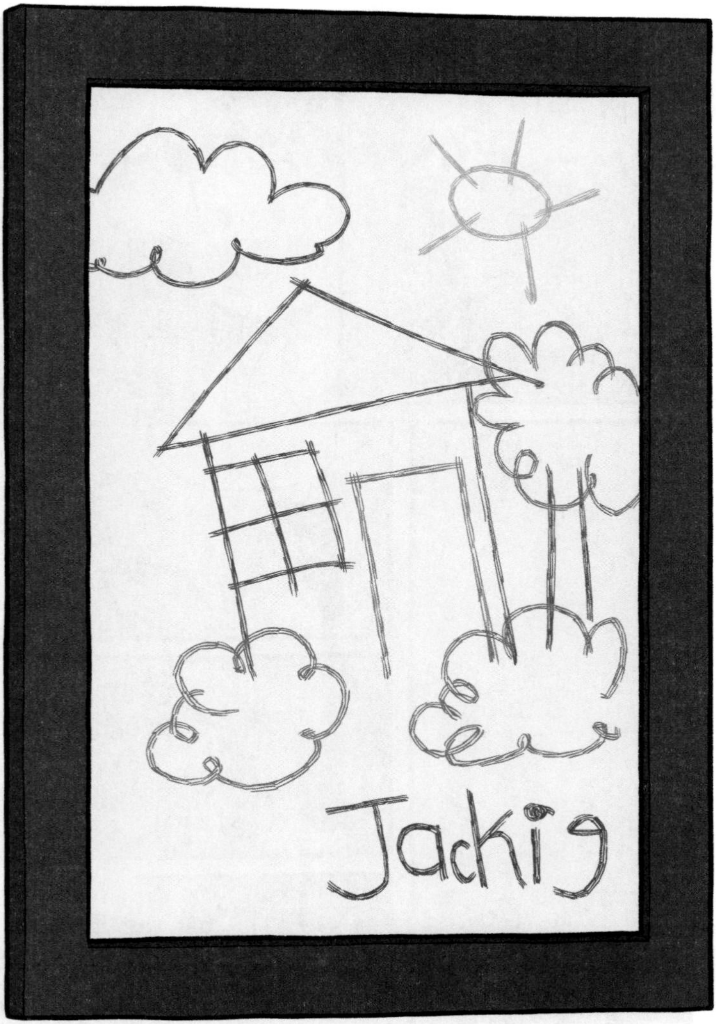
Jackie

CHAPTER 7

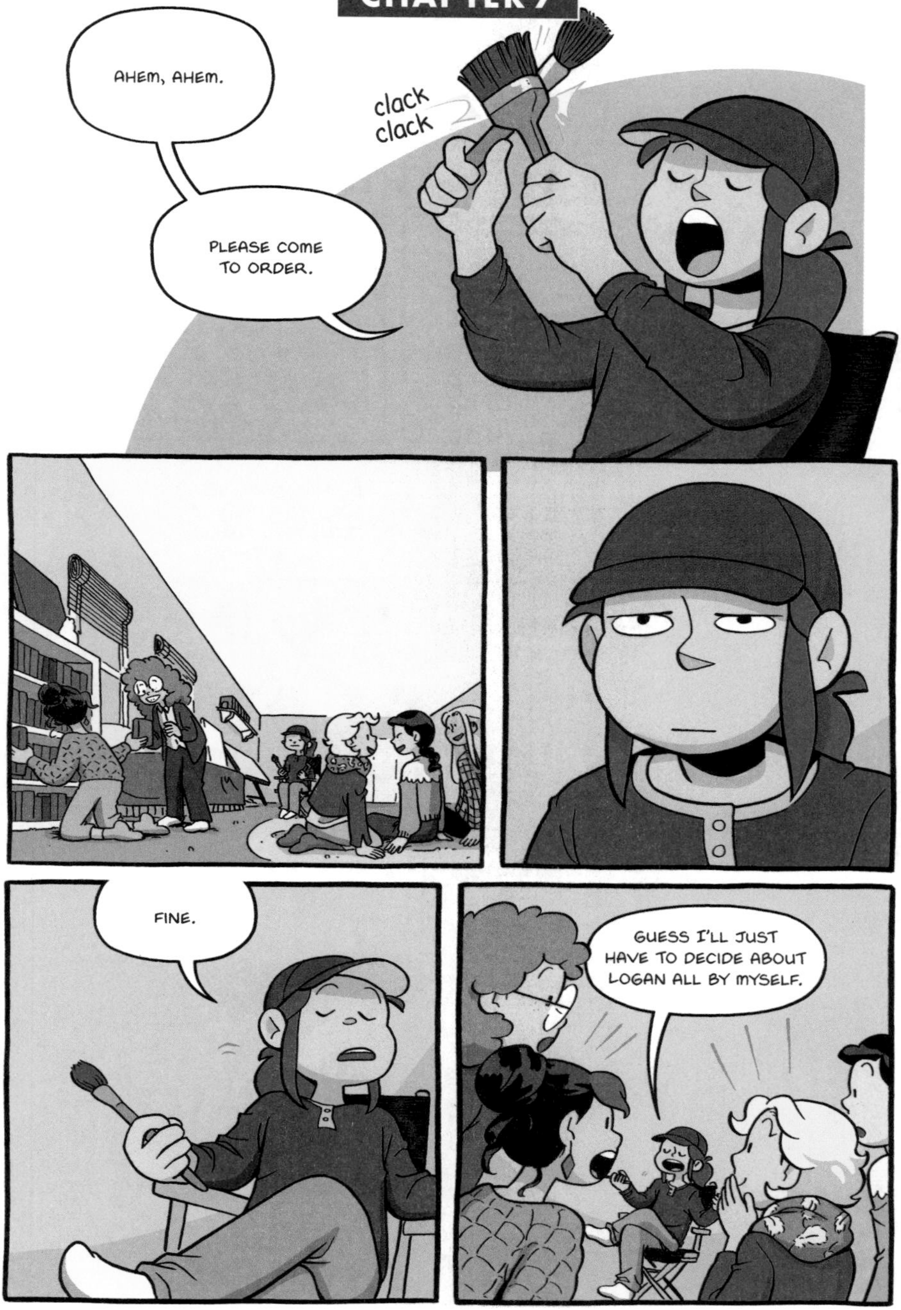
AHEM, AHEM.
clack clack
PLEASE COME TO ORDER.
FINE.
GUESS I'LL JUST HAVE TO DECIDE ABOUT LOGAN ALL BY MYSELF.

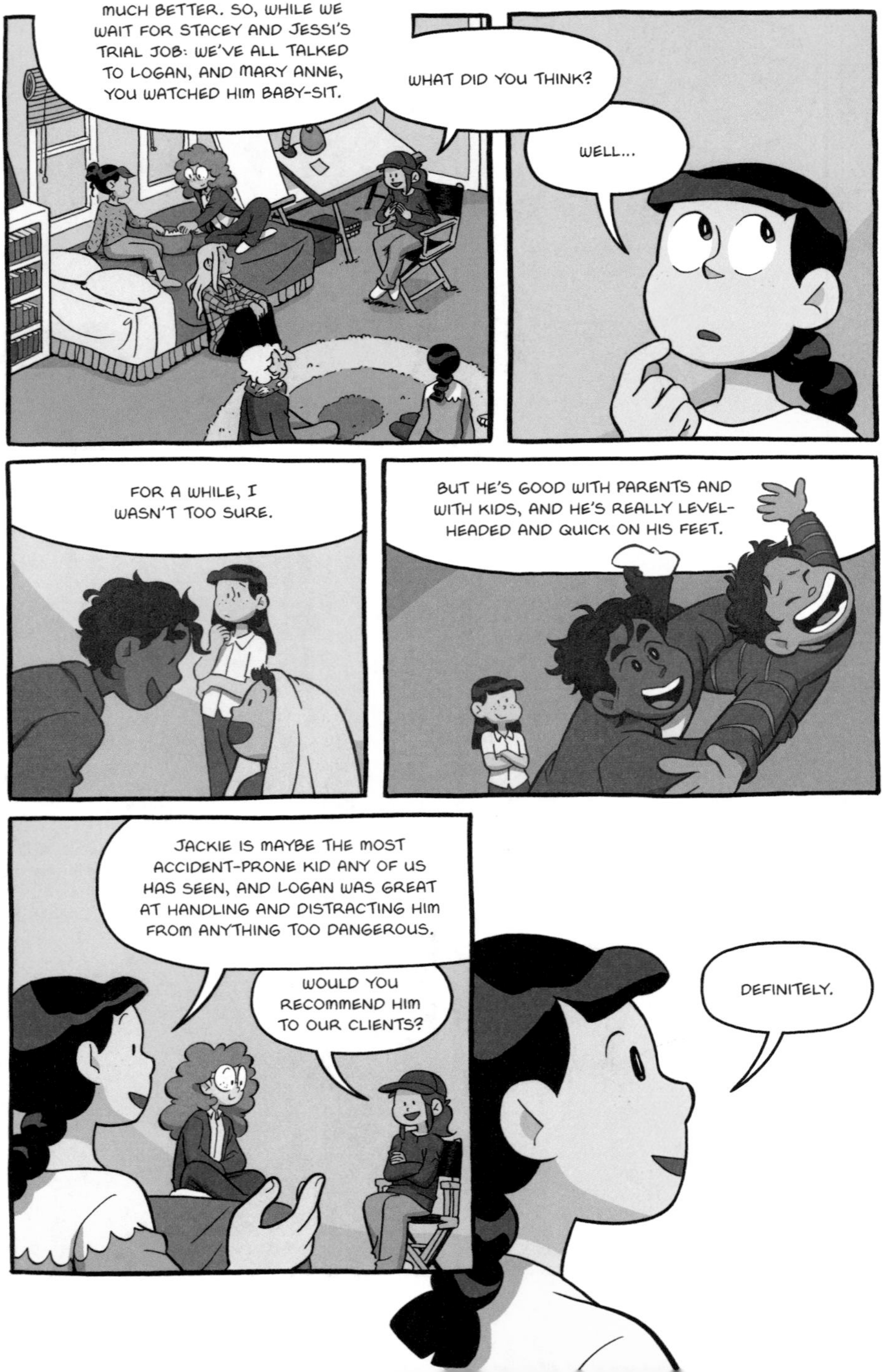
MUCH BETTER. SO, WHILE WE WAIT FOR STACEY AND JESSI'S TRIAL JOB: WE'VE ALL TALKED TO LOGAN, AND MARY ANNE, YOU WATCHED HIM BABY-SIT.
WHAT DID YOU THINK?
WELL...
FOR A WHILE, I WASN'T TOO SURE.
BUT HE'S GOOD WITH PARENTS AND WITH KIDS, AND HE'S REALLY LEVEL-HEADED AND QUICK ON HIS FEET.
JACKIE IS MAYBE THE MOST ACCIDENT-PRONE KID ANY OF US HAS SEEN, AND LOGAN WAS GREAT AT HANDLING AND DISTRACTING HIM FROM ANYTHING TOO DANGEROUS.
WOULD YOU RECOMMEND HIM TO OUR CLIENTS?
DEFINITELY.

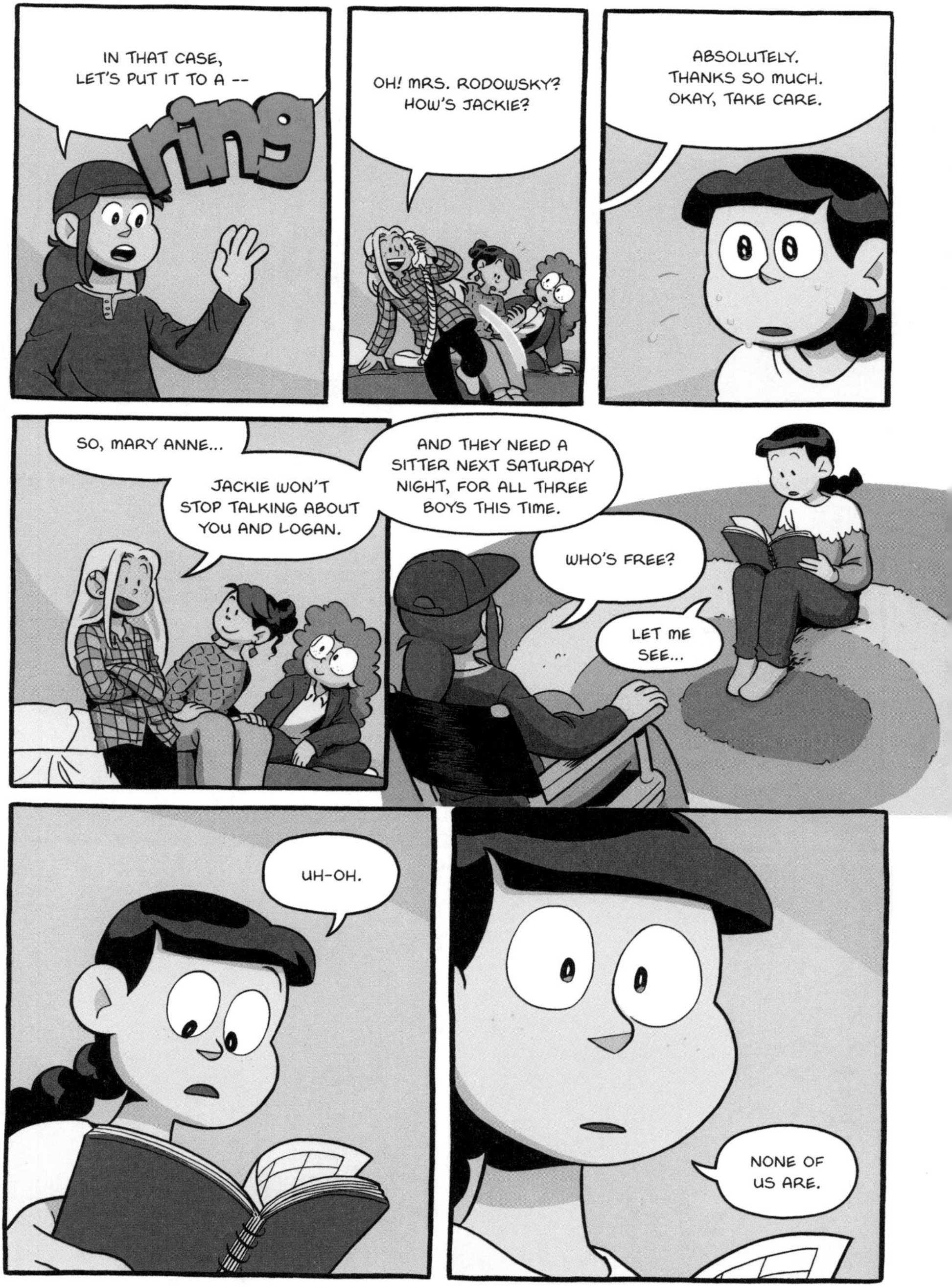
IN THAT CASE, LET'S PUT IT TO A --
ring
OH! MRS. RODOWSKY? HOW'S JACKIE?
ABSOLUTELY. THANKS SO MUCH. OKAY, TAKE CARE.
SO, MARY ANNE...
JACKIE WON'T STOP TALKING ABOUT YOU AND LOGAN.
AND THEY NEED A SITTER NEXT SATURDAY NIGHT, FOR ALL THREE BOYS THIS TIME.
WHO'S FREE?
LET ME SEE...
UH-OH.
NONE OF US ARE.

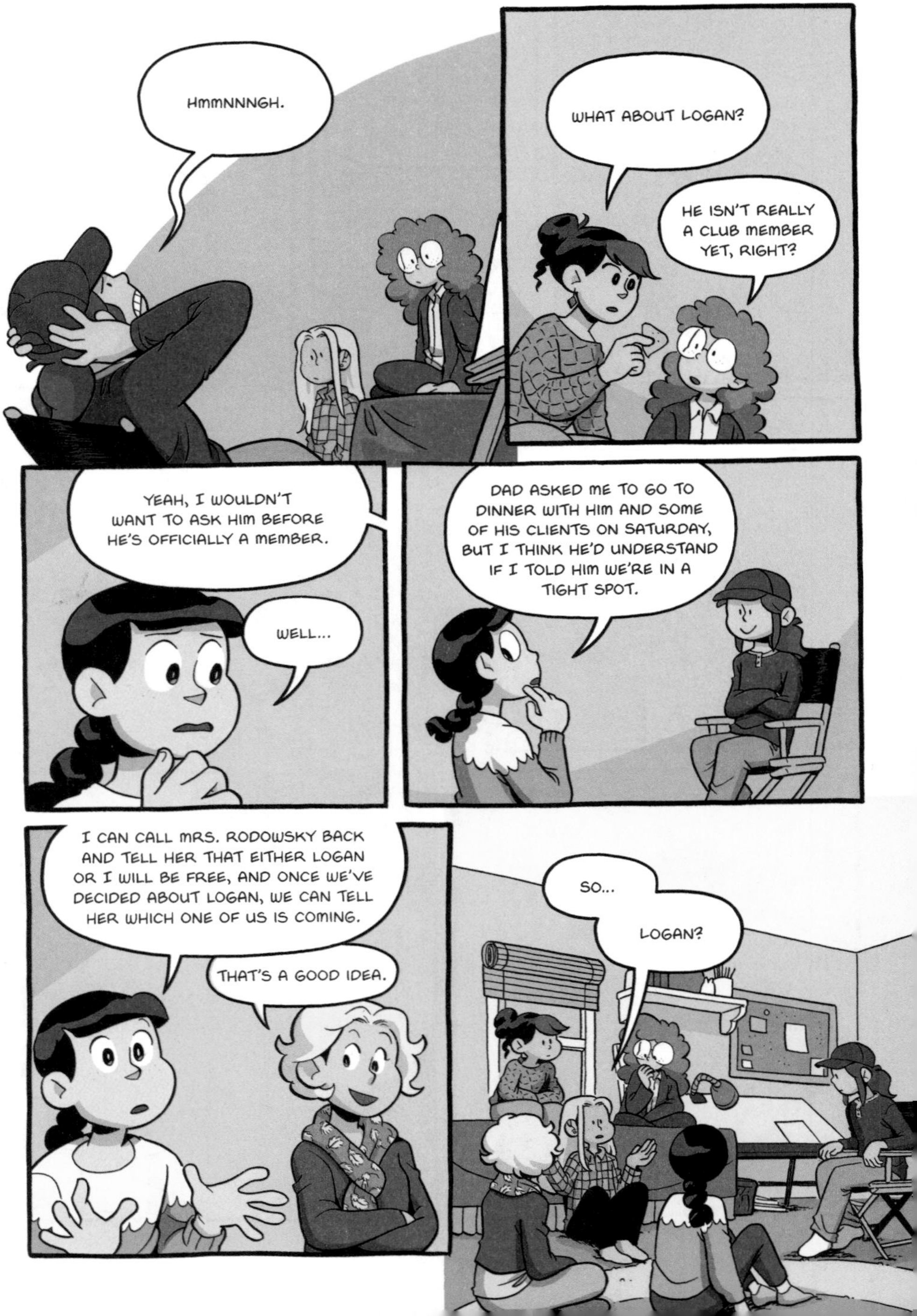
HMMNNNGH.
WHAT ABOUT LOGAN?
HE ISN'T REALLY A CLUB MEMBER YET, RIGHT?
YEAH, I WOULDN'T WANT TO ASK HIM BEFORE HE'S OFFICIALLY A MEMBER.
WELL...
DAD ASKED ME TO GO TO DINNER WITH HIM AND SOME OF HIS CLIENTS ON SATURDAY, BUT I THINK HE'D UNDERSTAND IF I TOLD HIM WE'RE IN A TIGHT SPOT.
I CAN CALL MRS. RODOWSKY BACK AND TELL HER THAT EITHER LOGAN OR I WILL BE FREE, AND ONCE WE'VE DECIDED ABOUT LOGAN, WE CAN TELL HER WHICH ONE OF US IS COMING.
THAT'S A GOOD IDEA.
SO...
LOGAN?

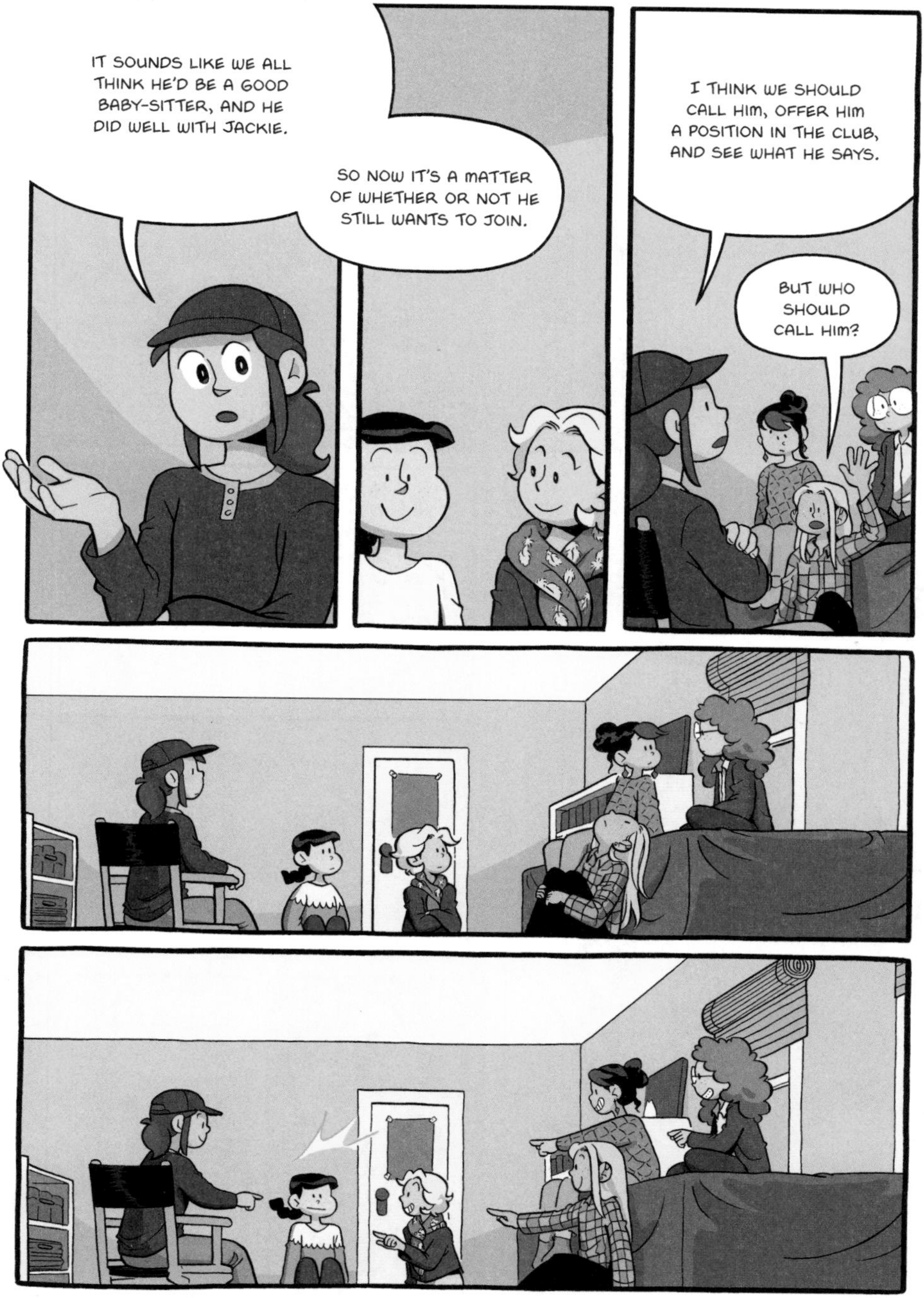
IT SOUNDS LIKE WE ALL THINK HE'D BE A GOOD BABY-SITTER, AND HE DID WELL WITH JACKIE.
SO NOW IT'S A MATTER OF WHETHER OR NOT HE STILL WANTS TO JOIN.
I THINK WE SHOULD CALL HIM, OFFER HIM A POSITION IN THE CLUB, AND SEE WHAT HE SAYS.
BUT WHO SHOULD CALL HIM?

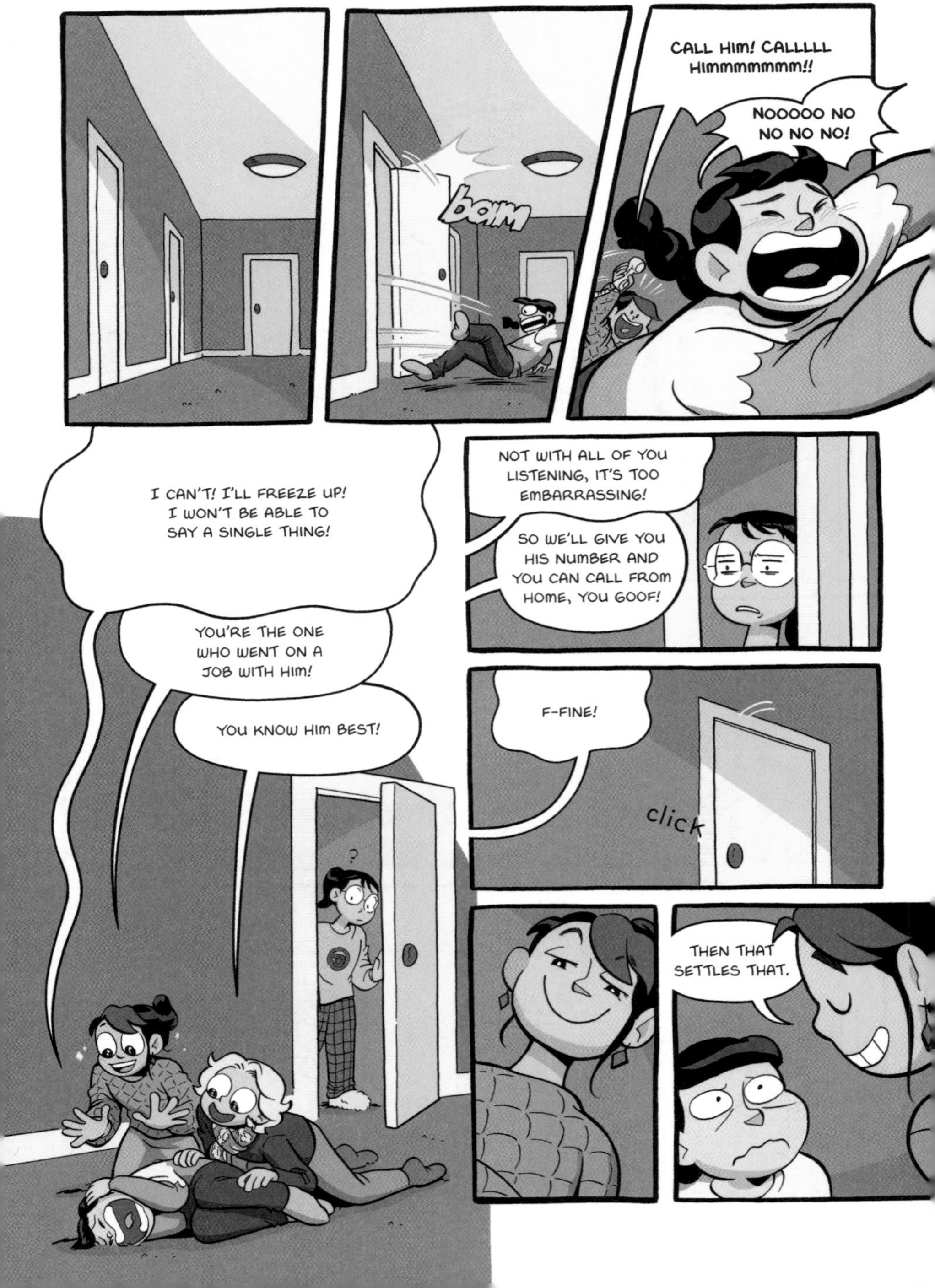
baim
CALL HIM! CALLLLL HIMMMMMMM!!
NOOOOO NO NO NO NO!
I CAN'T! I'LL FREEZE UP! I WON'T BE ABLE TO SAY A SINGLE THING!
NOT WITH ALL OF YOU LISTENING, IT'S TOO EMBARRASSING!
SO WE'LL GIVE YOU HIS NUMBER AND YOU CAN CALL FROM HOME, YOU GOOF!
YOU'RE THE ONE WHO WENT ON A JOB WITH HIM!
YOU KNOW HIM BEST!
F-FINE!
click
THEN THAT SETTLES THAT.

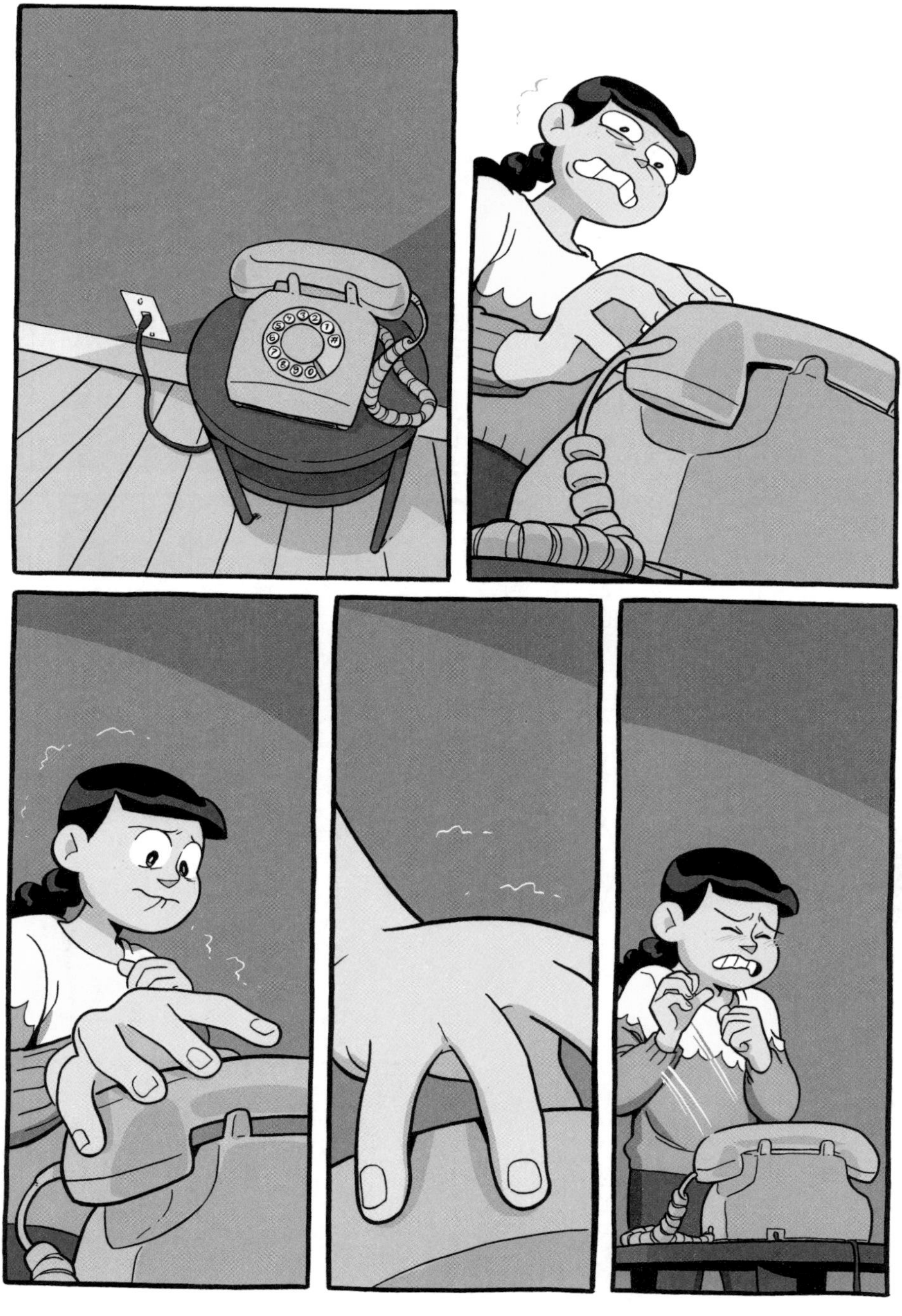

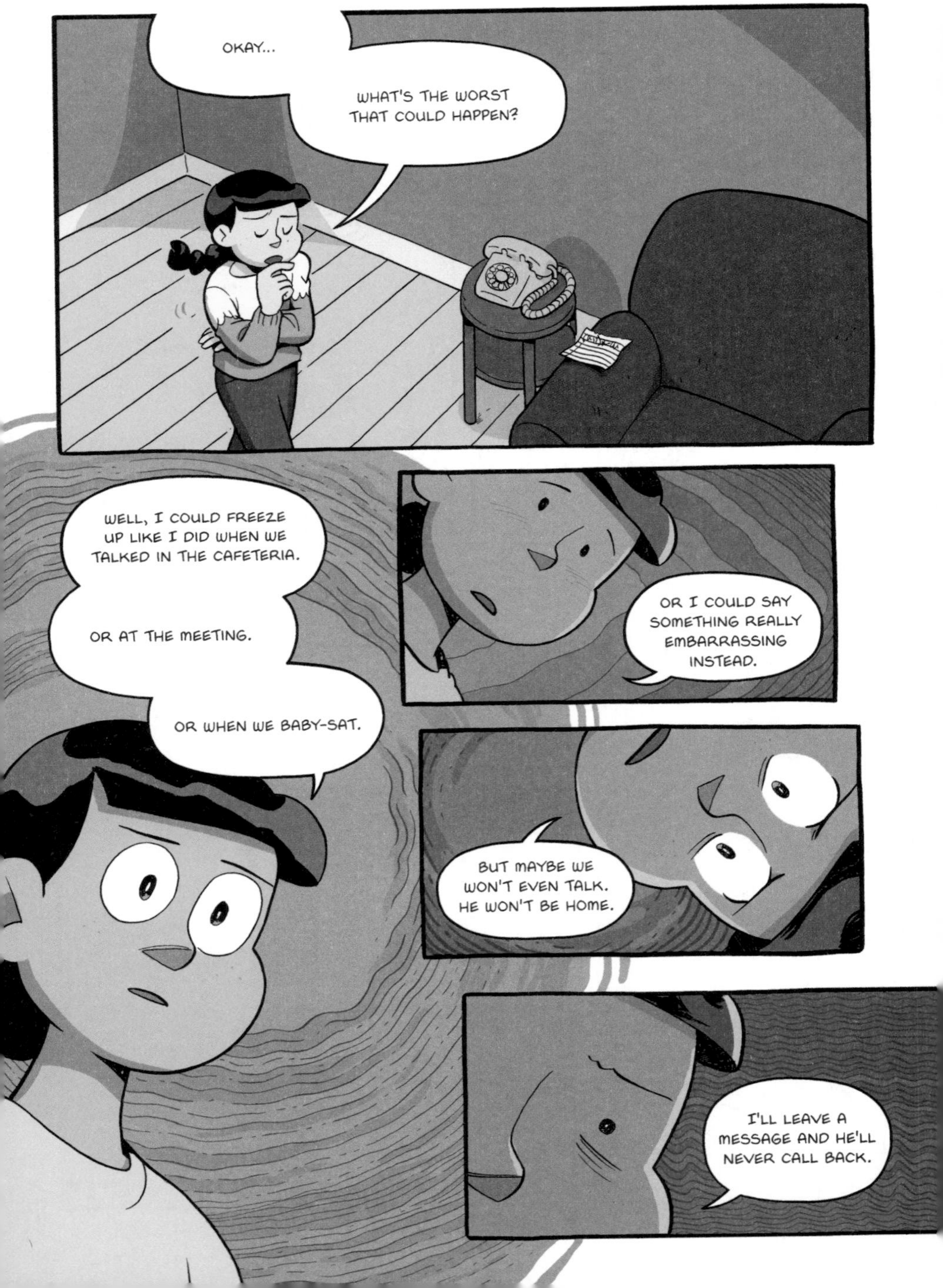
OKAY...
WHAT'S THE WORST THAT COULD HAPPEN?
WELL, I COULD FREEZE UP LIKE I DID WHEN WE TALKED IN THE CAFETERIA.
OR AT THE MEETING.
OR WHEN WE BABY-SAT.
OR I COULD SAY SOMETHING REALLY EMBARRASSING INSTEAD.
BUT MAYBE WE WON'T EVEN TALK. HE WON'T BE HOME.
I'LL LEAVE A MESSAGE AND HE'LL NEVER CALL BACK.

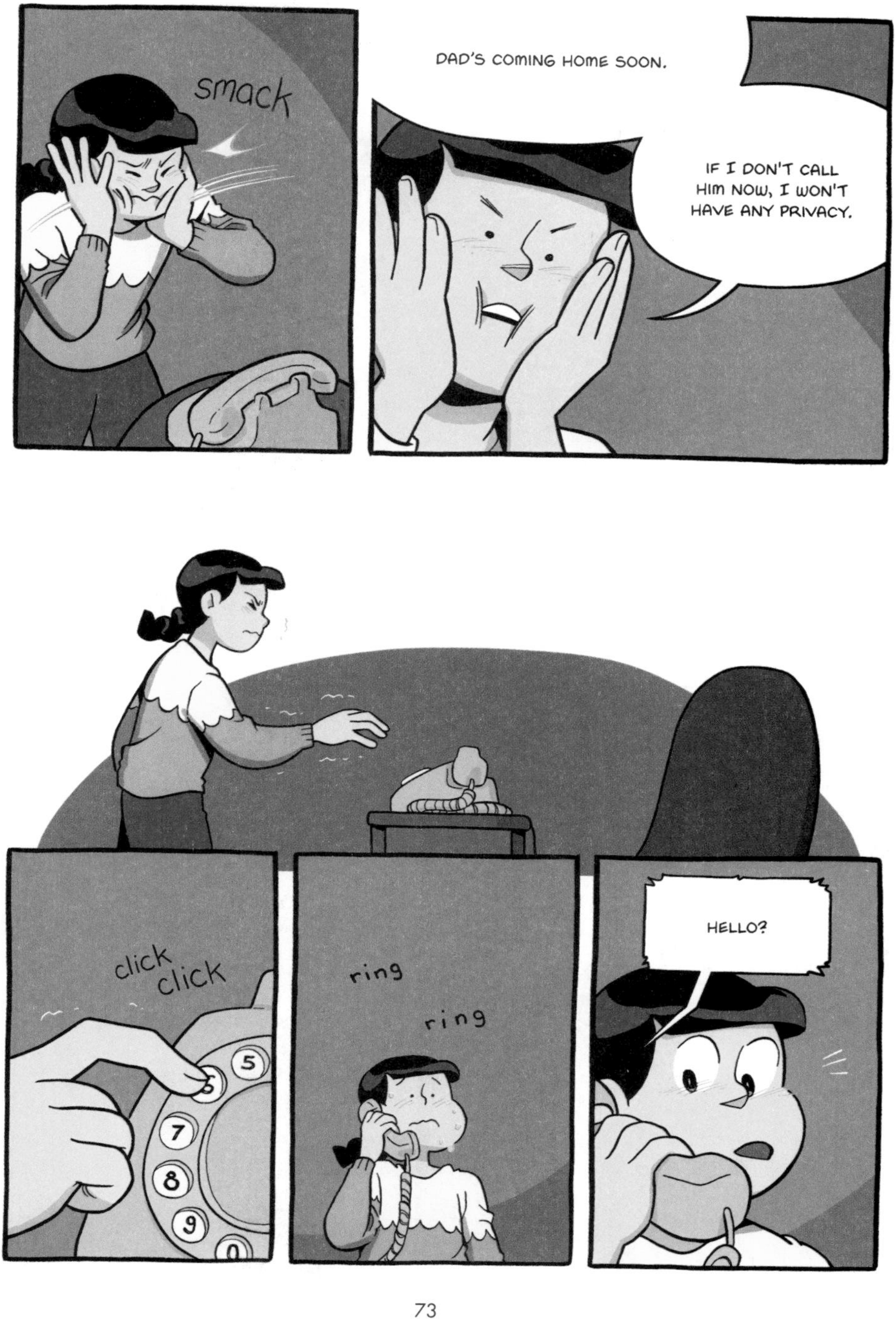
smack
DAD'S COMING HOME SOON.
IF I DON'T CALL HIM NOW, I WON'T HAVE ANY PRIVACY.
click click
ring
ring
HELLO?

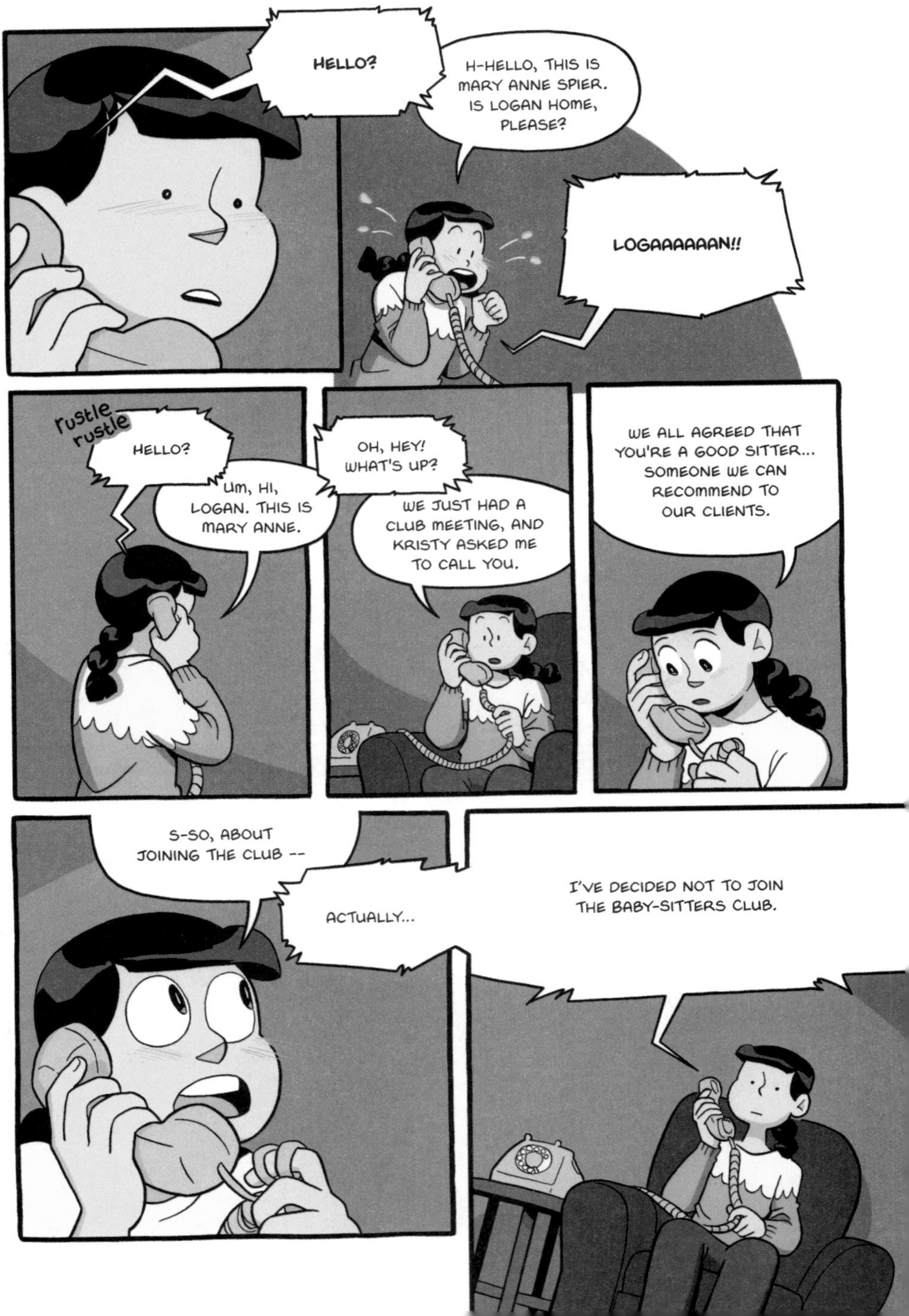
HELLO?
H-HELLO, THIS IS MARY ANNE SPIER. IS LOGAN HOME, PLEASE?
LOGAAAAAAN!!
rustle rustle
HELLO?
UM, HI, LOGAN. THIS IS MARY ANNE.
OH, HEY! WHAT'S UP?
WE JUST HAD A CLUB MEETING, AND KRISTY ASKED ME TO CALL YOU.
WE ALL AGREED THAT YOU'RE A GOOD SITTER... SOMEONE WE CAN RECOMMEND TO OUR CLIENTS.
S-SO, ABOUT JOINING THE CLUB --
ACTUALLY...
I'VE DECIDED NOT TO JOIN THE BABY-SITTERS CLUB.

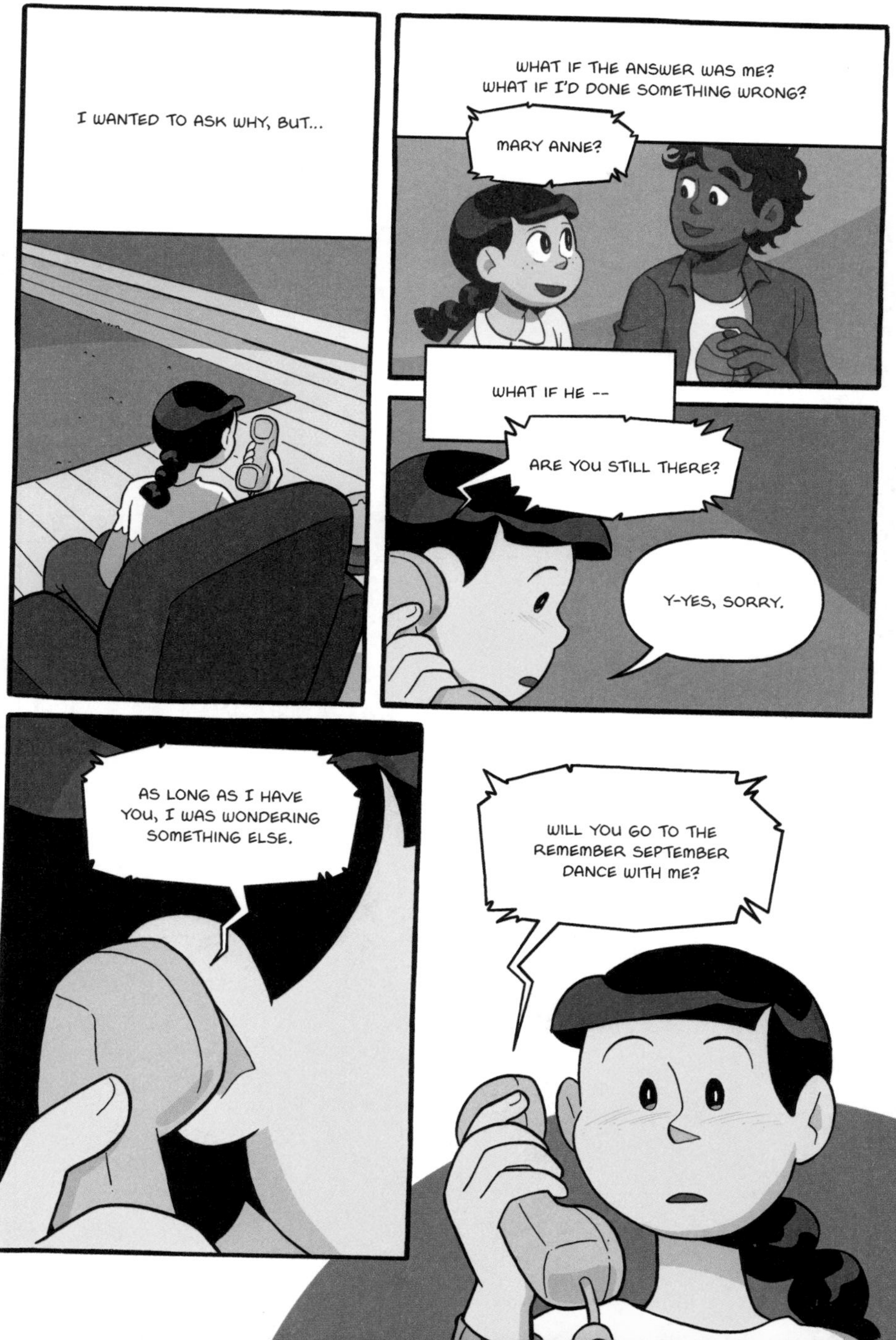
I WANTED TO ASK WHY, BUT...
WHAT IF THE ANSWER WAS ME? WHAT IF I'D DONE SOMETHING WRONG?
MARY ANNE?
WHAT IF HE --
ARE YOU STILL THERE?
Y-YES, SORRY.
AS LONG AS I HAVE YOU, I WAS WONDERING SOMETHING ELSE.
WILL YOU GO TO THE REMEMBER SEPTEMBER DANCE WITH ME?

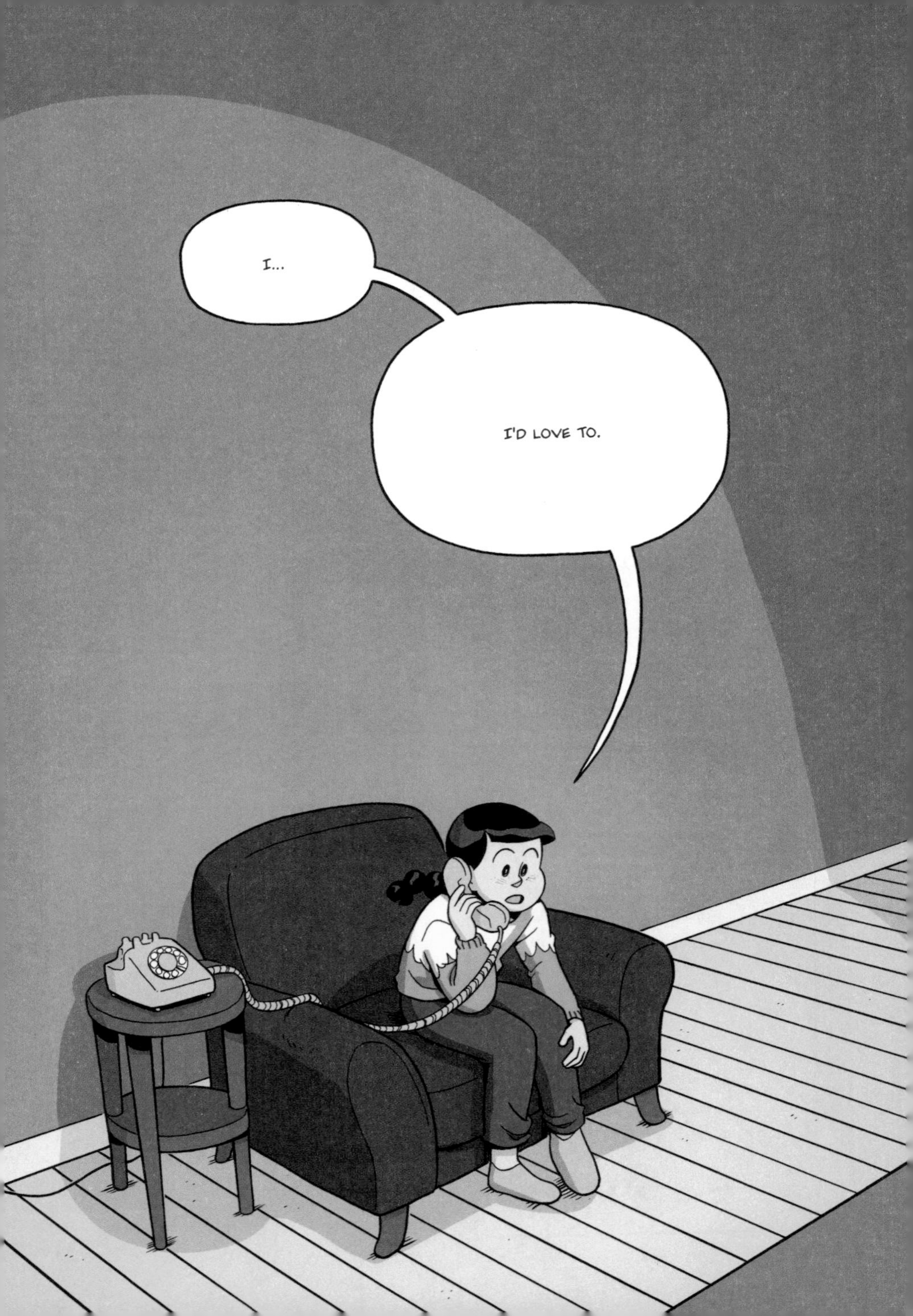
I...
I'D LOVE TO.

Tuesday

Boy, is the Charlotte Johanssen I baby-sat today different from the Charlotte I used to sit for last year. She has grown up so much! Skipping a grade was the right thing to do for her. She's bouncy and happy and full of ideas, and she even has a "best friend" - a girl in her class called Sophie McCann. (Last week her "best friend" was Vanessa Pike. I remember when "best friend" meant nothing - just whoever your current good friend was. Do you guys remember, too?)

Oh, well. I'm way off the subject. Anyway, there's not much to say. Charlotte's easy to sit for and she warmed up to Jessi right away, especially after hearing that Jessi has a sister her age (look out, Sophie McCann!). I brought the Kid-Kit over, and we all had a great afternoon.

Stacey

CHAPTER 8

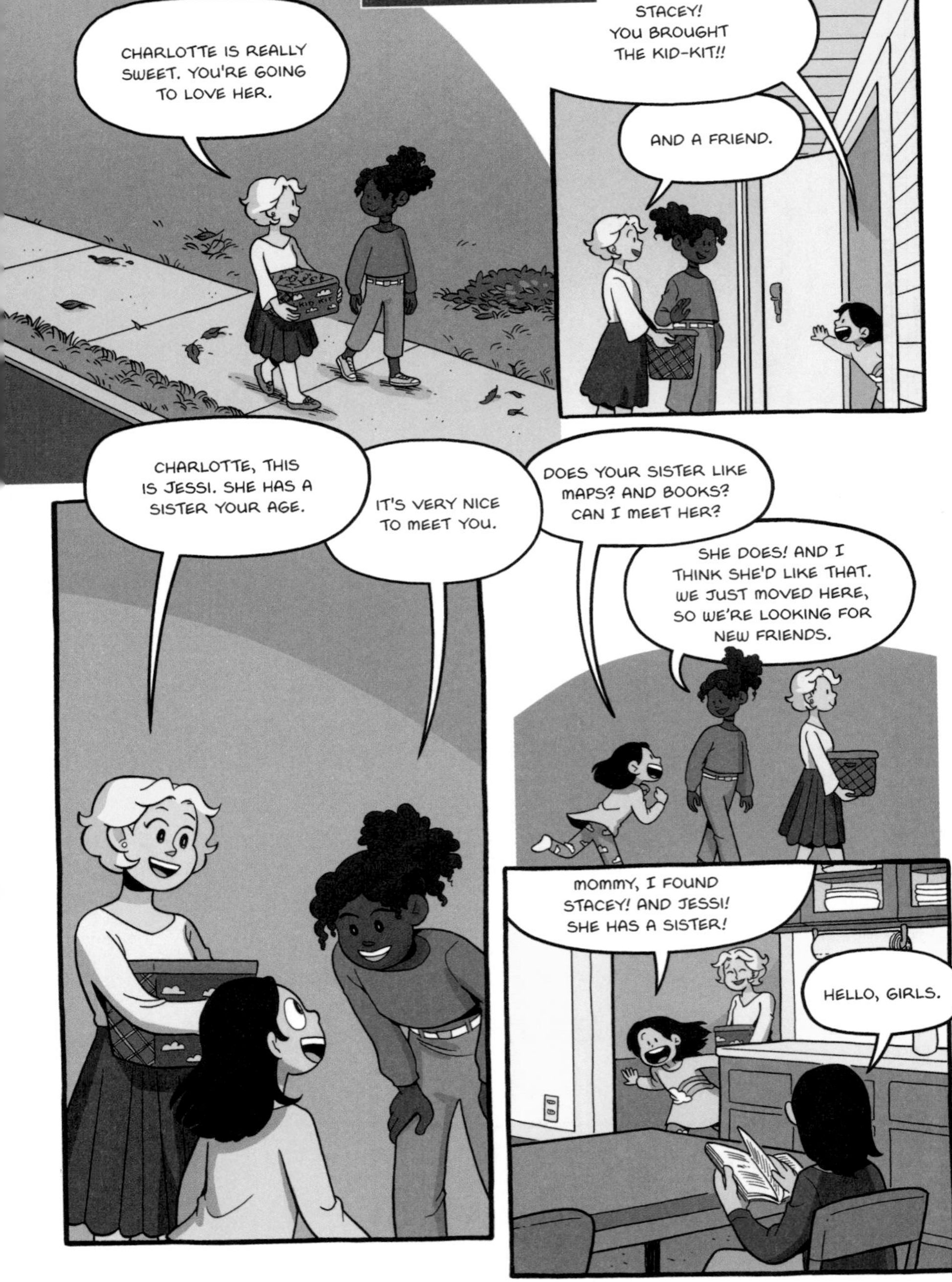
CHARLOTTE IS REALLY SWEET. YOU'RE GOING TO LOVE HER.
STACEY! YOU BROUGHT THE KID-KIT!!
AND A FRIEND.
CHARLOTTE, THIS IS JESSI. SHE HAS A SISTER YOUR AGE.
IT'S VERY NICE TO MEET YOU.
DOES YOUR SISTER LIKE MAPS? AND BOOKS? CAN I MEET HER?
SHE DOES! AND I THINK SHE'D LIKE THAT. WE JUST MOVED HERE, SO WE'RE LOOKING FOR NEW FRIENDS.
MOMMY, I FOUND STACEY! AND JESSI! SHE HAS A SISTER!
HELLO, GIRLS.

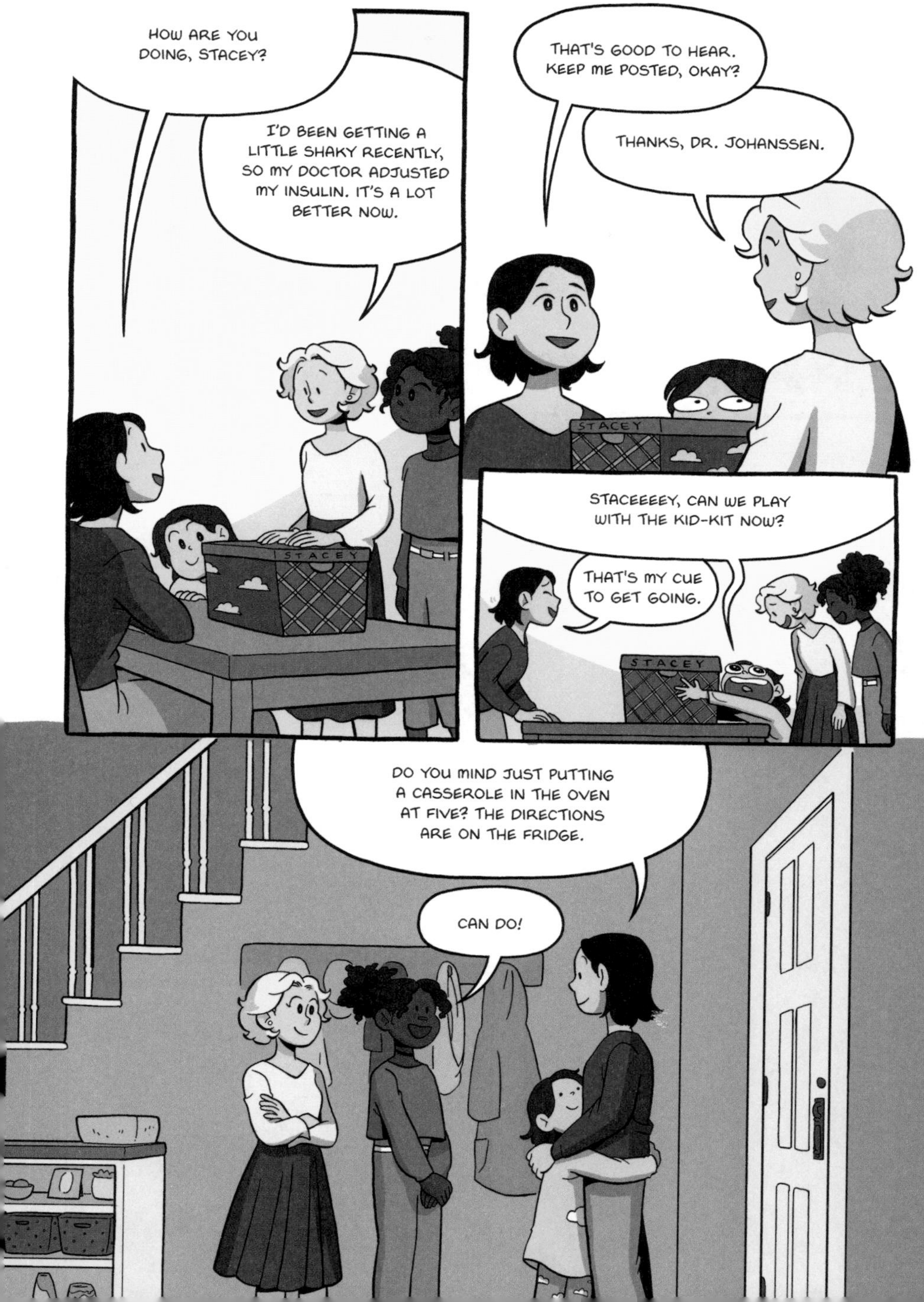
HOW ARE YOU DOING, STACEY?
I'D BEEN GETTING A LITTLE SHAKY RECENTLY, SO MY DOCTOR ADJUSTED MY INSULIN. IT'S A LOT BETTER NOW.
STACEY
THAT'S GOOD TO HEAR. KEEP ME POSTED, OKAY?
THANKS, DR. JOHANSSEN.
STACEY
STACEEEEY, CAN WE PLAY WITH THE KID-KIT NOW?
THAT'S MY CUE TO GET GOING.
STACEY
DO YOU MIND JUST PUTTING A CASSEROLE IN THE OVEN AT FIVE? THE DIRECTIONS ARE ON THE FRIDGE.
CAN DO!

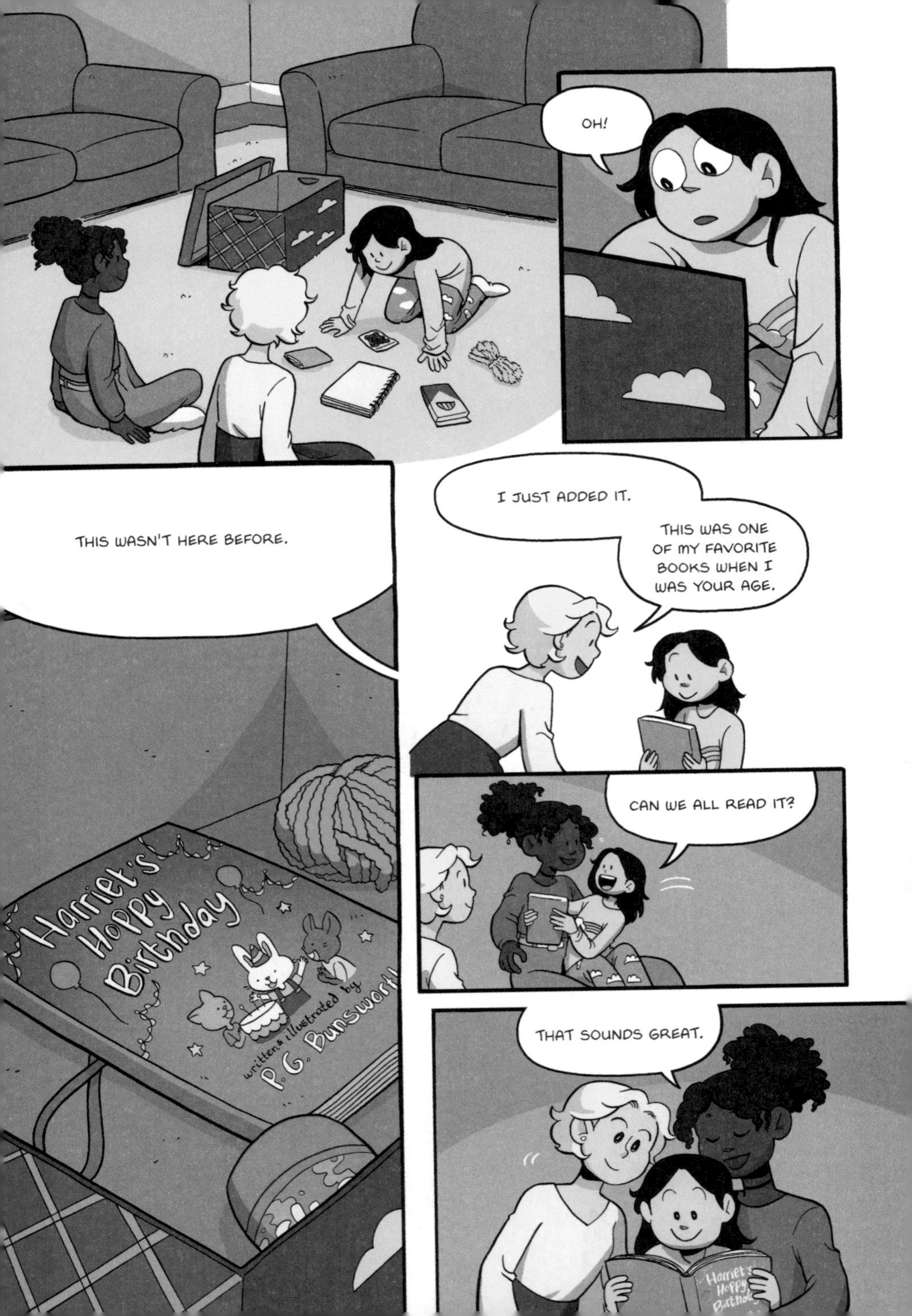
OH!
THIS WASN'T HERE BEFORE.
I JUST ADDED IT.
THIS WAS ONE OF MY FAVORITE BOOKS WHEN I WAS YOUR AGE.
Harriet's Hoppy Birthday
written & illustrated by P.G. Bunsworth
CAN WE ALL READ IT?
THAT SOUNDS GREAT.
Harriet's Hoppy Birthday

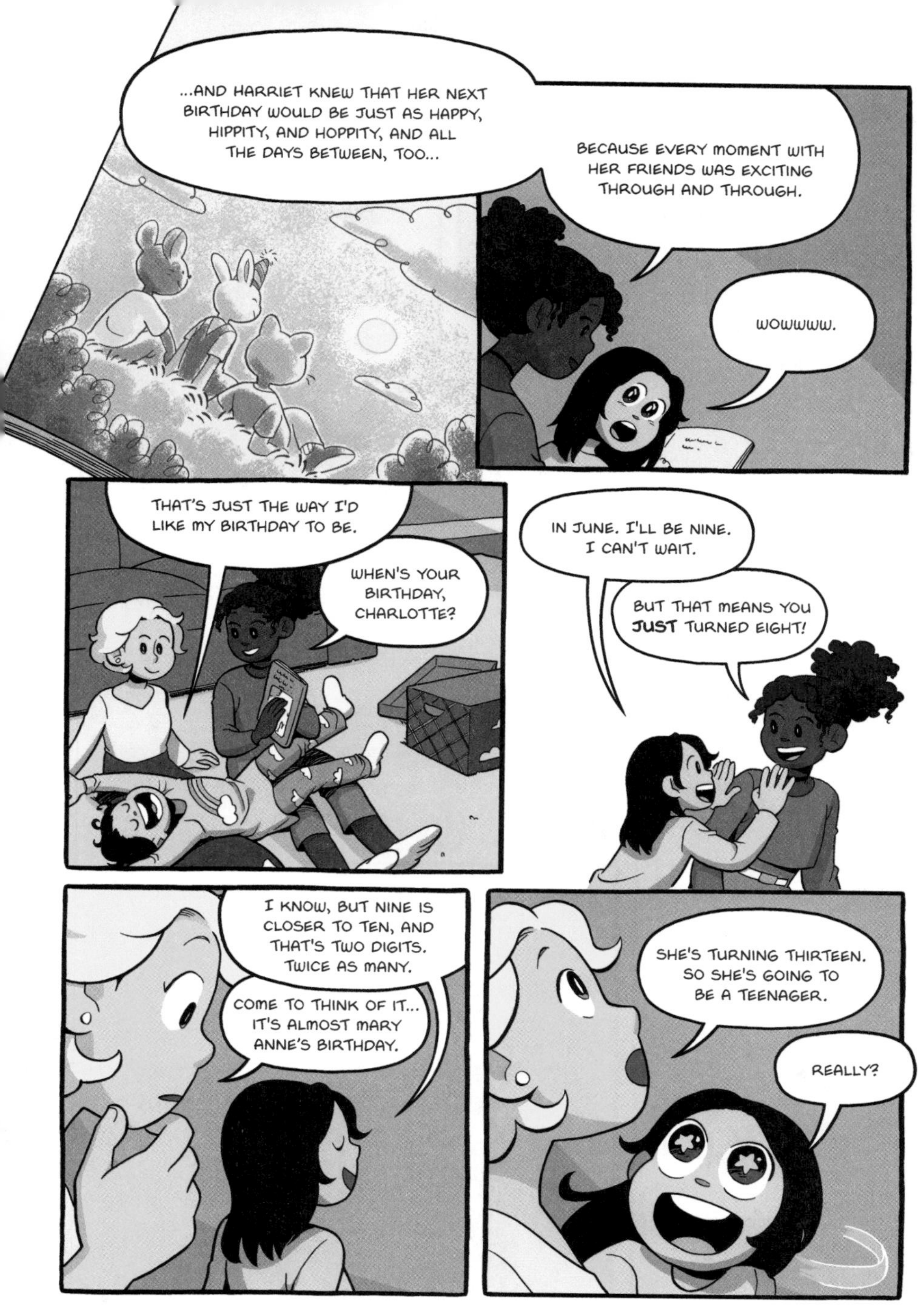
...AND HARRIET KNEW THAT HER NEXT BIRTHDAY WOULD BE JUST AS HAPPY, HIPPITY, AND HOPPITY, AND ALL THE DAYS BETWEEN, TOO...
BECAUSE EVERY MOMENT WITH HER FRIENDS WAS EXCITING THROUGH AND THROUGH.
WOWWWW.
THAT'S JUST THE WAY I'D LIKE MY BIRTHDAY TO BE.
WHEN'S YOUR BIRTHDAY, CHARLOTTE?
IN JUNE. I'LL BE NINE. I CAN'T WAIT.
BUT THAT MEANS YOU **JUST** TURNED EIGHT!
I KNOW, BUT NINE IS CLOSER TO TEN, AND THAT'S TWO DIGITS. TWICE AS MANY.
COME TO THINK OF IT... IT'S ALMOST MARY ANNE'S BIRTHDAY.
SHE'S TURNING THIRTEEN. SO SHE'S GOING TO BE A TEENAGER.
REALLY?

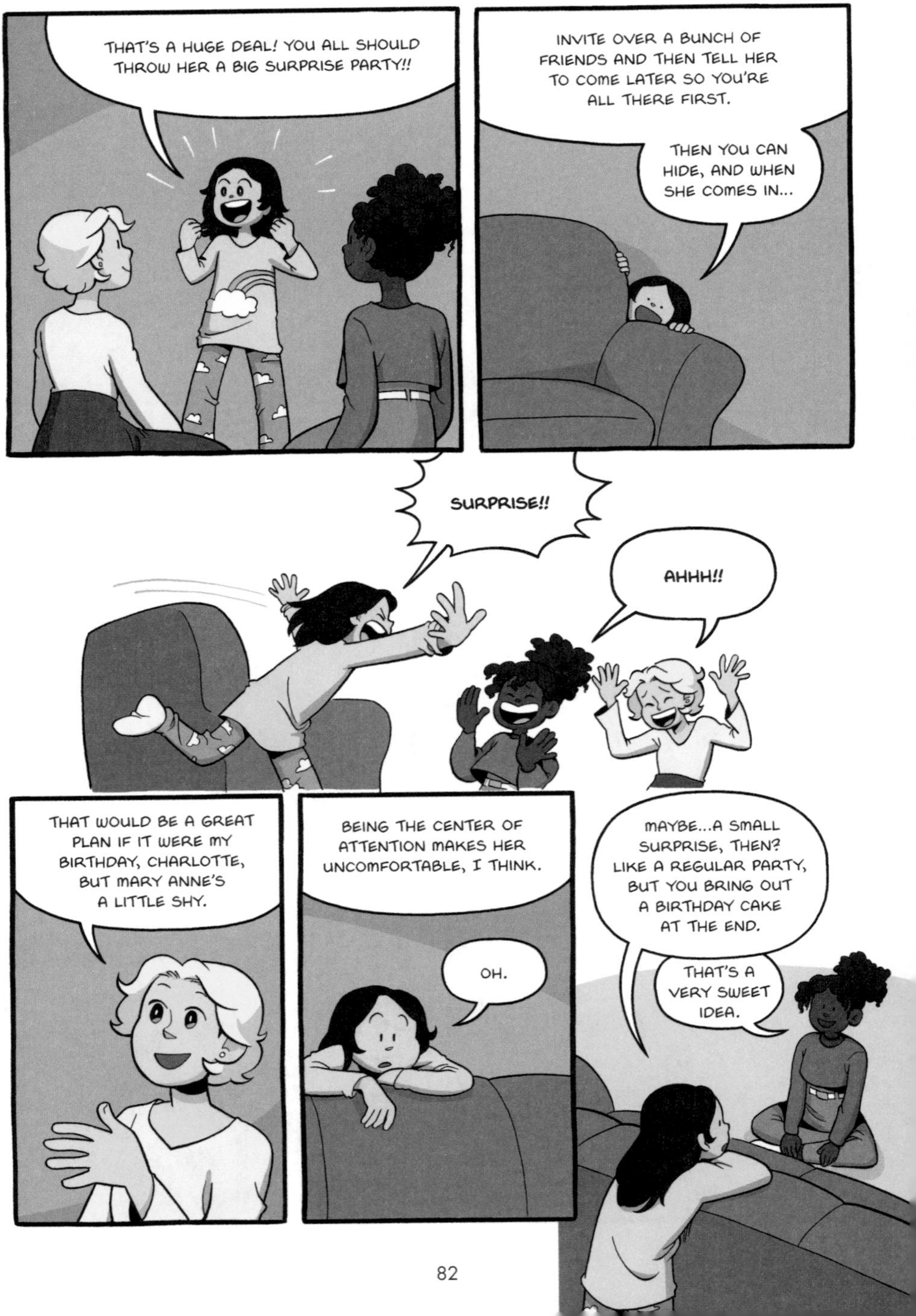
THAT'S A HUGE DEAL! YOU ALL SHOULD THROW HER A BIG SURPRISE PARTY!!
INVITE OVER A BUNCH OF FRIENDS AND THEN TELL HER TO COME LATER SO YOU'RE ALL THERE FIRST.
THEN YOU CAN HIDE, AND WHEN SHE COMES IN...
SURPRISE!!
AHHH!!
THAT WOULD BE A GREAT PLAN IF IT WERE MY BIRTHDAY, CHARLOTTE, BUT MARY ANNE'S A LITTLE SHY.
BEING THE CENTER OF ATTENTION MAKES HER UNCOMFORTABLE, I THINK.
OH.
MAYBE...A SMALL SURPRISE, THEN? LIKE A REGULAR PARTY, BUT YOU BRING OUT A BIRTHDAY CAKE AT THE END.
THAT'S A VERY SWEET IDEA.

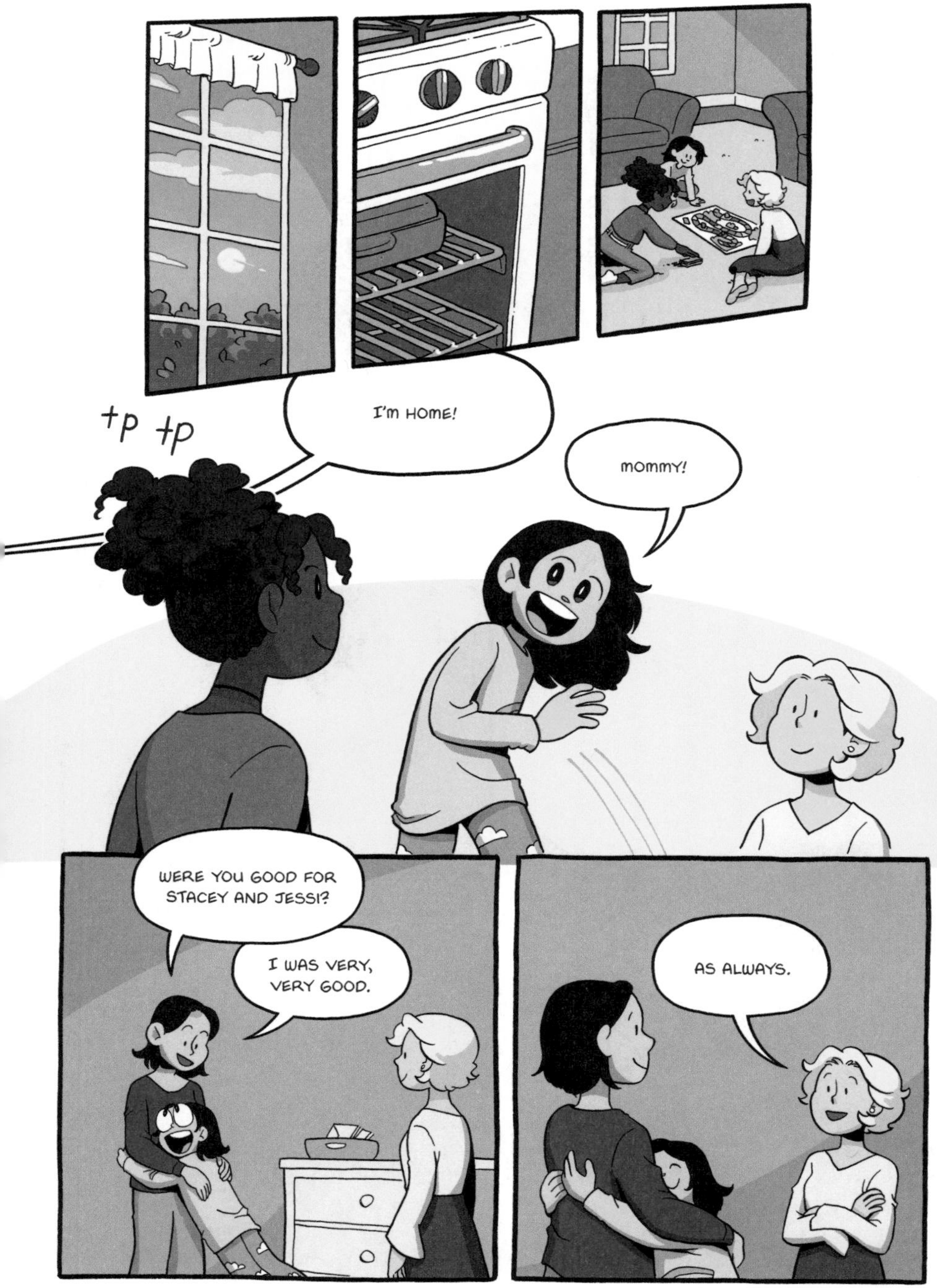

tp tp
I'm HOME!
MOMMY!
WERE YOU GOOD FOR STACEY AND JESSI?
I WAS VERY, VERY GOOD.
AS ALWAYS.

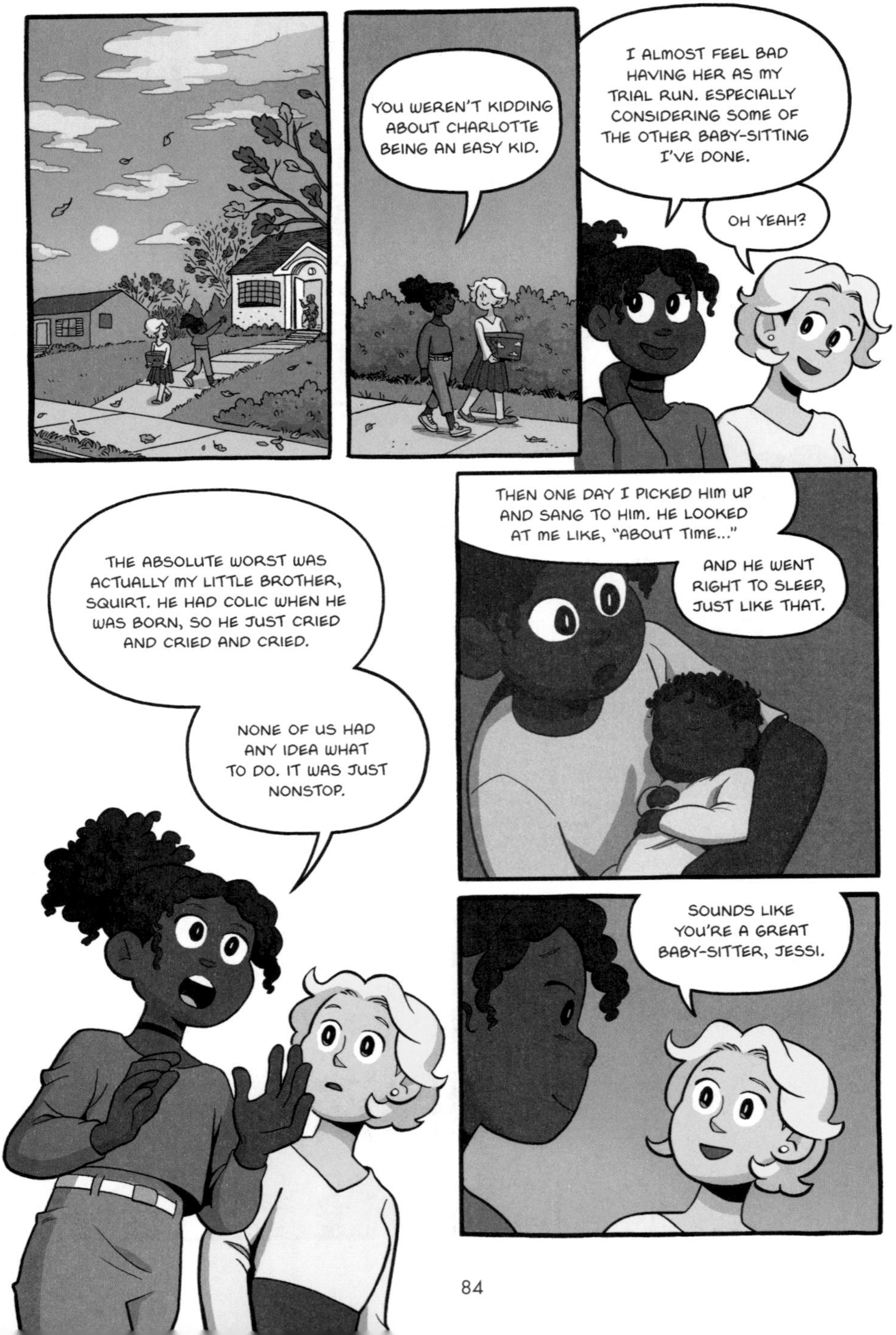
YOU WEREN'T KIDDING ABOUT CHARLOTTE BEING AN EASY KID.
I ALMOST FEEL BAD HAVING HER AS MY TRIAL RUN. ESPECIALLY CONSIDERING SOME OF THE OTHER BABY-SITTING I'VE DONE.
OH YEAH?
THE ABSOLUTE WORST WAS ACTUALLY MY LITTLE BROTHER, SQUIRT. HE HAD COLIC WHEN HE WAS BORN, SO HE JUST CRIED AND CRIED AND CRIED.
NONE OF US HAD ANY IDEA WHAT TO DO. IT WAS JUST NONSTOP.
THEN ONE DAY I PICKED HIM UP AND SANG TO HIM. HE LOOKED AT ME LIKE, "ABOUT TIME..."
AND HE WENT RIGHT TO SLEEP, JUST LIKE THAT.
SOUNDS LIKE YOU'RE A GREAT BABY-SITTER, JESSI.

CHAPTER 9

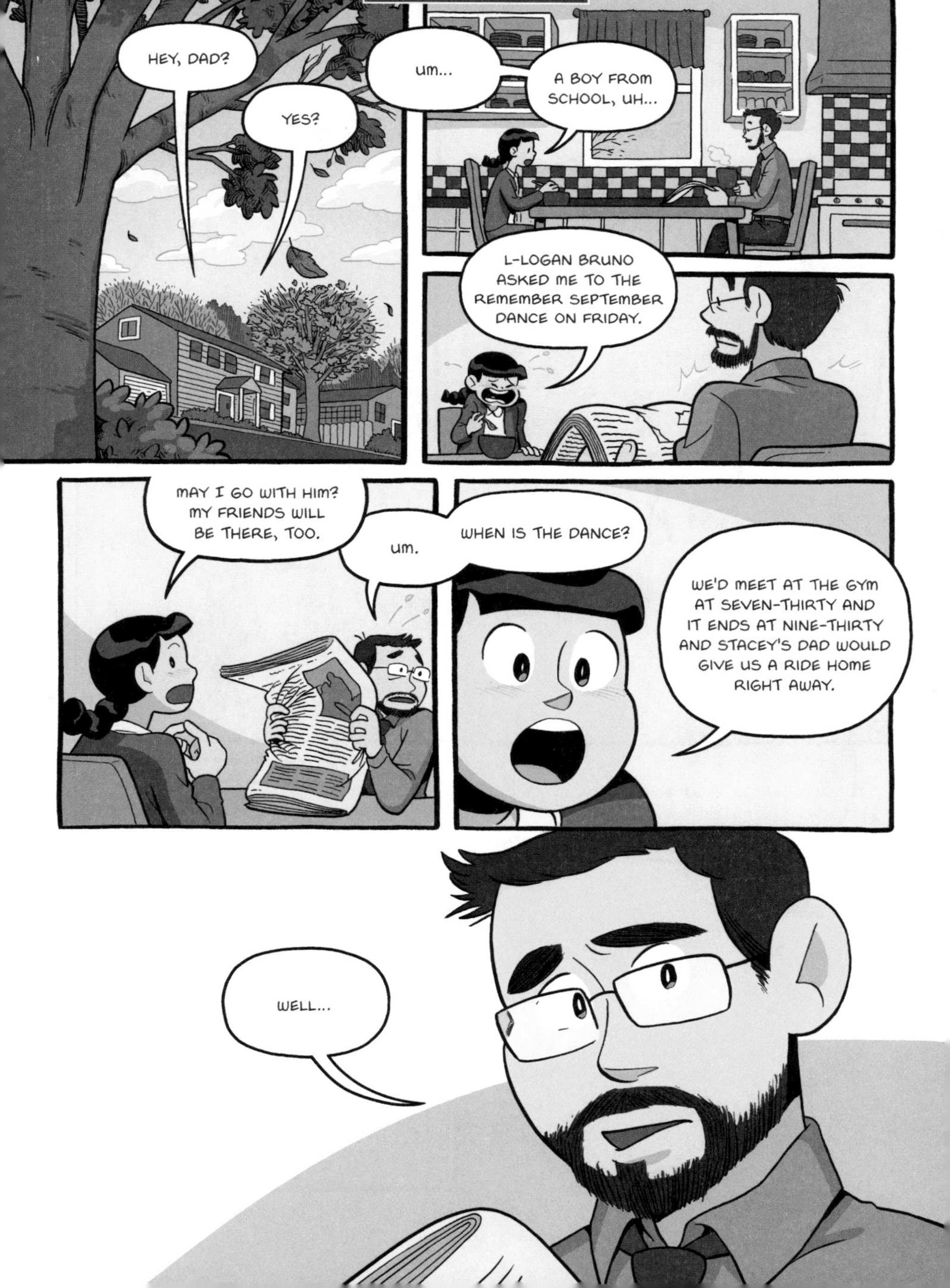
HEY, DAD?
YES?
UM...
A BOY FROM SCHOOL, UH...
L-LOGAN BRUNO ASKED ME TO THE REMEMBER SEPTEMBER DANCE ON FRIDAY.
MAY I GO WITH HIM? MY FRIENDS WILL BE THERE, TOO.
UM.
WHEN IS THE DANCE?
WE'D MEET AT THE GYM AT SEVEN-THIRTY AND IT ENDS AT NINE-THIRTY AND STACEY'S DAD WOULD GIVE US A RIDE HOME RIGHT AWAY.
WELL...

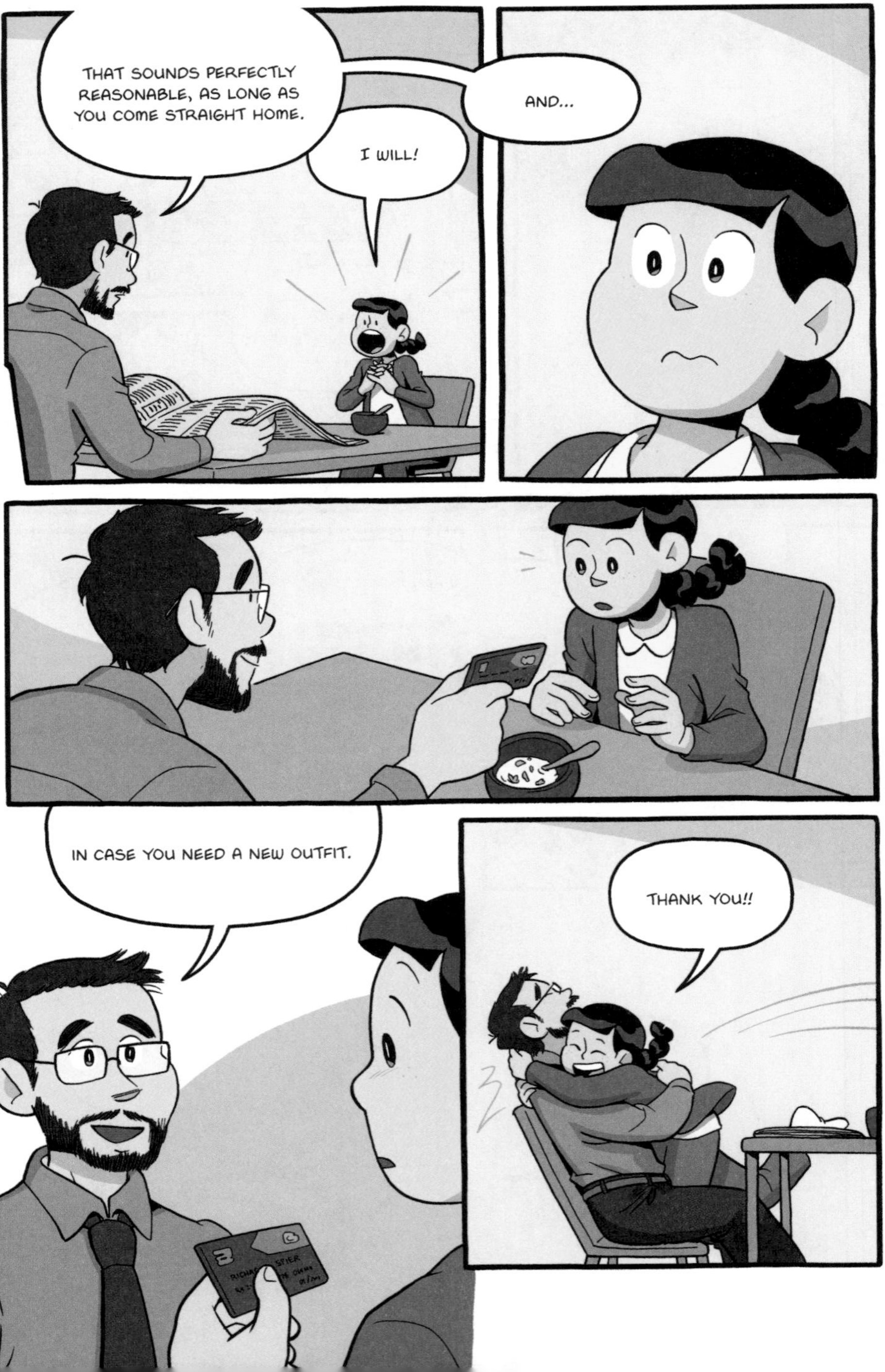
THAT SOUNDS PERFECTLY REASONABLE, AS LONG AS YOU COME STRAIGHT HOME.
I WILL!
AND...
IN CASE YOU NEED A NEW OUTFIT.
THANK YOU!!

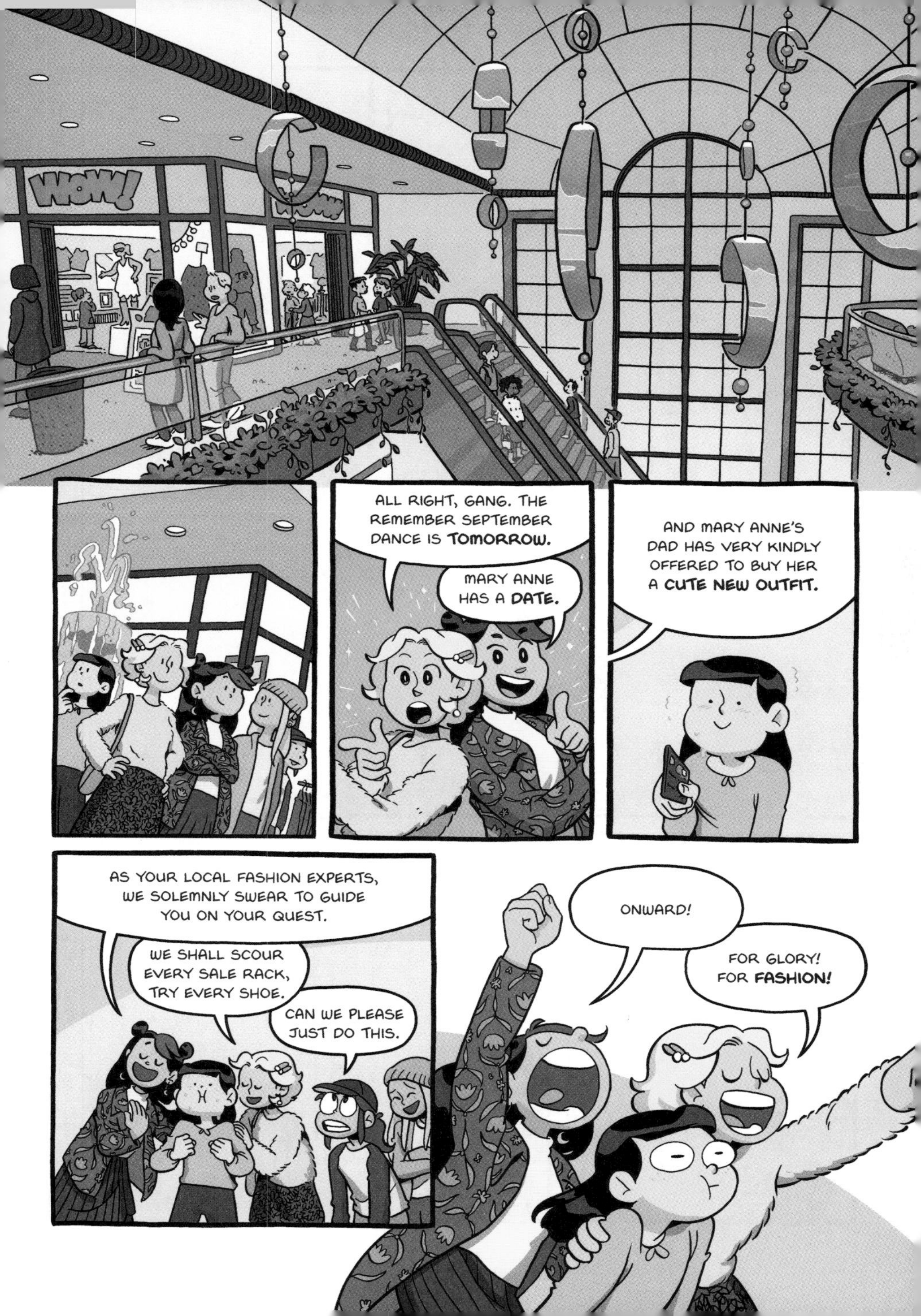
WOW!
ALL RIGHT, GANG. THE REMEMBER SEPTEMBER DANCE IS **TOMORROW.**
MARY ANNE HAS A **DATE.**
AND MARY ANNE'S DAD HAS VERY KINDLY OFFERED TO BUY HER A **CUTE NEW OUTFIT.**
AS YOUR LOCAL FASHION EXPERTS, WE SOLEMNLY SWEAR TO GUIDE YOU ON YOUR QUEST.
WE SHALL SCOUR EVERY SALE RACK, TRY EVERY SHOE.
CAN WE PLEASE JUST DO THIS.
ONWARD!
FOR GLORY! FOR **FASHION!**

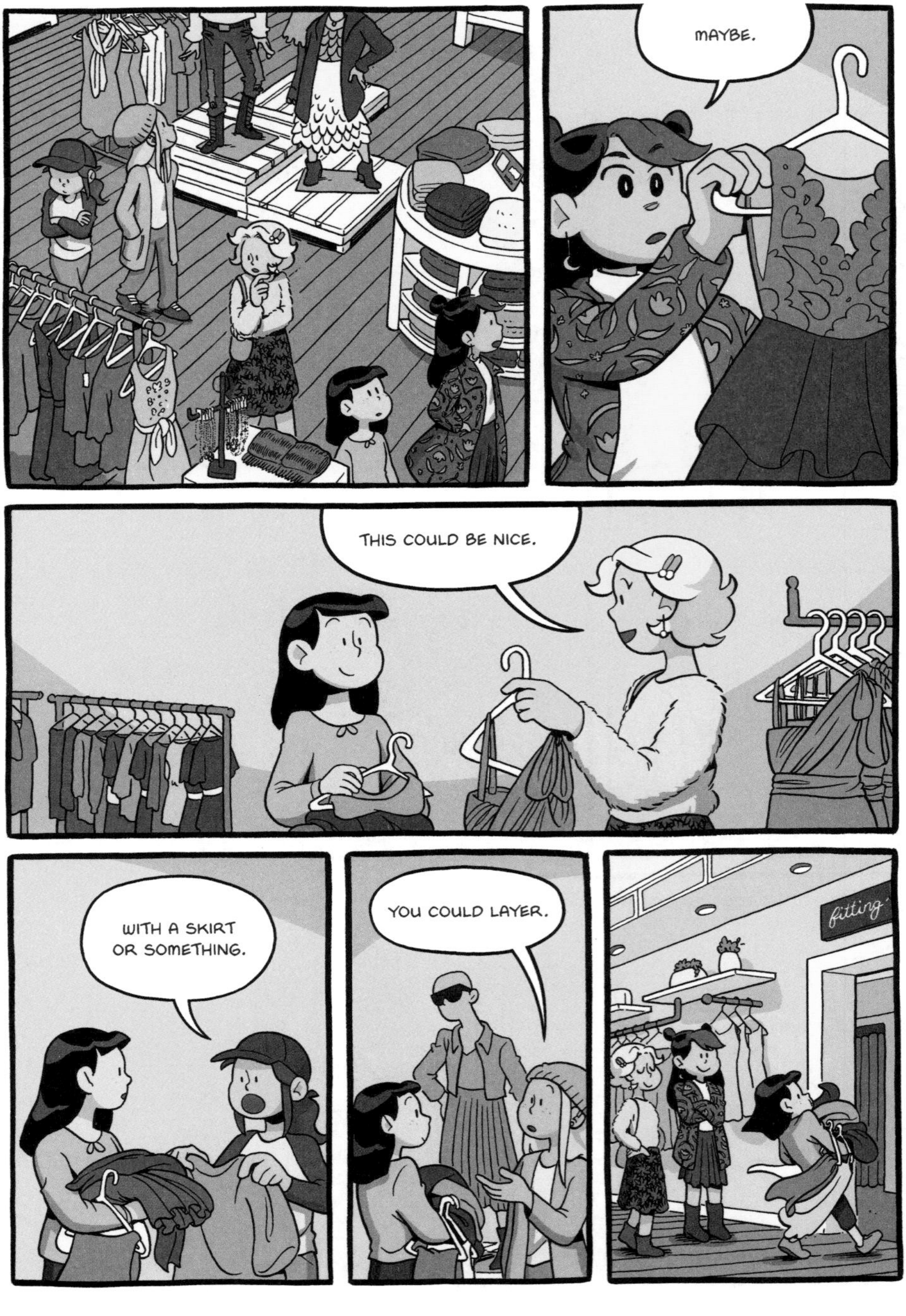
MAYBE.
THIS COULD BE NICE.
WITH A SKIRT OR SOMETHING.
YOU COULD LAYER.
fitting

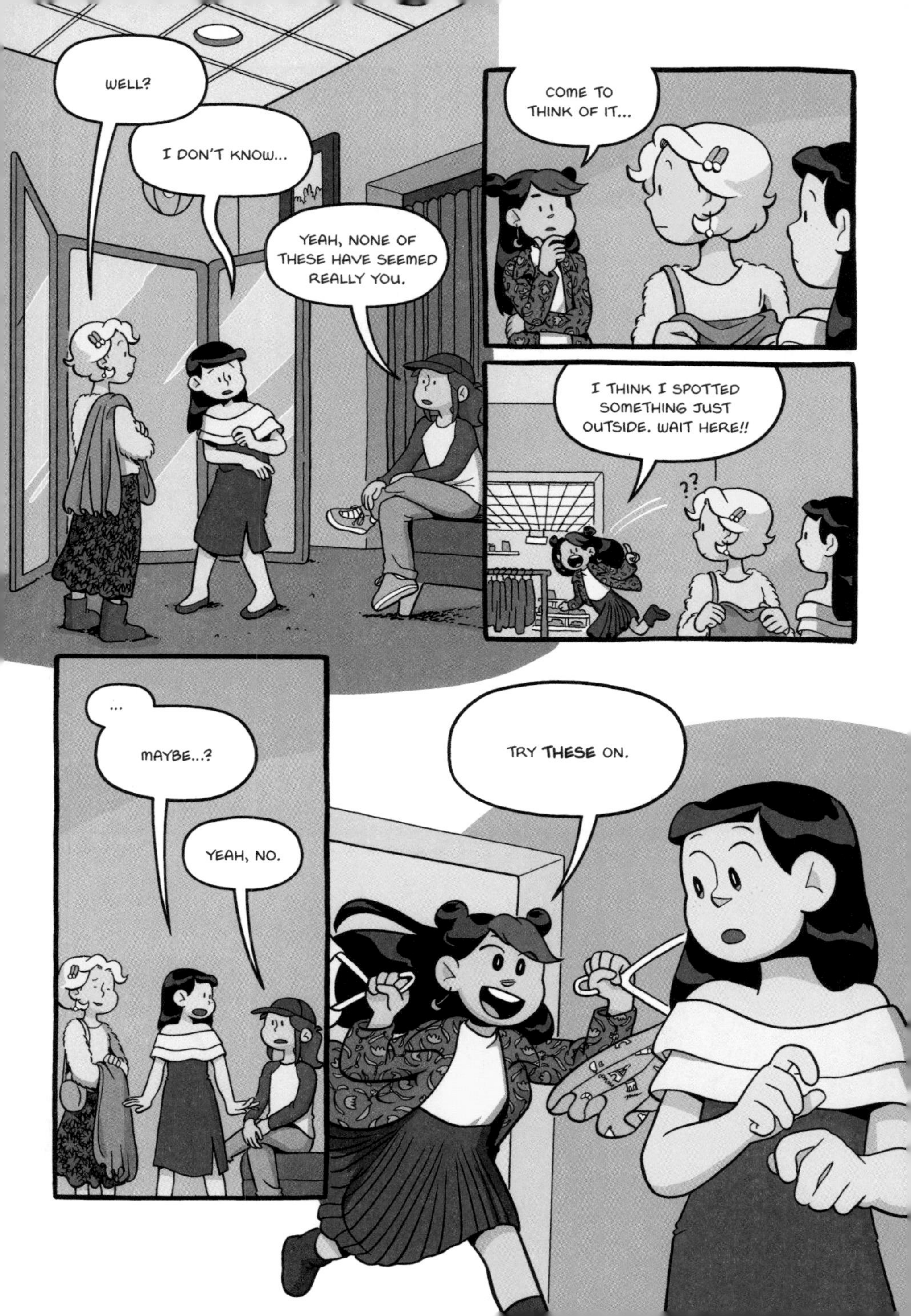
WELL?
I DON'T KNOW...
YEAH, NONE OF THESE HAVE SEEMED REALLY YOU.
COME TO THINK OF IT...
I THINK I SPOTTED SOMETHING JUST OUTSIDE. WAIT HERE!!
??
...
MAYBE...?
YEAH, NO.
TRY **THESE** ON.

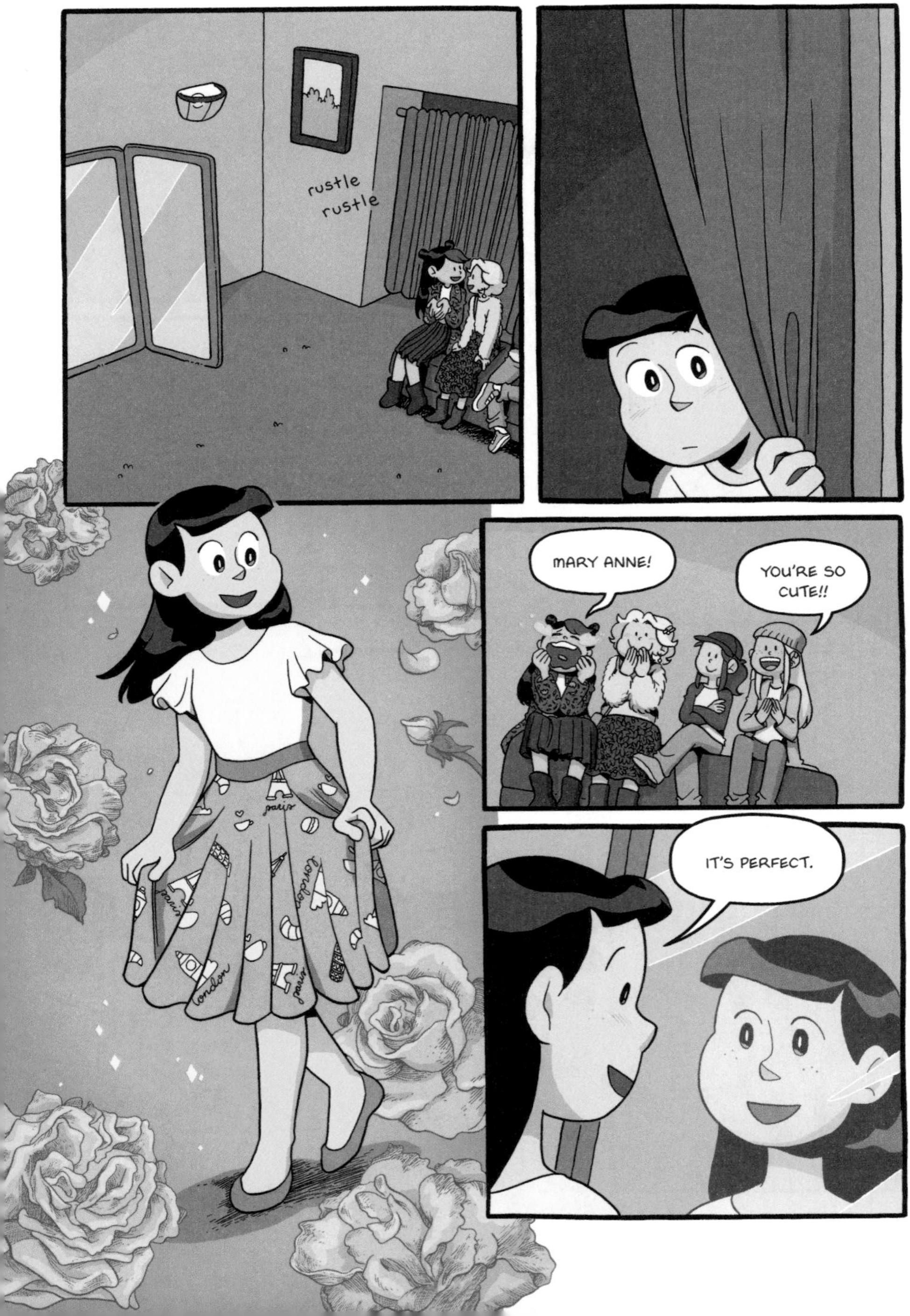
rustle
rustle
MARY ANNE!
YOU'RE SO CUTE!!
IT'S PERFECT.

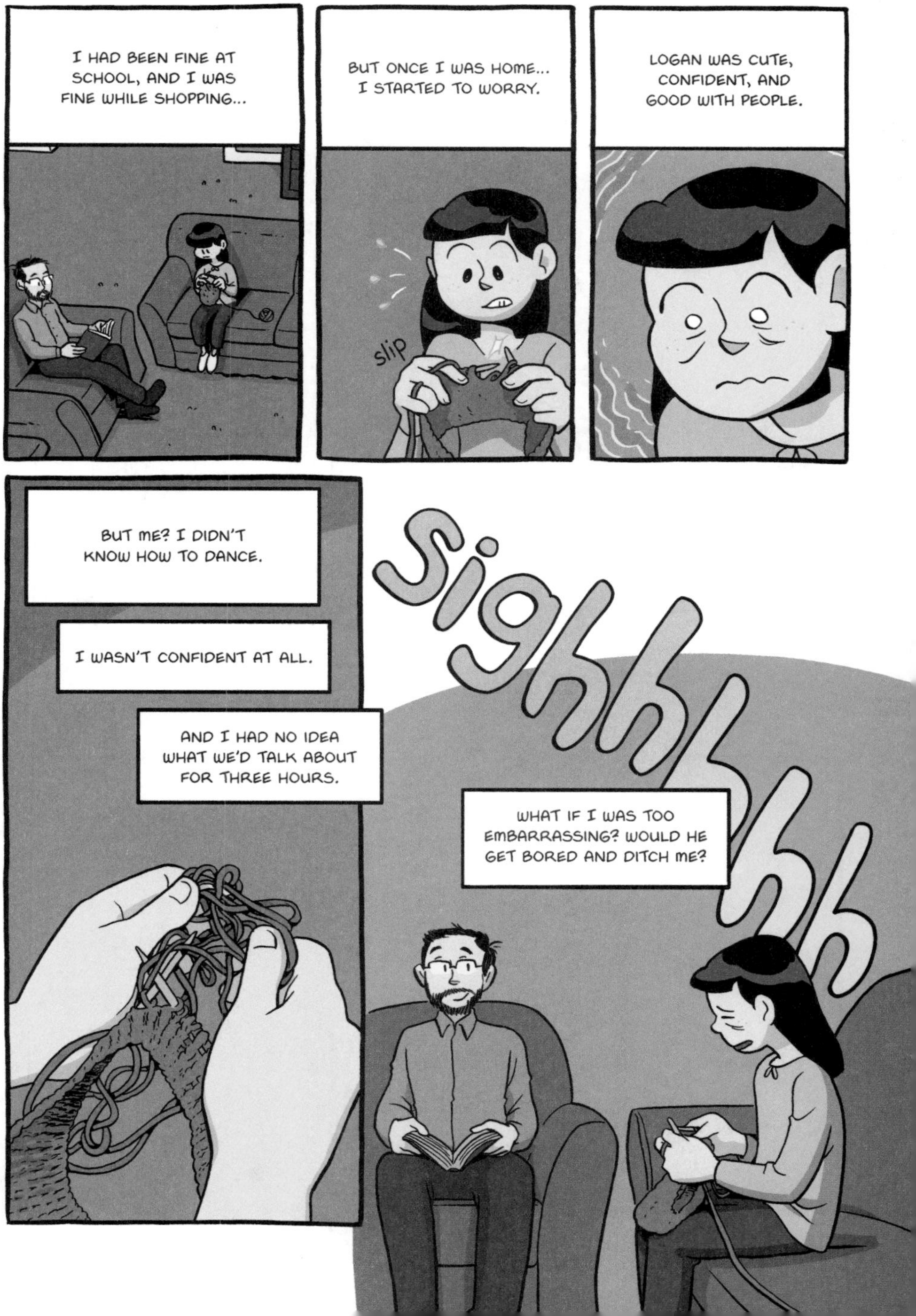
I HAD BEEN FINE AT SCHOOL, AND I WAS FINE WHILE SHOPPING...
BUT ONCE I WAS HOME... I STARTED TO WORRY.
slip
LOGAN WAS CUTE, CONFIDENT, AND GOOD WITH PEOPLE.
BUT ME? I DIDN'T KNOW HOW TO DANCE.
I WASN'T CONFIDENT AT ALL.
AND I HAD NO IDEA WHAT WE'D TALK ABOUT FOR THREE HOURS.
Sighhhhh
WHAT IF I WAS TOO EMBARRASSING? WOULD HE GET BORED AND DITCH ME?

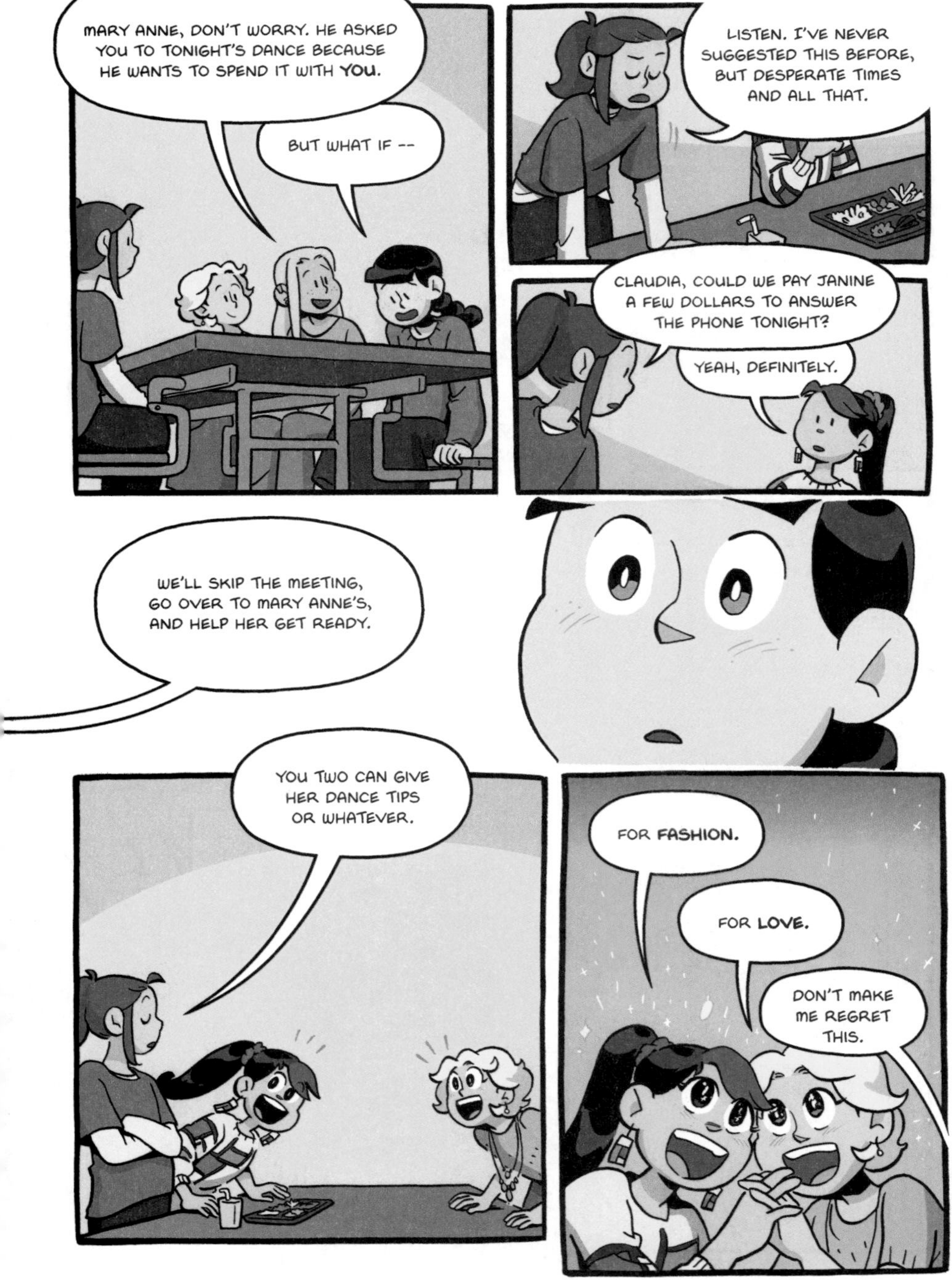
MARY ANNE, DON'T WORRY. HE ASKED YOU TO TONIGHT'S DANCE BECAUSE HE WANTS TO SPEND IT WITH **YOU**.
BUT WHAT IF --
LISTEN. I'VE NEVER SUGGESTED THIS BEFORE, BUT DESPERATE TIMES AND ALL THAT.
CLAUDIA, COULD WE PAY JANINE A FEW DOLLARS TO ANSWER THE PHONE TONIGHT?
YEAH, DEFINITELY.
WE'LL SKIP THE MEETING, GO OVER TO MARY ANNE'S, AND HELP HER GET READY.
YOU TWO CAN GIVE HER DANCE TIPS OR WHATEVER.
FOR **FASHION.**
FOR **LOVE.**
DON'T MAKE ME REGRET THIS.

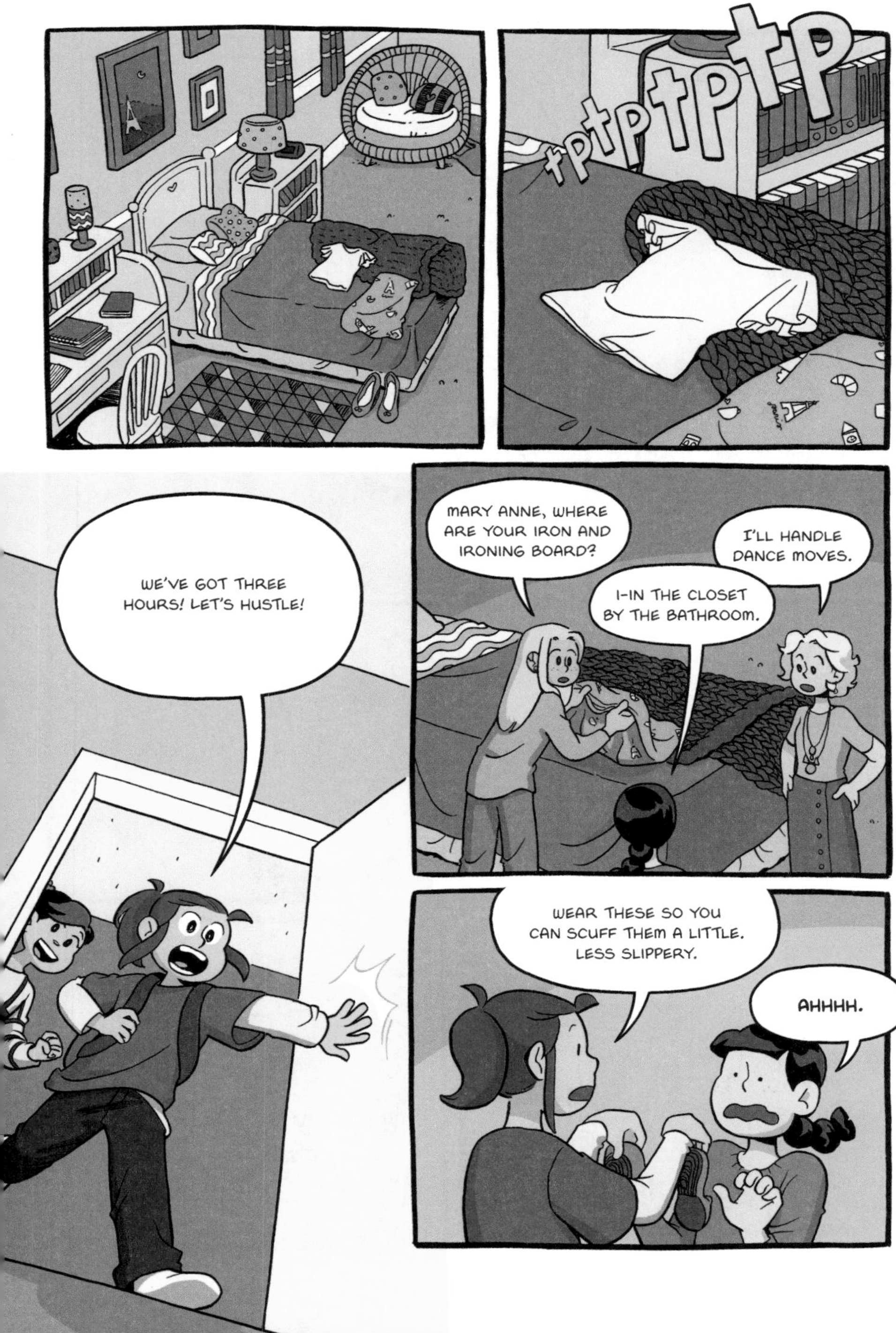
tptptptp
WE'VE GOT THREE HOURS! LET'S HUSTLE!
MARY ANNE, WHERE ARE YOUR IRON AND IRONING BOARD?
I'LL HANDLE DANCE MOVES.
I-IN THE CLOSET BY THE BATHROOM.
WEAR THESE SO YOU CAN SCUFF THEM A LITTLE. LESS SLIPPERY.
AHHHH.

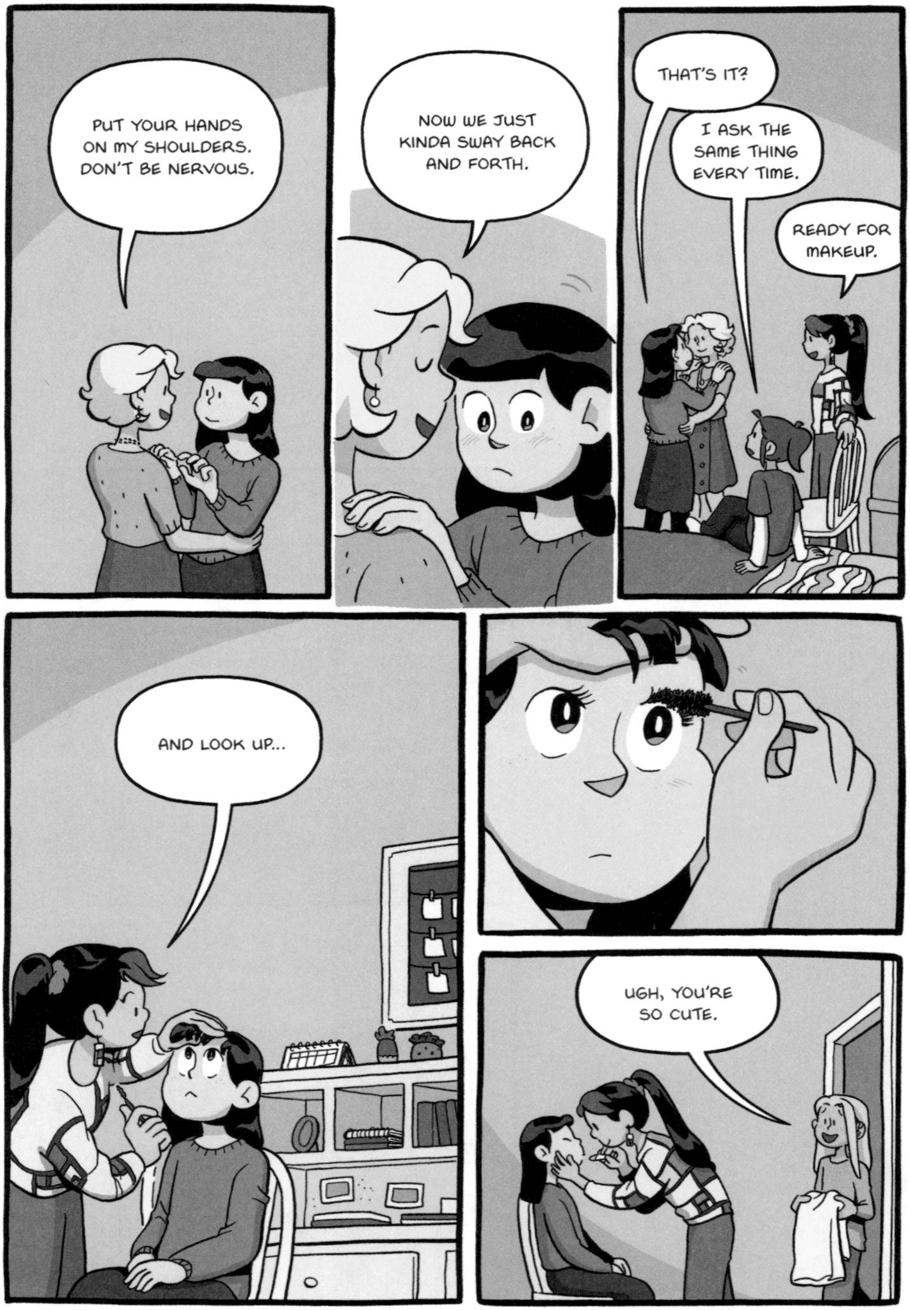
PUT YOUR HANDS ON MY SHOULDERS. DON'T BE NERVOUS.
NOW WE JUST KINDA SWAY BACK AND FORTH.
THAT'S IT?
I ASK THE SAME THING EVERY TIME.
READY FOR MAKEUP.
AND LOOK UP...
UGH, YOU'RE SO CUTE.

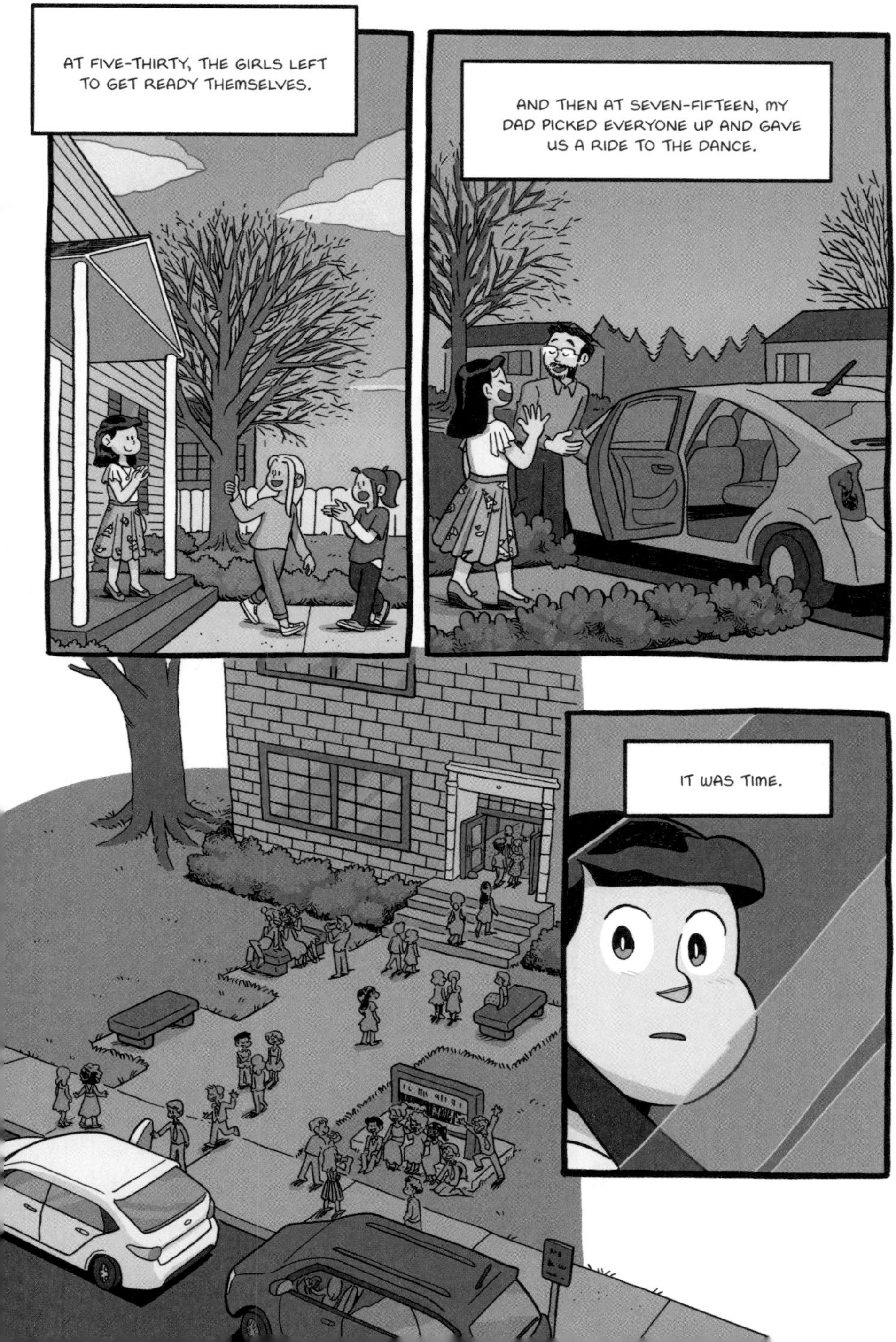
AT FIVE-THIRTY, THE GIRLS LEFT TO GET READY THEMSELVES.
AND THEN AT SEVEN-FIFTEEN, MY DAD PICKED EVERYONE UP AND GAVE US A RIDE TO THE DANCE.
IT WAS TIME.

CHAPTER 10

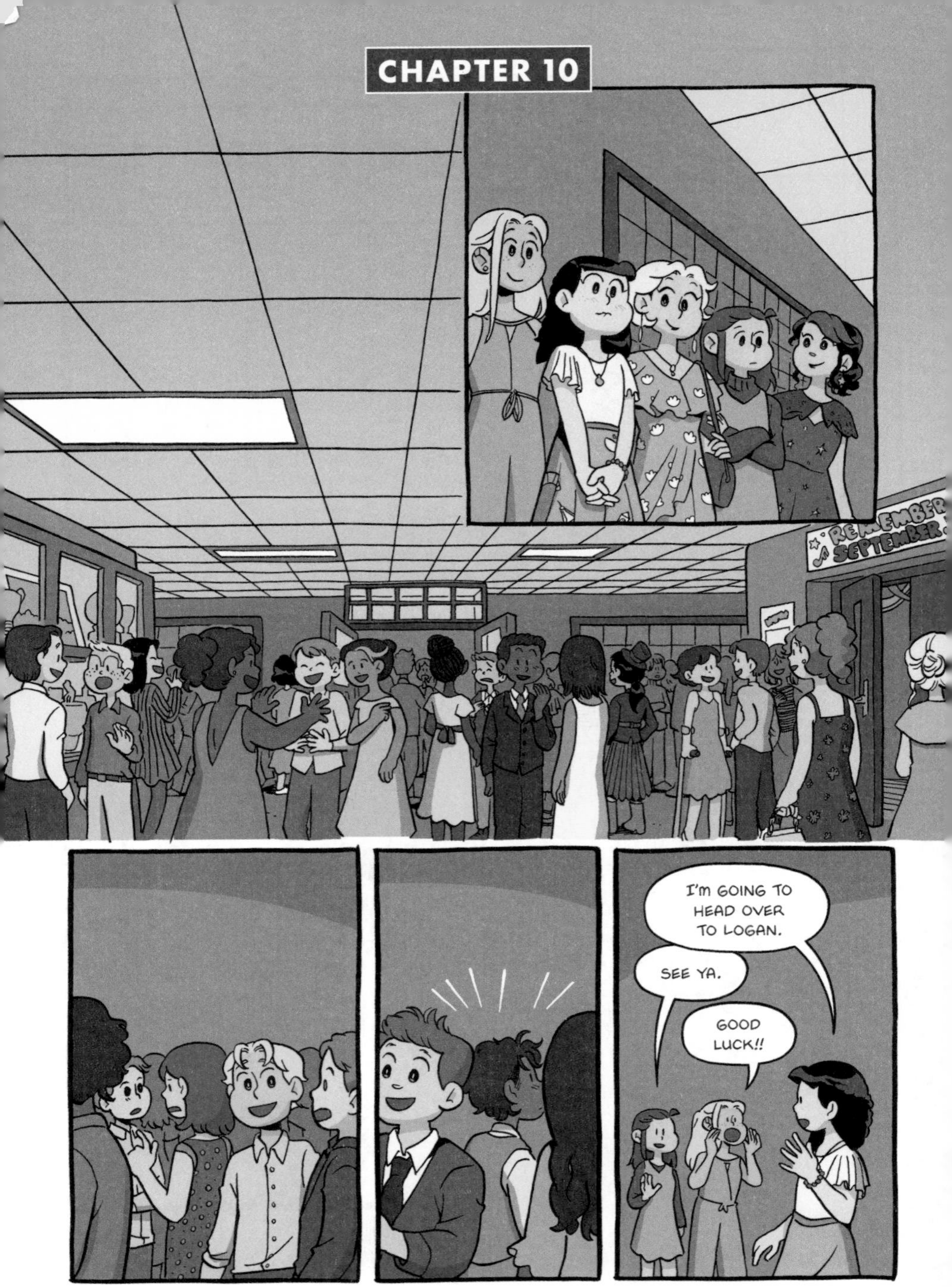
REMEMBER SEPTEMBER
I'm GOING TO HEAD OVER TO LOGAN.
SEE YA.
GOOD LUCK!!

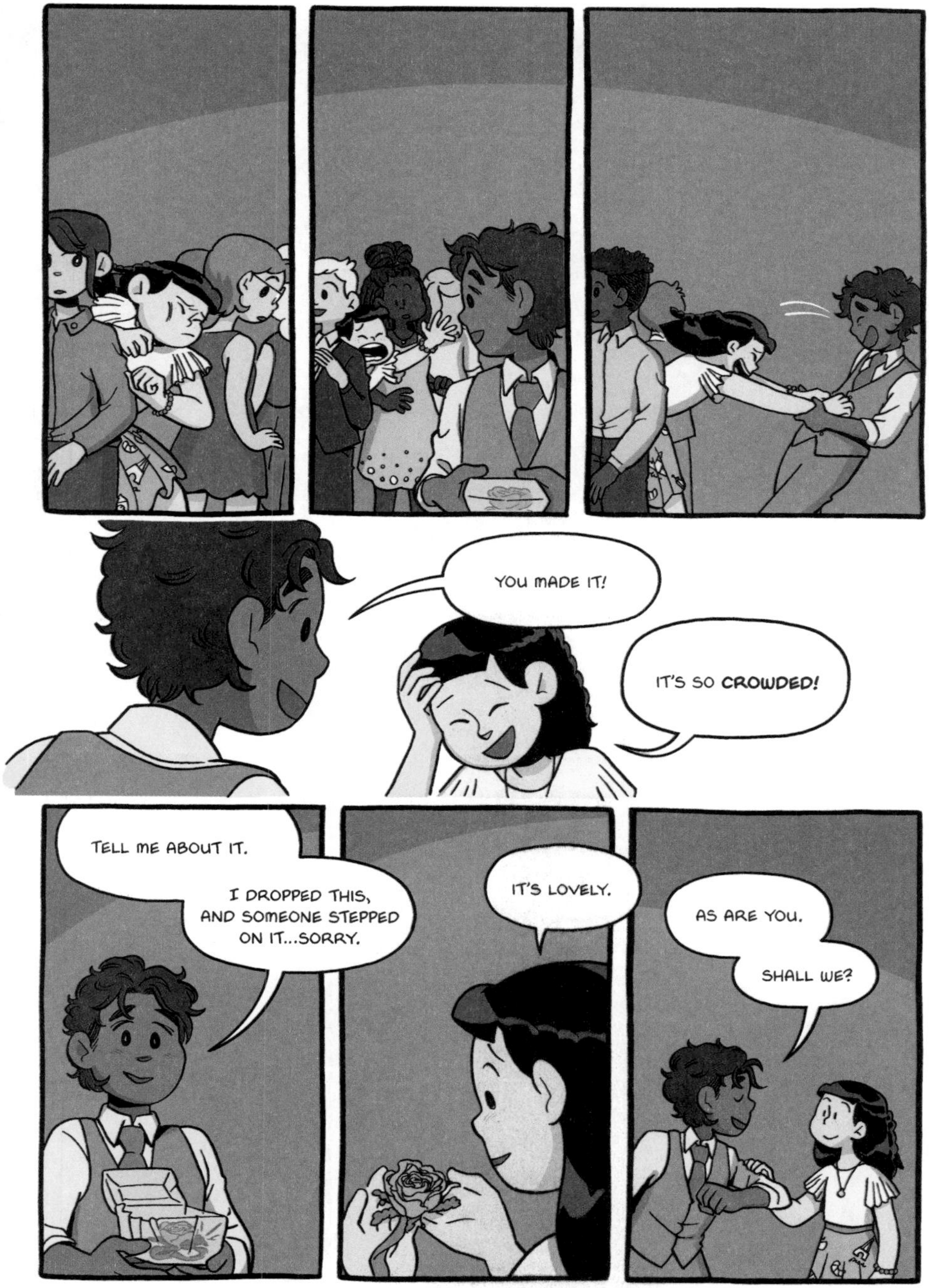
YOU MADE IT!
IT'S SO **CROWDED!**
TELL ME ABOUT IT.
I DROPPED THIS, AND SOMEONE STEPPED ON IT...SORRY.
IT'S LOVELY.
AS ARE YOU.
SHALL WE?

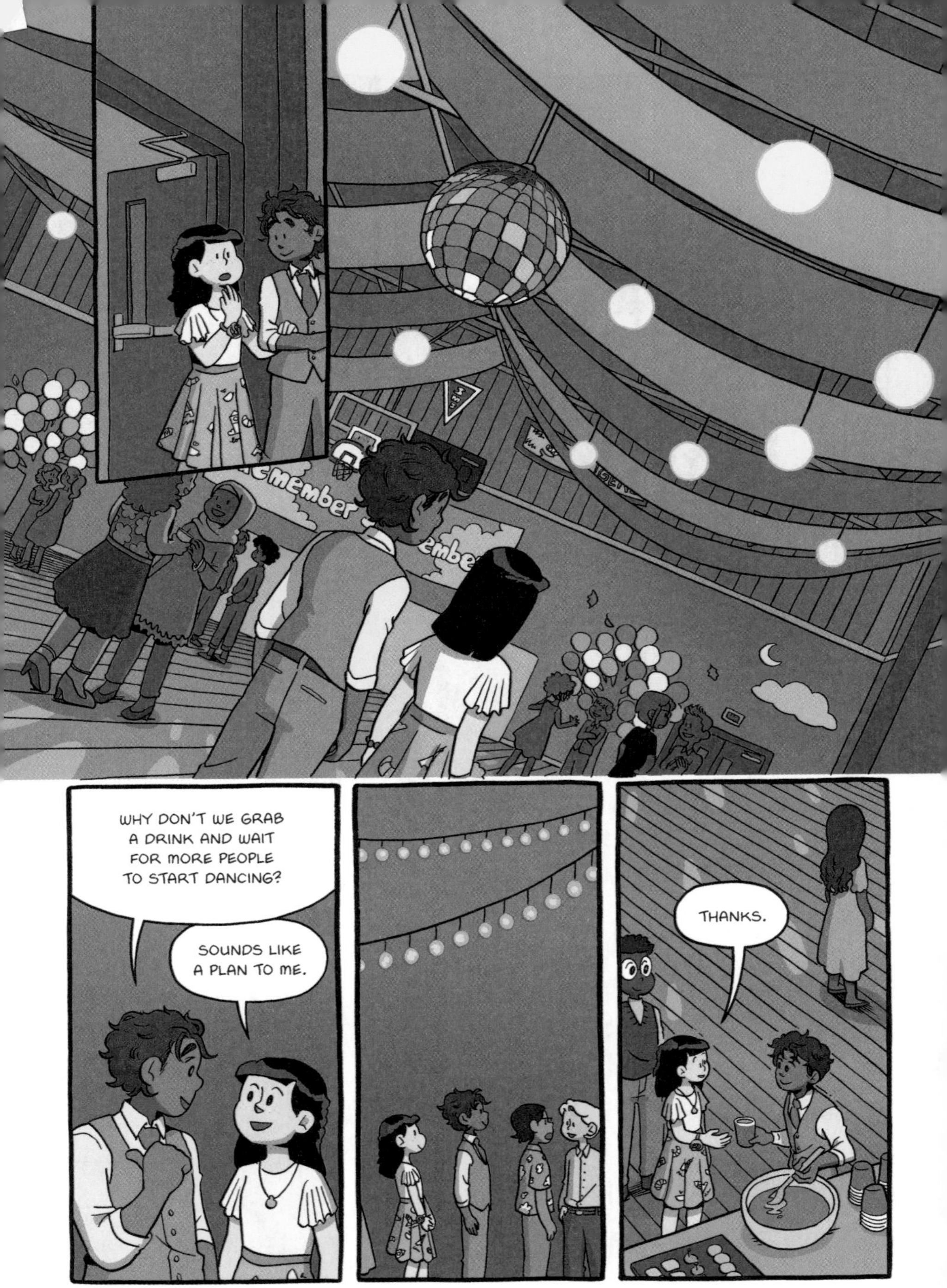
WHY DON'T WE GRAB A DRINK AND WAIT FOR MORE PEOPLE TO START DANCING?
SOUNDS LIKE A PLAN TO ME.
THANKS.

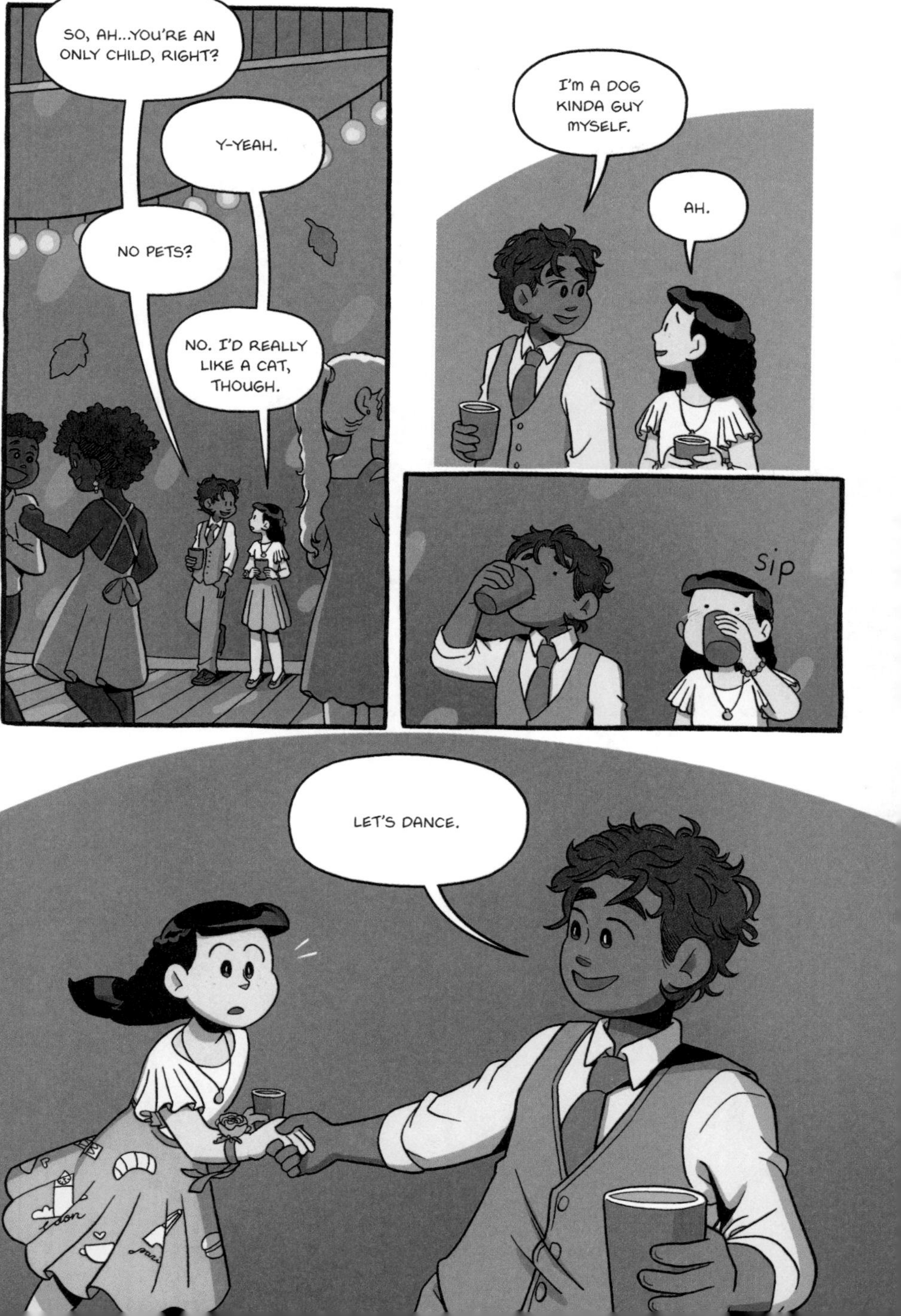
SO, AH...YOU'RE AN ONLY CHILD, RIGHT?
Y-YEAH.
NO PETS?
NO. I'D REALLY LIKE A CAT, THOUGH.
I'M A DOG KINDA GUY MYSELF.
AH.
sip
LET'S DANCE.

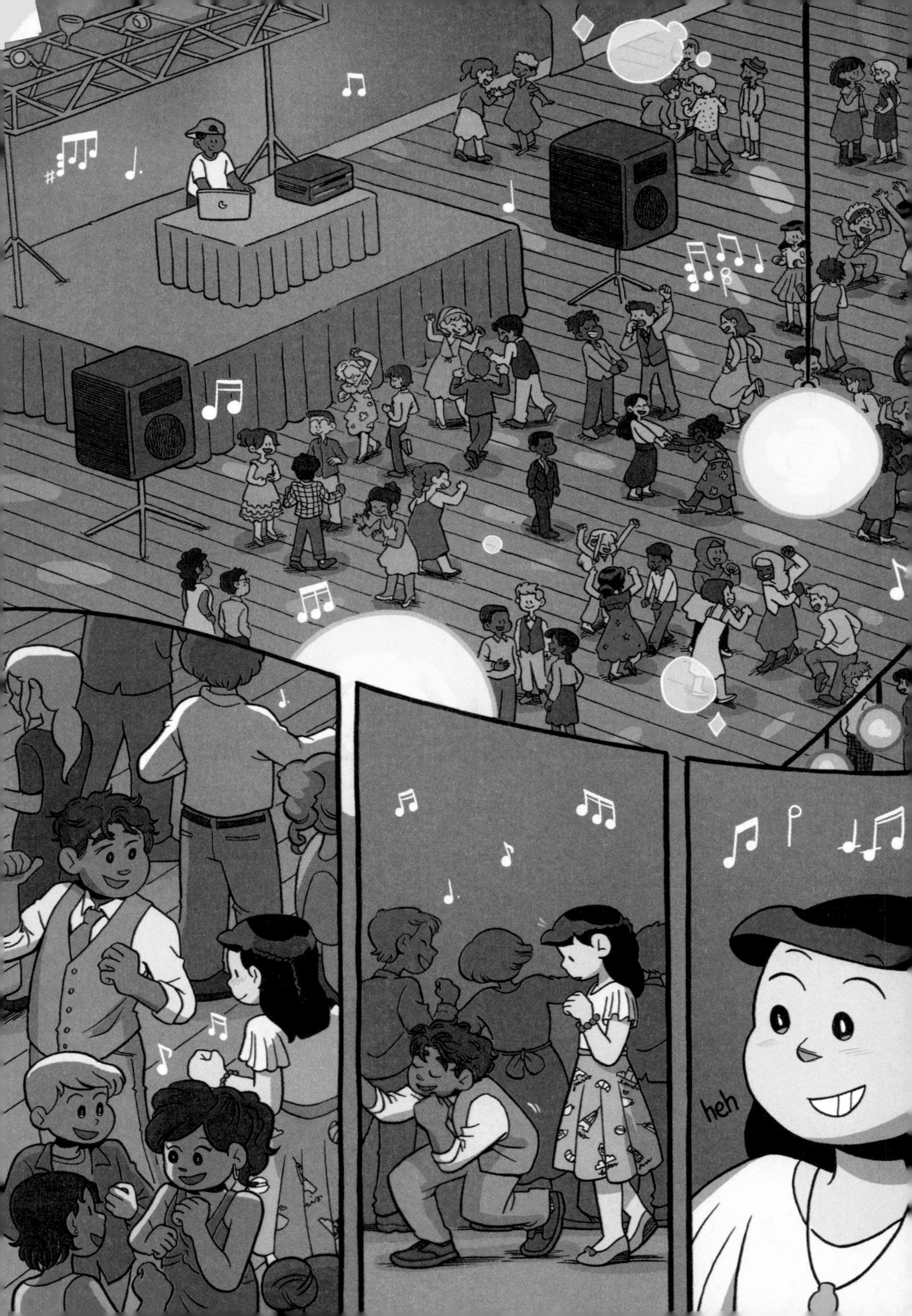
heh

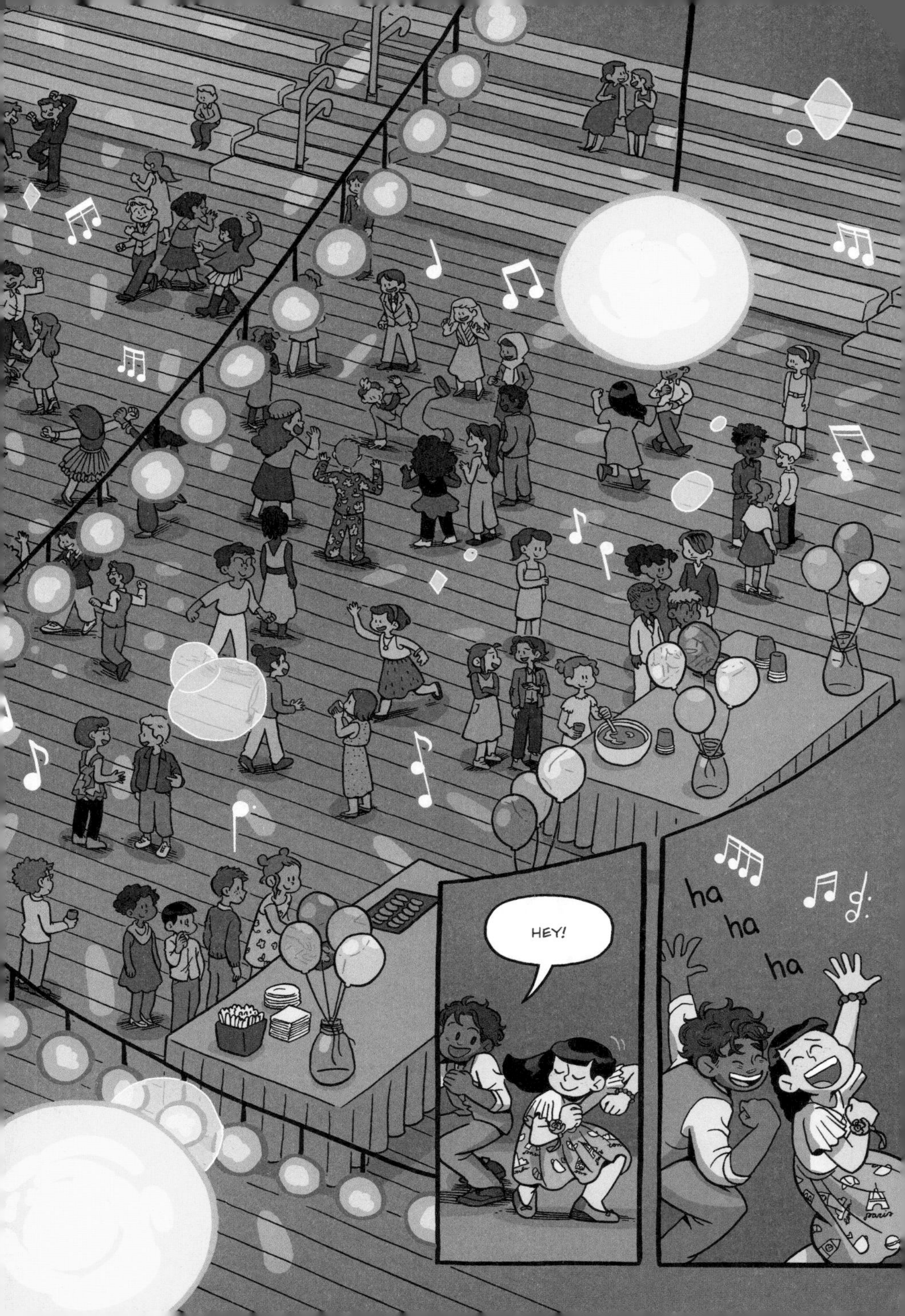
HEY!
ha
ha
ha

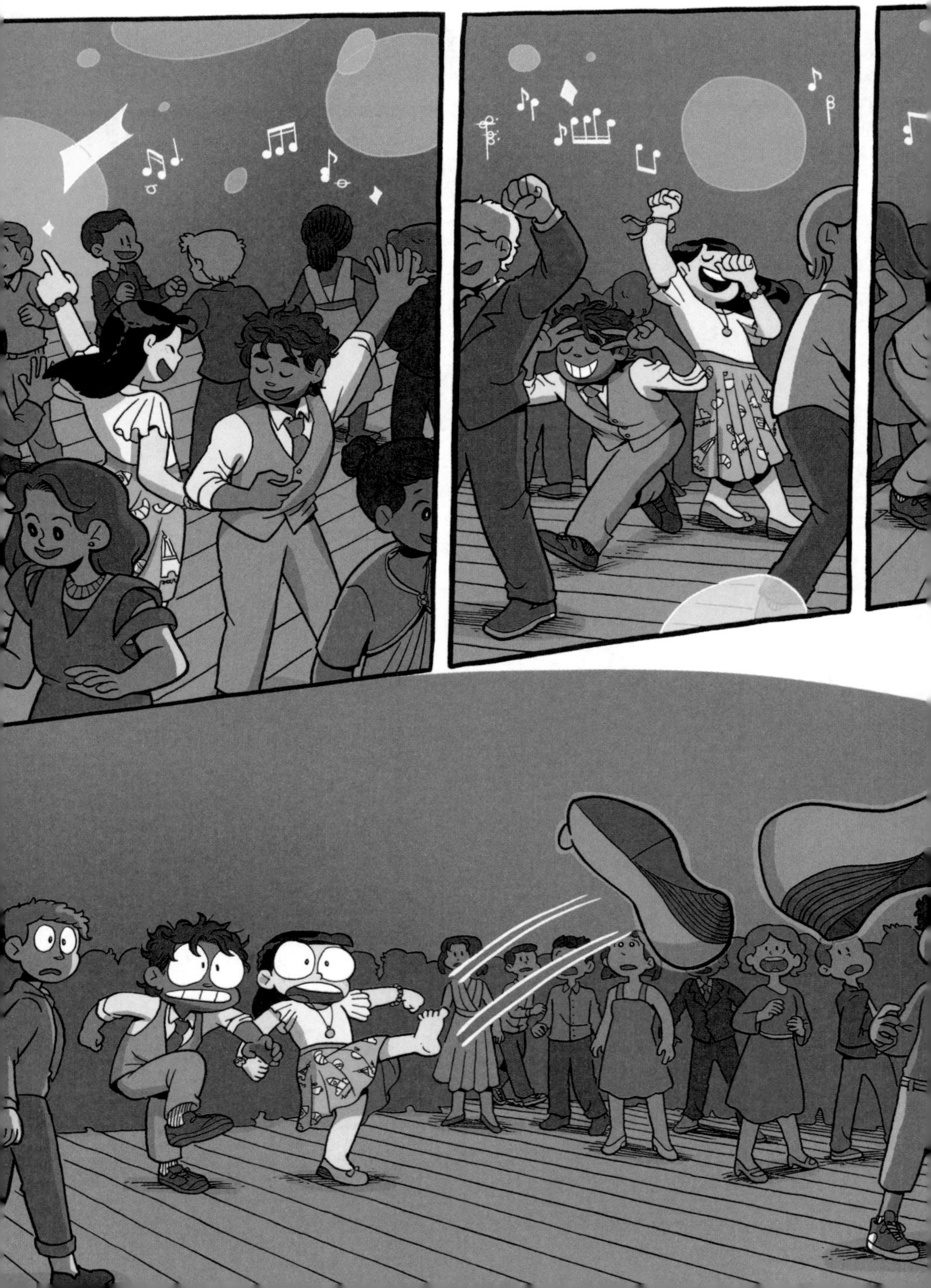

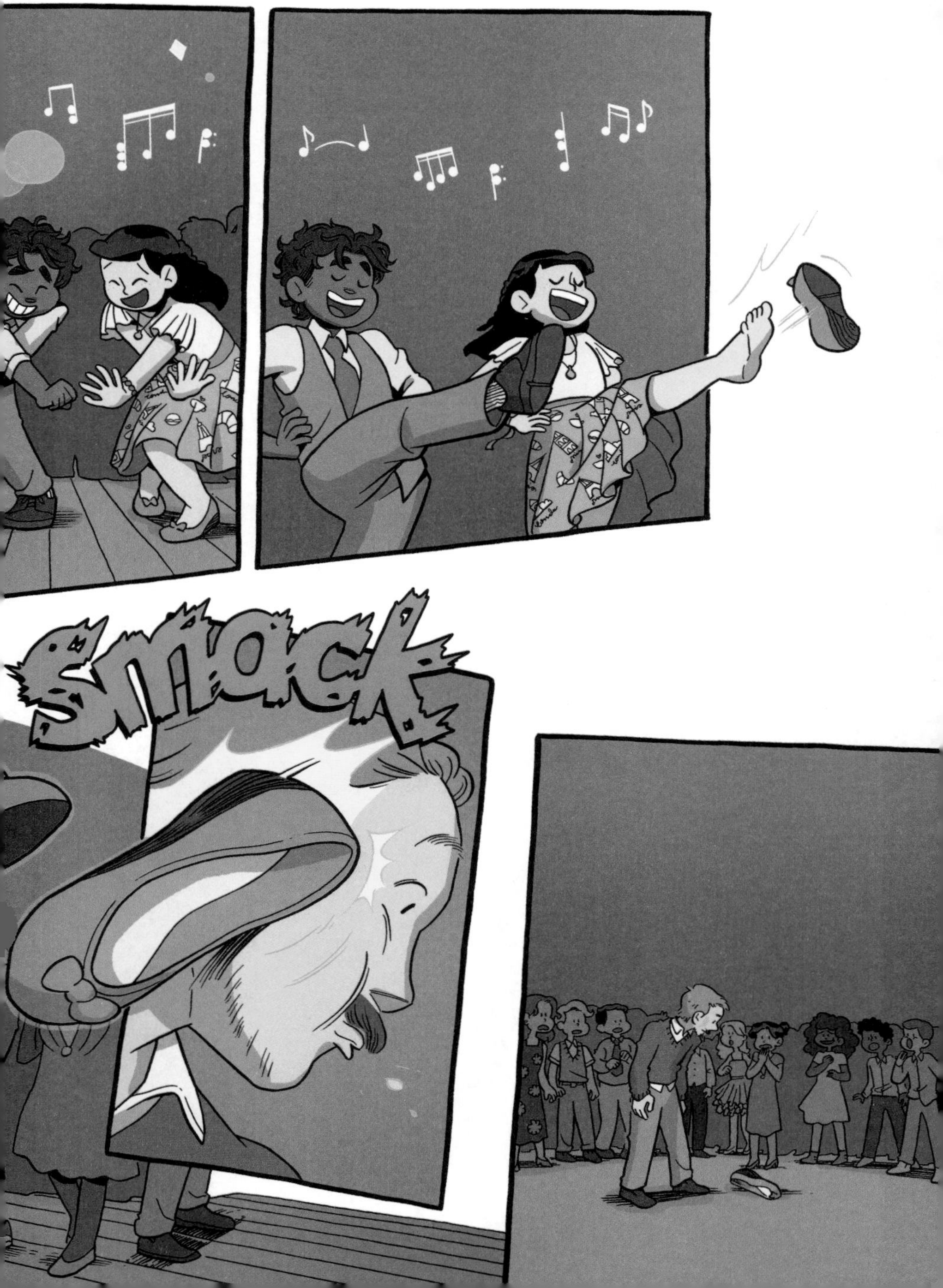
SMACK

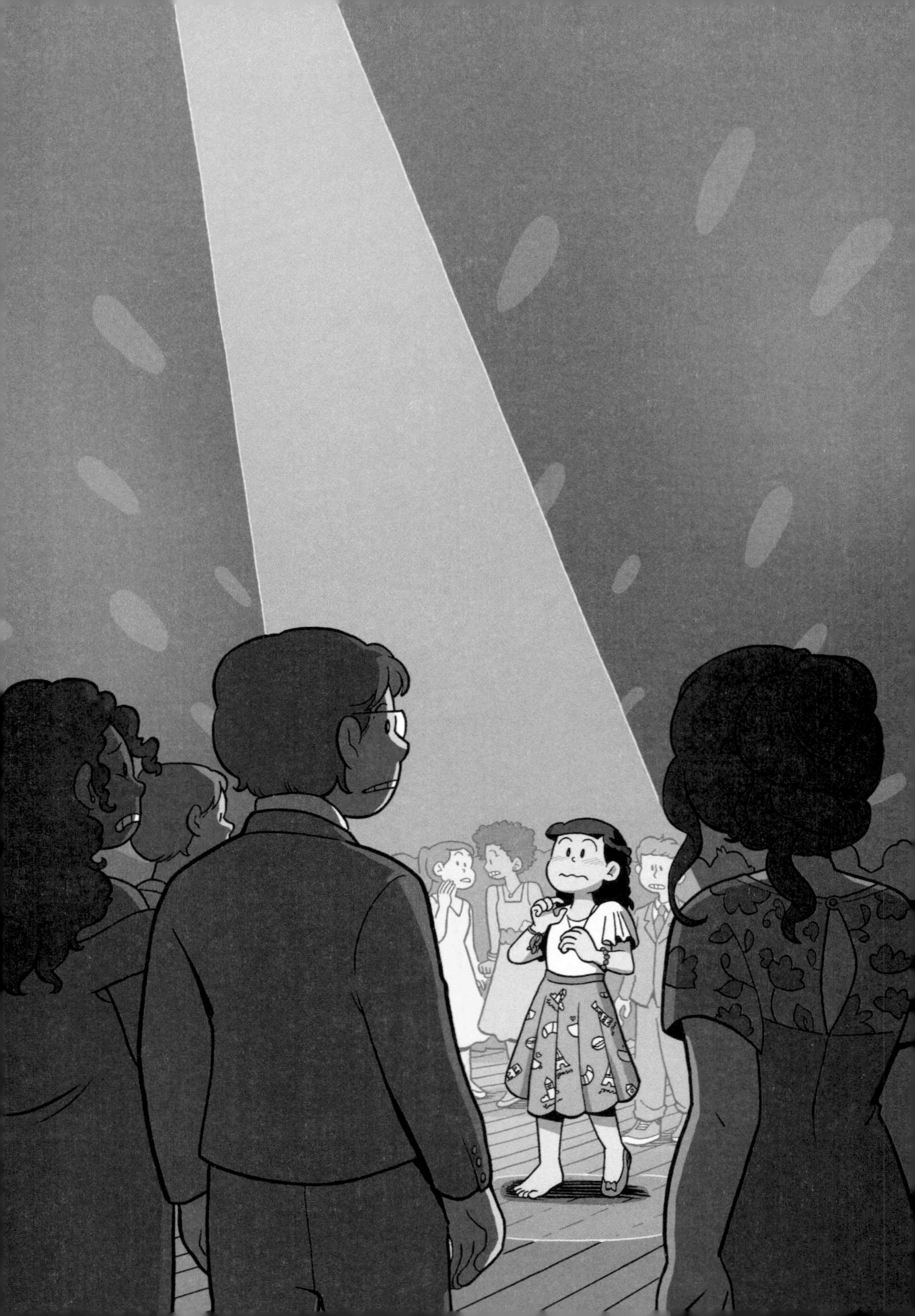

CHAPTER 11

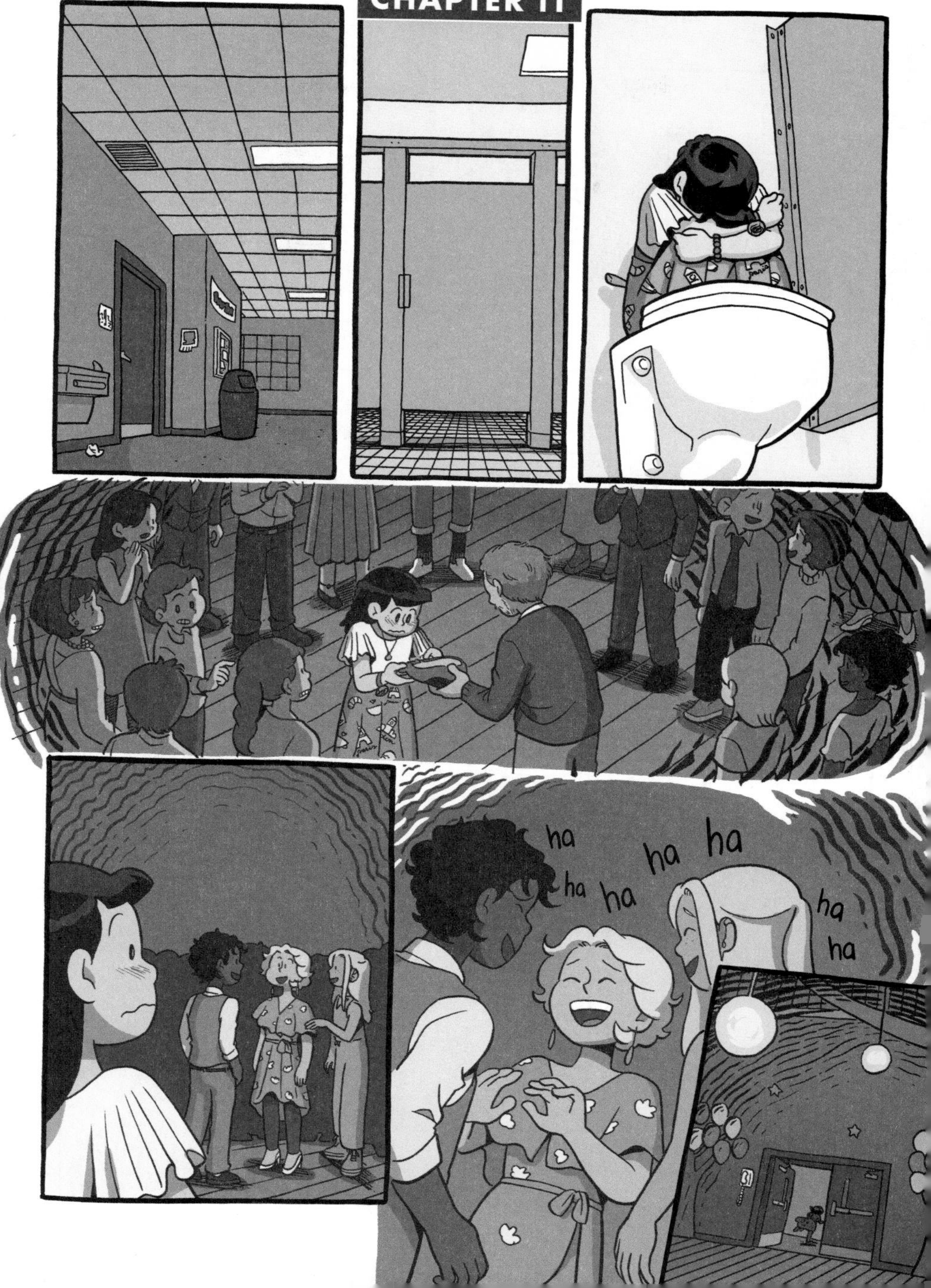
ha
ha
ha
ha
ha
ha
ha

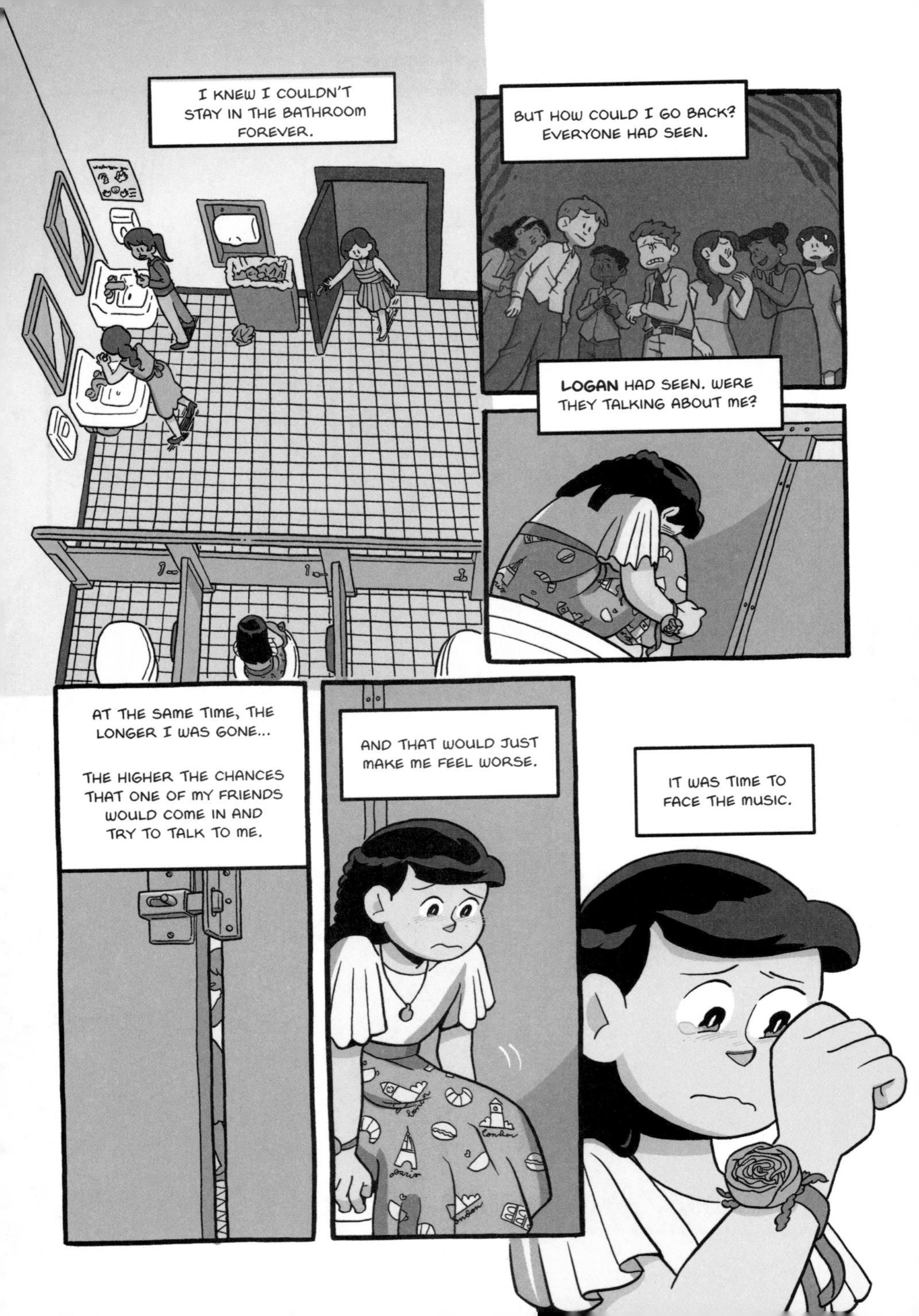
I KNEW I COULDN'T STAY IN THE BATHROOM FOREVER.
BUT HOW COULD I GO BACK? EVERYONE HAD SEEN.
LOGAN HAD SEEN. WERE THEY TALKING ABOUT ME?
AT THE SAME TIME, THE LONGER I WAS GONE...
THE HIGHER THE CHANCES THAT ONE OF MY FRIENDS WOULD COME IN AND TRY TO TALK TO ME.
AND THAT WOULD JUST MAKE ME FEEL WORSE.
IT WAS TIME TO FACE THE MUSIC.

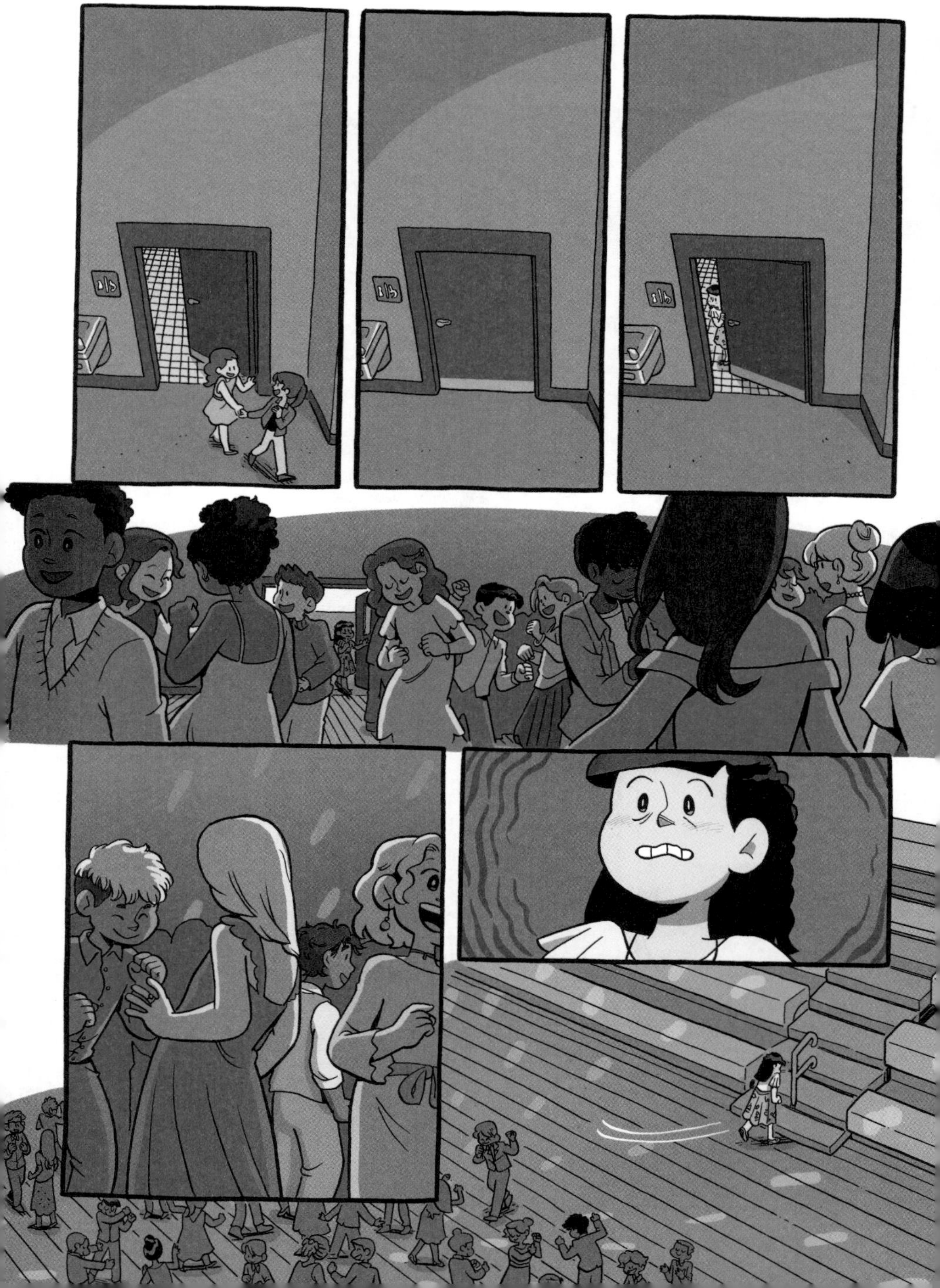

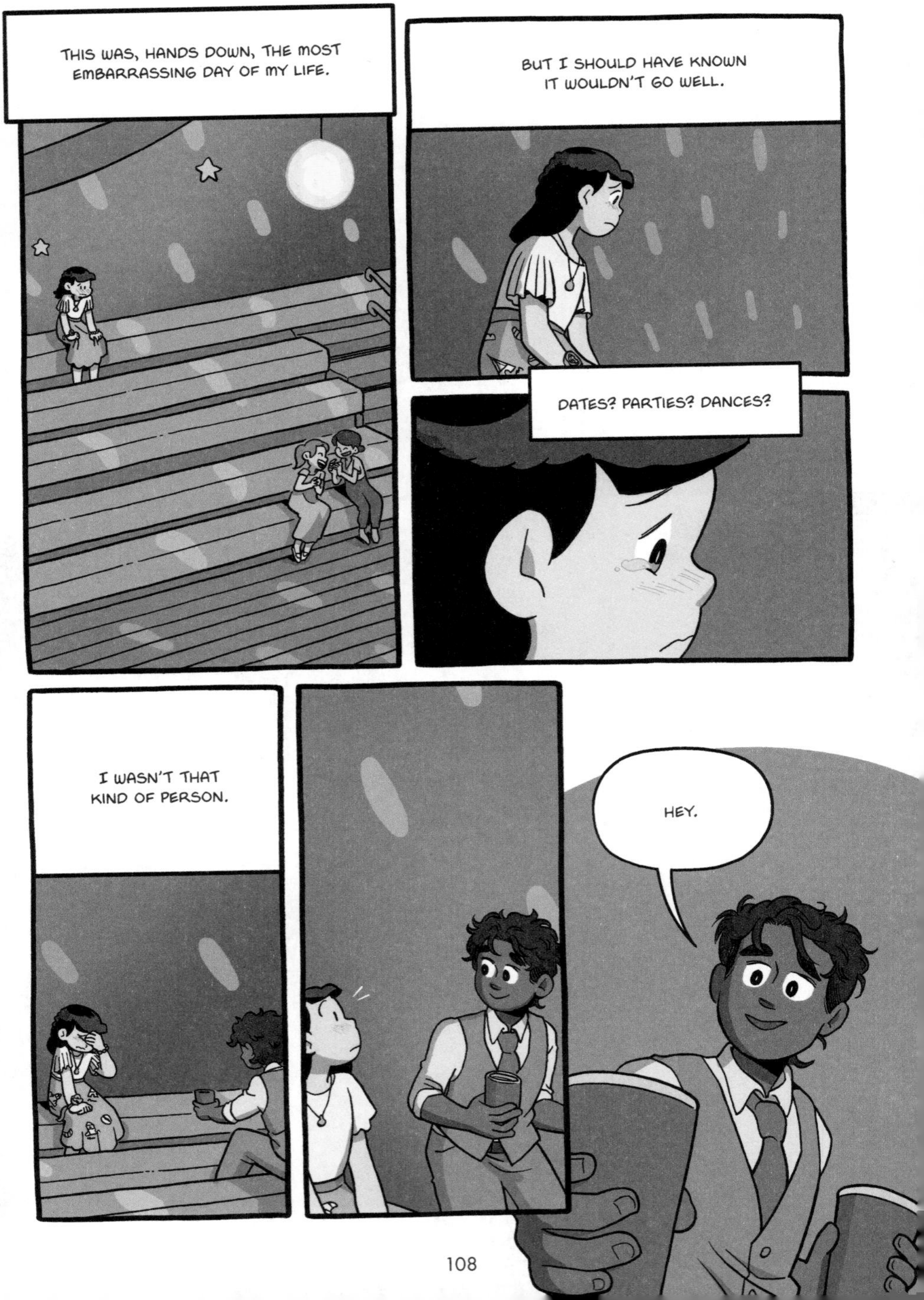
THIS WAS, HANDS DOWN, THE MOST EMBARRASSING DAY OF MY LIFE.
BUT I SHOULD HAVE KNOWN IT WOULDN'T GO WELL.
DATES? PARTIES? DANCES?
I WASN'T THAT KIND OF PERSON.
HEY.

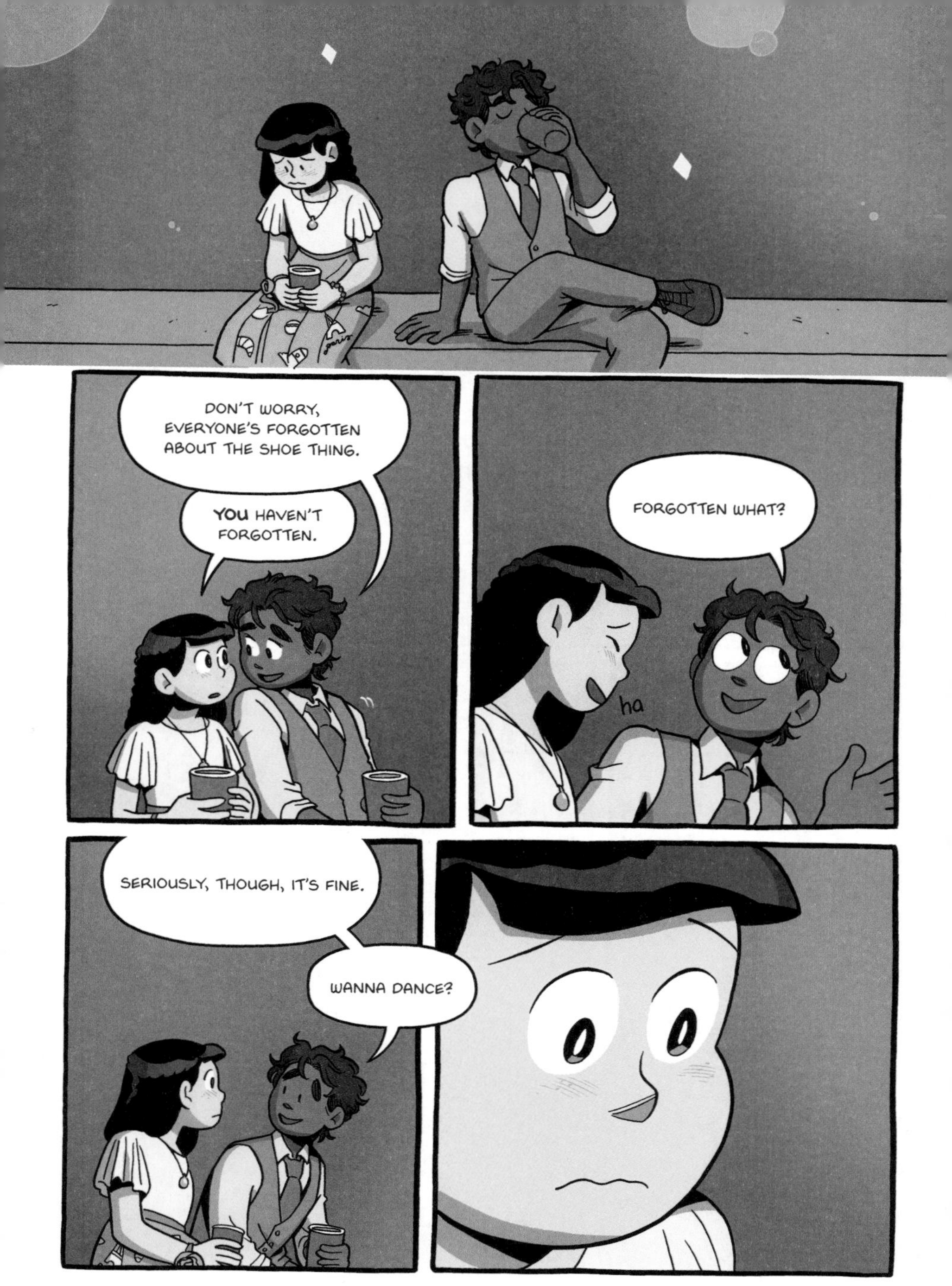
DON'T WORRY, EVERYONE'S FORGOTTEN ABOUT THE SHOE THING.
YOU HAVEN'T FORGOTTEN.
FORGOTTEN WHAT?
ha
SERIOUSLY, THOUGH, IT'S FINE.
WANNA DANCE?

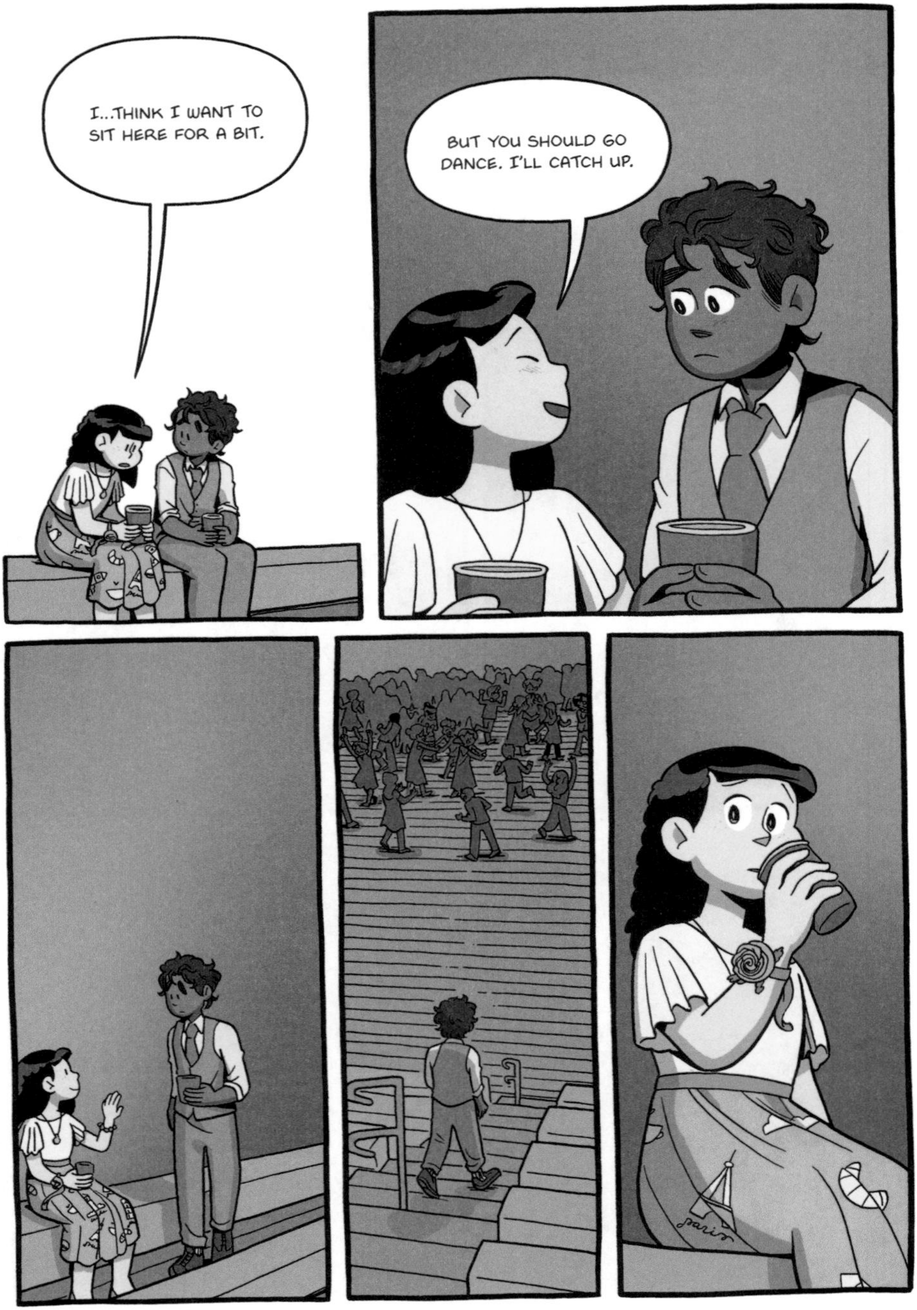
I...THINK I WANT TO SIT HERE FOR A BIT.
BUT YOU SHOULD GO DANCE. I'LL CATCH UP.
paris

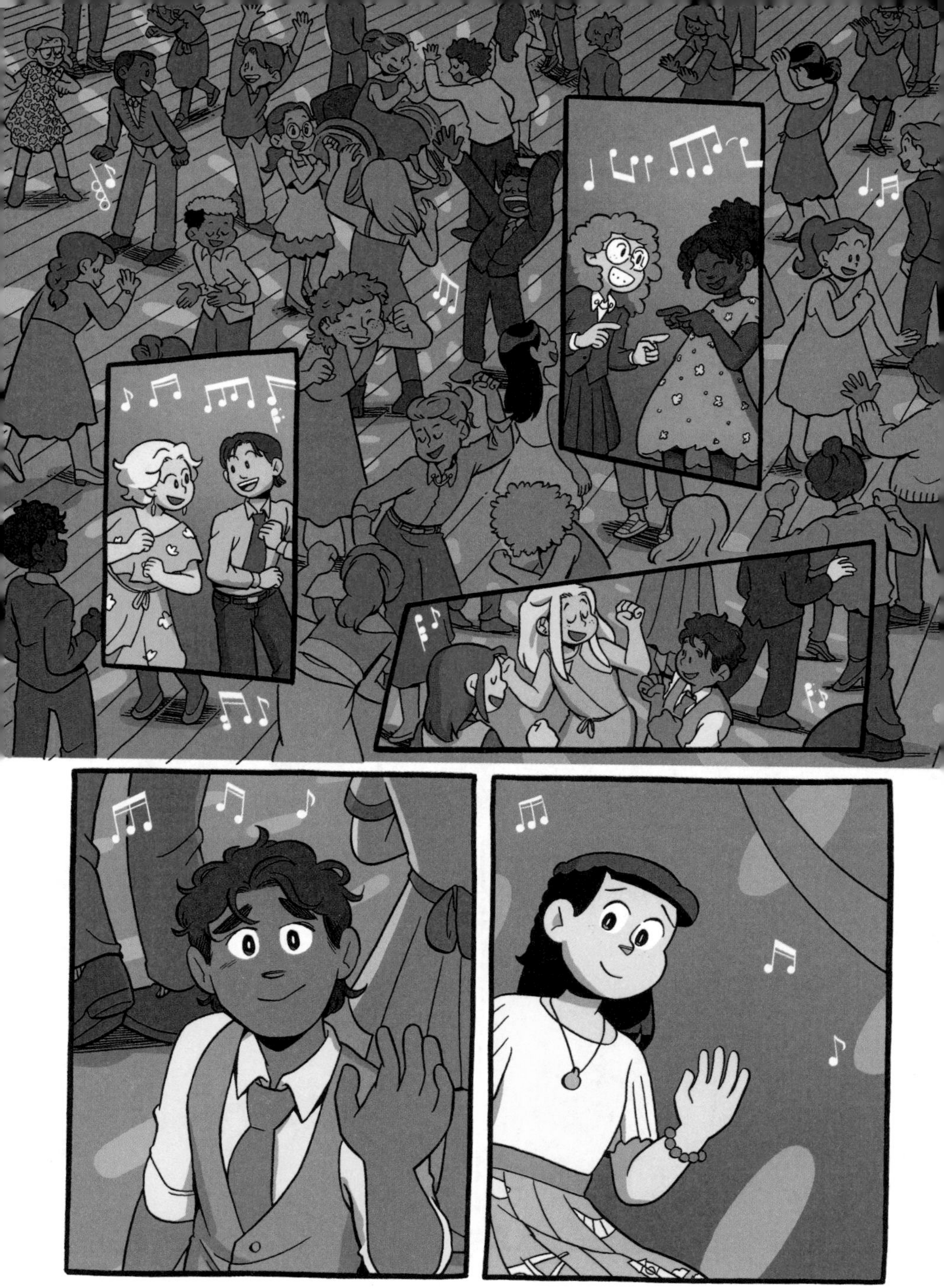

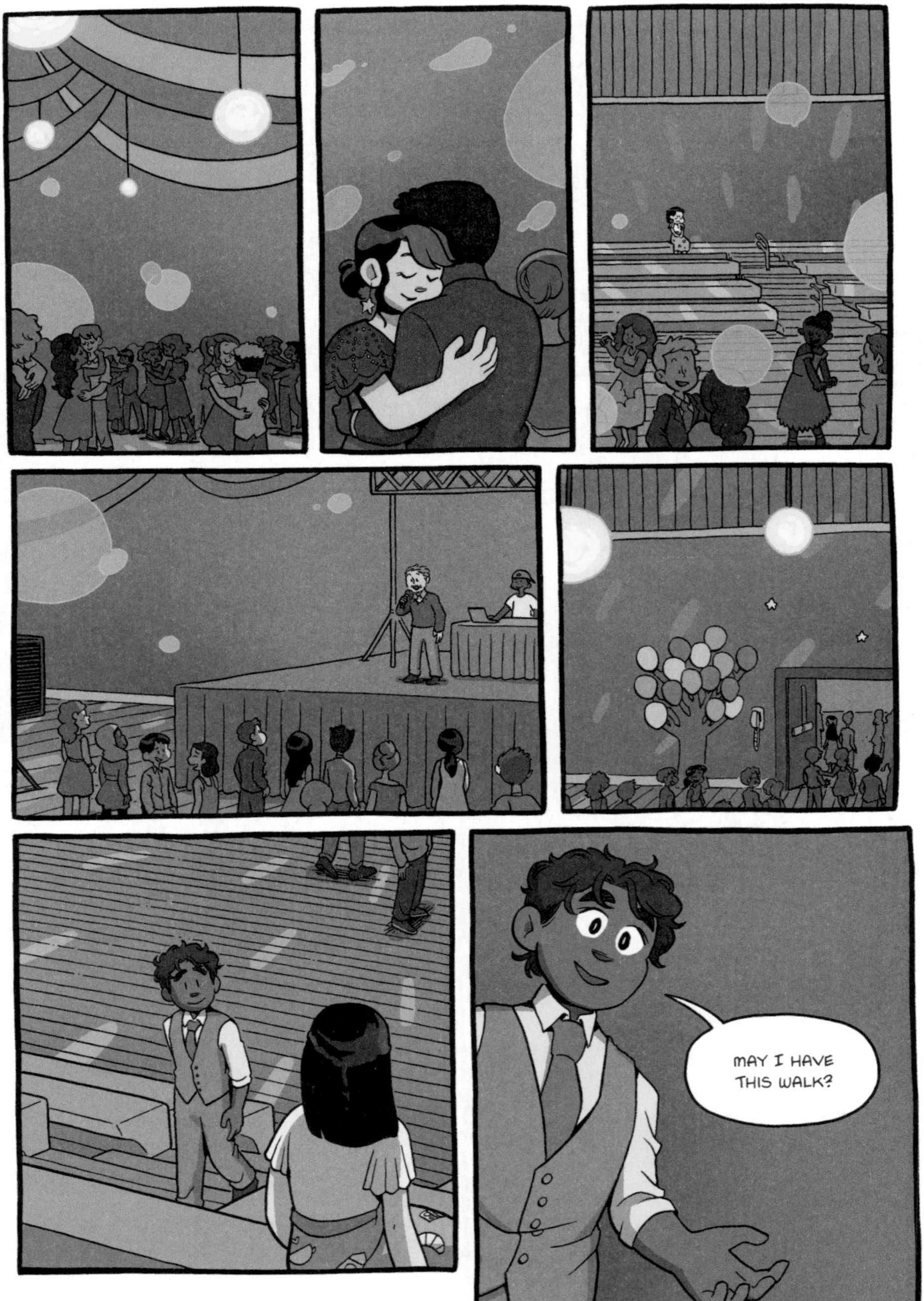
MAY I HAVE
THIS WALK?

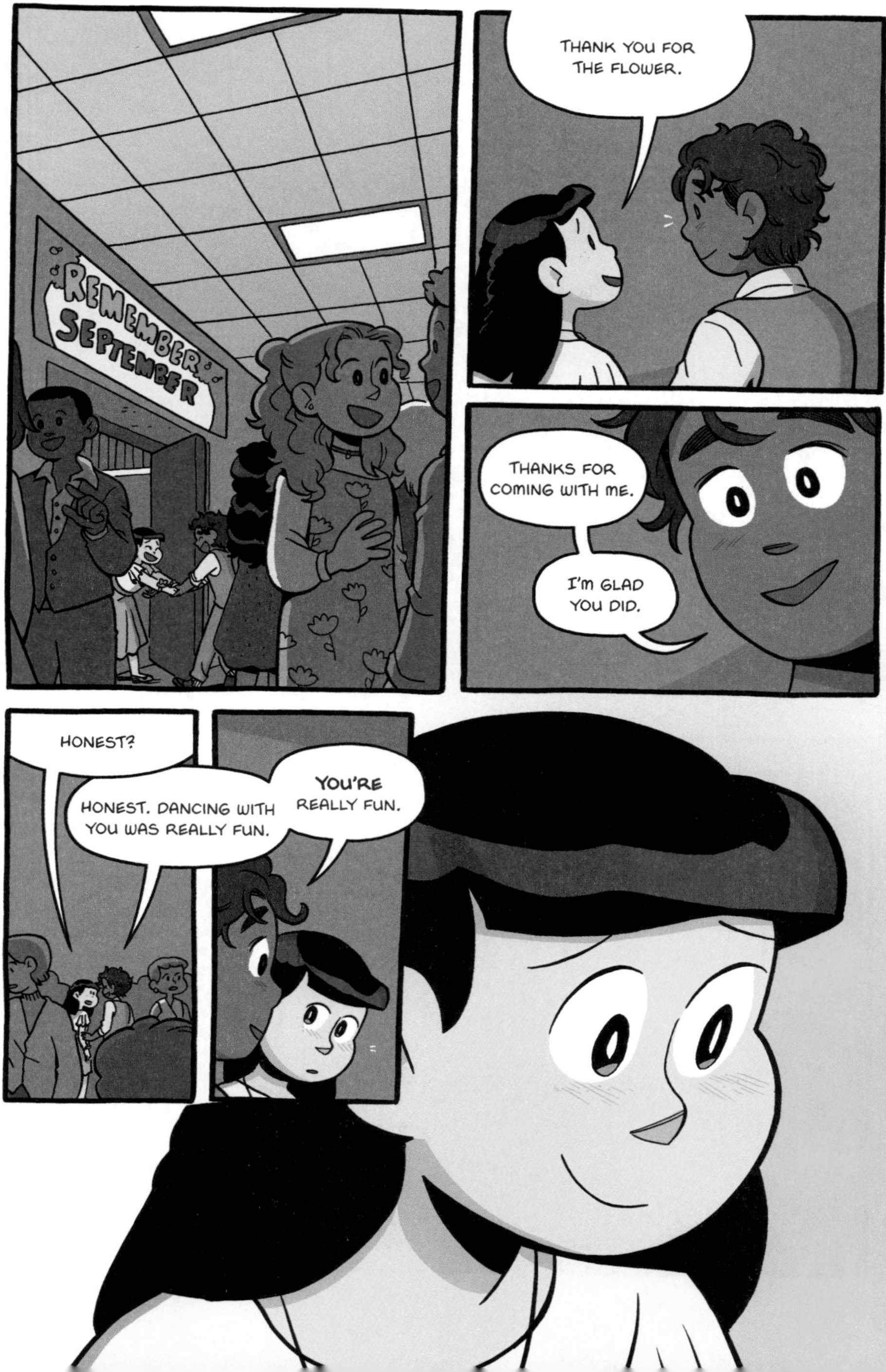

REMEMBER SEPTEMBER
THANK YOU FOR THE FLOWER.
THANKS FOR COMING WITH ME.
I'M GLAD YOU DID.
HONEST?
HONEST. DANCING WITH YOU WAS REALLY FUN.
YOU'RE REALLY FUN.

CHAPTER 12

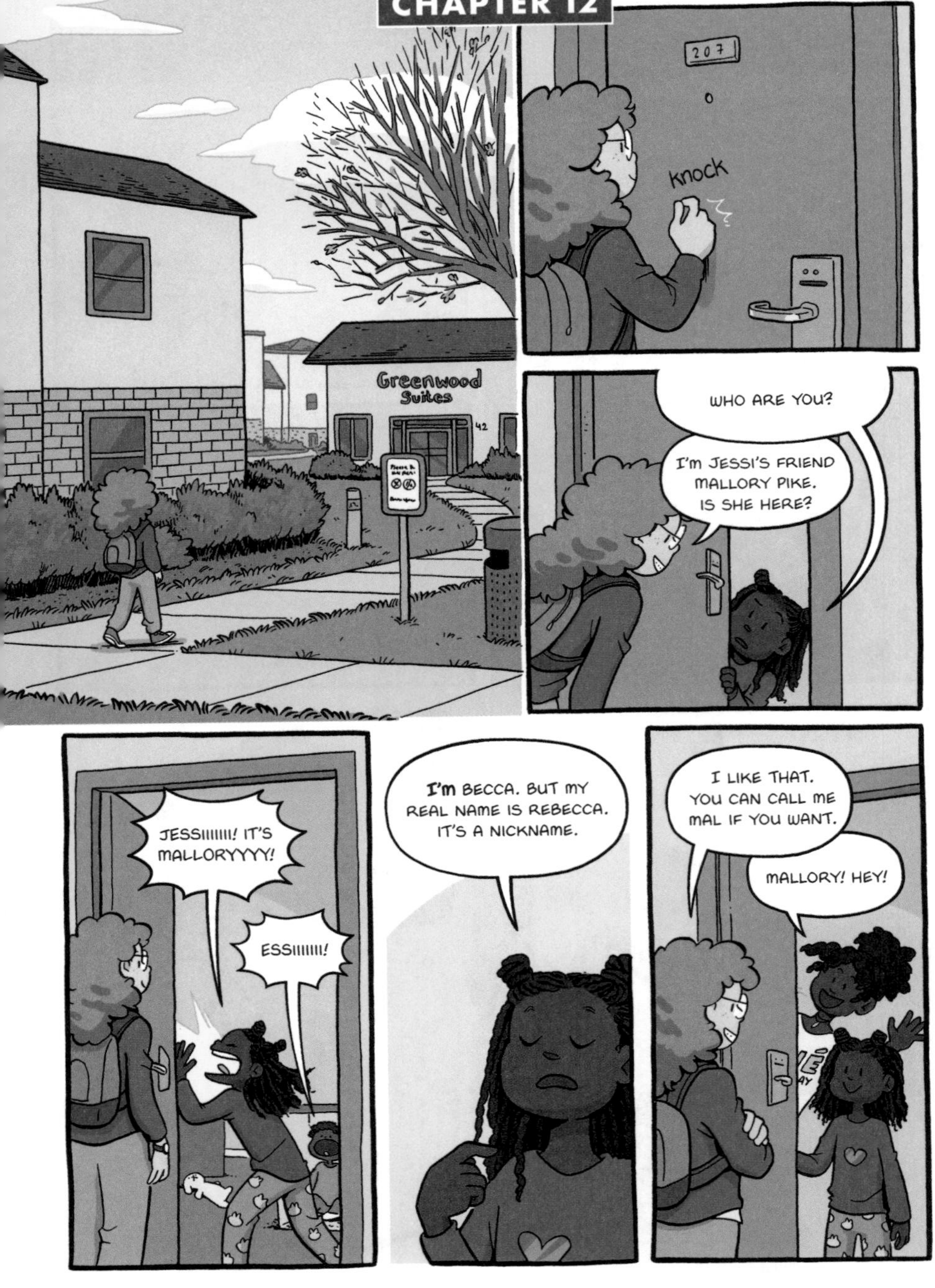
Greenwood Suites
knock
WHO ARE YOU?
I'M JESSI'S FRIEND MALLORY PIKE. IS SHE HERE?
JESSIIIIIII! IT'S MALLORYYYY!
ESSIIIIIII!
I'M BECCA. BUT MY REAL NAME IS REBECCA. IT'S A NICKNAME.
I LIKE THAT. YOU CAN CALL ME MAL IF YOU WANT.
MALLORY! HEY!

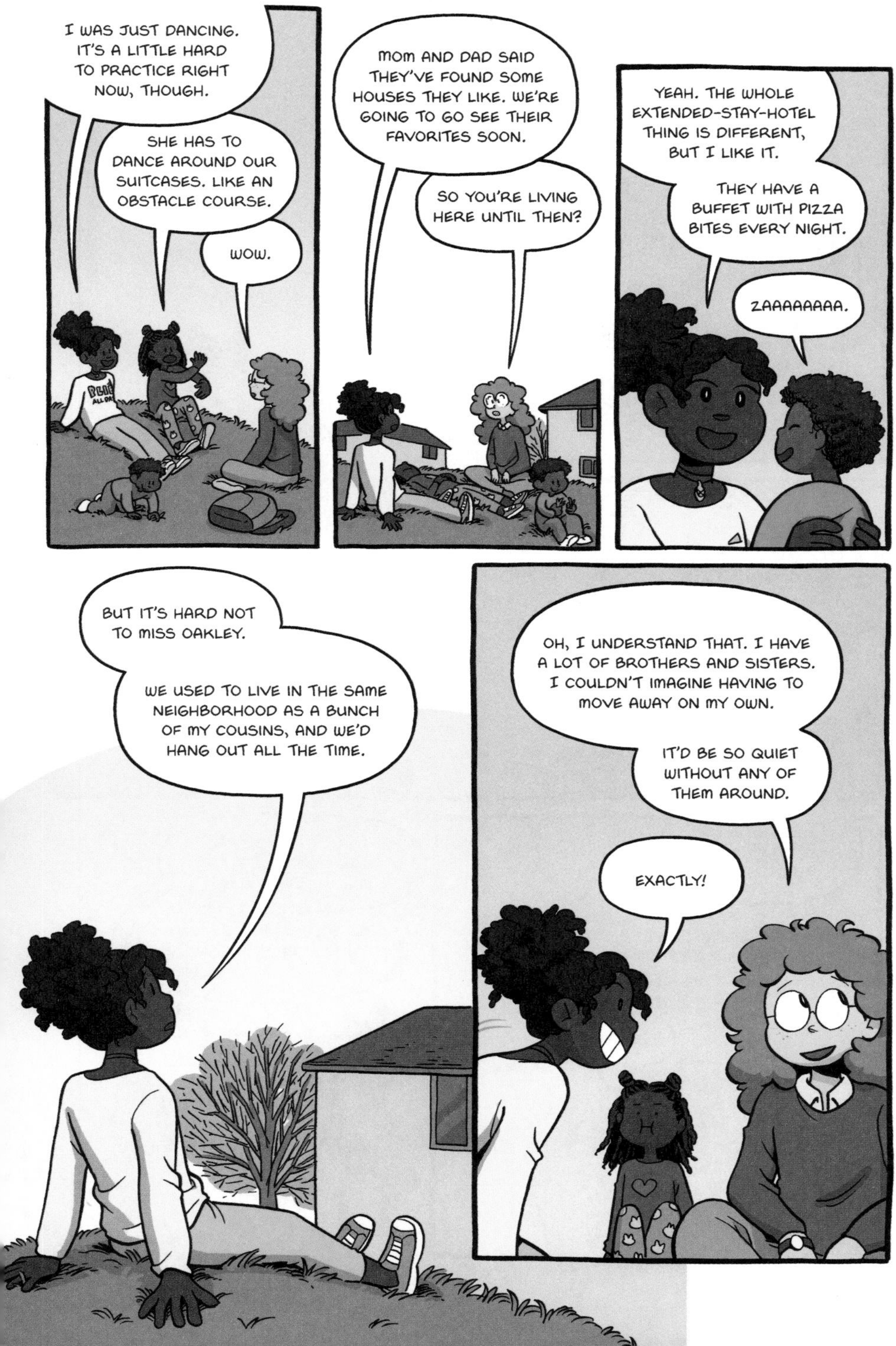

I WAS JUST DANCING. IT'S A LITTLE HARD TO PRACTICE RIGHT NOW, THOUGH.
SHE HAS TO DANCE AROUND OUR SUITCASES. LIKE AN OBSTACLE COURSE.
WOW.
MOM AND DAD SAID THEY'VE FOUND SOME HOUSES THEY LIKE. WE'RE GOING TO GO SEE THEIR FAVORITES SOON.
SO YOU'RE LIVING HERE UNTIL THEN?
YEAH. THE WHOLE EXTENDED-STAY-HOTEL THING IS DIFFERENT, BUT I LIKE IT.
THEY HAVE A BUFFET WITH PIZZA BITES EVERY NIGHT.
ZAAAAAAAA.
BUT IT'S HARD NOT TO MISS OAKLEY.
WE USED TO LIVE IN THE SAME NEIGHBORHOOD AS A BUNCH OF MY COUSINS, AND WE'D HANG OUT ALL THE TIME.
OH, I UNDERSTAND THAT. I HAVE A LOT OF BROTHERS AND SISTERS. I COULDN'T IMAGINE HAVING TO MOVE AWAY ON MY OWN.
IT'D BE SO QUIET WITHOUT ANY OF THEM AROUND.
EXACTLY!

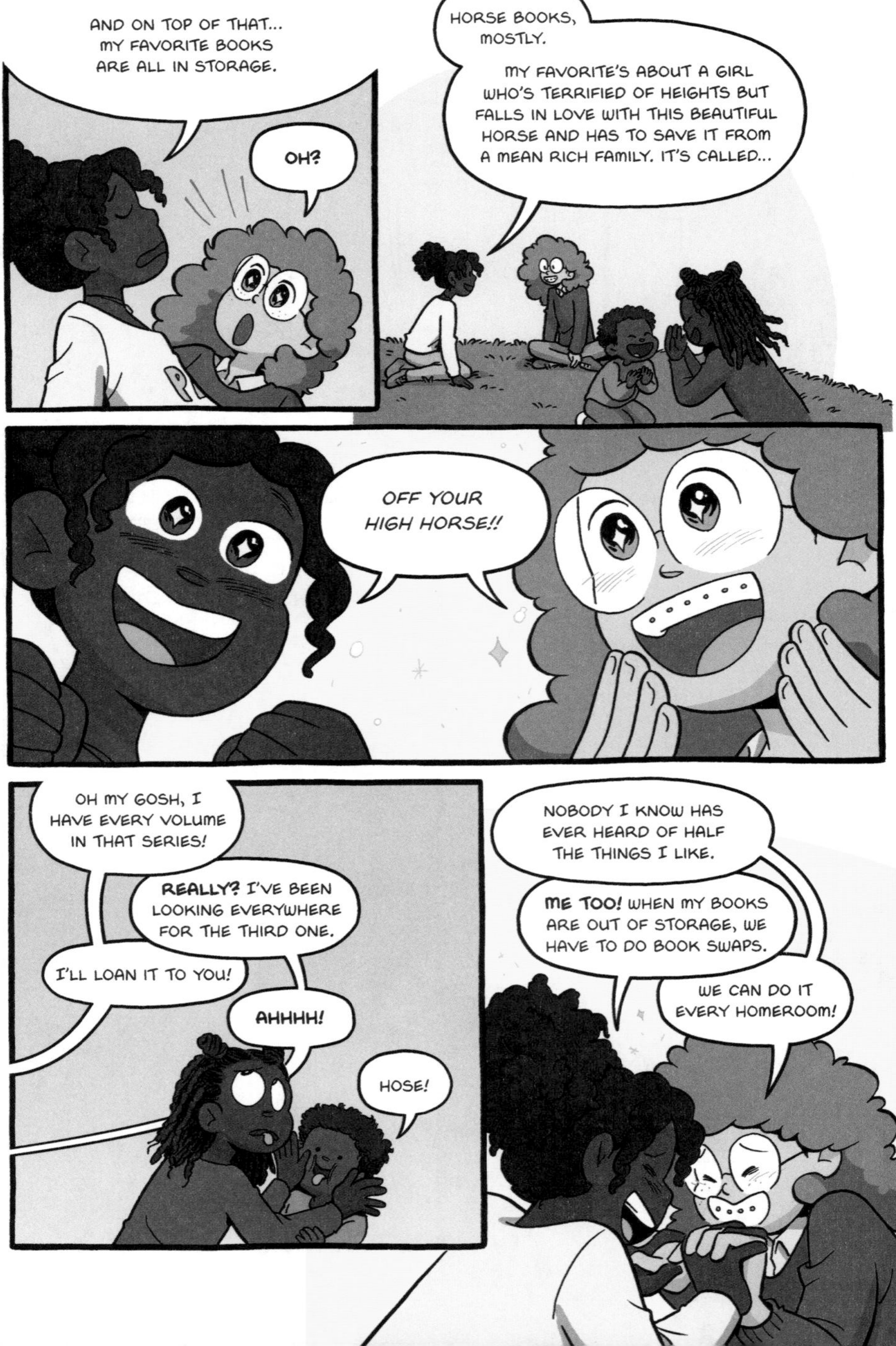
AND ON TOP OF THAT... MY FAVORITE BOOKS ARE ALL IN STORAGE.
OH?
HORSE BOOKS, MOSTLY.
MY FAVORITE'S ABOUT A GIRL WHO'S TERRIFIED OF HEIGHTS BUT FALLS IN LOVE WITH THIS BEAUTIFUL HORSE AND HAS TO SAVE IT FROM A MEAN RICH FAMILY. IT'S CALLED...
OFF YOUR HIGH HORSE!!
OH MY GOSH, I HAVE EVERY VOLUME IN THAT SERIES!
REALLY? I'VE BEEN LOOKING EVERYWHERE FOR THE THIRD ONE.
I'LL LOAN IT TO YOU!
AHHHH!
HOSE!
NOBODY I KNOW HAS EVER HEARD OF HALF THE THINGS I LIKE.
ME TOO! WHEN MY BOOKS ARE OUT OF STORAGE, WE HAVE TO DO BOOK SWAPS.
WE CAN DO IT EVERY HOMEROOM!

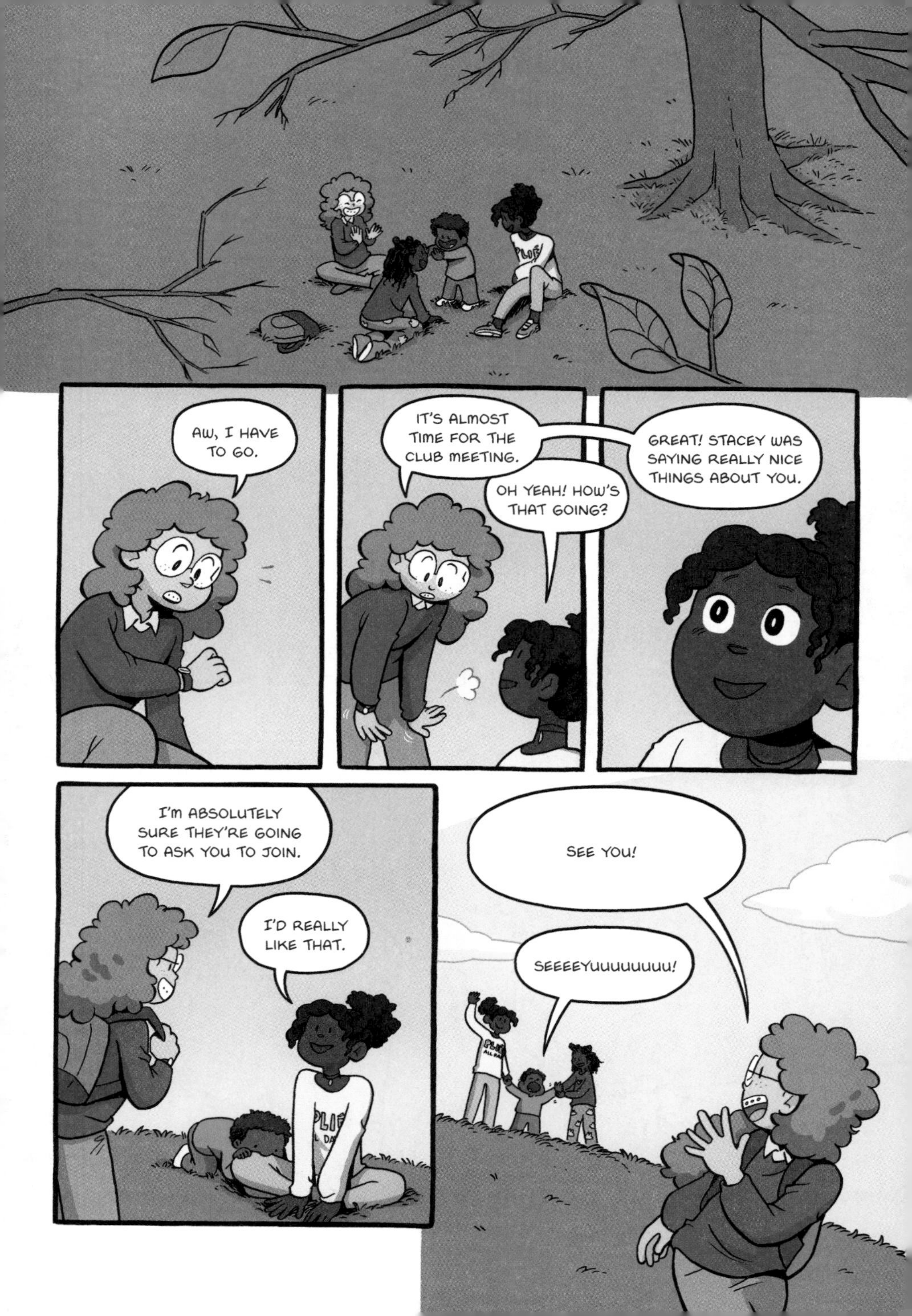
AW, I HAVE TO GO.
IT'S ALMOST TIME FOR THE CLUB MEETING.
OH YEAH! HOW'S THAT GOING?
GREAT! STACEY WAS SAYING REALLY NICE THINGS ABOUT YOU.
I'M ABSOLUTELY SURE THEY'RE GOING TO ASK YOU TO JOIN.
I'D REALLY LIKE THAT.
SEE YOU!
SEEEEYUUUUUUUU!

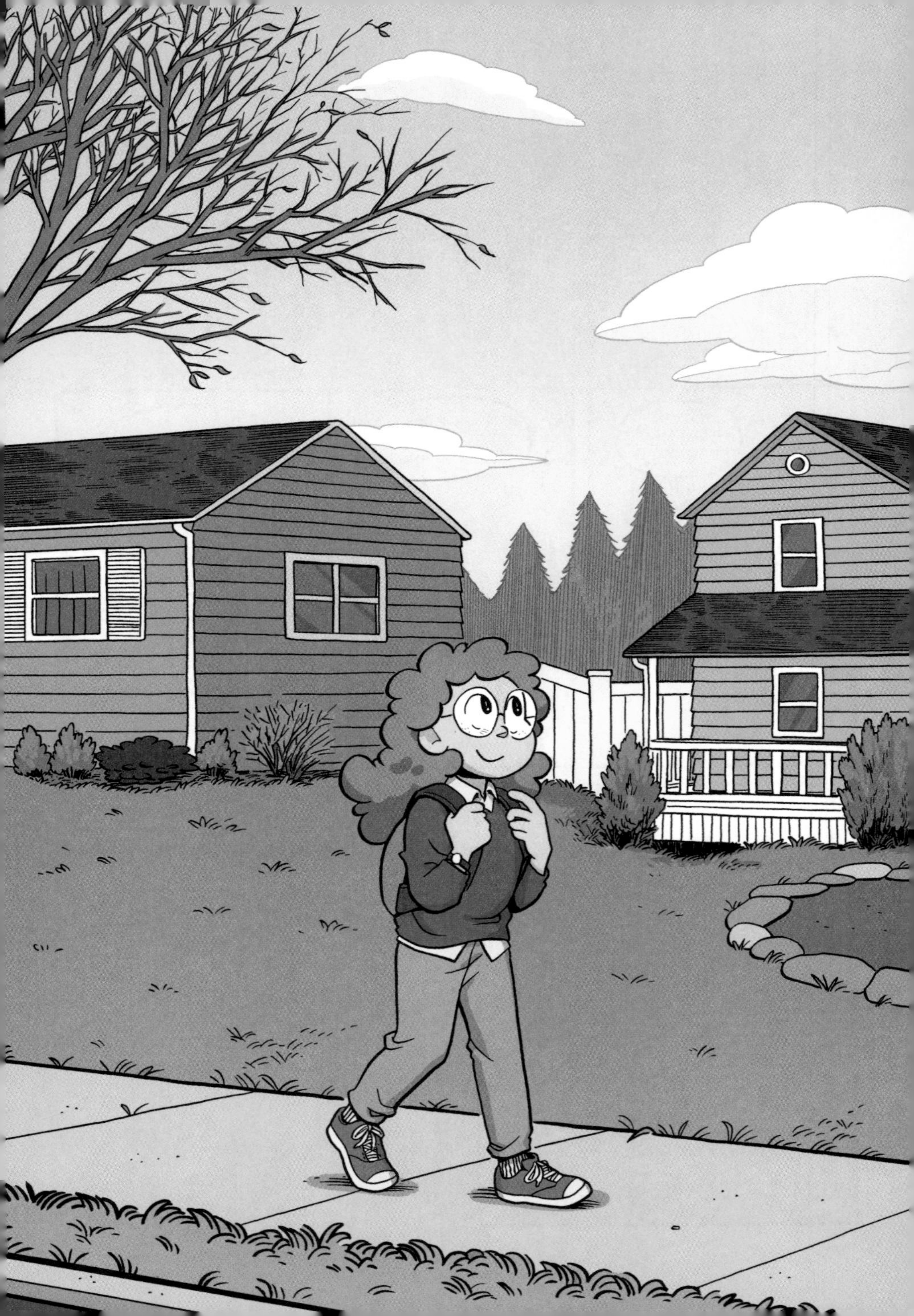

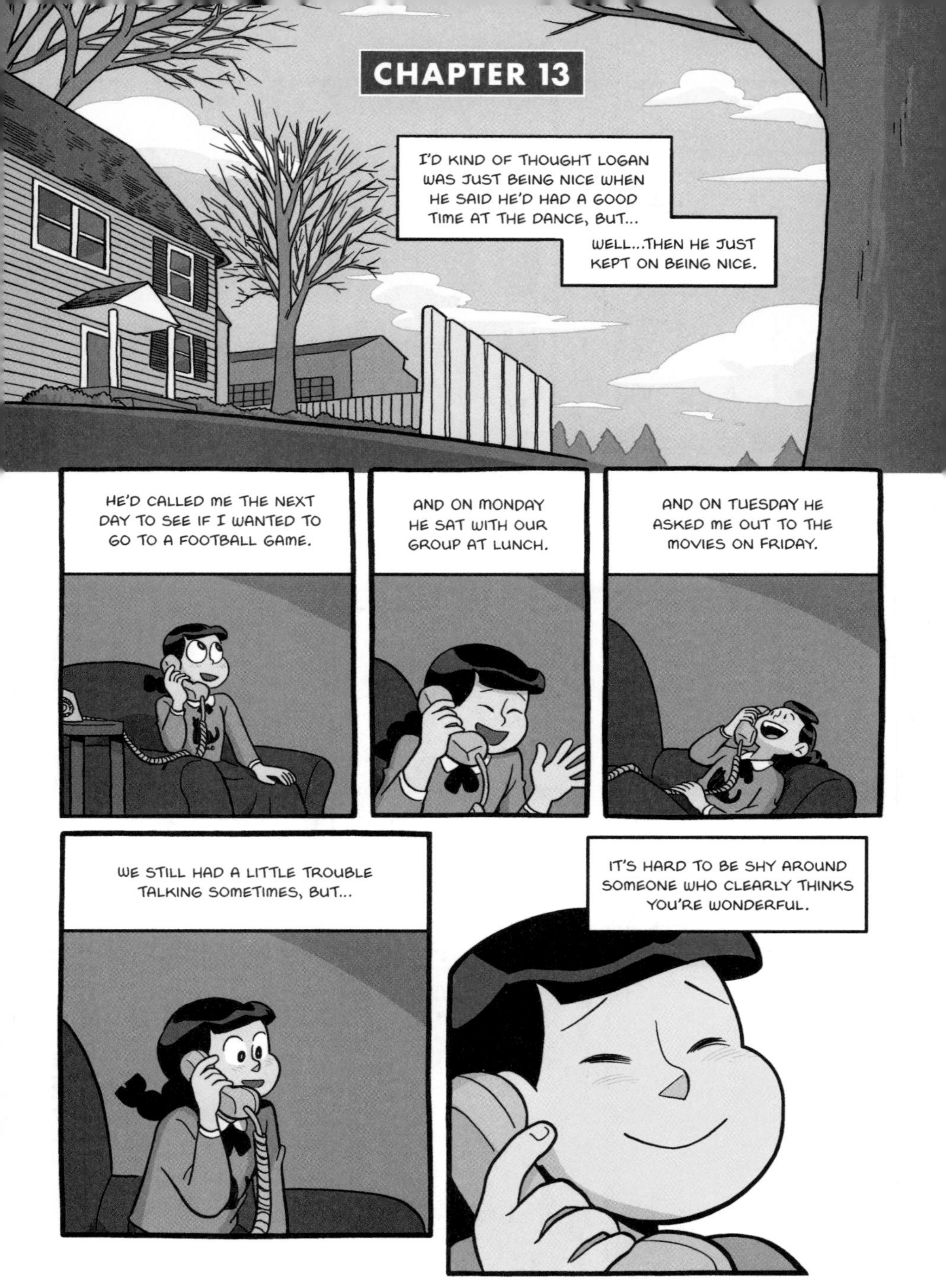
CHAPTER 13
I'D KIND OF THOUGHT LOGAN WAS JUST BEING NICE WHEN HE SAID HE'D HAD A GOOD TIME AT THE DANCE, BUT...
WELL...THEN HE JUST KEPT ON BEING NICE.
HE'D CALLED ME THE NEXT DAY TO SEE IF I WANTED TO GO TO A FOOTBALL GAME.
AND ON MONDAY HE SAT WITH OUR GROUP AT LUNCH.
AND ON TUESDAY HE ASKED ME OUT TO THE MOVIES ON FRIDAY.
WE STILL HAD A LITTLE TROUBLE TALKING SOMETIMES, BUT...
IT'S HARD TO BE SHY AROUND SOMEONE WHO CLEARLY THINKS YOU'RE WONDERFUL.

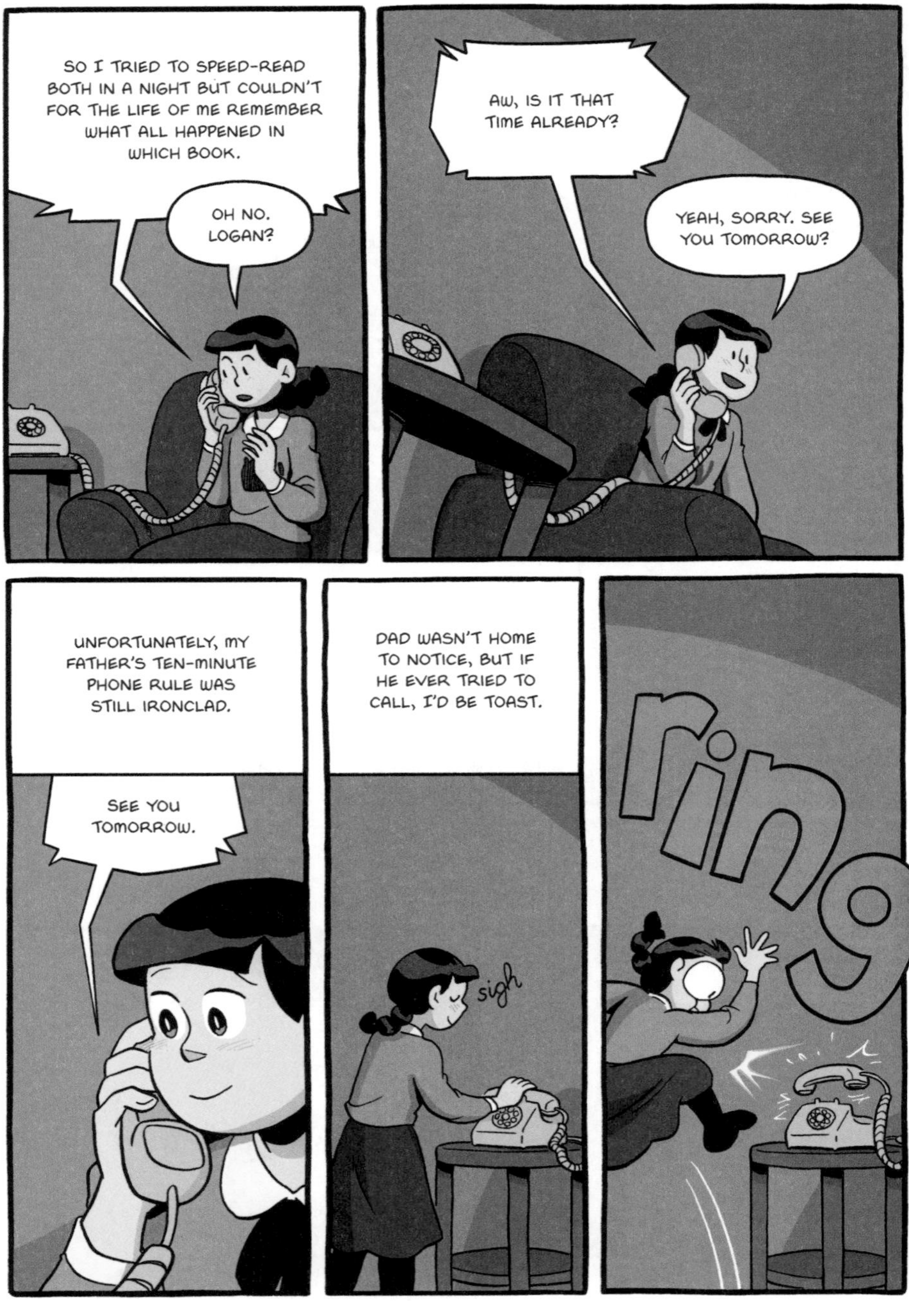
SO I TRIED TO SPEED-READ BOTH IN A NIGHT BUT COULDN'T FOR THE LIFE OF ME REMEMBER WHAT ALL HAPPENED IN WHICH BOOK.
OH NO. LOGAN?
AW, IS IT THAT TIME ALREADY?
YEAH, SORRY. SEE YOU TOMORROW?
UNFORTUNATELY, MY FATHER'S TEN-MINUTE PHONE RULE WAS STILL IRONCLAD.
SEE YOU TOMORROW.
DAD WASN'T HOME TO NOTICE, BUT IF HE EVER TRIED TO CALL, I'D BE TOAST.
sigh
ring

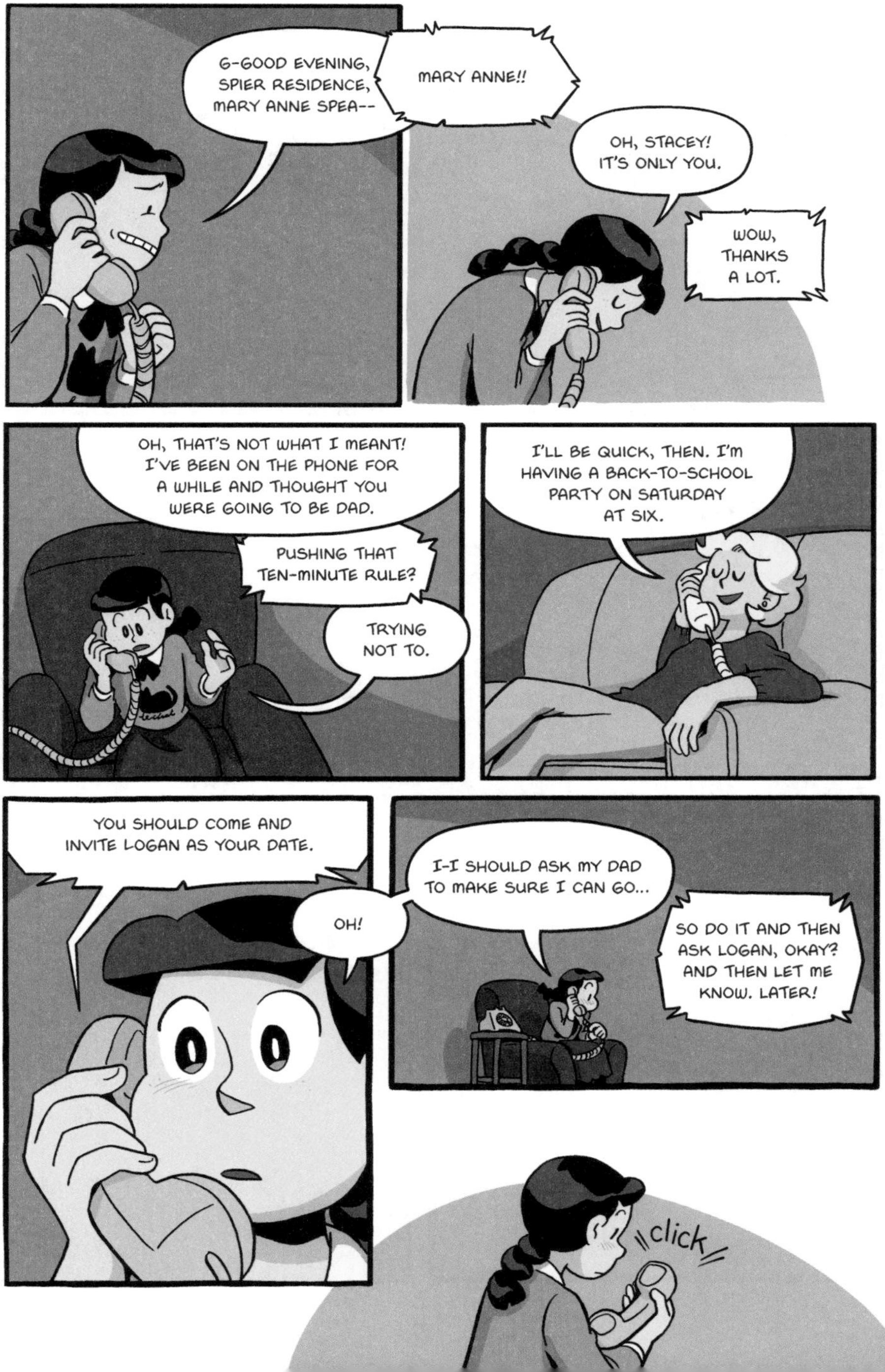
G-GOOD EVENING, SPIER RESIDENCE, MARY ANNE SPEA--
MARY ANNE!!
OH, STACEY! IT'S ONLY YOU.
WOW, THANKS A LOT.
OH, THAT'S NOT WHAT I MEANT! I'VE BEEN ON THE PHONE FOR A WHILE AND THOUGHT YOU WERE GOING TO BE DAD.
PUSHING THAT TEN-MINUTE RULE?
TRYING NOT TO.
I'LL BE QUICK, THEN. I'M HAVING A BACK-TO-SCHOOL PARTY ON SATURDAY AT SIX.
YOU SHOULD COME AND INVITE LOGAN AS YOUR DATE.
OH!
I-I SHOULD ASK MY DAD TO MAKE SURE I CAN GO...
SO DO IT AND THEN ASK LOGAN, OKAY? AND THEN LET ME KNOW. LATER!
click

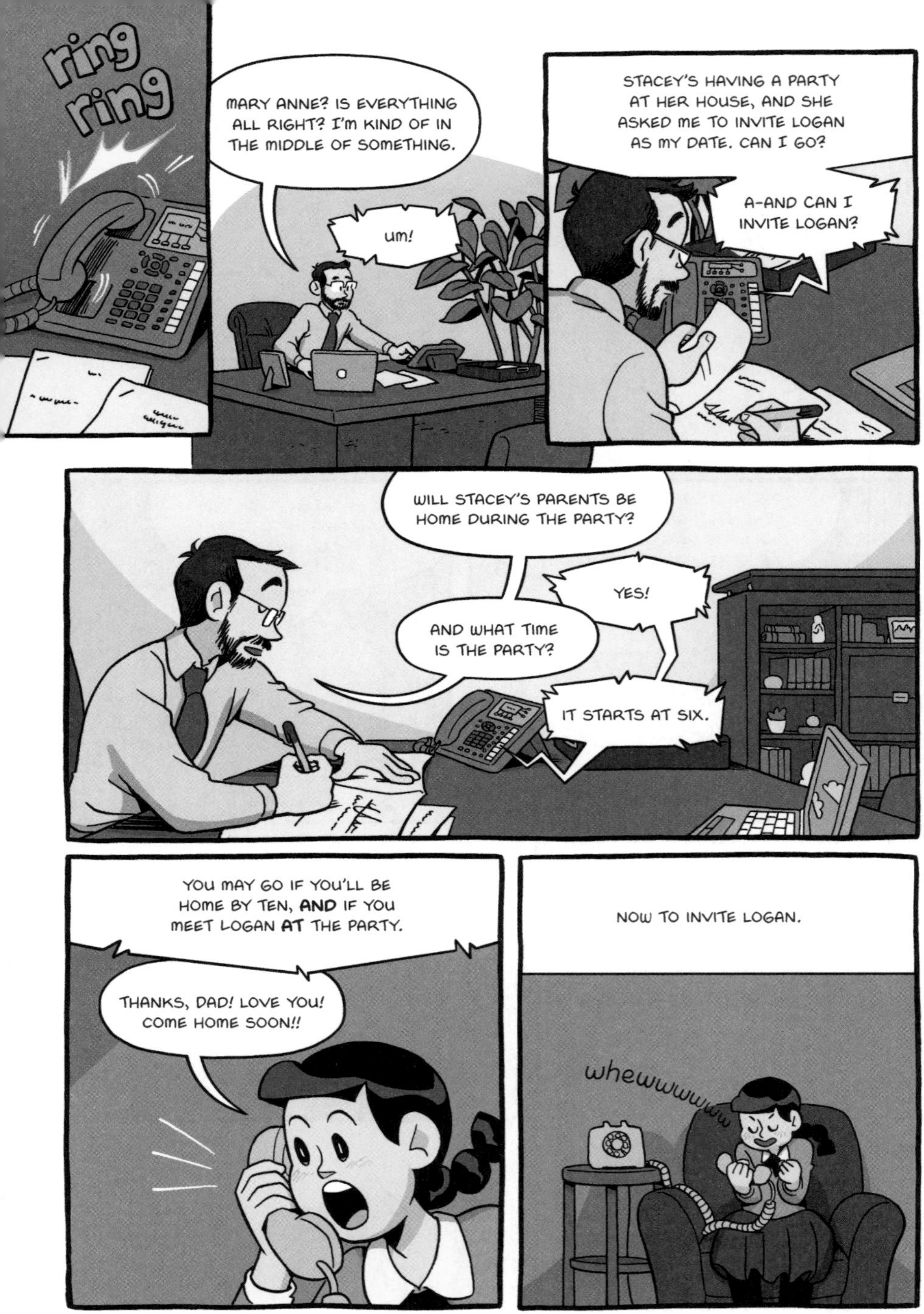
ring ring
MARY ANNE? IS EVERYTHING ALL RIGHT? I'M KIND OF IN THE MIDDLE OF SOMETHING.
um!
STACEY'S HAVING A PARTY AT HER HOUSE, AND SHE ASKED ME TO INVITE LOGAN AS MY DATE. CAN I GO?
A-AND CAN I INVITE LOGAN?
WILL STACEY'S PARENTS BE HOME DURING THE PARTY?
YES!
AND WHAT TIME IS THE PARTY?
IT STARTS AT SIX.
YOU MAY GO IF YOU'LL BE HOME BY TEN, AND IF YOU MEET LOGAN AT THE PARTY.
THANKS, DAD! LOVE YOU! COME HOME SOON!!
NOW TO INVITE LOGAN.
whewwwwww

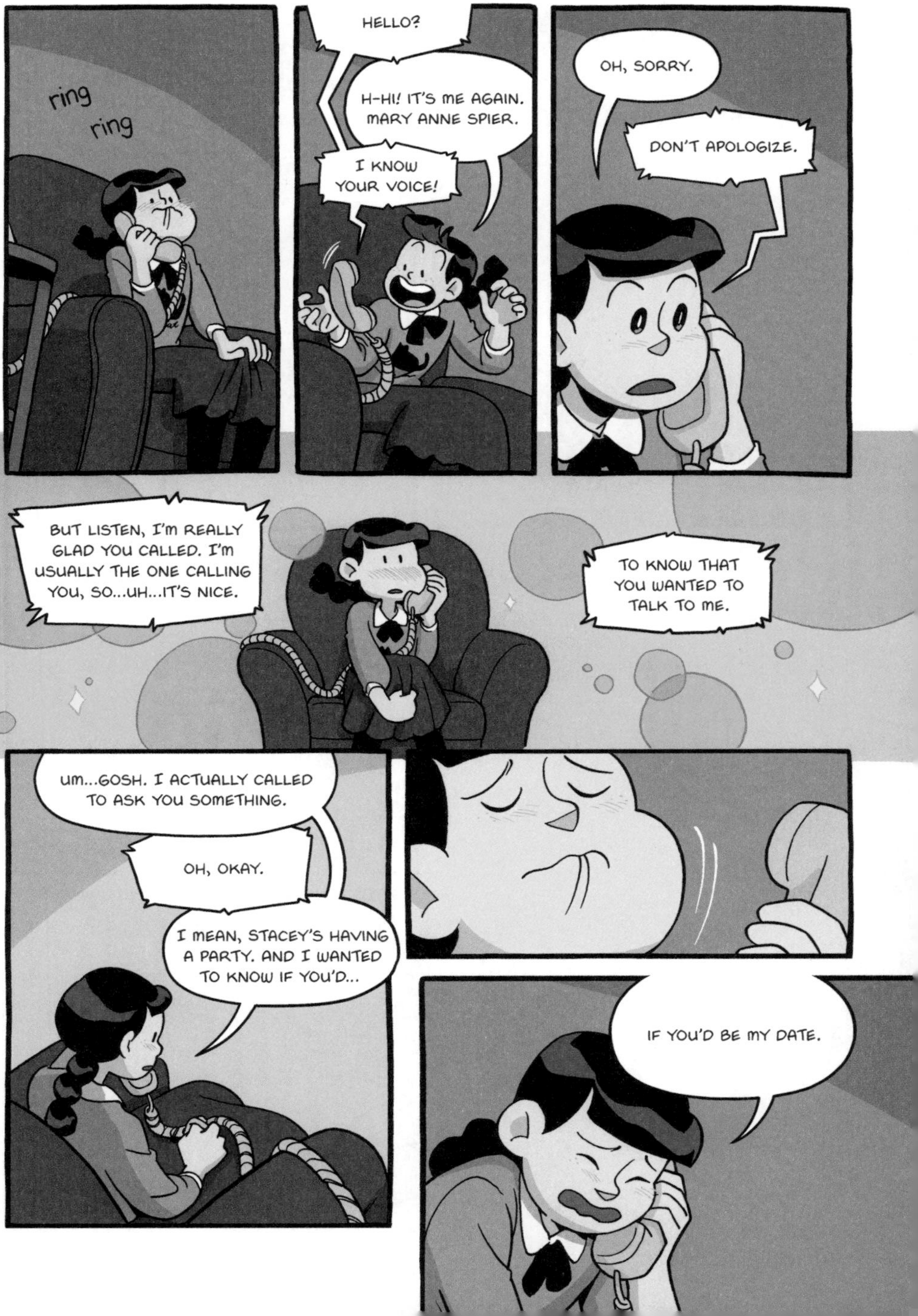
ring
ring
HELLO?
H-HI! IT'S ME AGAIN. MARY ANNE SPIER.
I KNOW YOUR VOICE!
OH, SORRY.
DON'T APOLOGIZE.
BUT LISTEN, I'M REALLY GLAD YOU CALLED. I'M USUALLY THE ONE CALLING YOU, SO...UH...IT'S NICE.
TO KNOW THAT YOU WANTED TO TALK TO ME.
UM...GOSH. I ACTUALLY CALLED TO ASK YOU SOMETHING.
OH, OKAY.
I MEAN, STACEY'S HAVING A PARTY. AND I WANTED TO KNOW IF YOU'D...
IF YOU'D BE MY DATE.

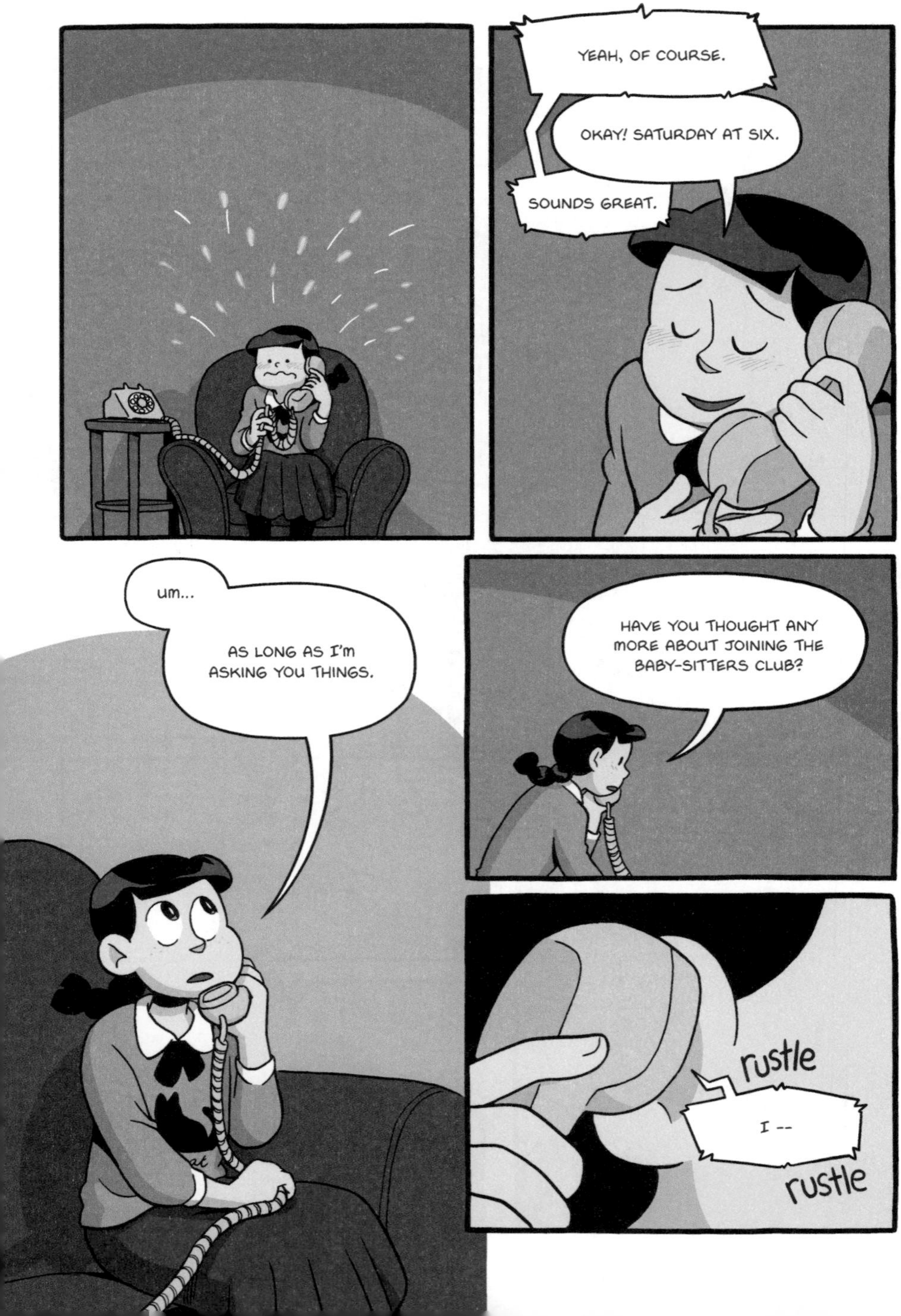

YEAH, OF COURSE.
OKAY! SATURDAY AT SIX.
SOUNDS GREAT.
um...
AS LONG AS I'm ASKING YOU THINGS.
HAVE YOU THOUGHT ANY MORE ABOUT JOINING THE BABY-SITTERS CLUB?
rustle
I --
rustle

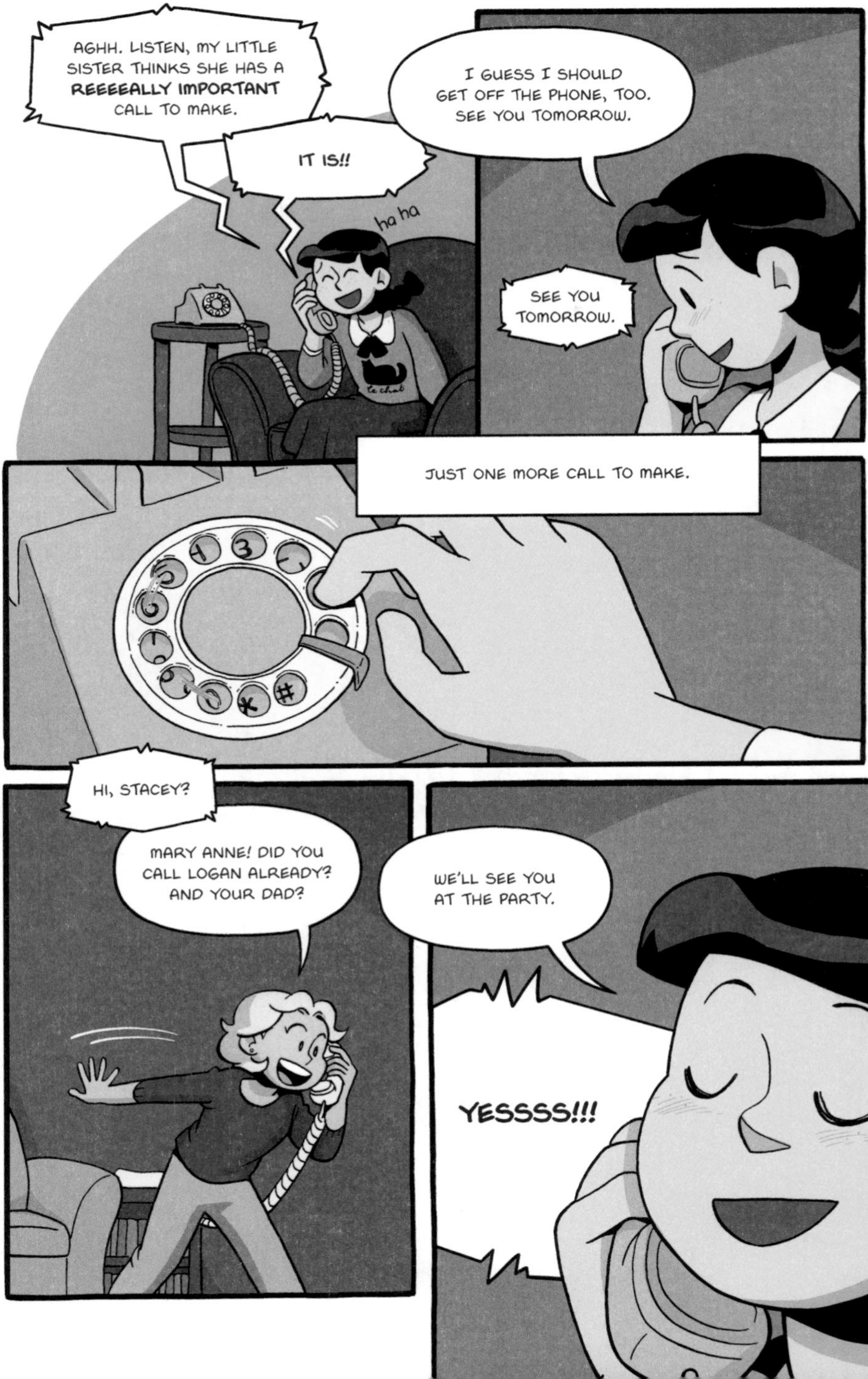
AGHH. LISTEN, MY LITTLE SISTER THINKS SHE HAS A **REEEEALLY IMPORTANT** CALL TO MAKE.
IT IS!!
ha ha
le chat
I GUESS I SHOULD GET OFF THE PHONE, TOO. SEE YOU TOMORROW.
SEE YOU TOMORROW.
JUST ONE MORE CALL TO MAKE.
HI, STACEY?
MARY ANNE! DID YOU CALL LOGAN ALREADY? AND YOUR DAD?
WE'LL SEE YOU AT THE PARTY.
YESSSS!!!

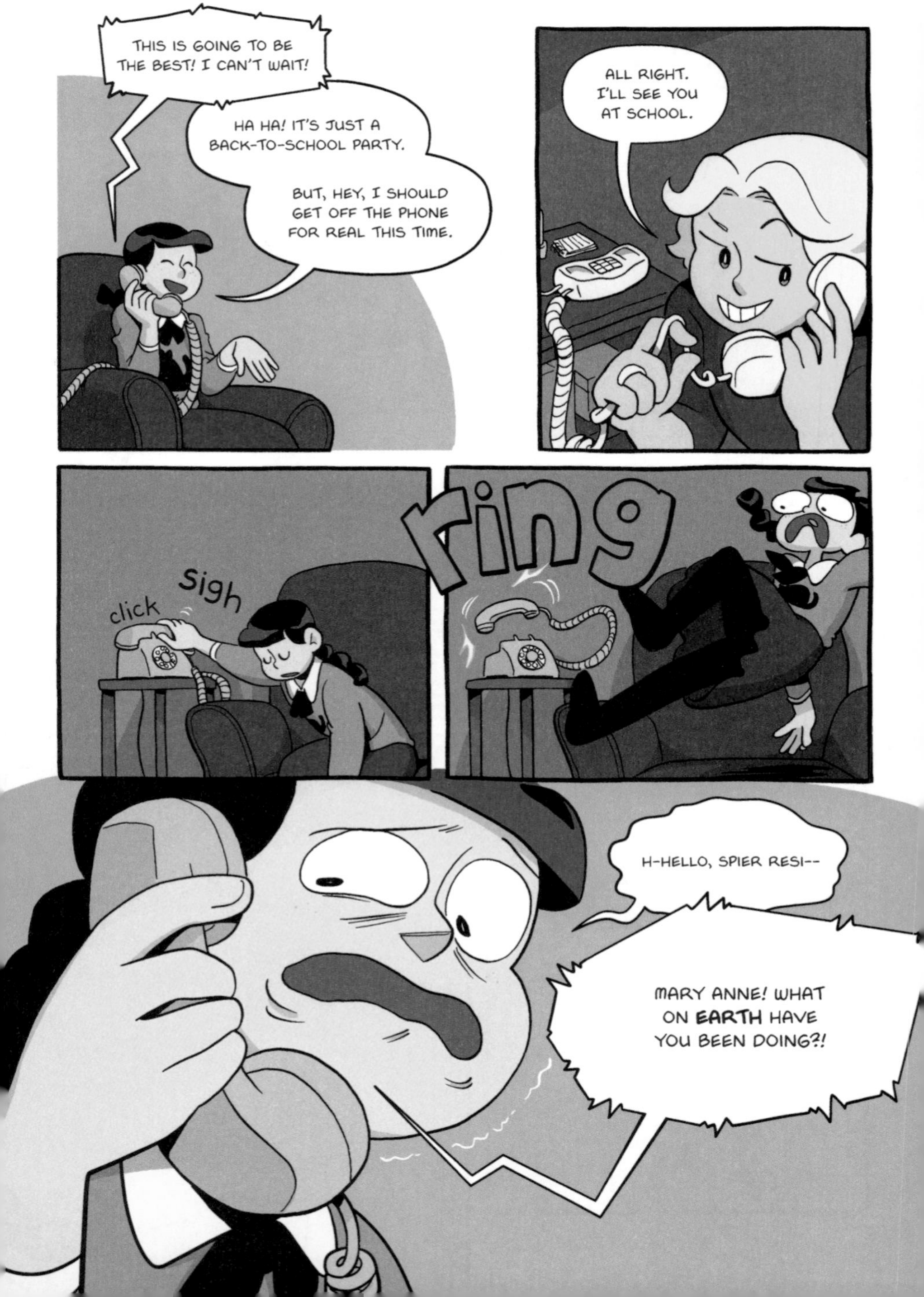
THIS IS GOING TO BE THE BEST! I CAN'T WAIT!
HA HA! IT'S JUST A BACK-TO-SCHOOL PARTY.
BUT, HEY, I SHOULD GET OFF THE PHONE FOR REAL THIS TIME.
ALL RIGHT. I'LL SEE YOU AT SCHOOL.
click
sigh
ring
H-HELLO, SPIER RESI--
MARY ANNE! WHAT ON **EARTH** HAVE YOU BEEN DOING?!

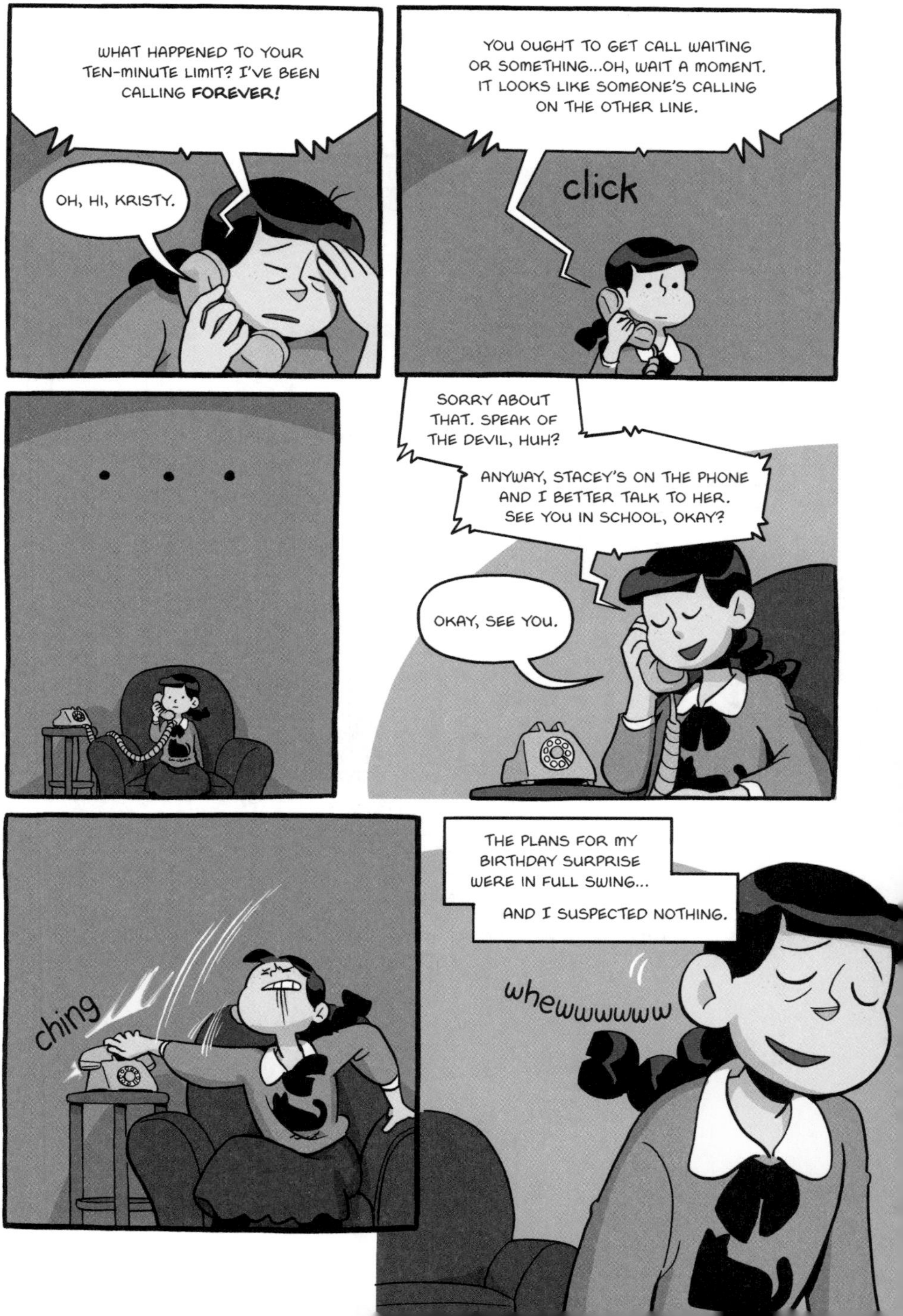
WHAT HAPPENED TO YOUR TEN-MINUTE LIMIT? I'VE BEEN CALLING **FOREVER!**
OH, HI, KRISTY.
YOU OUGHT TO GET CALL WAITING OR SOMETHING...OH, WAIT A MOMENT. IT LOOKS LIKE SOMEONE'S CALLING ON THE OTHER LINE.
click
• • •
SORRY ABOUT THAT. SPEAK OF THE DEVIL, HUH?
ANYWAY, STACEY'S ON THE PHONE AND I BETTER TALK TO HER. SEE YOU IN SCHOOL, OKAY?
OKAY, SEE YOU.
ching
THE PLANS FOR MY BIRTHDAY SURPRISE WERE IN FULL SWING...
AND I SUSPECTED NOTHING.
whewwwwww

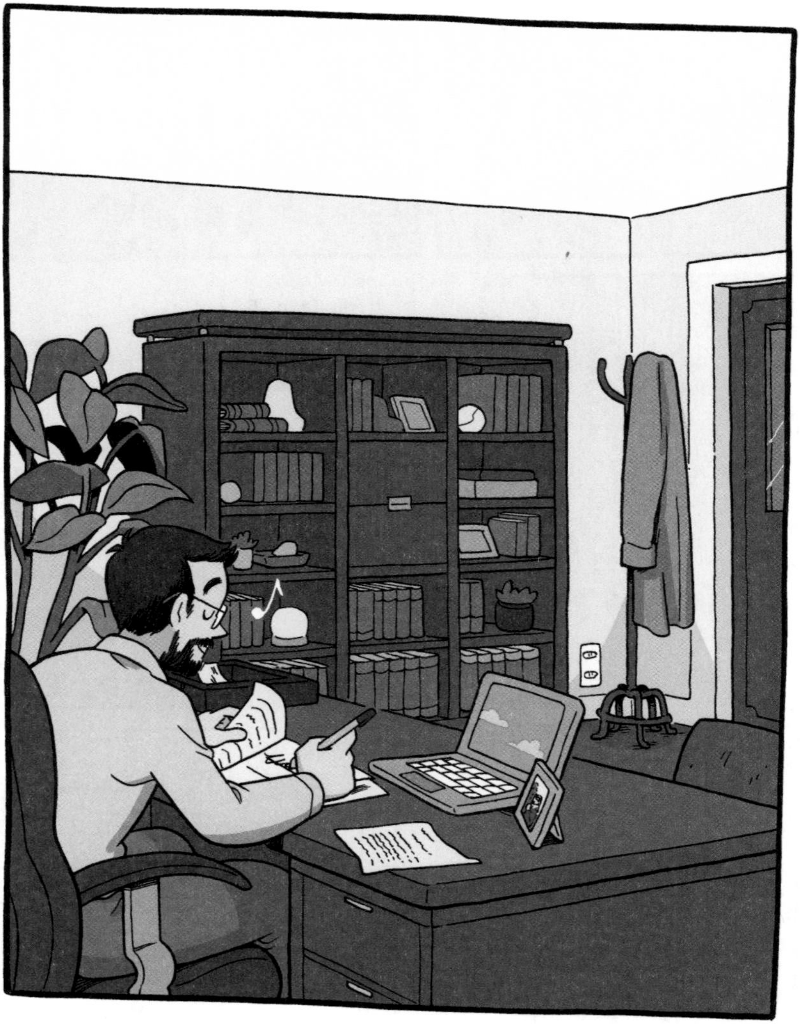

CHAPTER 14

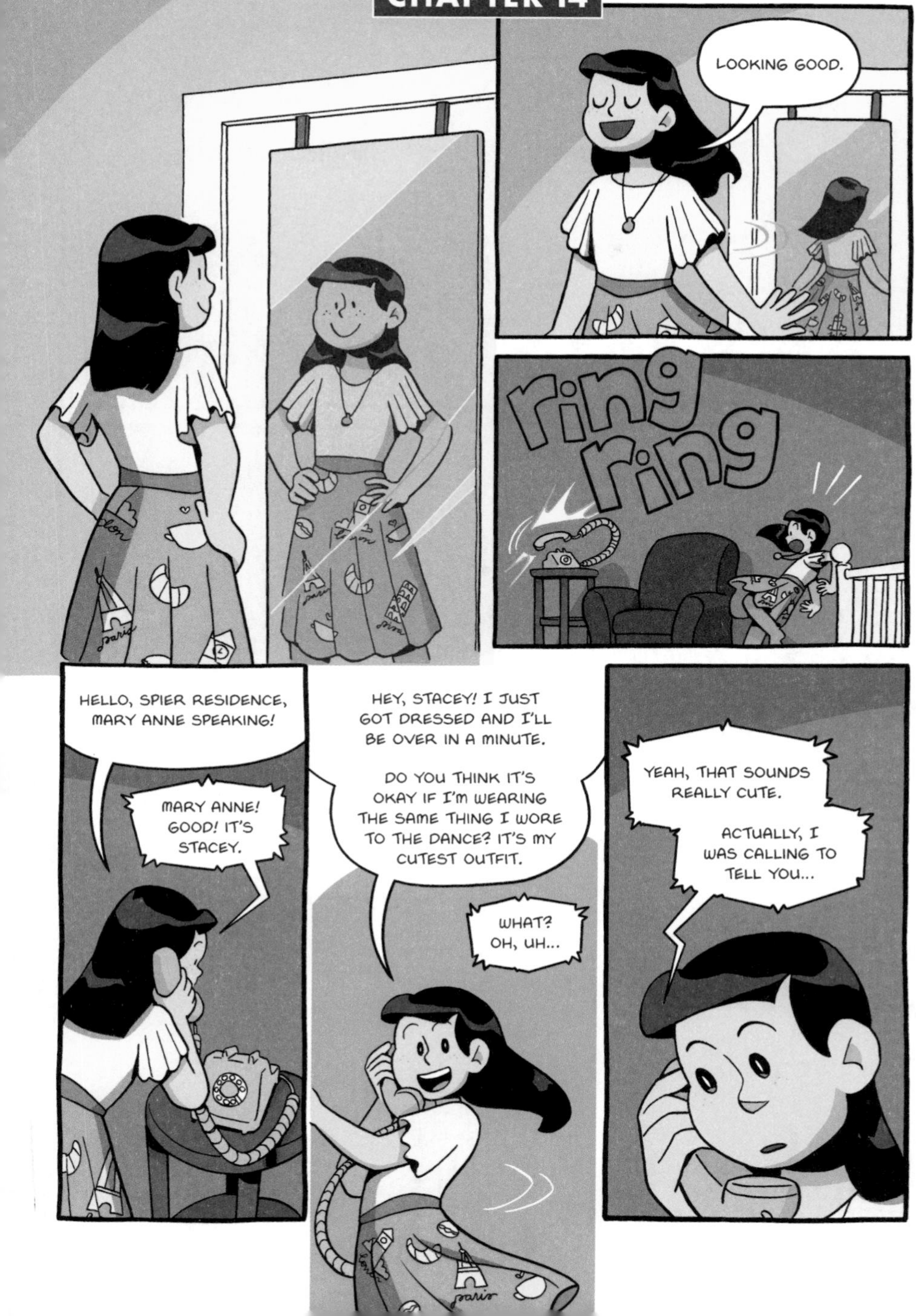

LOOKING GOOD.
ring ring
HELLO, SPIER RESIDENCE, MARY ANNE SPEAKING!
MARY ANNE! GOOD! IT'S STACEY.
HEY, STACEY! I JUST GOT DRESSED AND I'LL BE OVER IN A MINUTE.
DO YOU THINK IT'S OKAY IF I'M WEARING THE SAME THING I WORE TO THE DANCE? IT'S MY CUTEST OUTFIT.
WHAT? OH, UH...
YEAH, THAT SOUNDS REALLY CUTE.
ACTUALLY, I WAS CALLING TO TELL YOU...

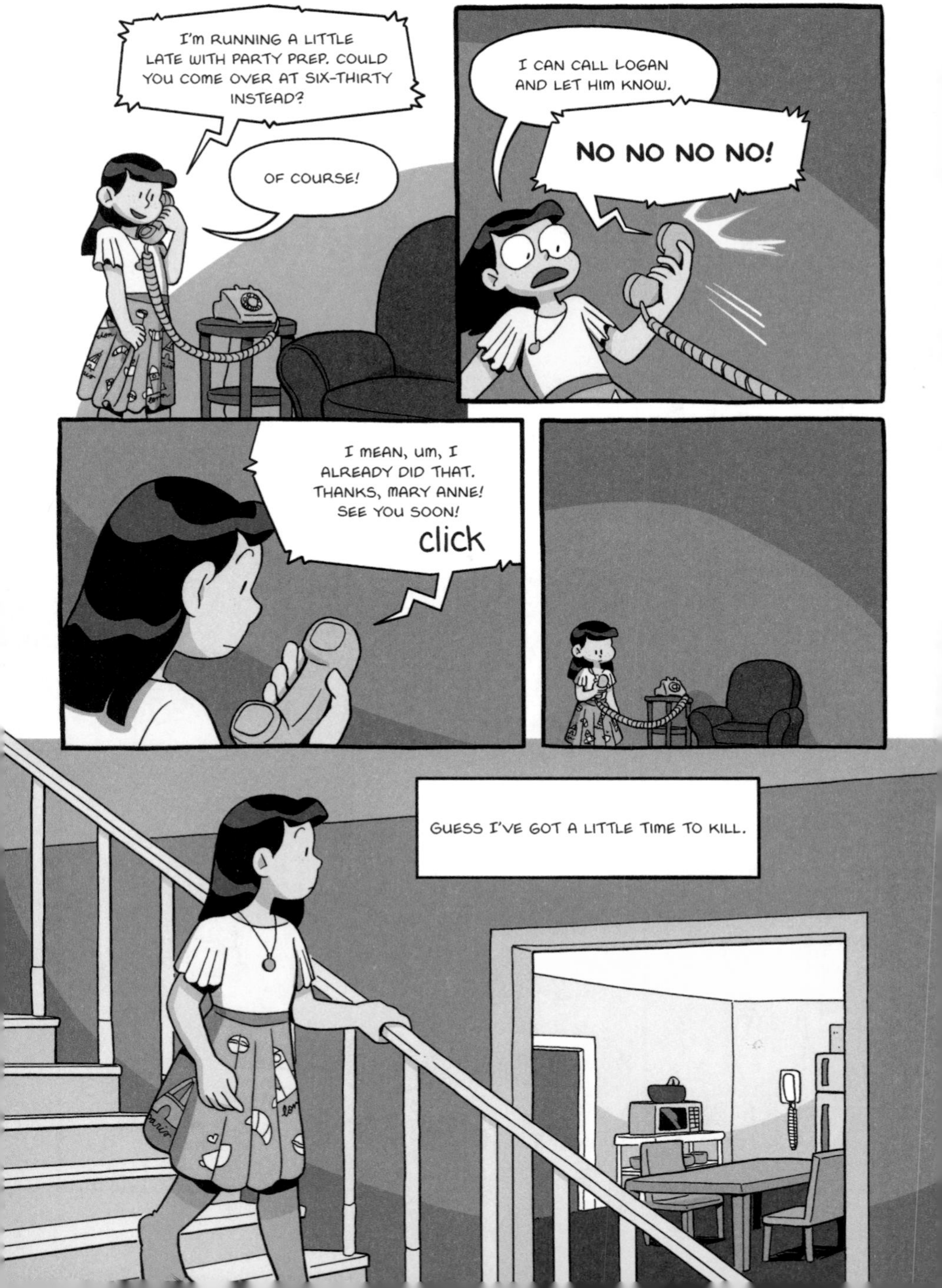
I'M RUNNING A LITTLE LATE WITH PARTY PREP. COULD YOU COME OVER AT SIX-THIRTY INSTEAD?
OF COURSE!
I CAN CALL LOGAN AND LET HIM KNOW.
NO NO NO NO!
I MEAN, UM, I ALREADY DID THAT. THANKS, MARY ANNE! SEE YOU SOON!
click
GUESS I'VE GOT A LITTLE TIME TO KILL.

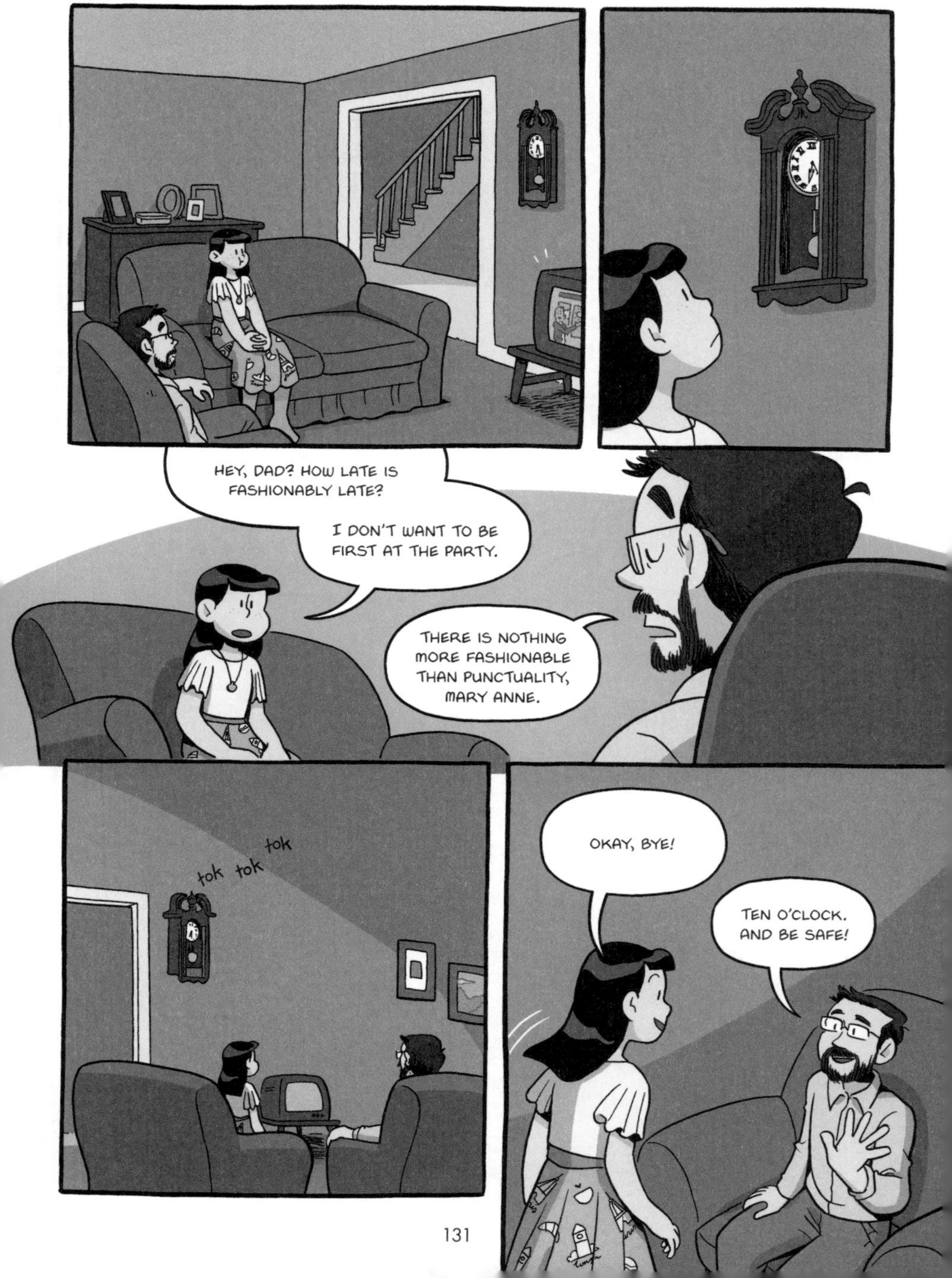
HEY, DAD? HOW LATE IS FASHIONABLY LATE?
I DON'T WANT TO BE FIRST AT THE PARTY.
THERE IS NOTHING MORE FASHIONABLE THAN PUNCTUALITY, MARY ANNE.
tok tok tok
OKAY, BYE!
TEN O'CLOCK. AND BE SAFE!

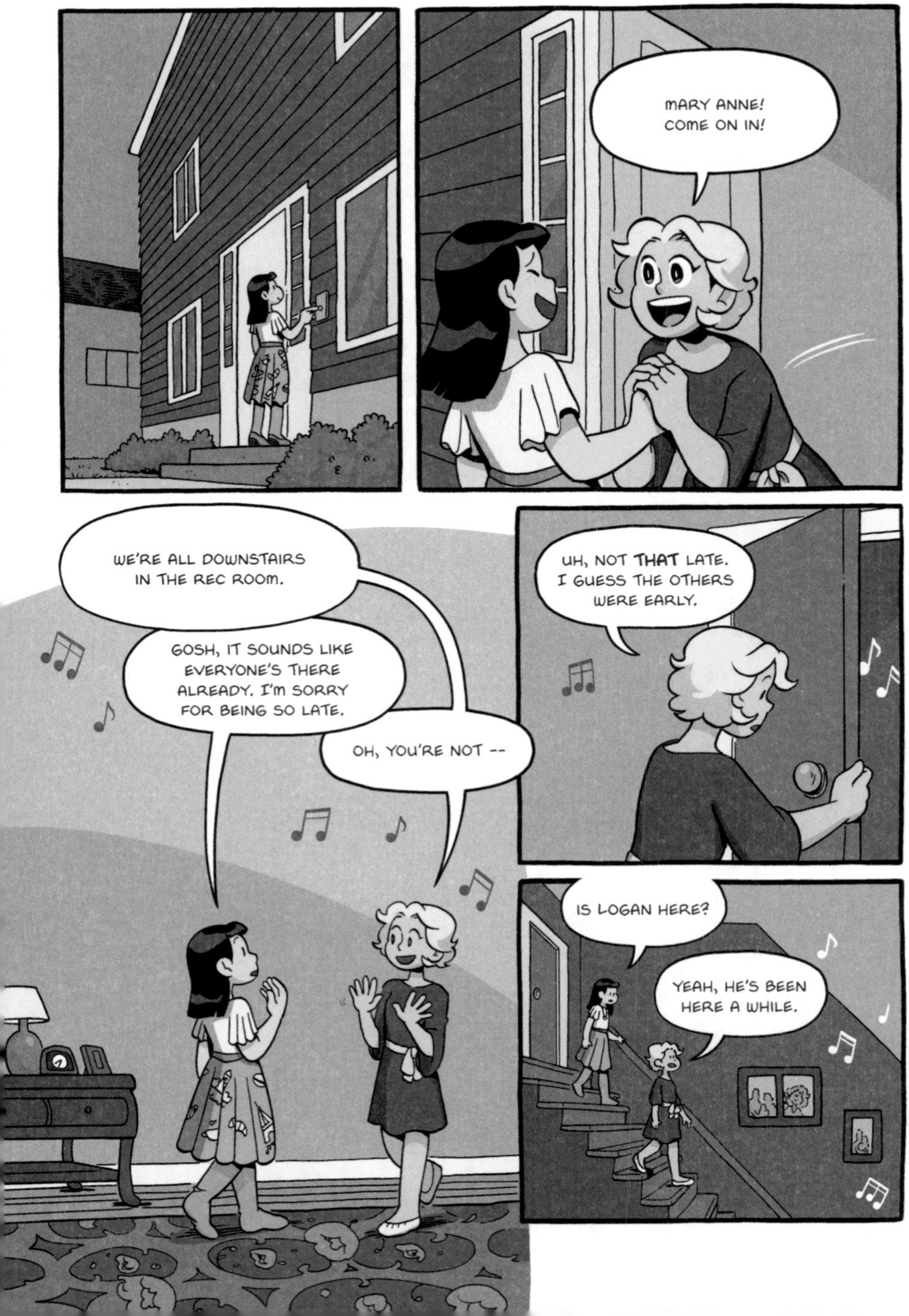
MARY ANNE! COME ON IN!
WE'RE ALL DOWNSTAIRS IN THE REC ROOM.
GOSH, IT SOUNDS LIKE EVERYONE'S THERE ALREADY. I'M SORRY FOR BEING SO LATE.
OH, YOU'RE NOT --
UH, NOT **THAT** LATE. I GUESS THE OTHERS WERE EARLY.
IS LOGAN HERE?
YEAH, HE'S BEEN HERE A WHILE.

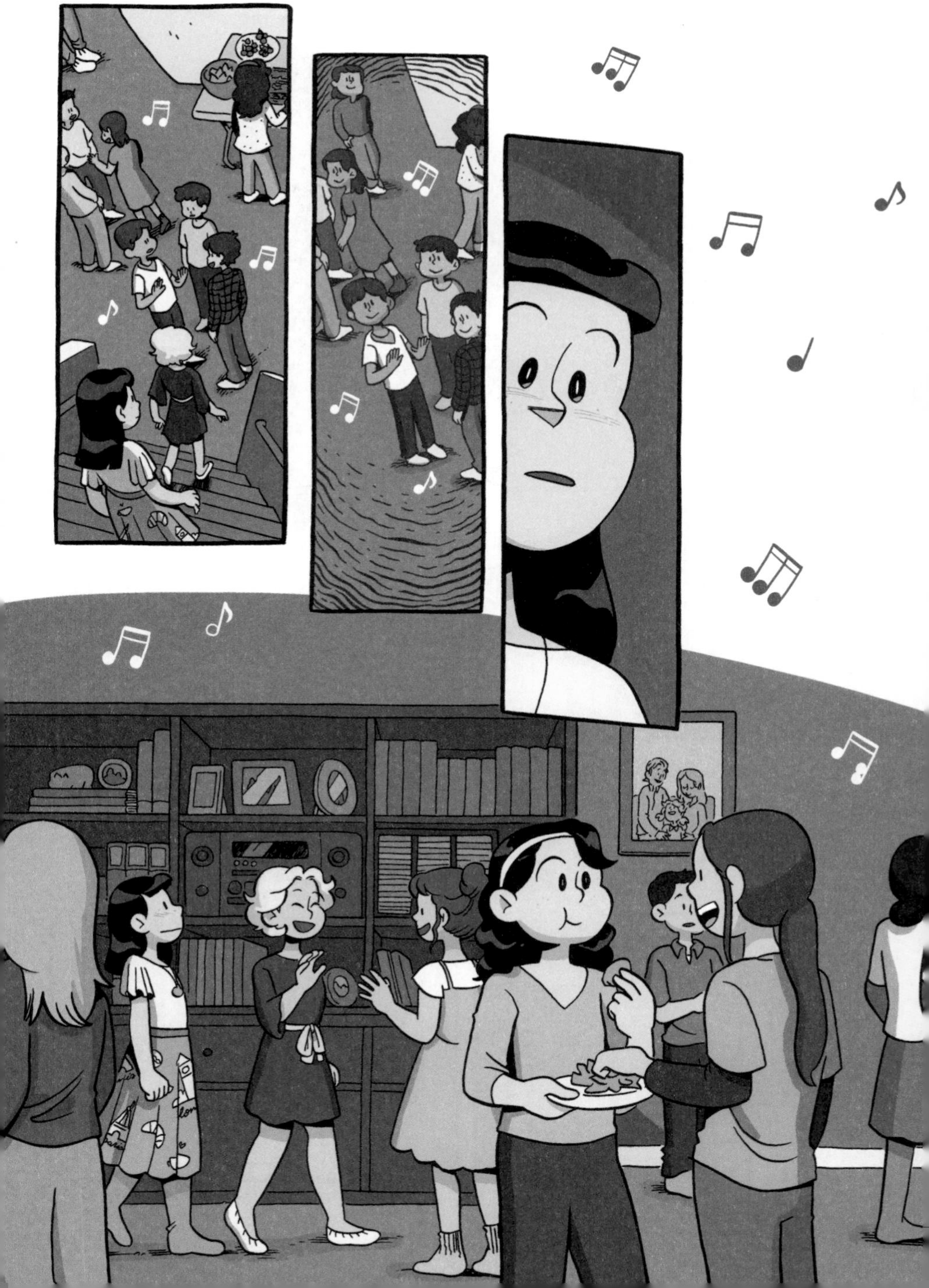

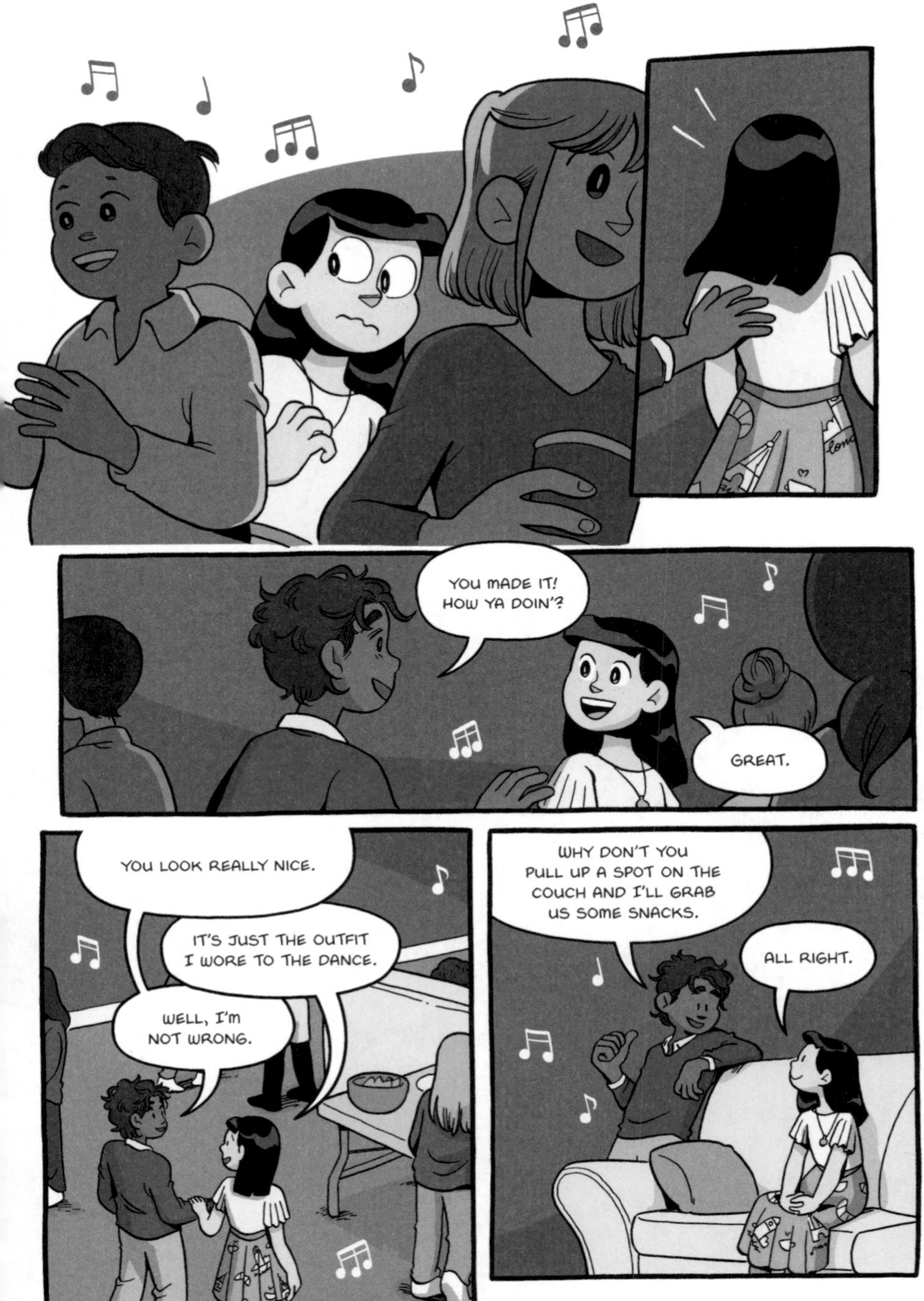
YOU MADE IT! HOW YA DOIN'?
GREAT.
YOU LOOK REALLY NICE.
IT'S JUST THE OUTFIT I WORE TO THE DANCE.
WELL, I'M NOT WRONG.
WHY DON'T YOU PULL UP A SPOT ON THE COUCH AND I'LL GRAB US SOME SNACKS.
ALL RIGHT.

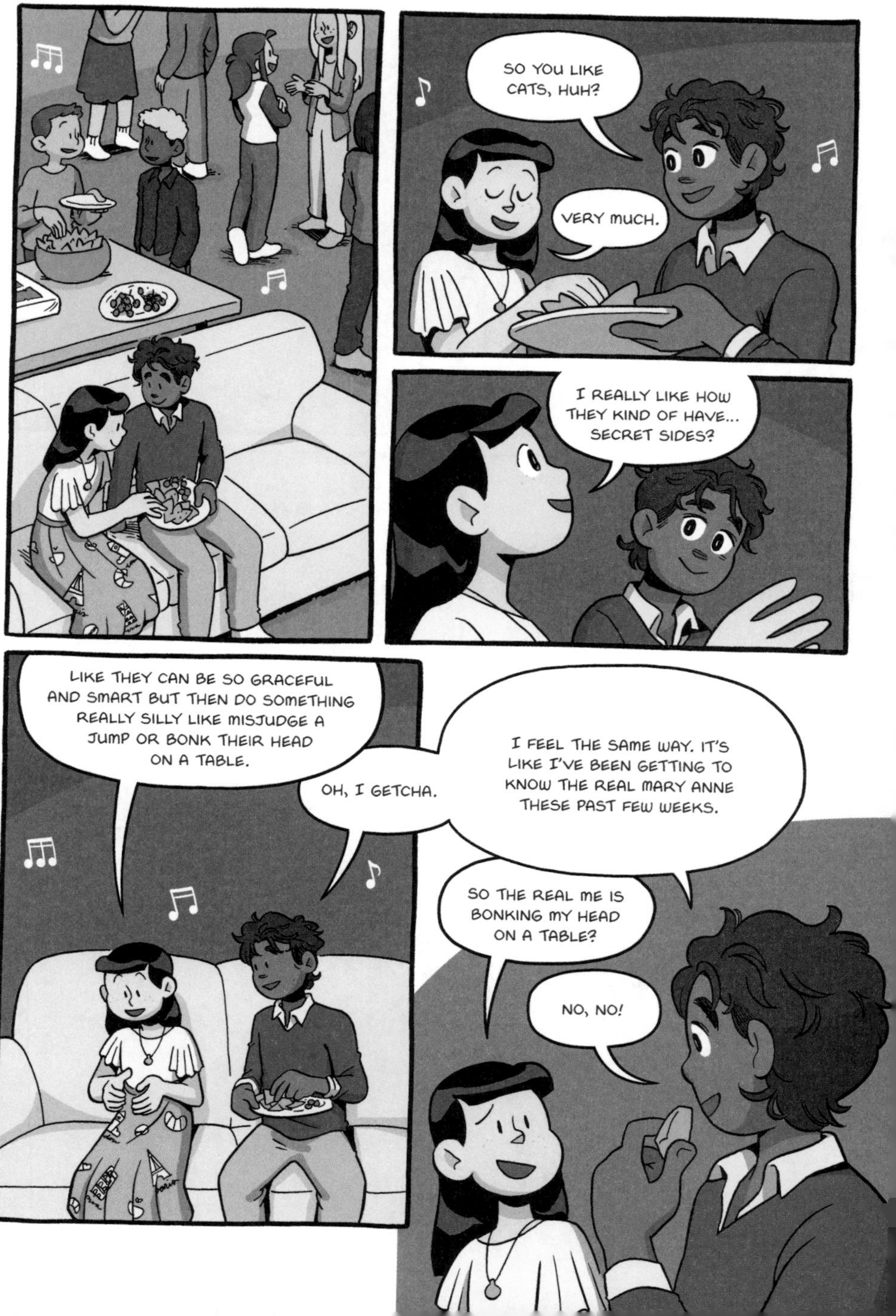
SO YOU LIKE CATS, HUH?
VERY MUCH.
I REALLY LIKE HOW THEY KIND OF HAVE... SECRET SIDES?
LIKE THEY CAN BE SO GRACEFUL AND SMART BUT THEN DO SOMETHING REALLY SILLY LIKE MISJUDGE A JUMP OR BONK THEIR HEAD ON A TABLE.
OH, I GETCHA.
I FEEL THE SAME WAY. IT'S LIKE I'VE BEEN GETTING TO KNOW THE REAL MARY ANNE THESE PAST FEW WEEKS.
SO THE REAL ME IS BONKING MY HEAD ON A TABLE?
NO, NO!

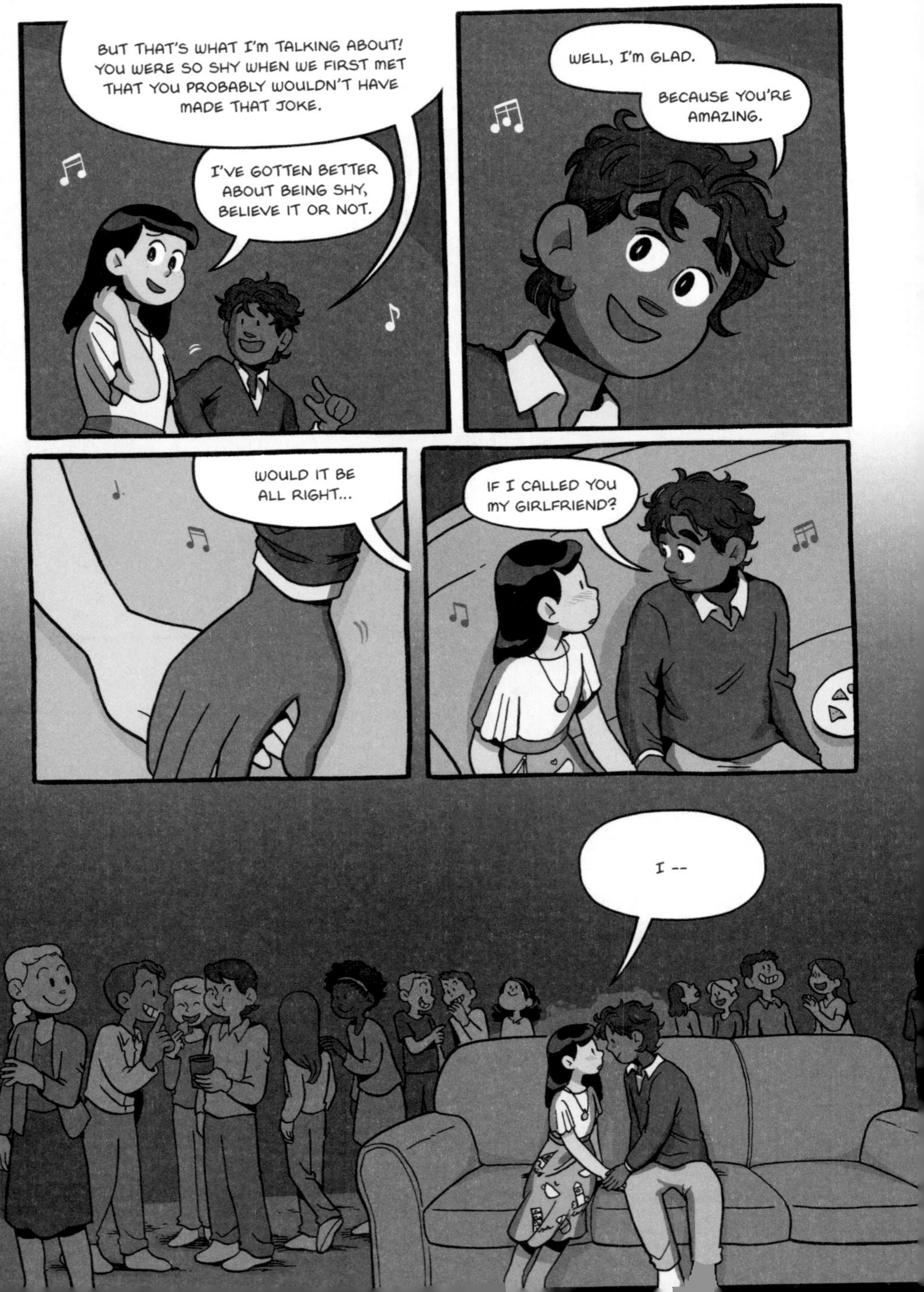
BUT THAT'S WHAT I'M TALKING ABOUT! YOU WERE SO SHY WHEN WE FIRST MET THAT YOU PROBABLY WOULDN'T HAVE MADE THAT JOKE.
I'VE GOTTEN BETTER ABOUT BEING SHY, BELIEVE IT OR NOT.
WELL, I'M GLAD.
BECAUSE YOU'RE AMAZING.
WOULD IT BE ALL RIGHT...
IF I CALLED YOU MY GIRLFRIEND?
I --

click!

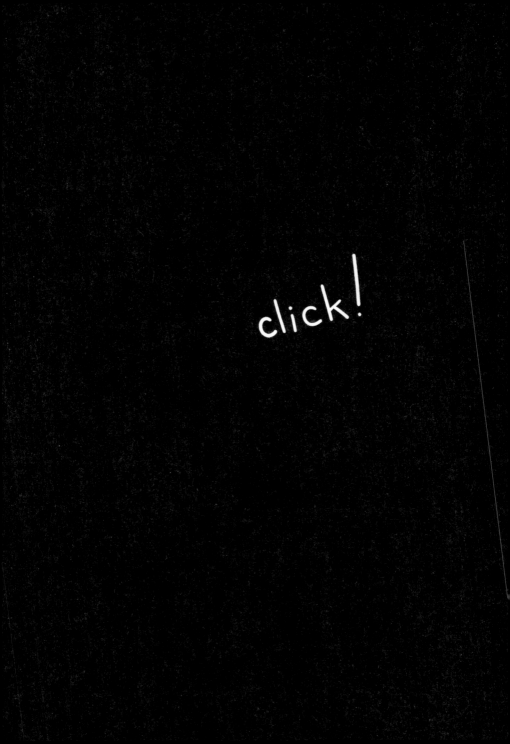

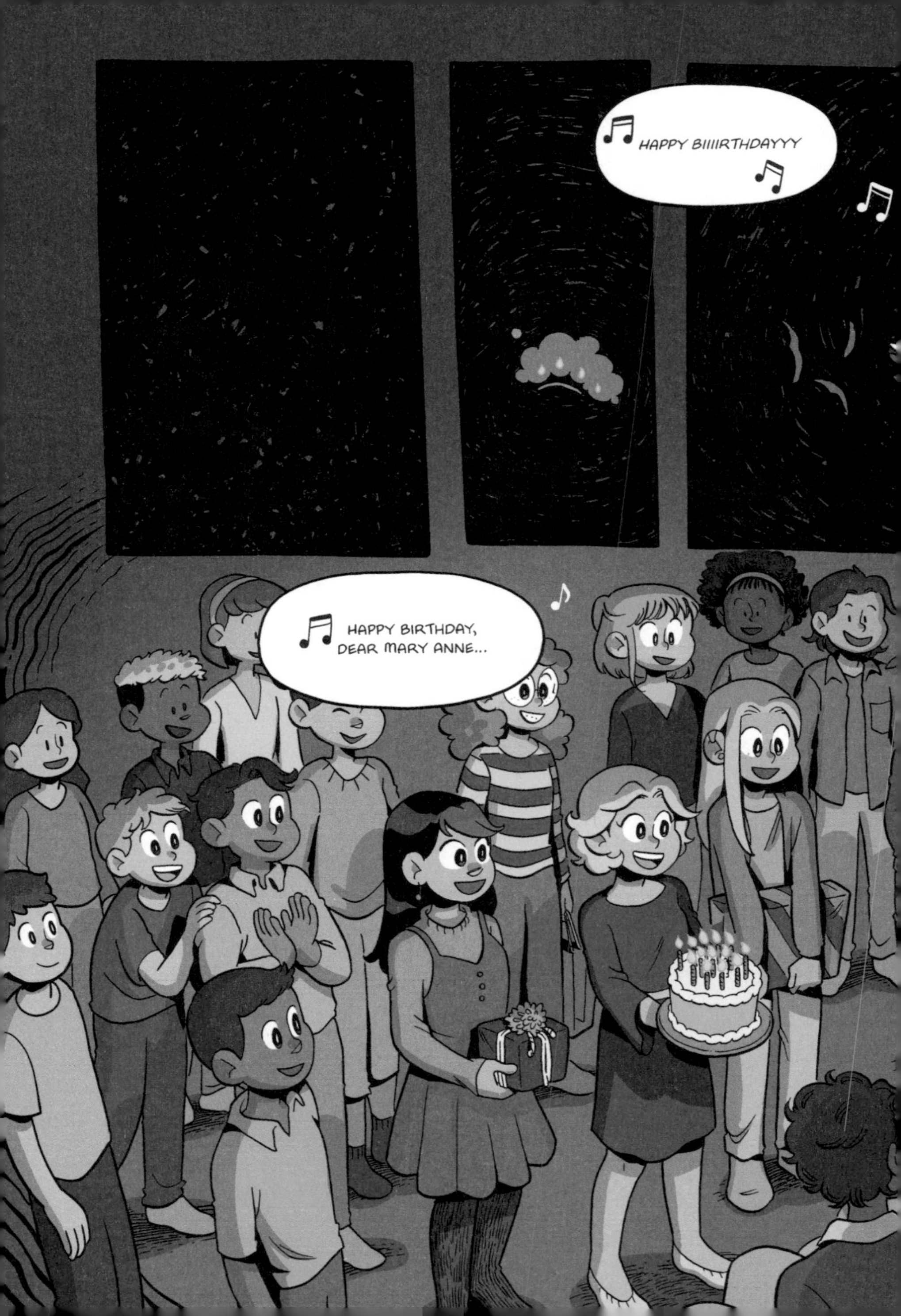
HAPPY BIIIIRTHDAYYY
HAPPY BIRTHDAY, DEAR MARY ANNE...

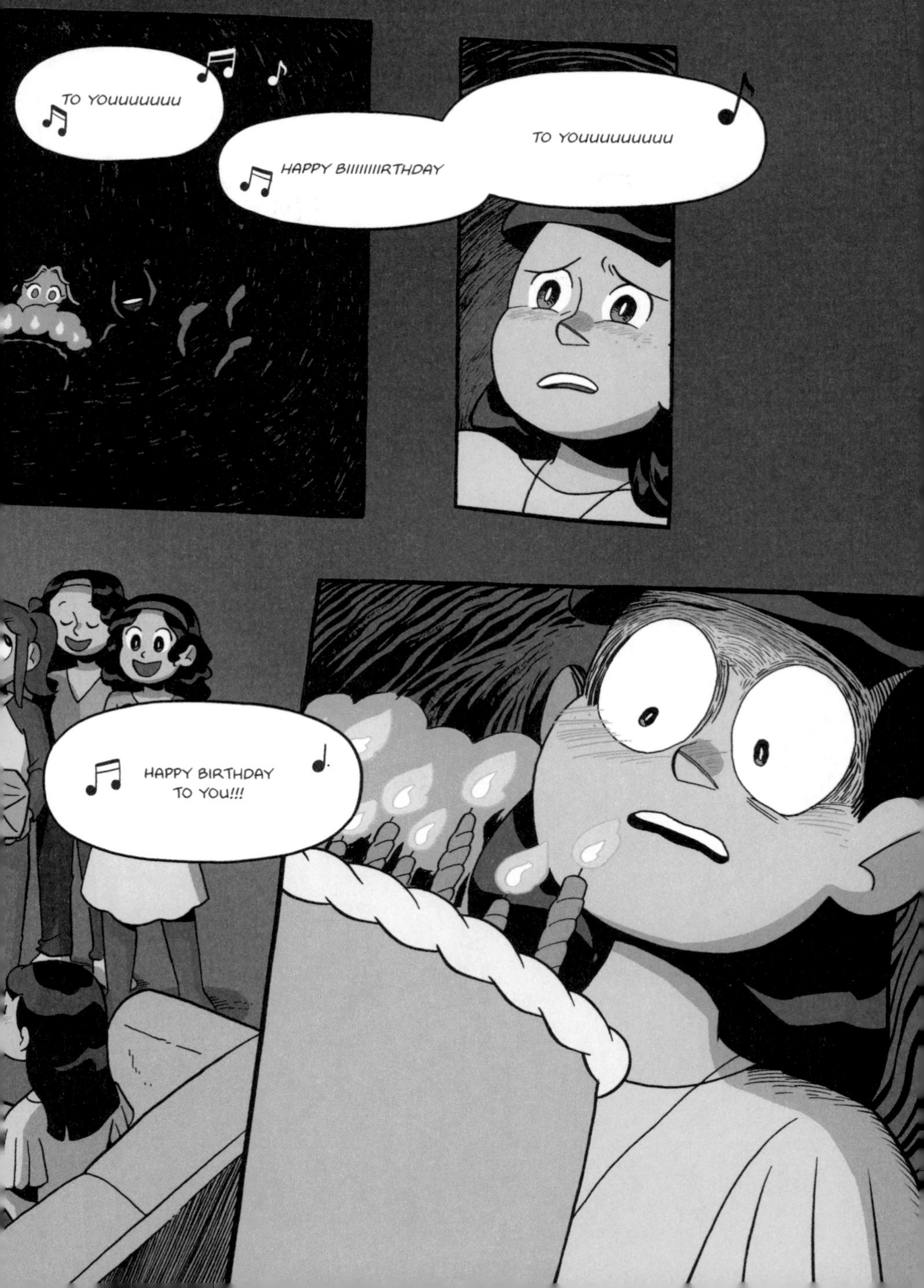
TO YOUUUUUUU
HAPPY BIIIIIIIRTHDAY
TO YOUUUUUUUUU
HAPPY BIRTHDAY
TO YOU!!!

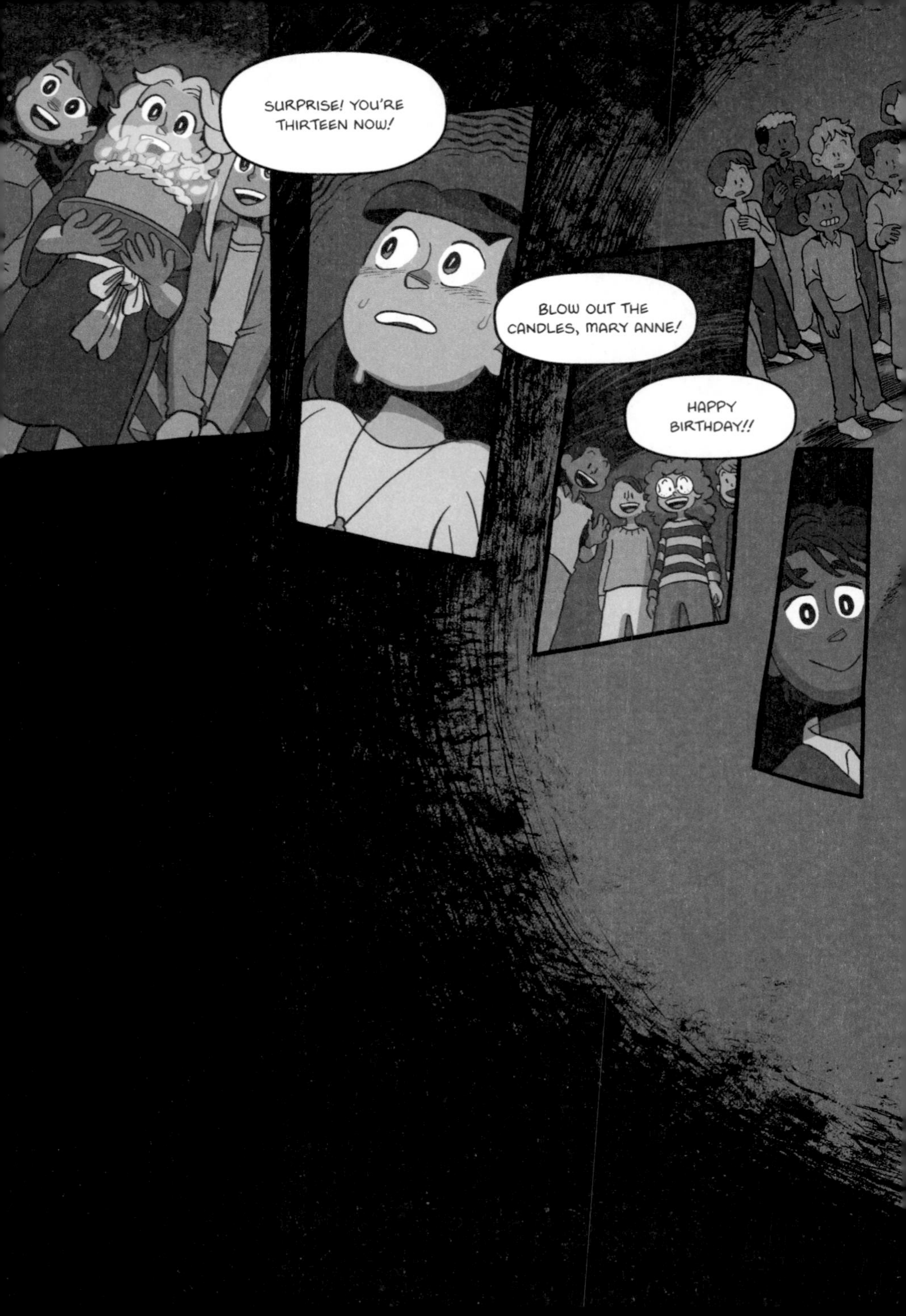
SURPRISE! YOU'RE THIRTEEN NOW!
BLOW OUT THE CANDLES, MARY ANNE!
HAPPY BIRTHDAY!!

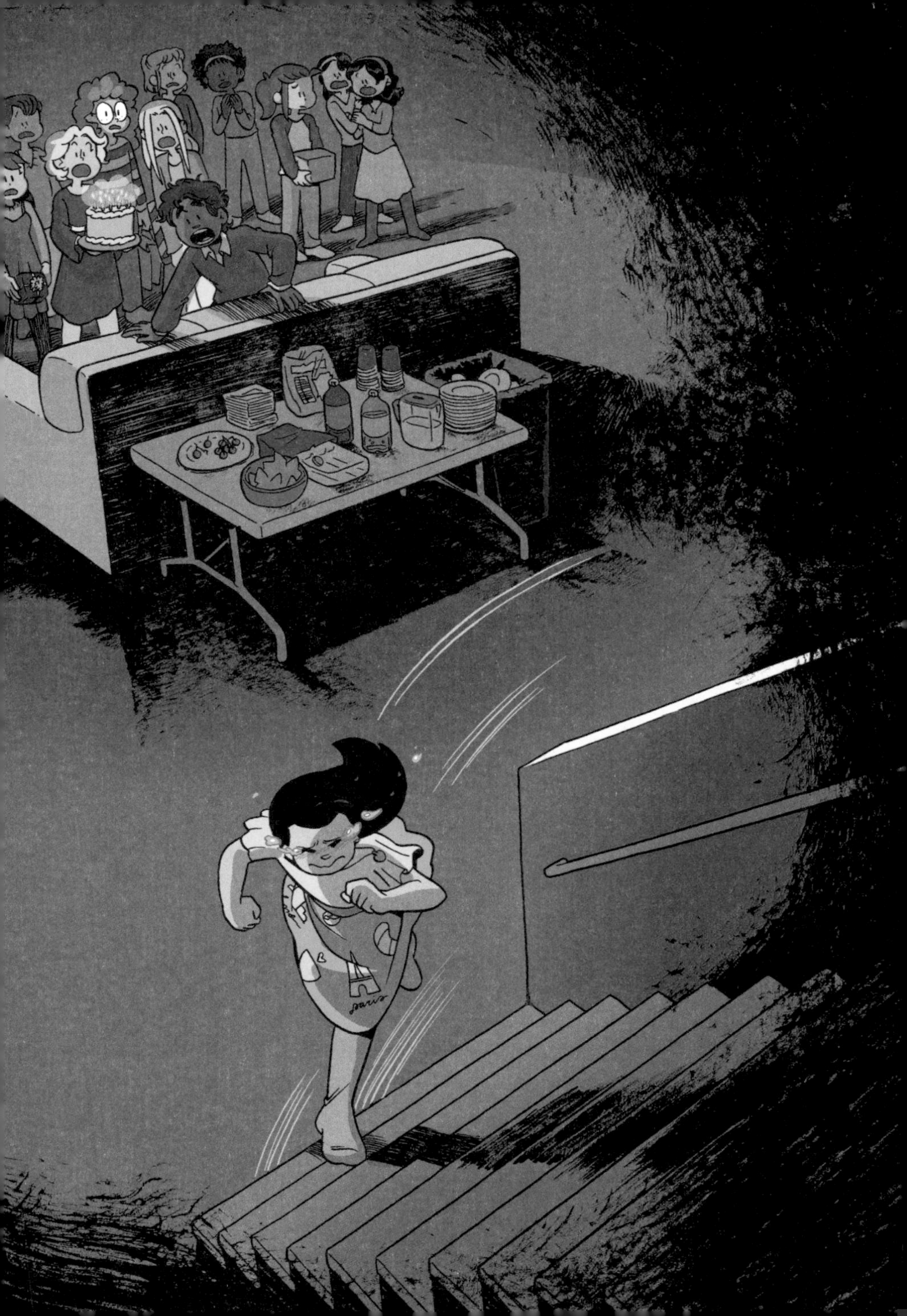
paris

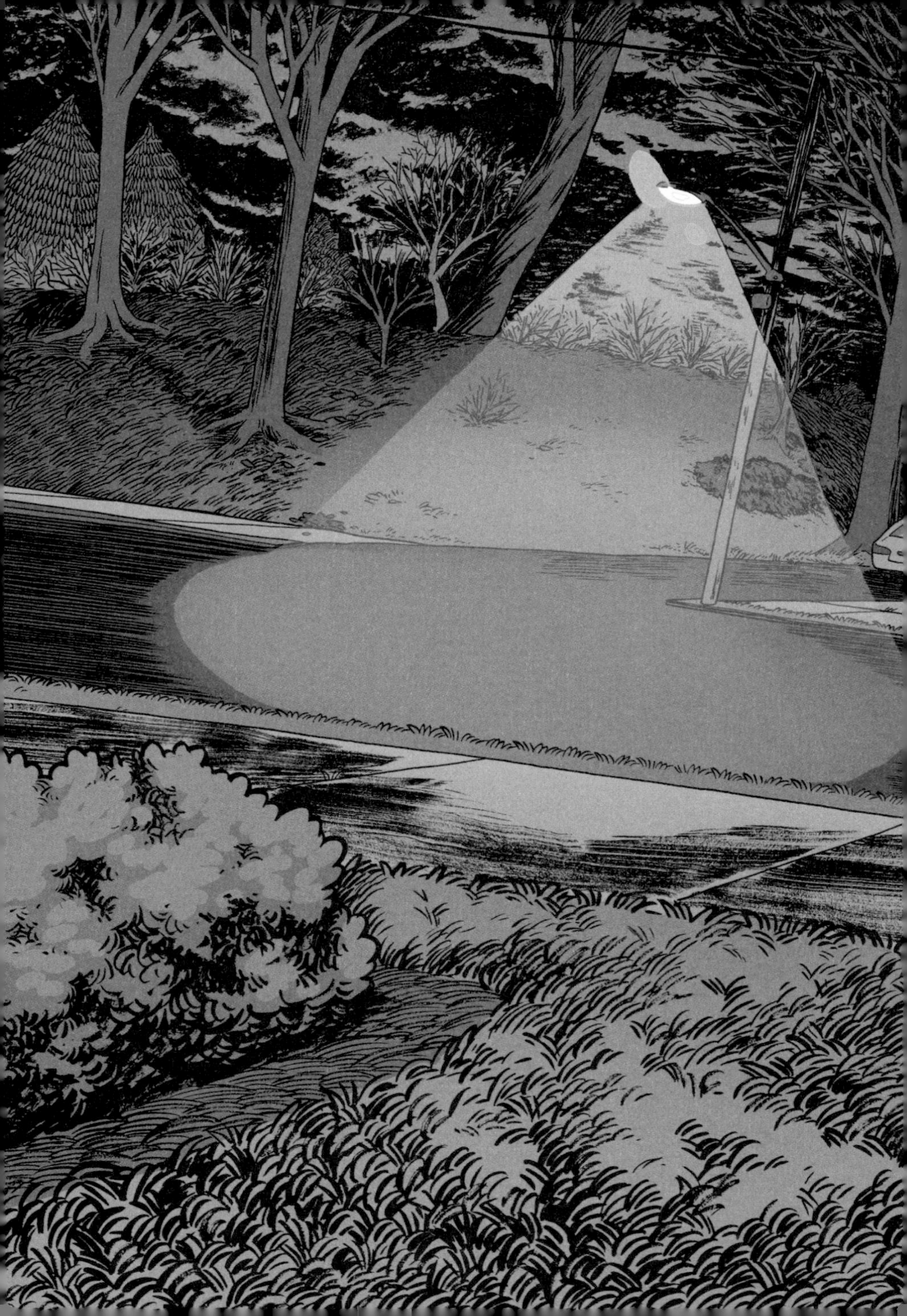

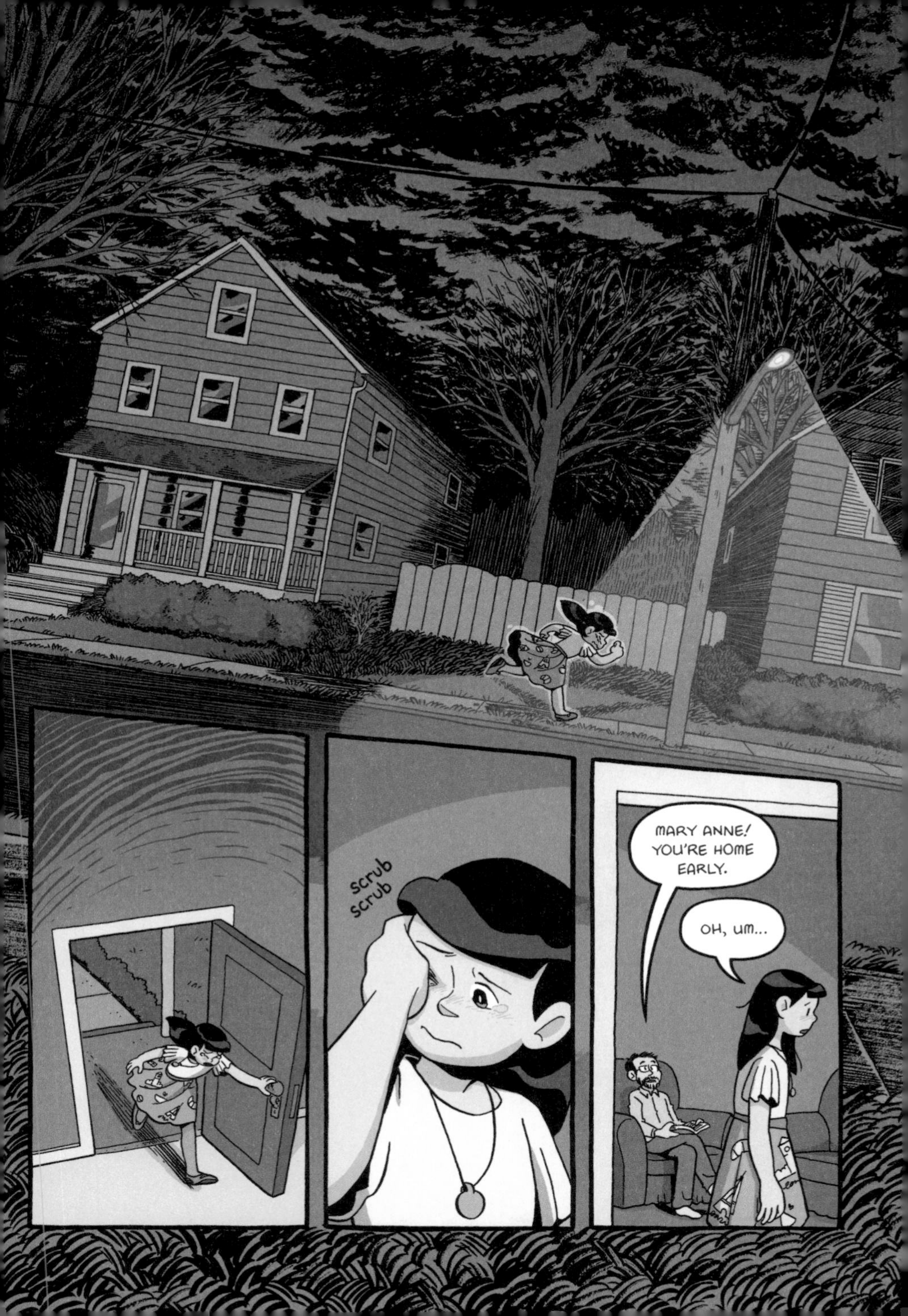
scrub scrub
MARY ANNE! YOU'RE HOME EARLY.
OH, UM...

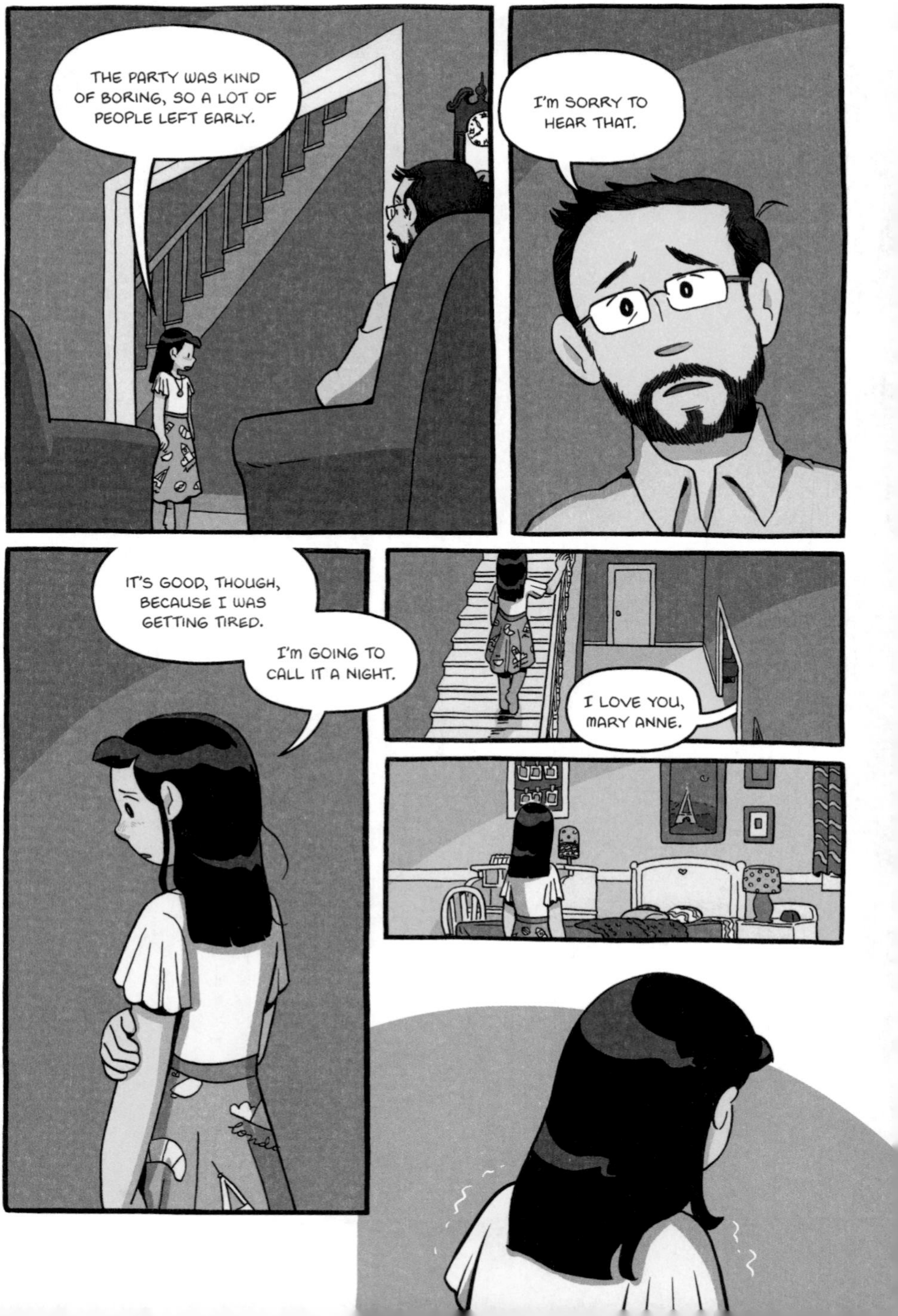
THE PARTY WAS KIND OF BORING, SO A LOT OF PEOPLE LEFT EARLY.
I'M SORRY TO HEAR THAT.
IT'S GOOD, THOUGH, BECAUSE I WAS GETTING TIRED.
I'M GOING TO CALL IT A NIGHT.
I LOVE YOU, MARY ANNE.

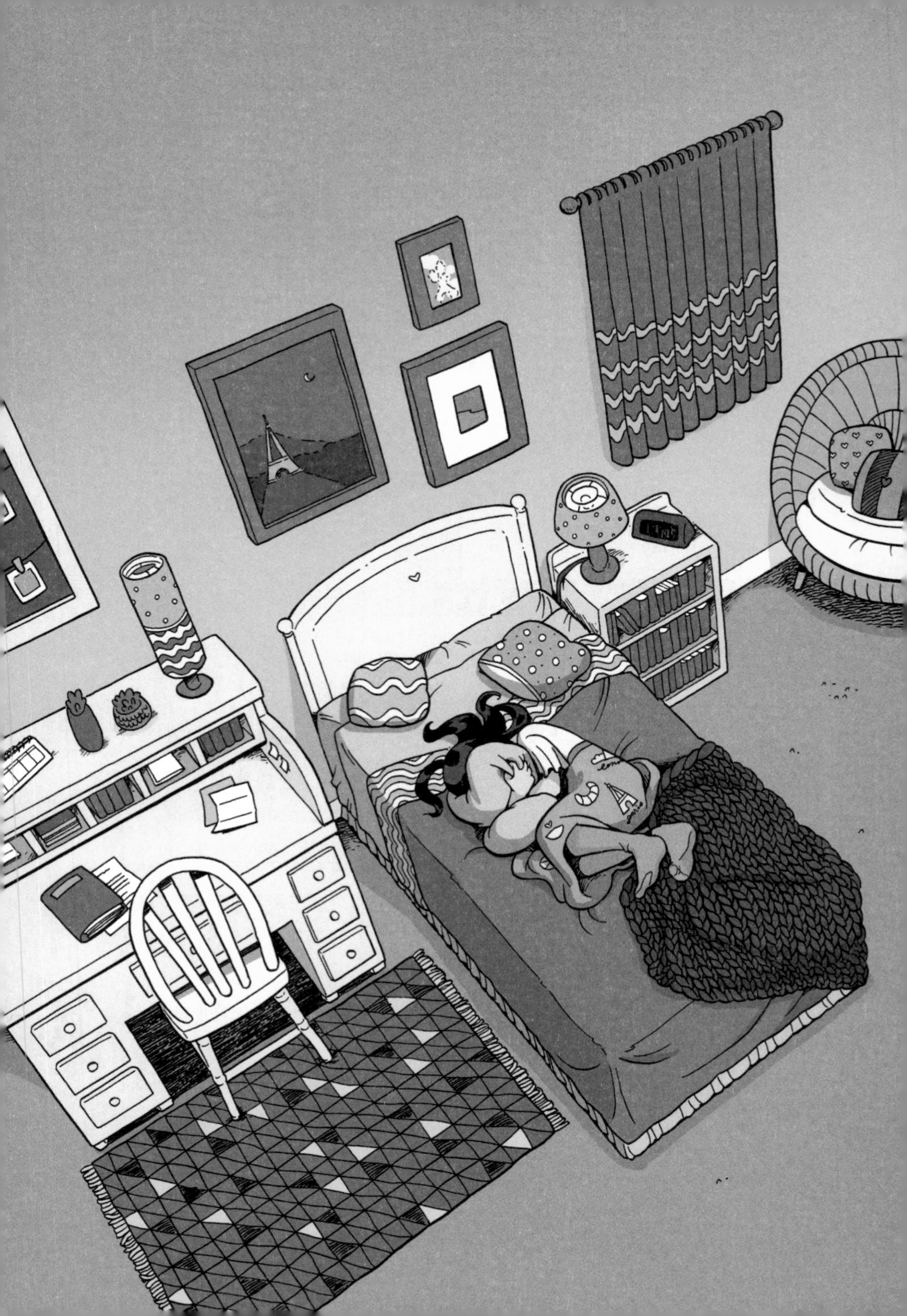

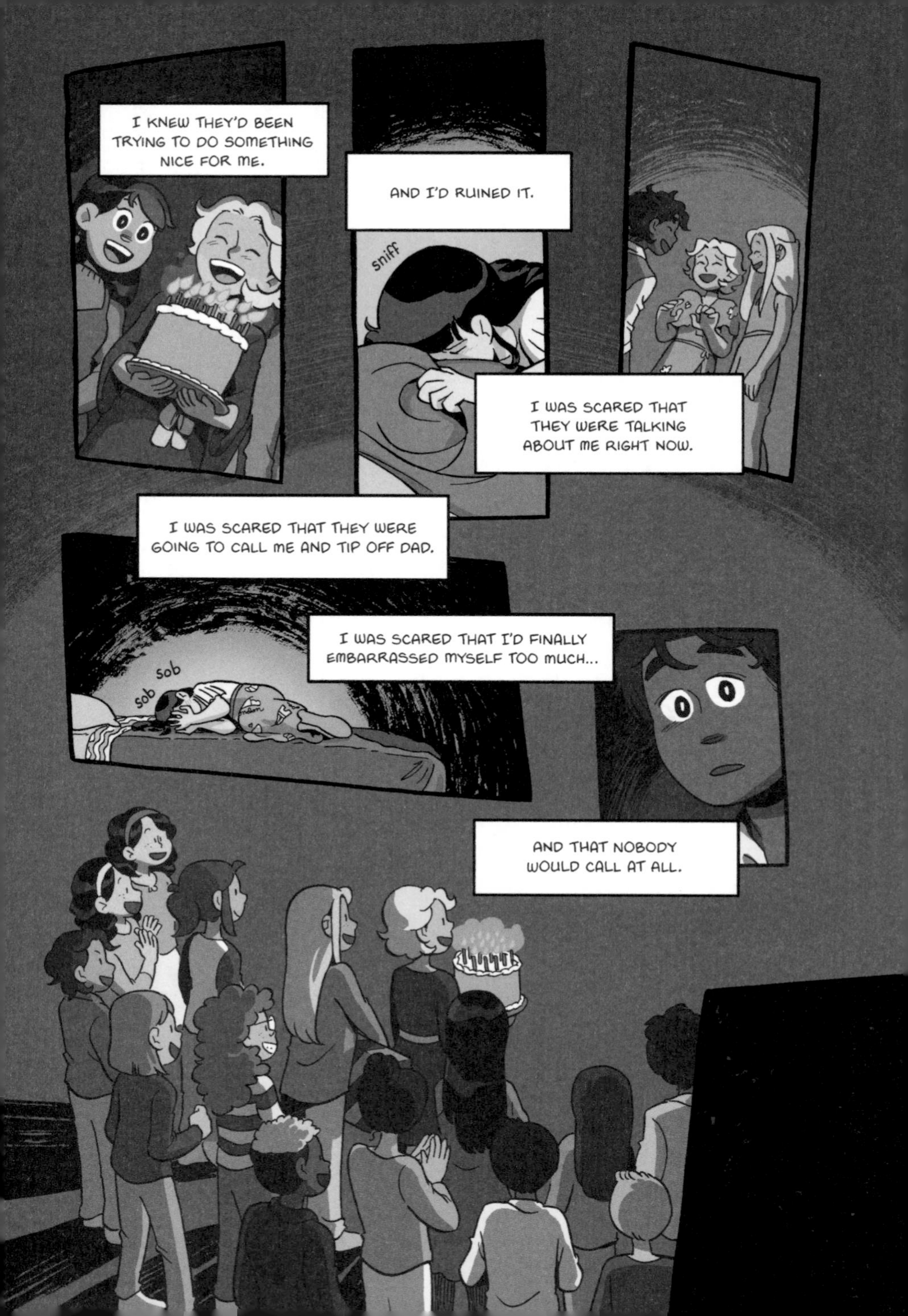
I KNEW THEY'D BEEN TRYING TO DO SOMETHING NICE FOR ME.
AND I'D RUINED IT.
sniff
I WAS SCARED THAT THEY WERE TALKING ABOUT ME RIGHT NOW.
I WAS SCARED THAT THEY WERE GOING TO CALL ME AND TIP OFF DAD.
sob sob
I WAS SCARED THAT I'D FINALLY EMBARRASSED MYSELF TOO MUCH...
AND THAT NOBODY WOULD CALL AT ALL.

CHAPTER 15

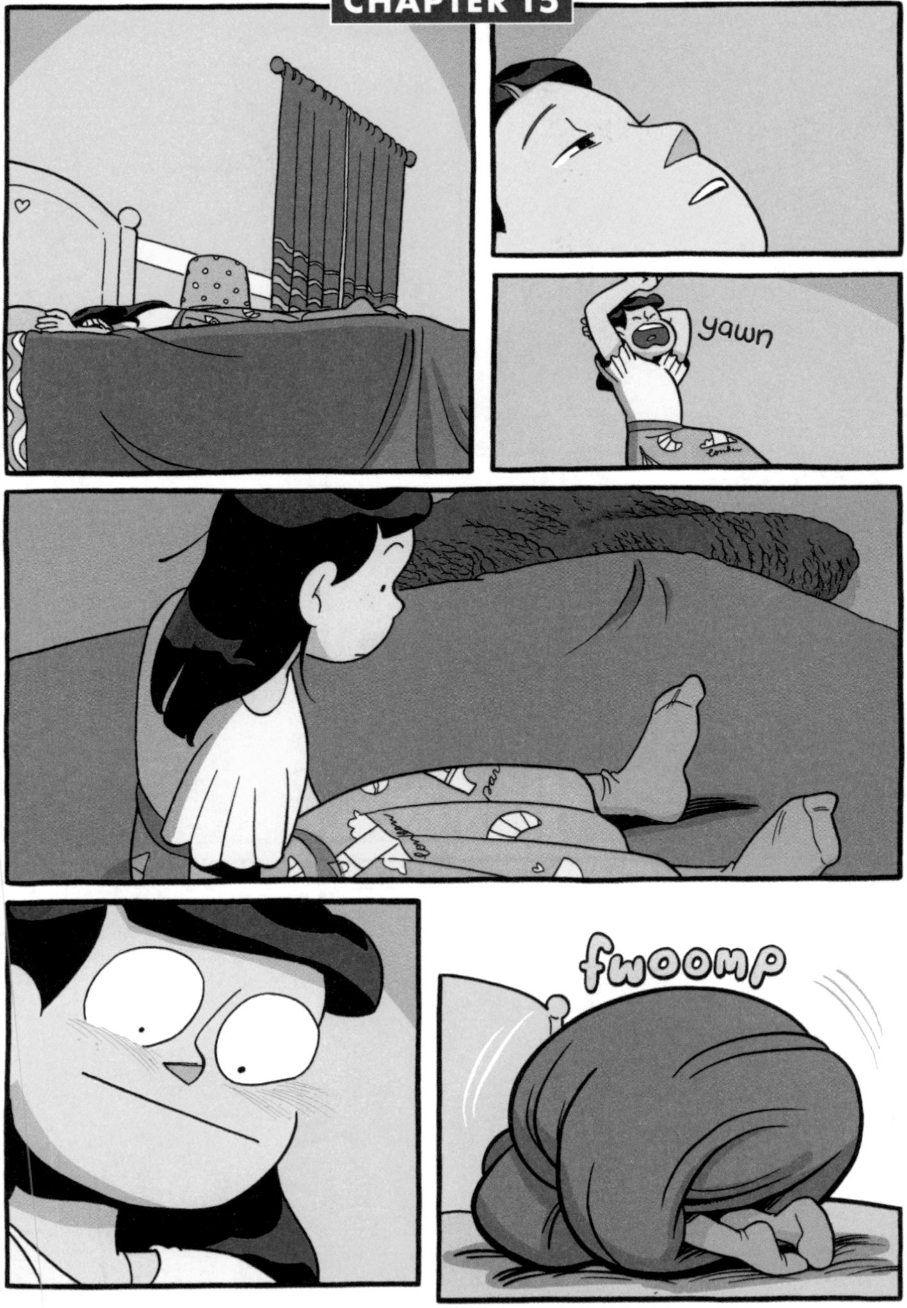
yawn
fwoomp

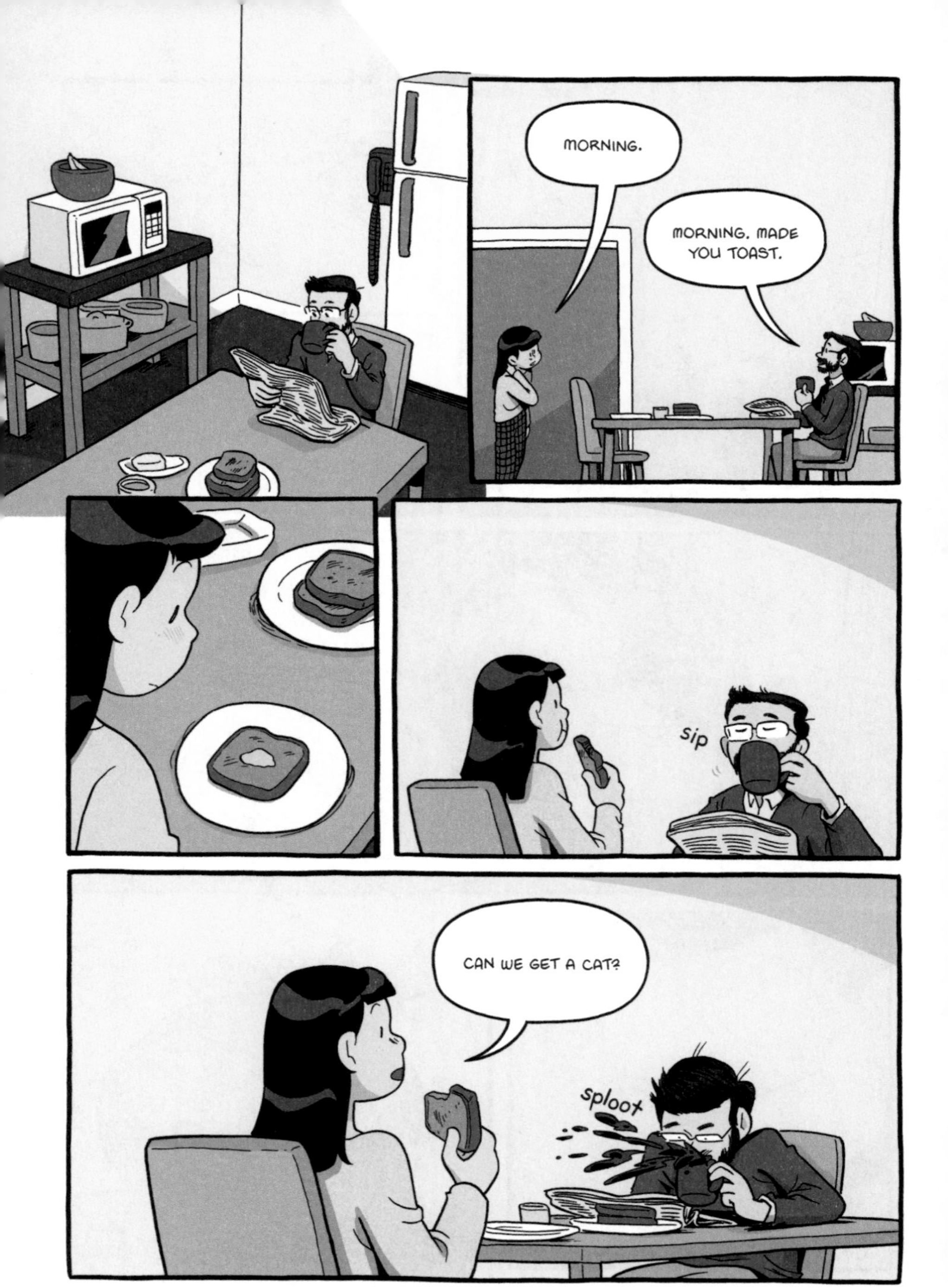
MORNING.
MORNING. MADE YOU TOAST.
sip
CAN WE GET A CAT?
sploot

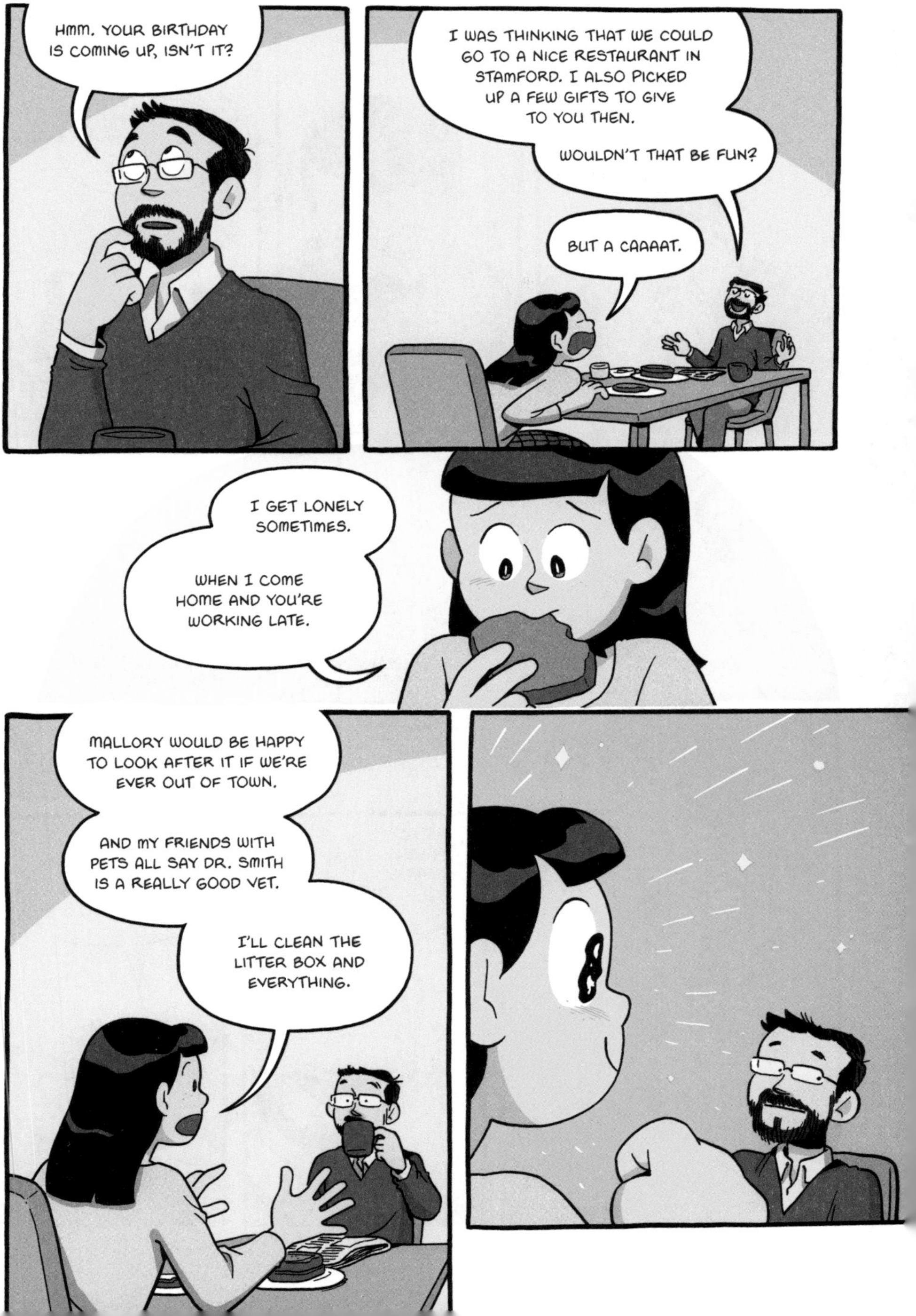
HMM. YOUR BIRTHDAY IS COMING UP, ISN'T IT?
I WAS THINKING THAT WE COULD GO TO A NICE RESTAURANT IN STAMFORD. I ALSO PICKED UP A FEW GIFTS TO GIVE TO YOU THEN.
WOULDN'T THAT BE FUN?
BUT A CAAAAT.
I GET LONELY SOMETIMES.
WHEN I COME HOME AND YOU'RE WORKING LATE.
MALLORY WOULD BE HAPPY TO LOOK AFTER IT IF WE'RE EVER OUT OF TOWN.
AND MY FRIENDS WITH PETS ALL SAY DR. SMITH IS A REALLY GOOD VET.
I'LL CLEAN THE LITTER BOX AND EVERYTHING.

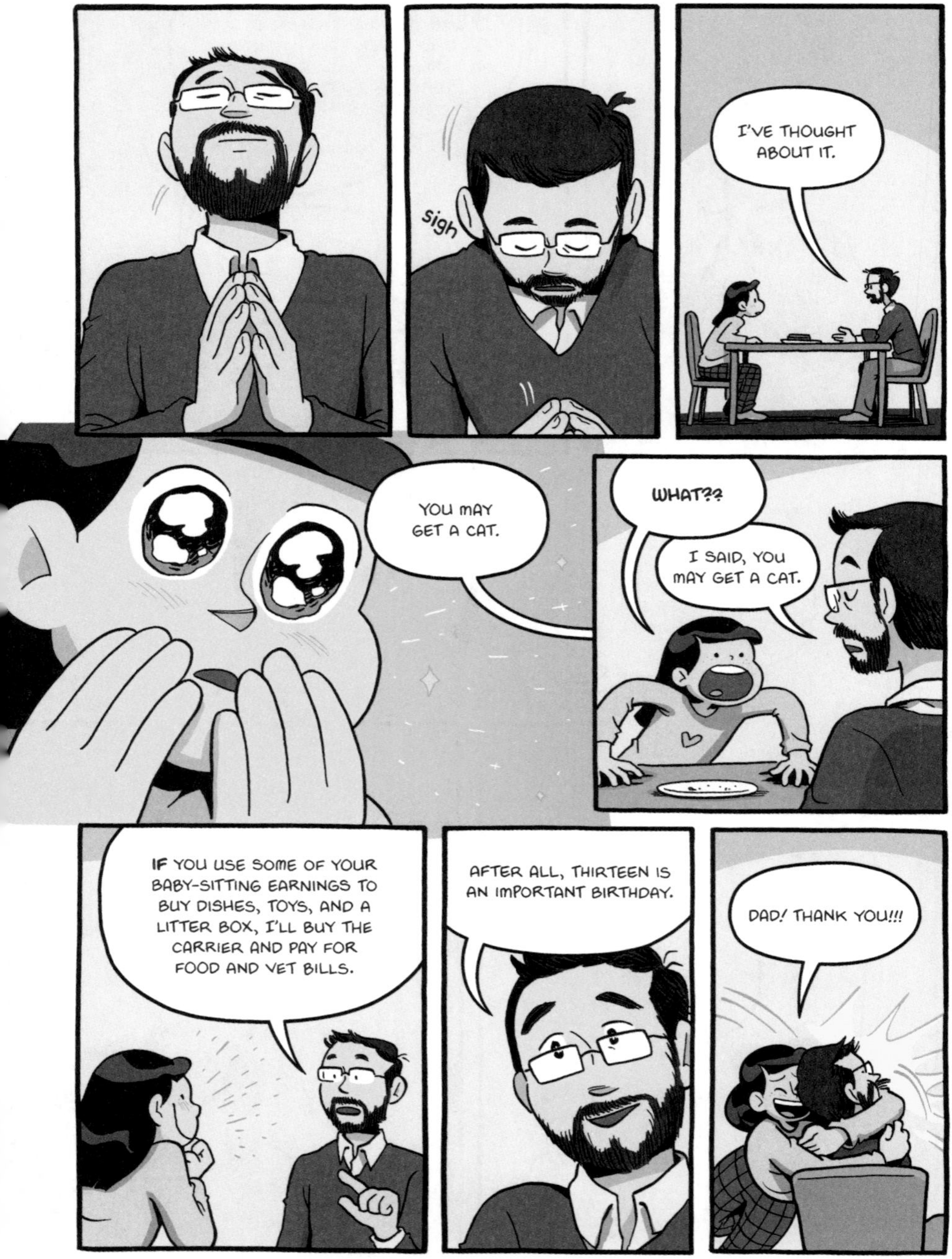
sigh
I'VE THOUGHT ABOUT IT.
YOU MAY GET A CAT.
WHAT??
I SAID, YOU MAY GET A CAT.
IF YOU USE SOME OF YOUR BABY-SITTING EARNINGS TO BUY DISHES, TOYS, AND A LITTER BOX, I'LL BUY THE CARRIER AND PAY FOR FOOD AND VET BILLS.
AFTER ALL, THIRTEEN IS AN IMPORTANT BIRTHDAY.
DAD! THANK YOU!!!

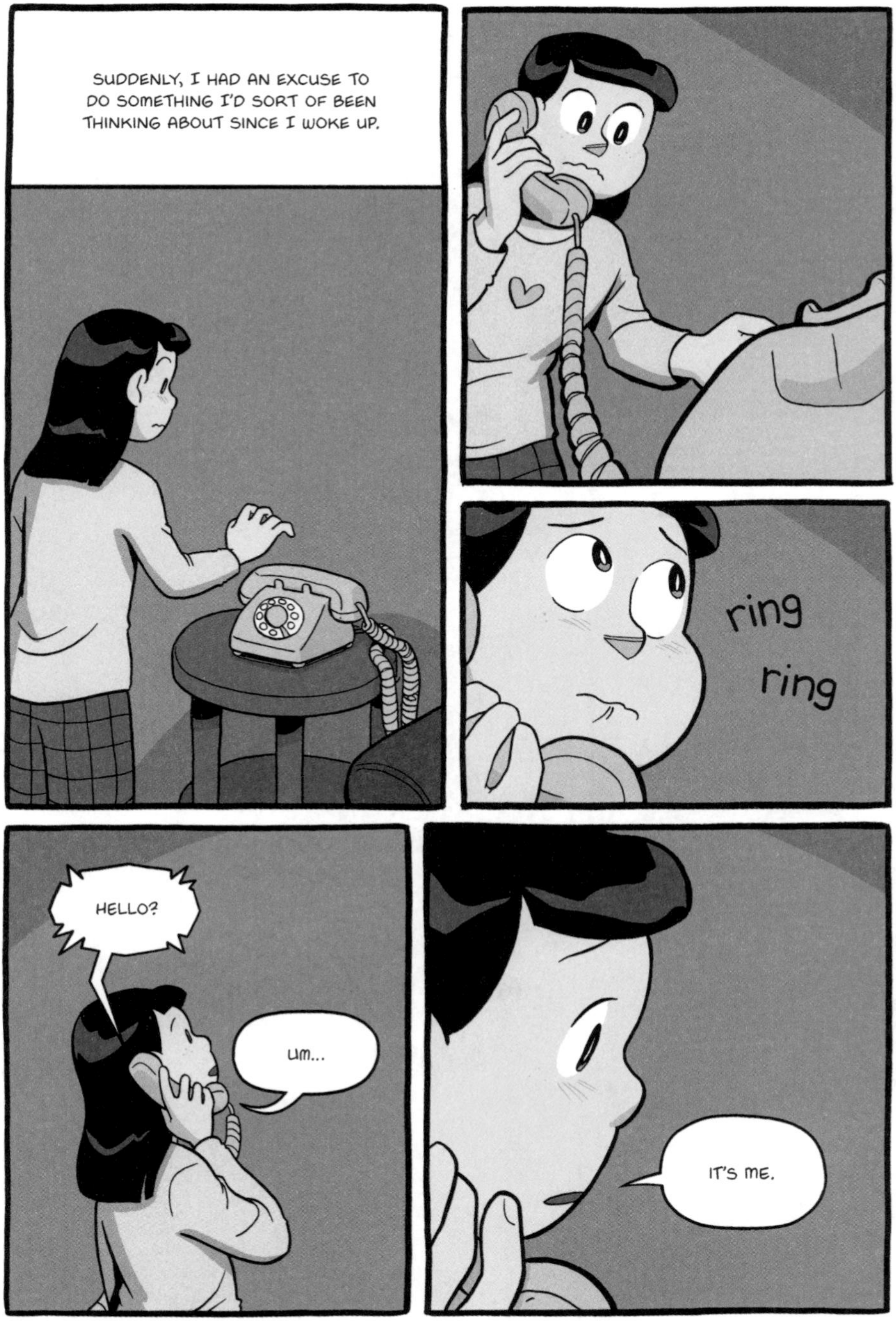
SUDDENLY, I HAD AN EXCUSE TO DO SOMETHING I'D SORT OF BEEN THINKING ABOUT SINCE I WOKE UP.
ring
ring
HELLO?
um...
IT'S ME.

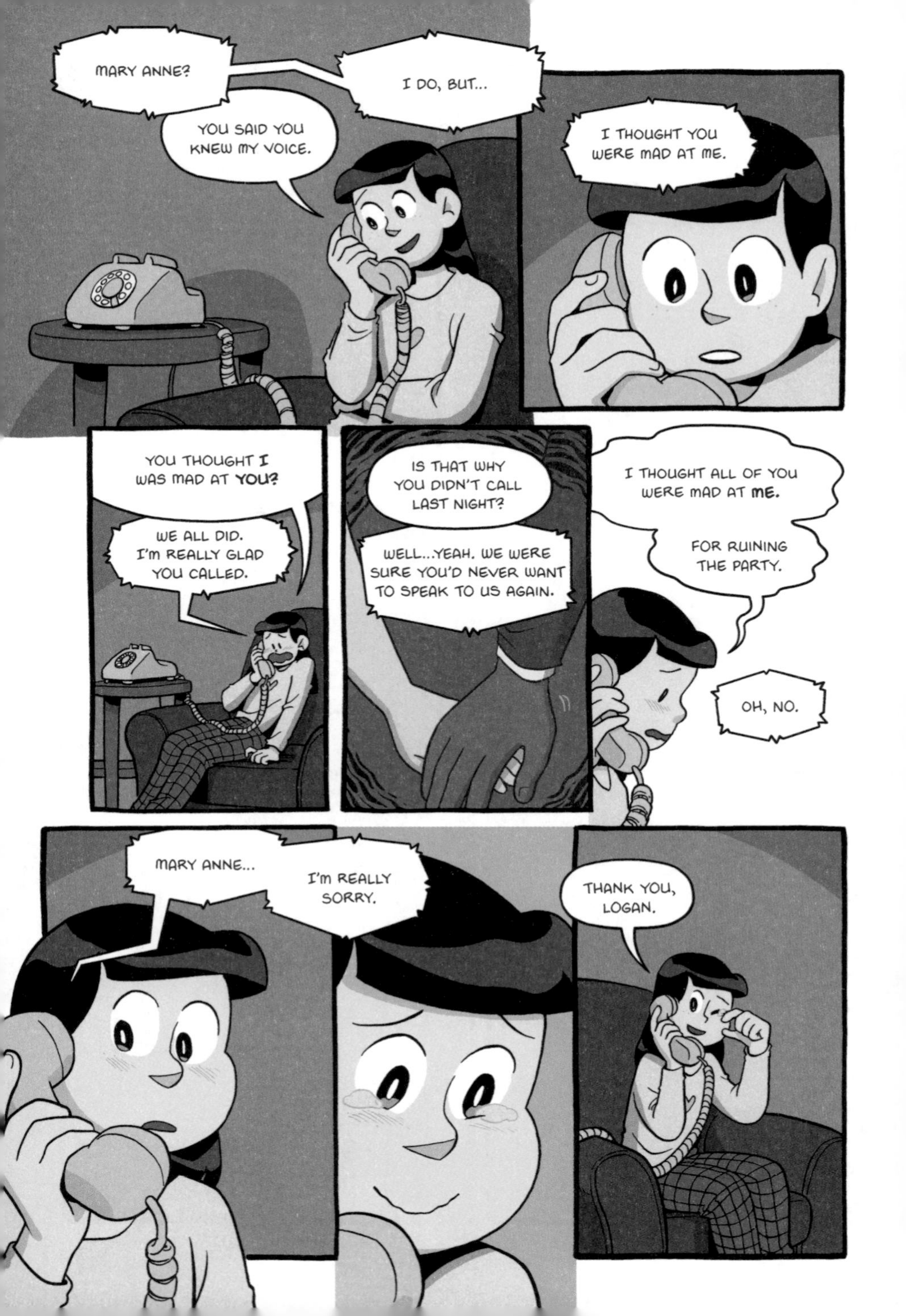
MARY ANNE?
I DO, BUT...
YOU SAID YOU KNEW MY VOICE.
I THOUGHT YOU WERE MAD AT ME.
YOU THOUGHT **I** WAS MAD AT **YOU?**
WE ALL DID. I'M REALLY GLAD YOU CALLED.
IS THAT WHY YOU DIDN'T CALL LAST NIGHT?
WELL...YEAH. WE WERE SURE YOU'D NEVER WANT TO SPEAK TO US AGAIN.
I THOUGHT ALL OF YOU WERE MAD AT **ME.**
FOR RUINING THE PARTY.
OH, NO.
MARY ANNE...
I'M REALLY SORRY.
THANK YOU, LOGAN.

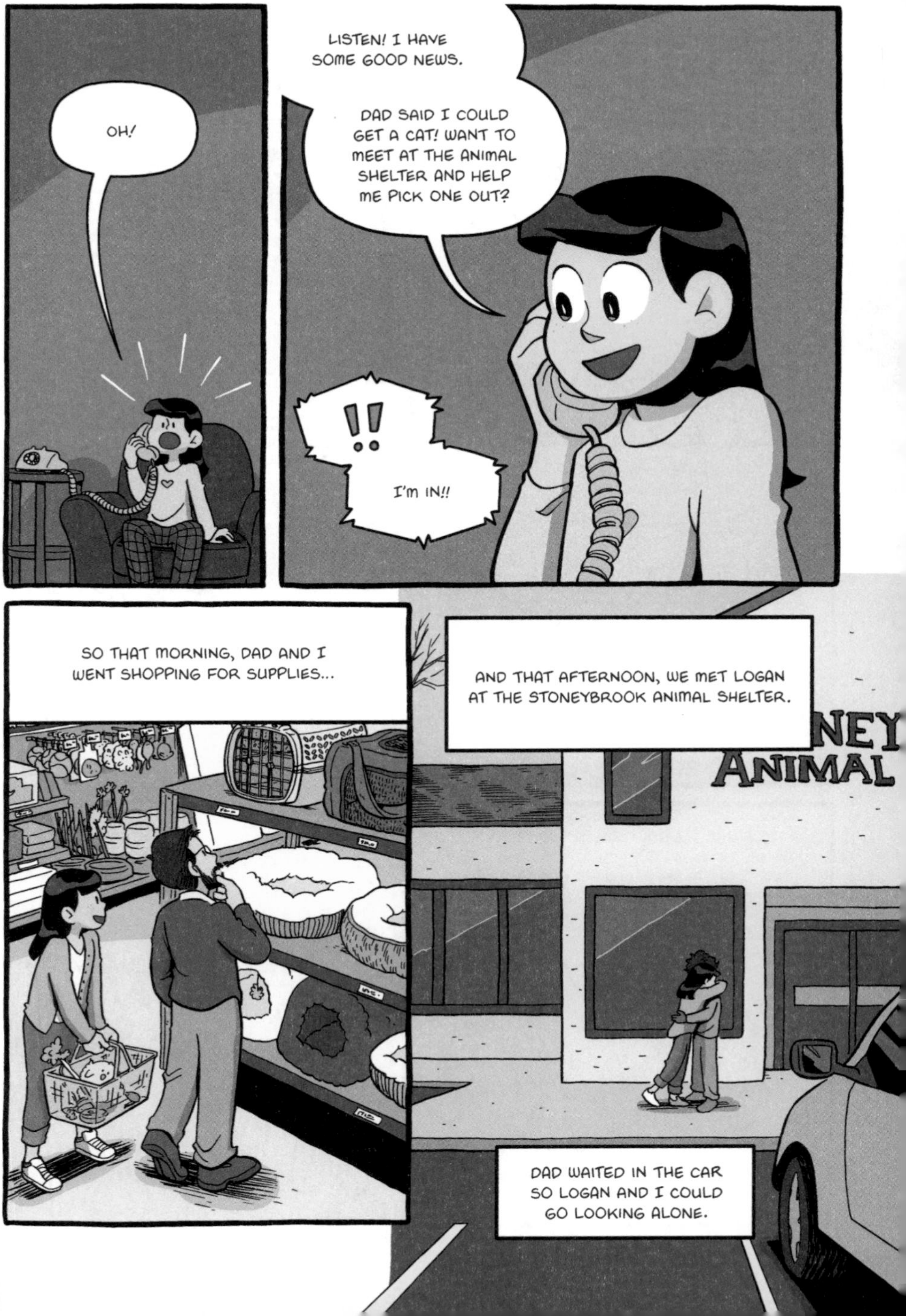
OH!
LISTEN! I HAVE SOME GOOD NEWS.
DAD SAID I COULD GET A CAT! WANT TO MEET AT THE ANIMAL SHELTER AND HELP ME PICK ONE OUT?
!!
I'M IN!!
SO THAT MORNING, DAD AND I WENT SHOPPING FOR SUPPLIES...
AND THAT AFTERNOON, WE MET LOGAN AT THE STONEYBROOK ANIMAL SHELTER.
NEY
ANIMAL
DAD WAITED IN THE CAR SO LOGAN AND I COULD GO LOOKING ALONE.

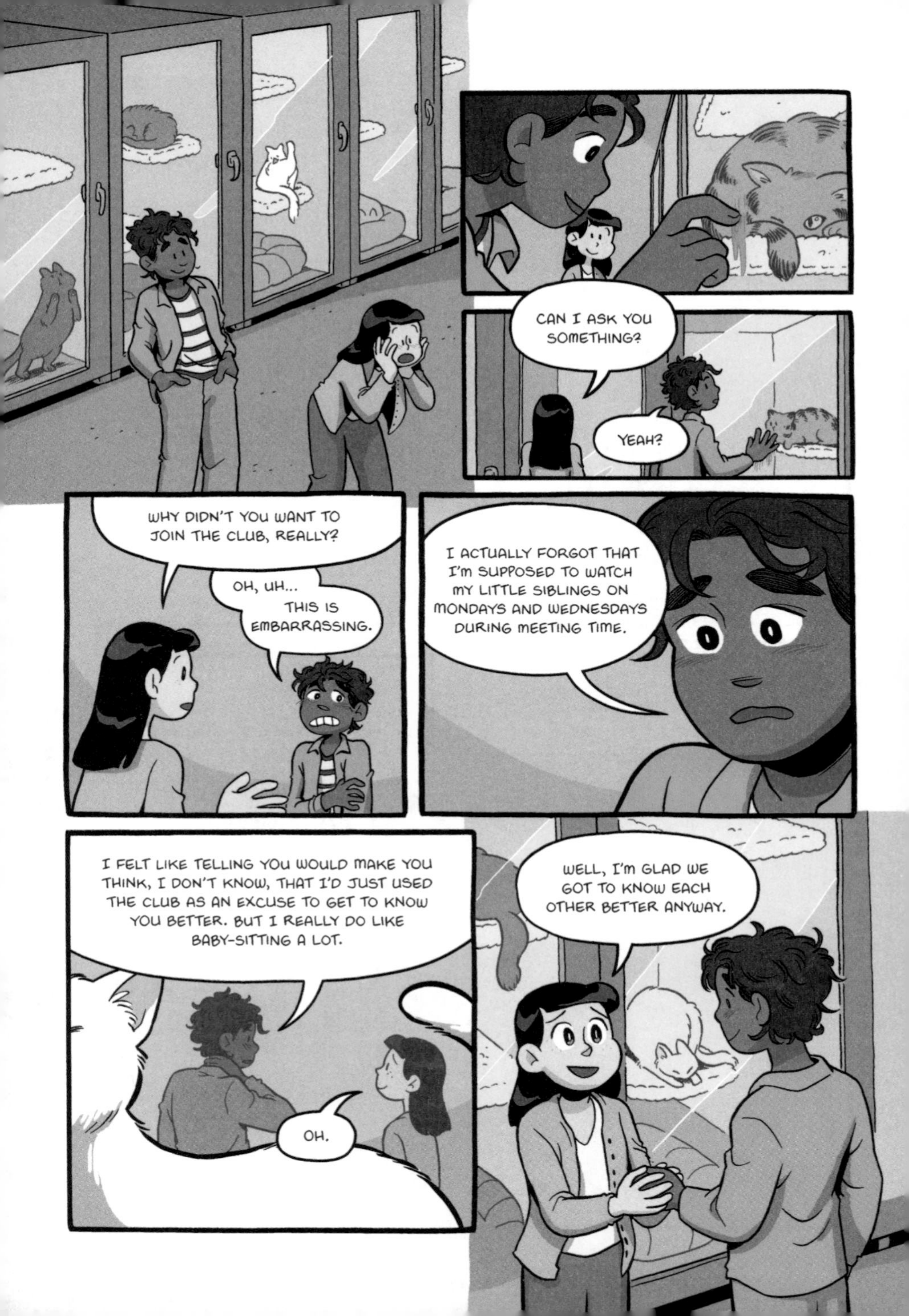
CAN I ASK YOU SOMETHING?
YEAH?
WHY DIDN'T YOU WANT TO JOIN THE CLUB, REALLY?
OH, UH... THIS IS EMBARRASSING.
I ACTUALLY FORGOT THAT I'M SUPPOSED TO WATCH MY LITTLE SIBLINGS ON MONDAYS AND WEDNESDAYS DURING MEETING TIME.
I FELT LIKE TELLING YOU WOULD MAKE YOU THINK, I DON'T KNOW, THAT I'D JUST USED THE CLUB AS AN EXCUSE TO GET TO KNOW YOU BETTER. BUT I REALLY DO LIKE BABY-SITTING A LOT.
OH.
WELL, I'M GLAD WE GOT TO KNOW EACH OTHER BETTER ANYWAY.

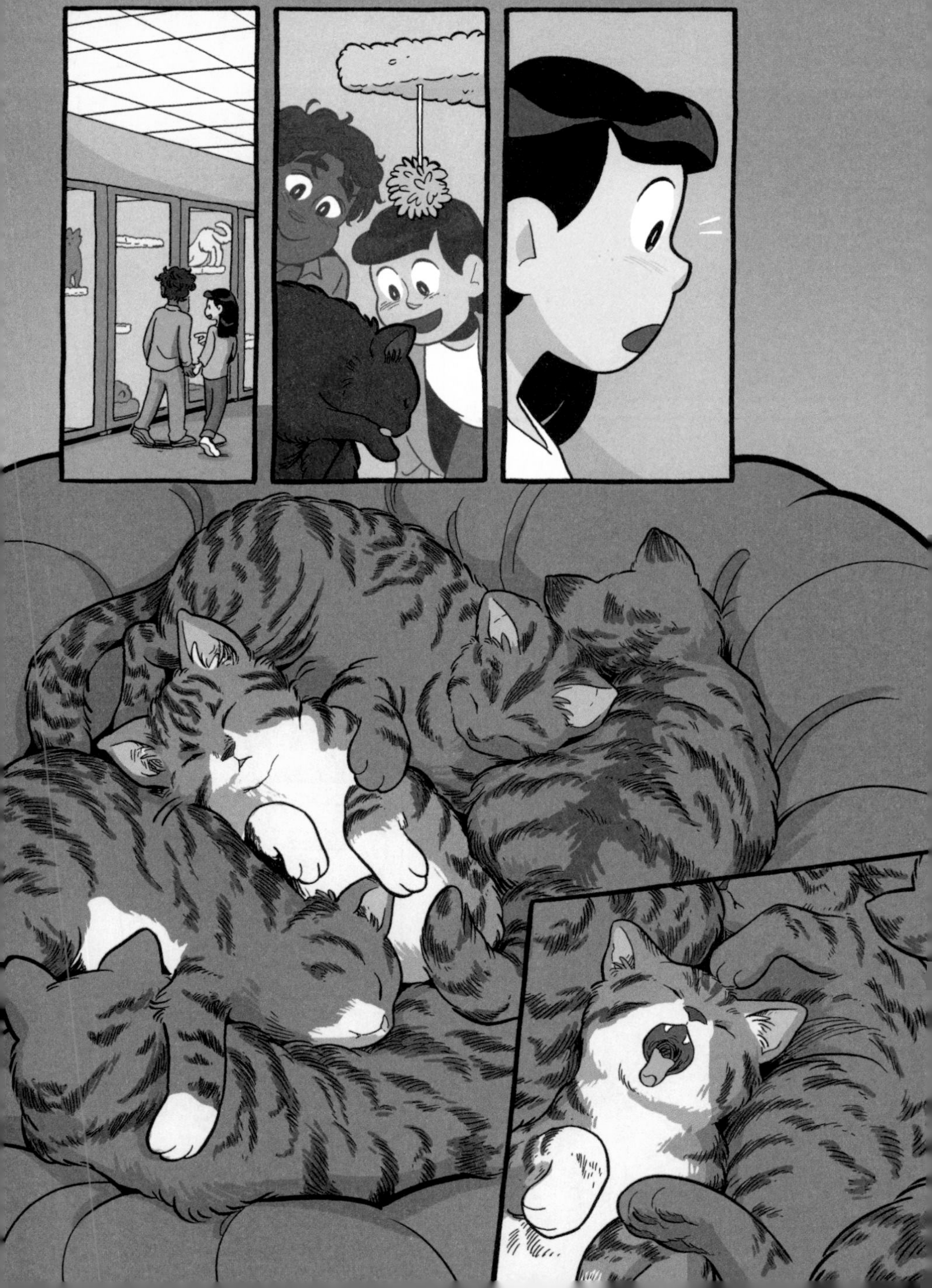

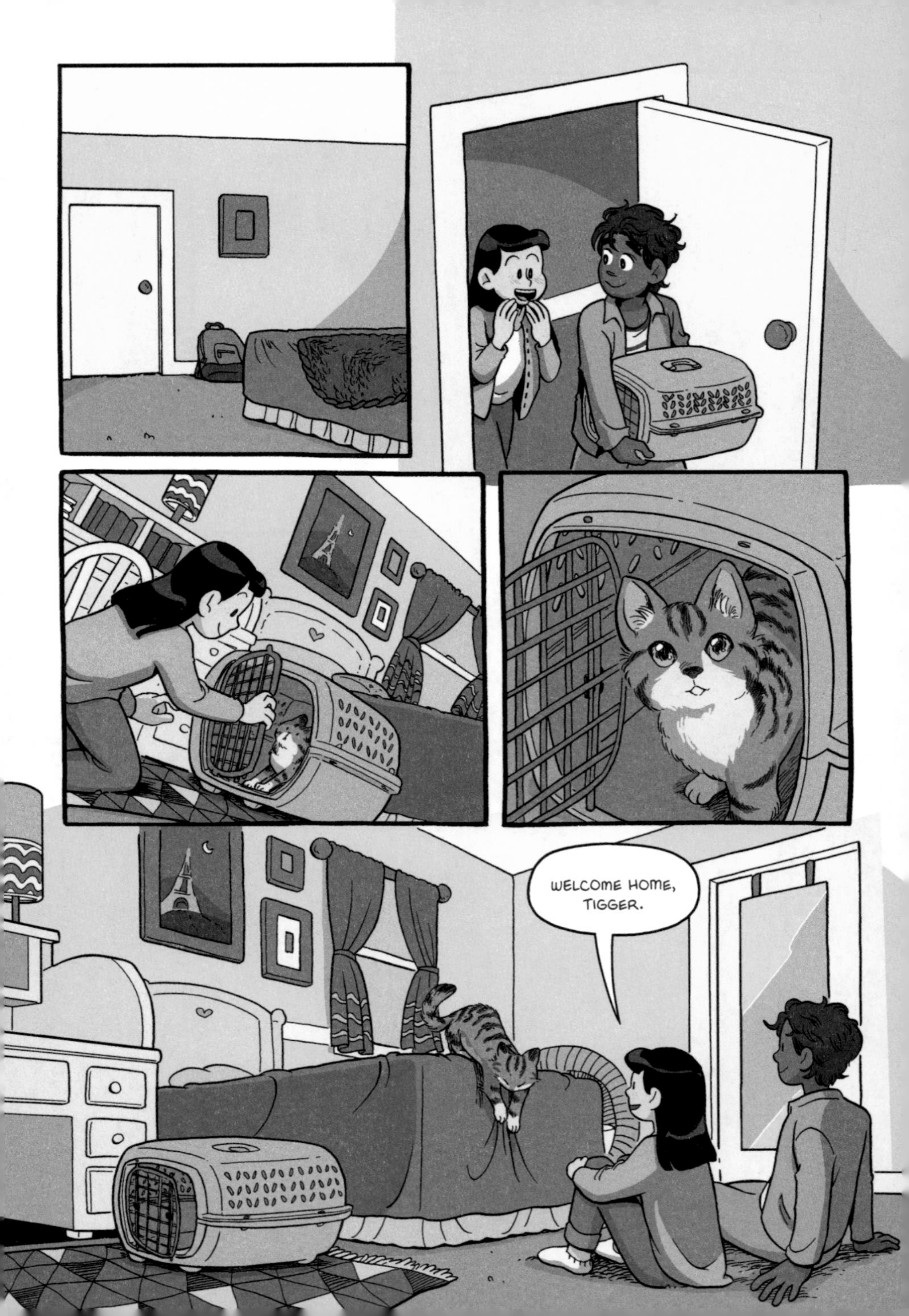
WELCOME HOME, TIGGER.

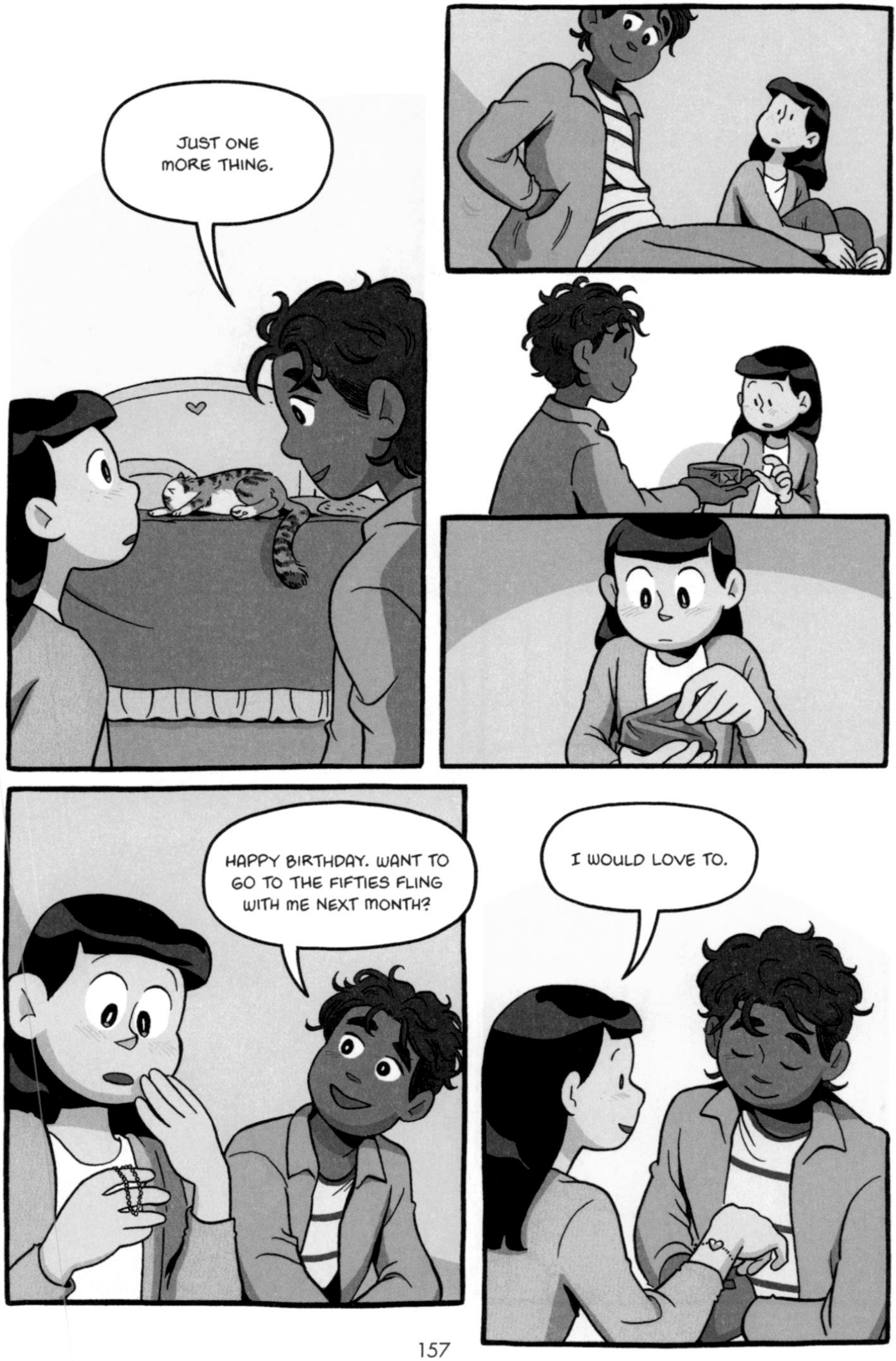
JUST ONE MORE THING.
HAPPY BIRTHDAY. WANT TO GO TO THE FIFTIES FLING WITH ME NEXT MONTH?
I WOULD LOVE TO.

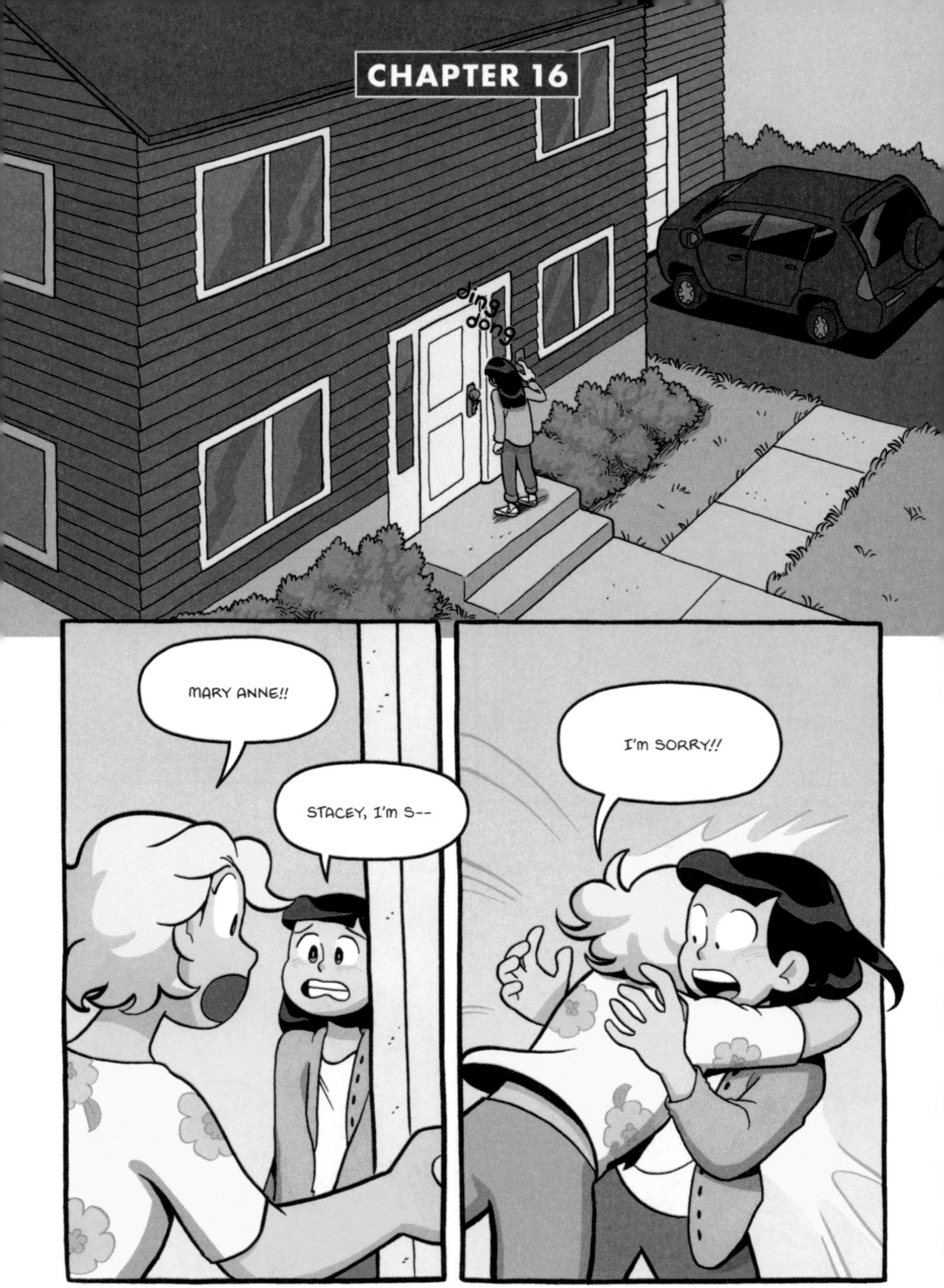
CHAPTER 16
ding dong
MARY ANNE!!
STACEY, I'M S--
I'M SORRY!!

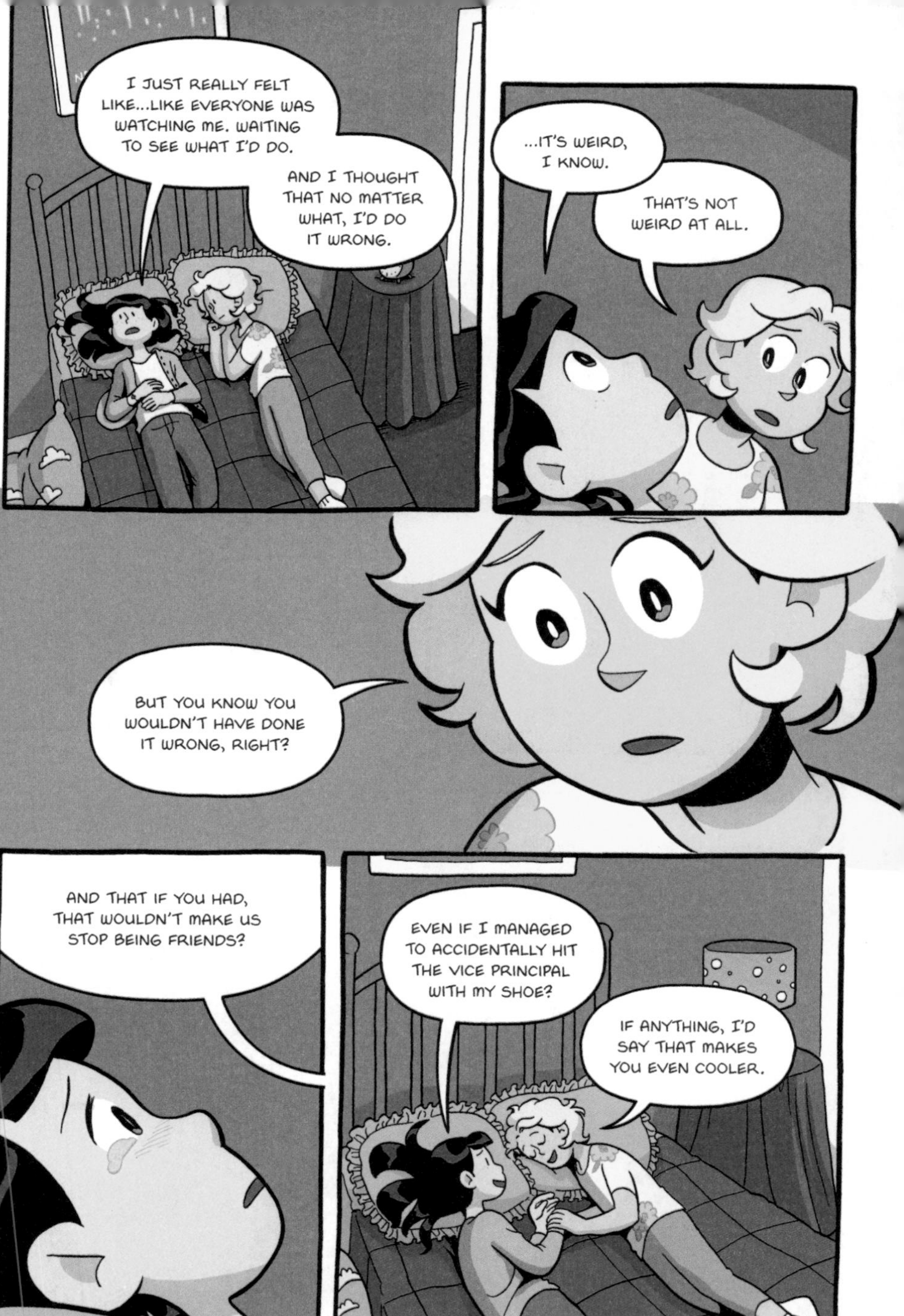
I JUST REALLY FELT LIKE...LIKE EVERYONE WAS WATCHING ME. WAITING TO SEE WHAT I'D DO.
AND I THOUGHT THAT NO MATTER WHAT, I'D DO IT WRONG.
...IT'S WEIRD, I KNOW.
THAT'S NOT WEIRD AT ALL.
BUT YOU KNOW YOU WOULDN'T HAVE DONE IT WRONG, RIGHT?
AND THAT IF YOU HAD, THAT WOULDN'T MAKE US STOP BEING FRIENDS?
EVEN IF I MANAGED TO ACCIDENTALLY HIT THE VICE PRINCIPAL WITH MY SHOE?
IF ANYTHING, I'D SAY THAT MAKES YOU EVEN COOLER.

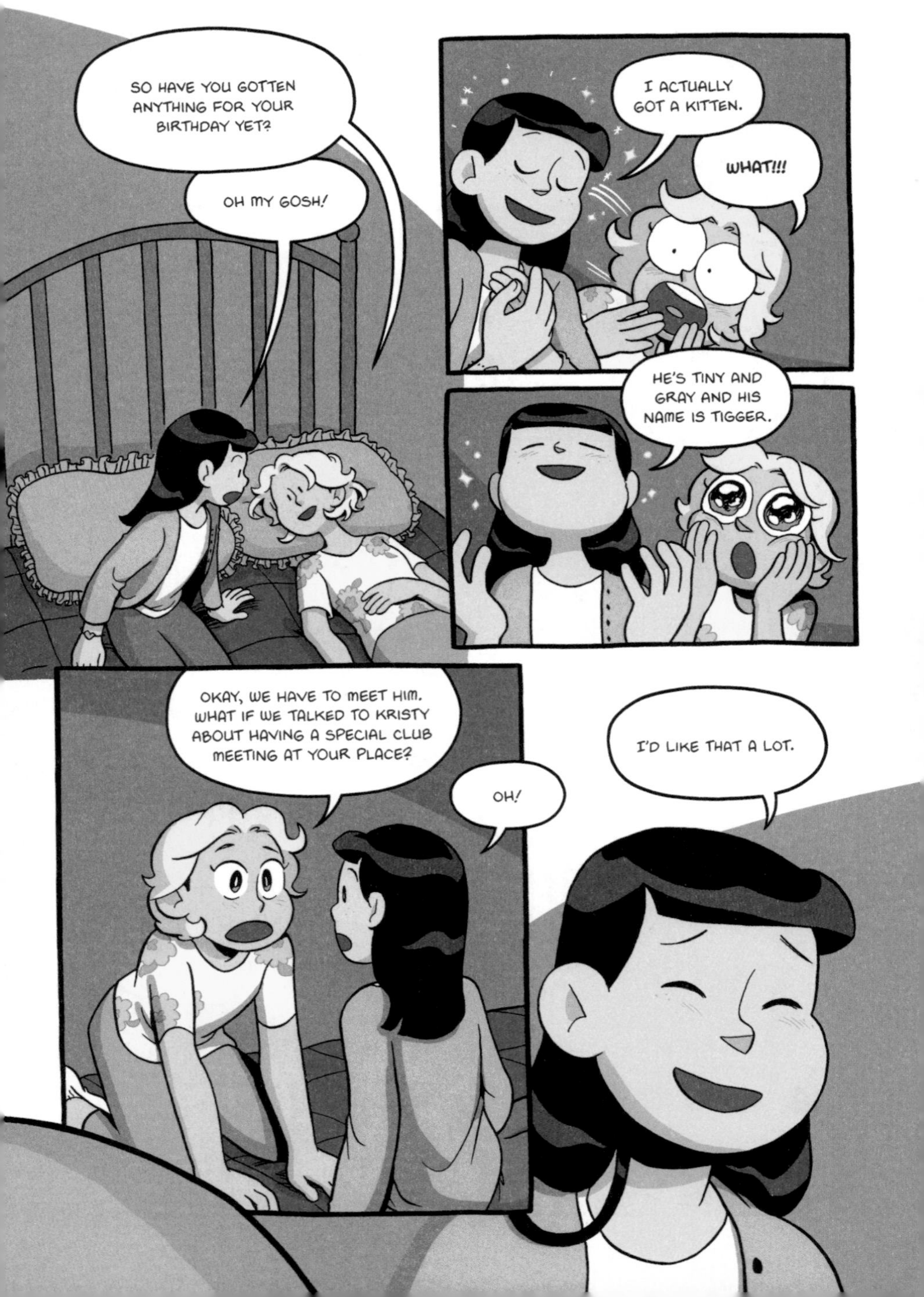
SO HAVE YOU GOTTEN ANYTHING FOR YOUR BIRTHDAY YET?
OH MY GOSH!
I ACTUALLY GOT A KITTEN.
WHAT!!!
HE'S TINY AND GRAY AND HIS NAME IS TIGGER.
OKAY, WE HAVE TO MEET HIM. WHAT IF WE TALKED TO KRISTY ABOUT HAVING A SPECIAL CLUB MEETING AT YOUR PLACE?
OH!
I'D LIKE THAT A LOT.

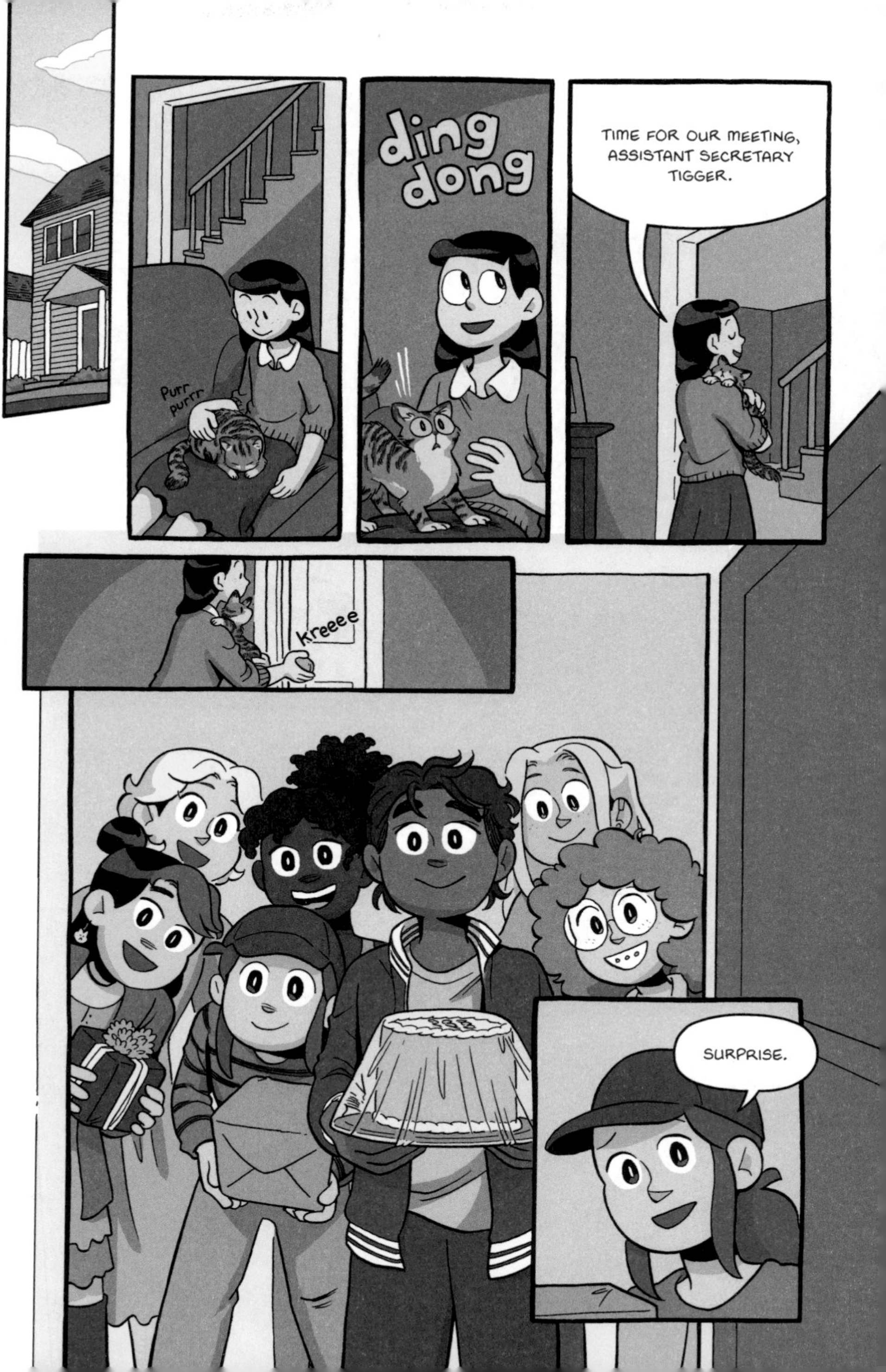
Purr purrr
ding dong
TIME FOR OUR MEETING, ASSISTANT SECRETARY TIGGER.
kreeee
SURPRISE.

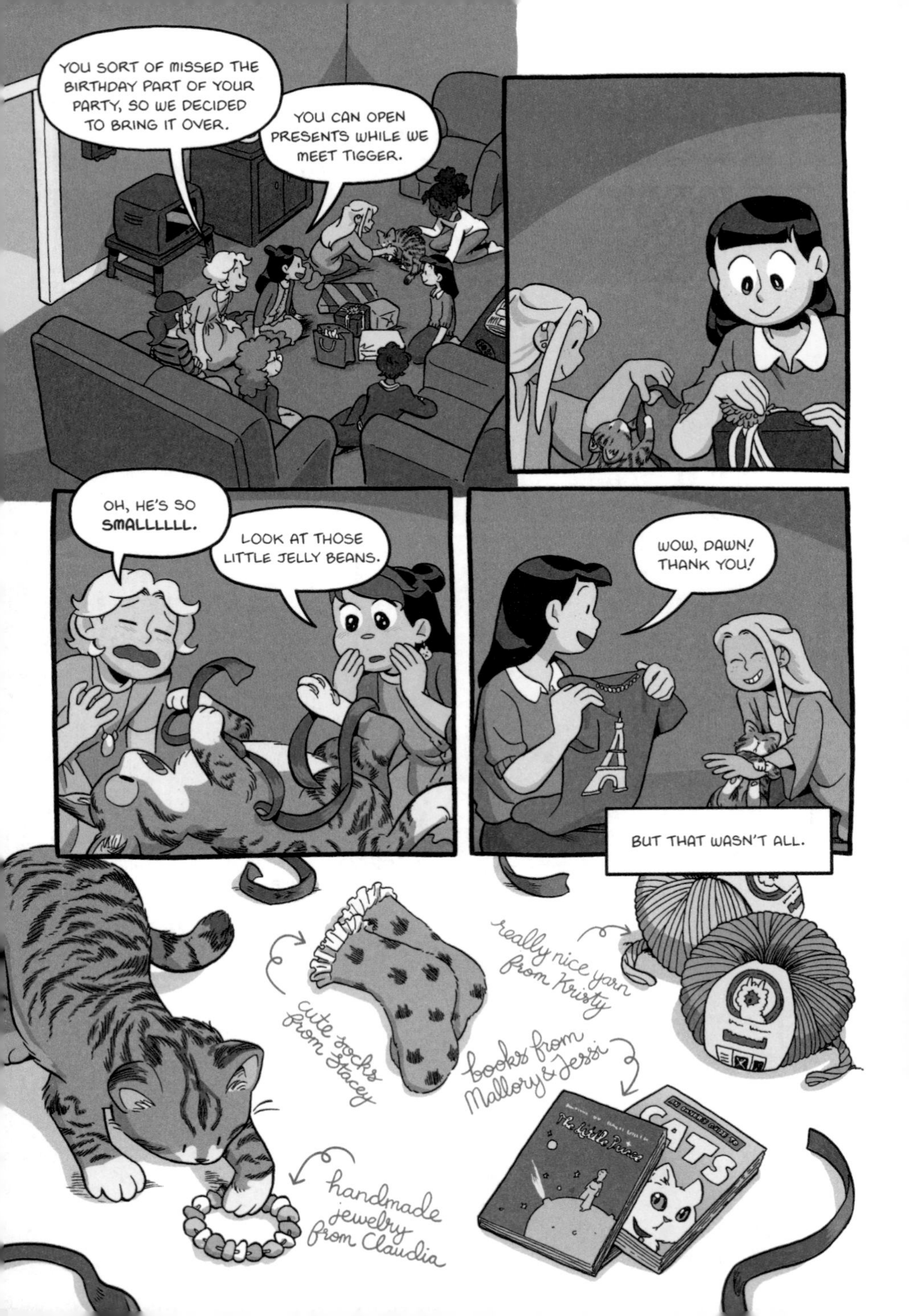
YOU SORT OF MISSED THE BIRTHDAY PART OF YOUR PARTY, SO WE DECIDED TO BRING IT OVER.
YOU CAN OPEN PRESENTS WHILE WE MEET TIGGER.
OH, HE'S SO SMALLLLLLL.
LOOK AT THOSE LITTLE JELLY BEANS.
WOW, DAWN! THANK YOU!
BUT THAT WASN'T ALL.
really nice yarn from Kristy
cute socks from Stacey
books from Mallory & Jessi
The Little Prince
CATS
handmade jewelry from Claudia

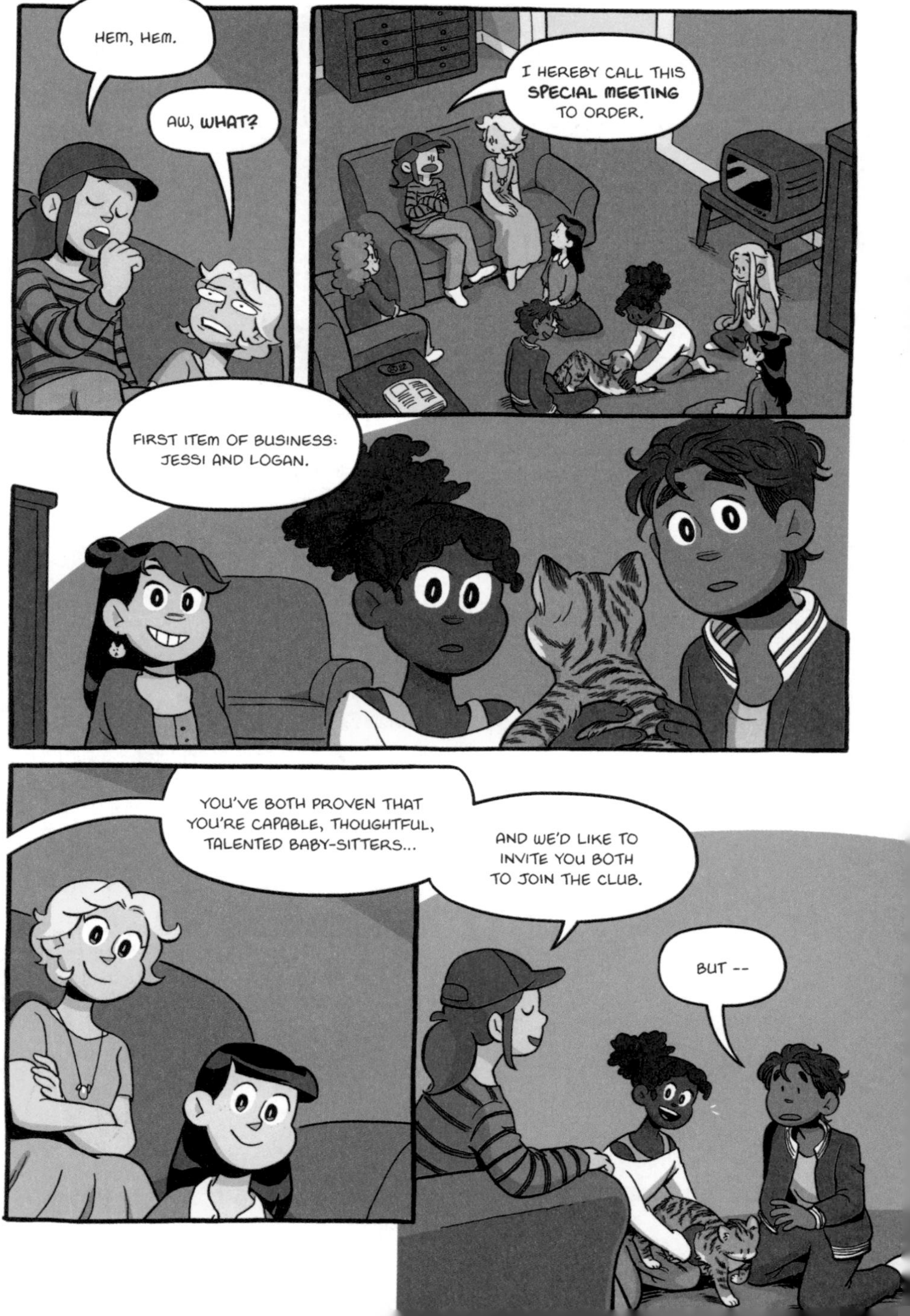
HEM, HEM.
AW, WHAT?
I HEREBY CALL THIS SPECIAL MEETING TO ORDER.
FIRST ITEM OF BUSINESS: JESSI AND LOGAN.
YOU'VE BOTH PROVEN THAT YOU'RE CAPABLE, THOUGHTFUL, TALENTED BABY-SITTERS...
AND WE'D LIKE TO INVITE YOU BOTH TO JOIN THE CLUB.
BUT --

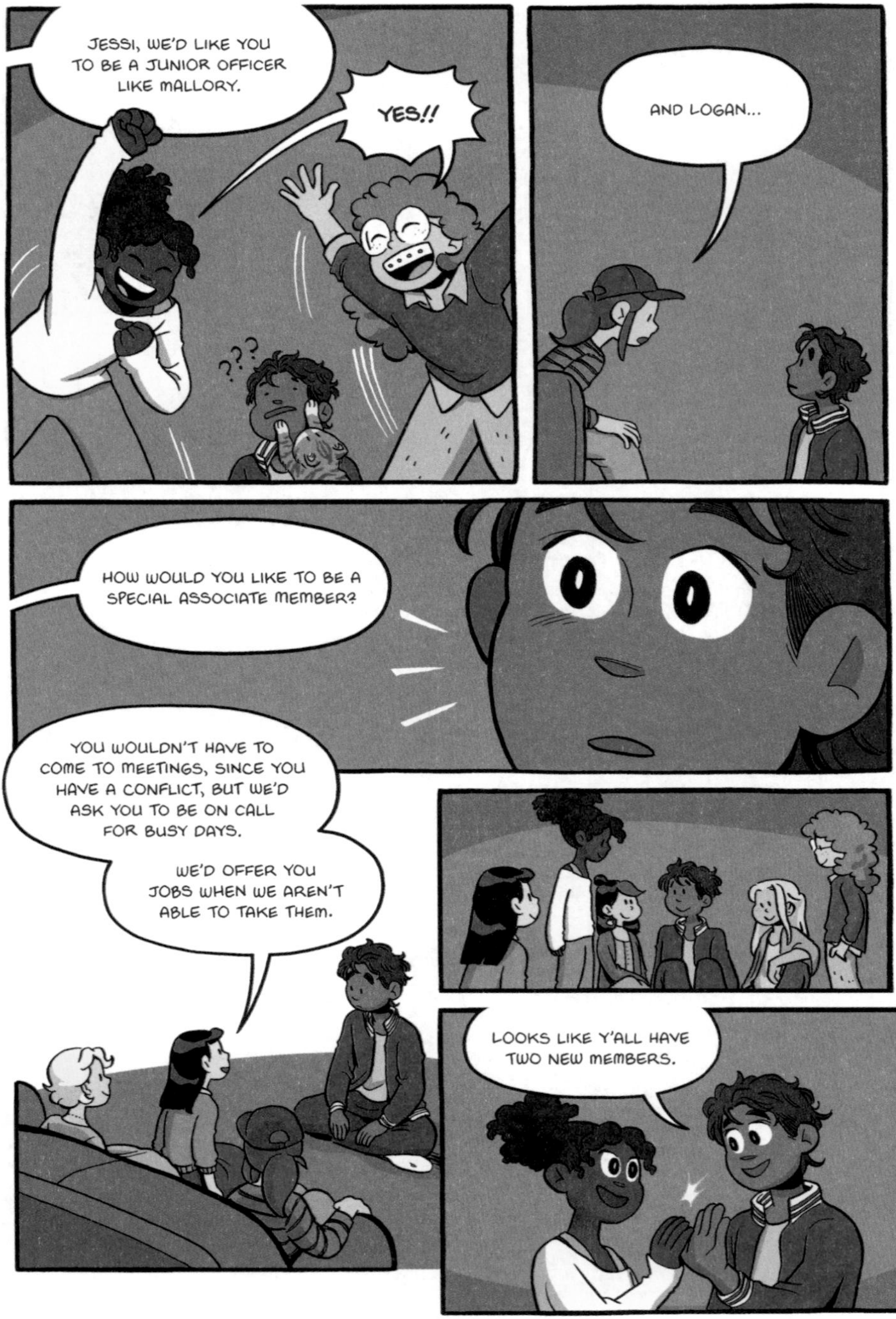
JESSI, WE'D LIKE YOU TO BE A JUNIOR OFFICER LIKE MALLORY.
YES!!
???
AND LOGAN...
HOW WOULD YOU LIKE TO BE A SPECIAL ASSOCIATE MEMBER?
YOU WOULDN'T HAVE TO COME TO MEETINGS, SINCE YOU HAVE A CONFLICT, BUT WE'D ASK YOU TO BE ON CALL FOR BUSY DAYS.
WE'D OFFER YOU JOBS WHEN WE AREN'T ABLE TO TAKE THEM.
LOOKS LIKE Y'ALL HAVE TWO NEW MEMBERS.

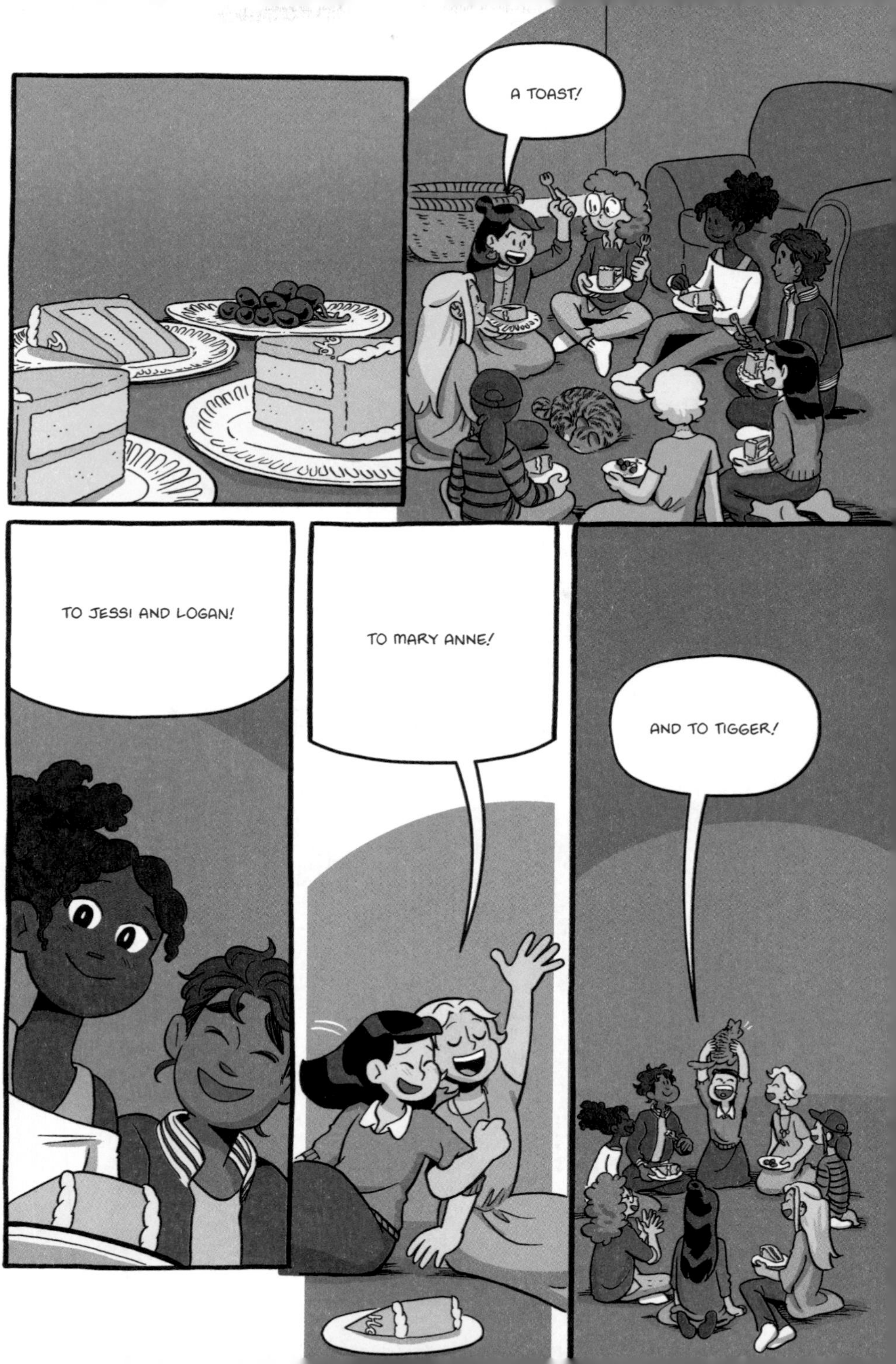
A TOAST!
TO JESSI AND LOGAN!
TO MARY ANNE!
AND TO TIGGER!

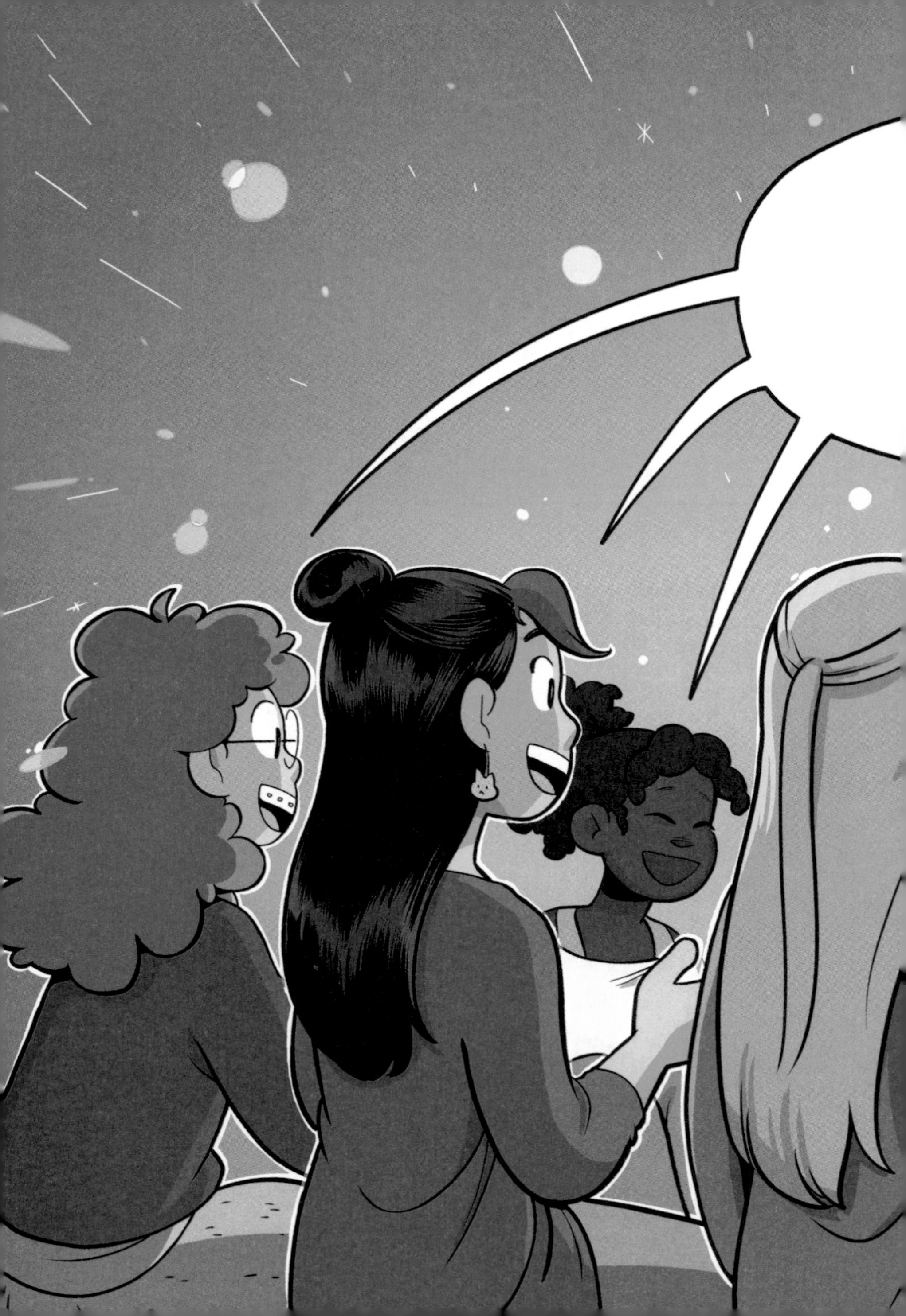

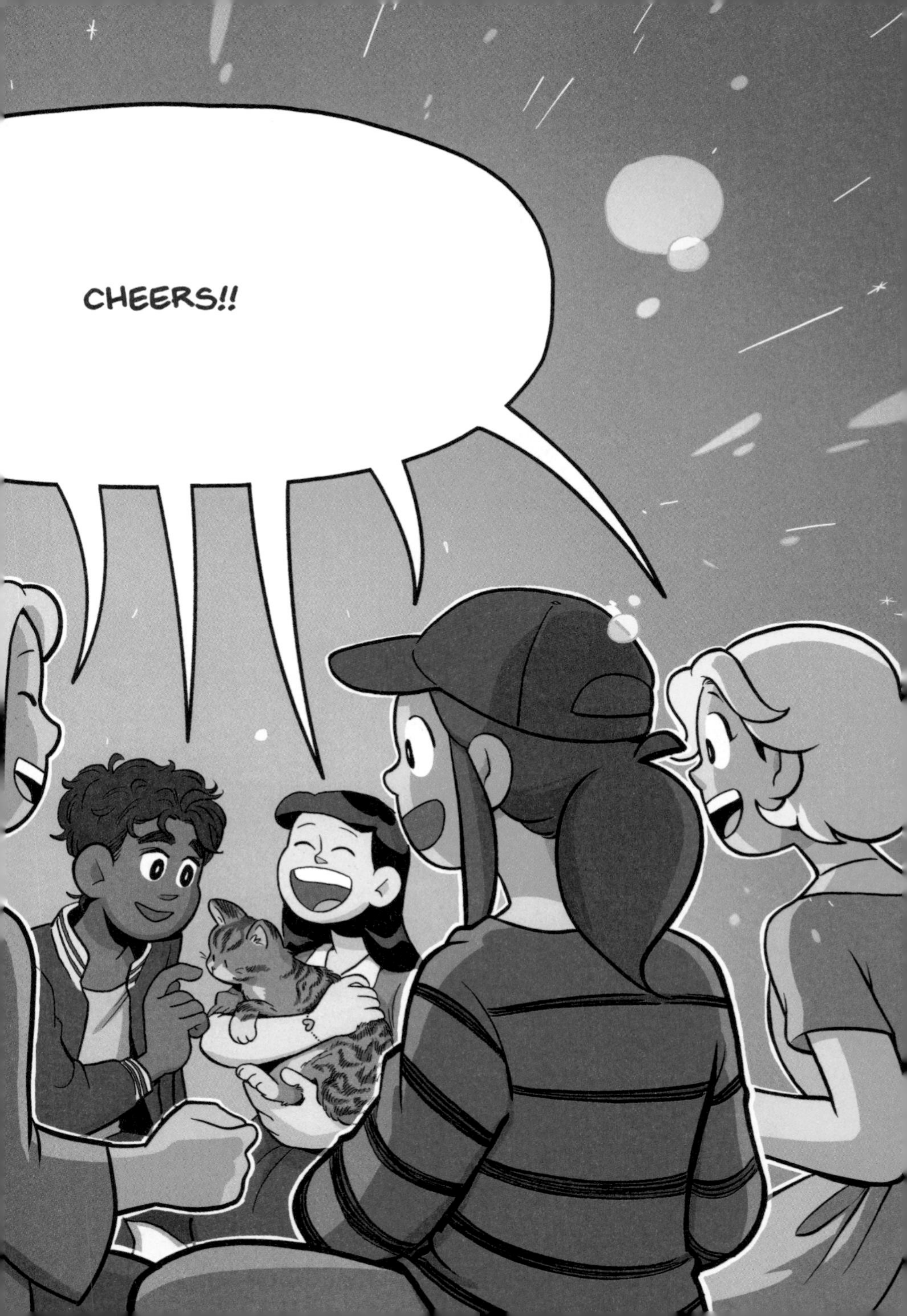
CHEERS!!

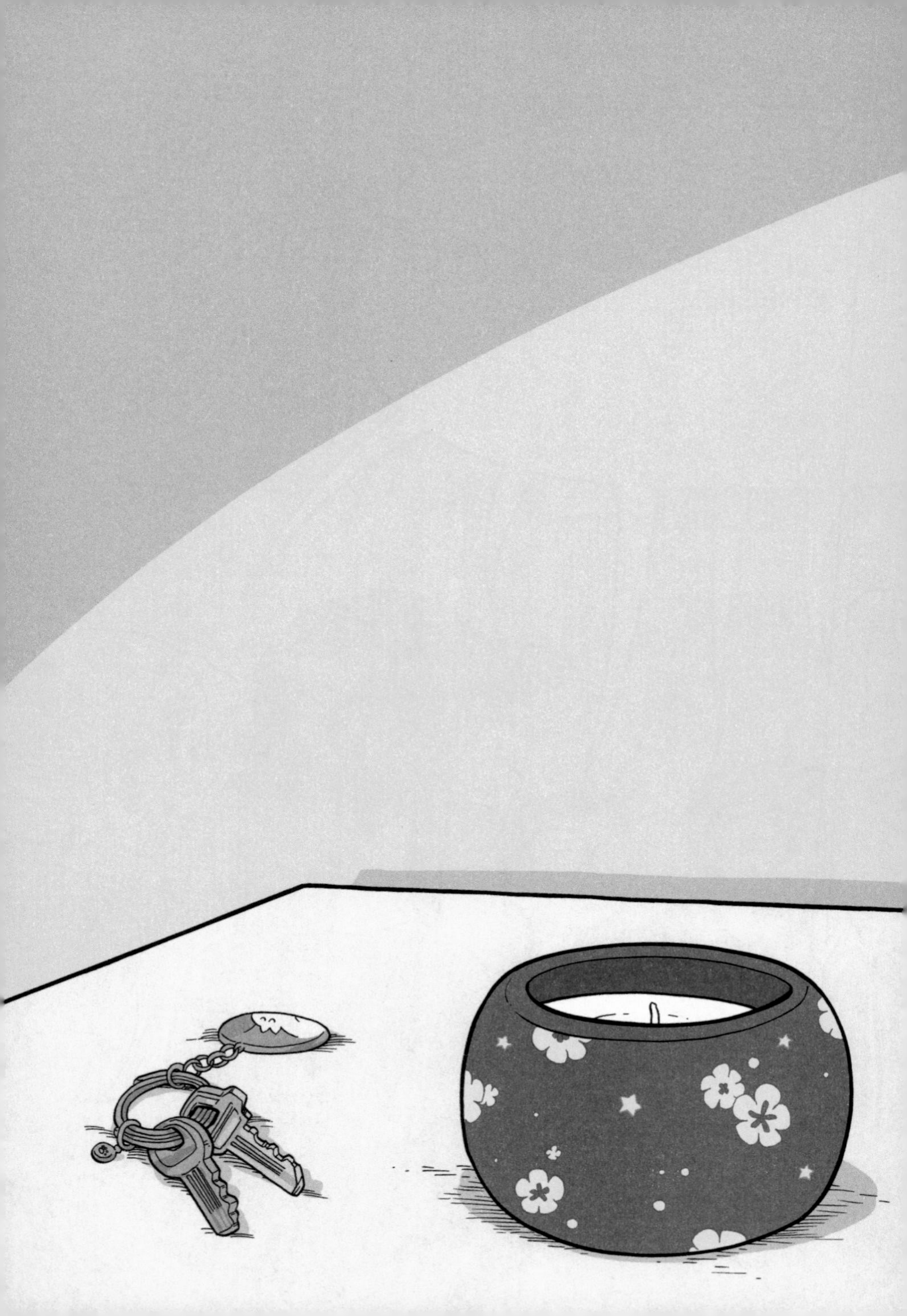

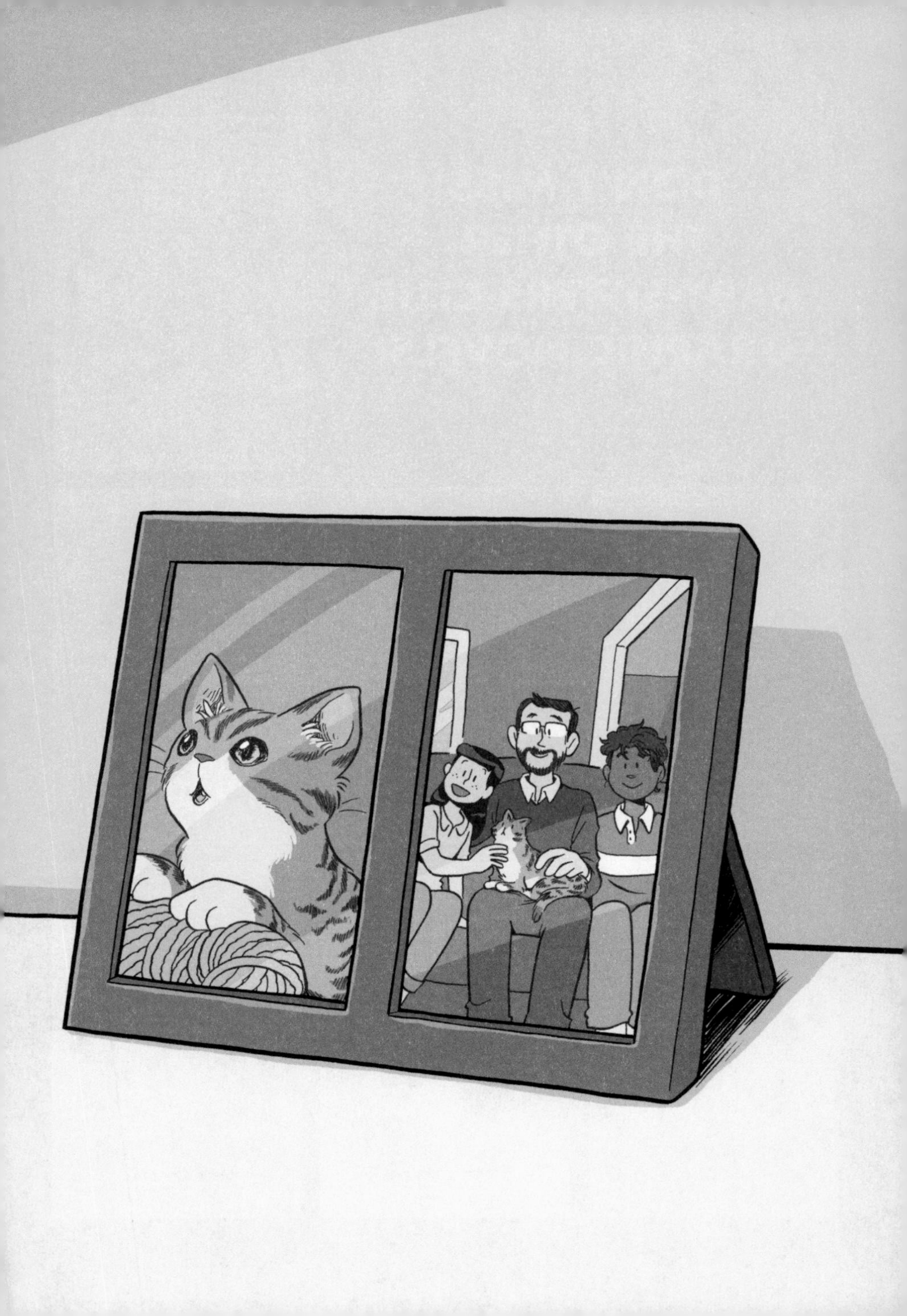

DON'T MISS THE OTHER BABY-SITTERS CLUB GRAPHIC NOVELS!

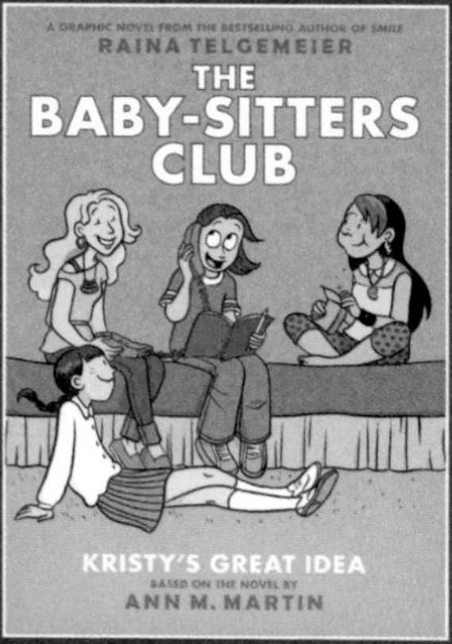
A GRAPHIC NOVEL FROM THE BESTSELLING AUTHOR OF SMILE
RAINA TELGEMEIER
THE BABY-SITTERS CLUB
KRISTY'S GREAT IDEA
BASED ON THE NOVEL BY
ANN M. MARTIN

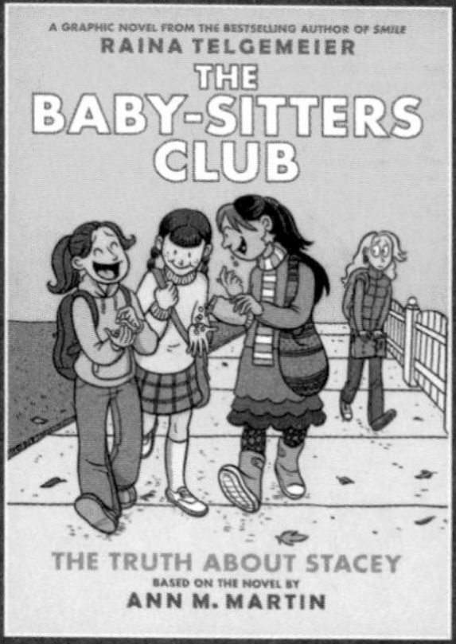
A GRAPHIC NOVEL FROM THE BESTSELLING AUTHOR OF SMILE
RAINA TELGEMEIER
THE BABY-SITTERS CLUB
THE TRUTH ABOUT STACEY
BASED ON THE NOVEL BY
ANN M. MARTIN

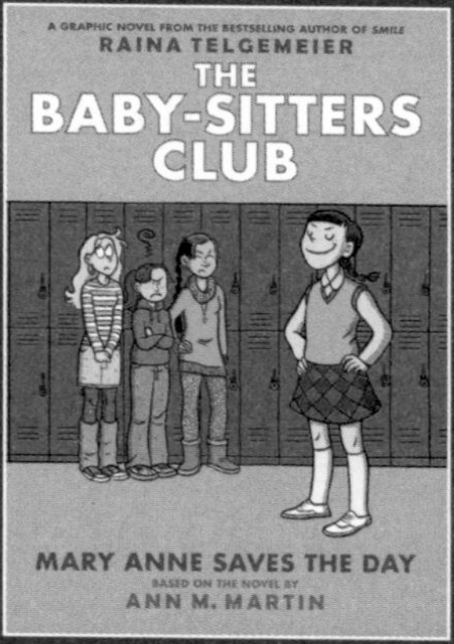
A GRAPHIC NOVEL FROM THE BESTSELLING AUTHOR OF SMILE
RAINA TELGEMEIER
THE BABY-SITTERS CLUB
MARY ANNE SAVES THE DAY
BASED ON THE NOVEL BY
ANN M. MARTIN

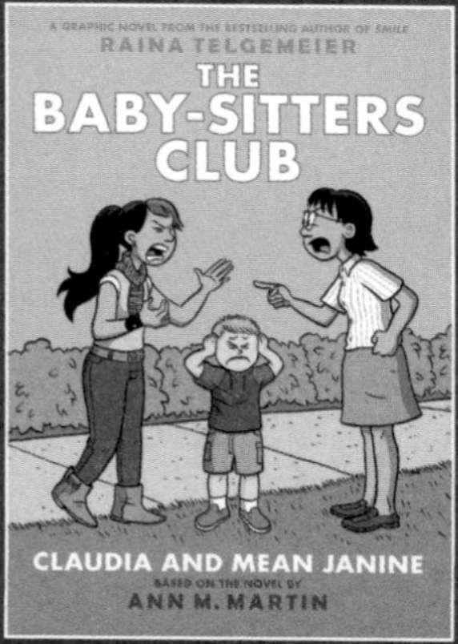
A GRAPHIC NOVEL FROM THE BESTSELLING AUTHOR OF SMILE
RAINA TELGEMEIER
THE BABY-SITTERS CLUB
CLAUDIA AND MEAN JANINE
BASED ON THE NOVEL BY
ANN M. MARTIN

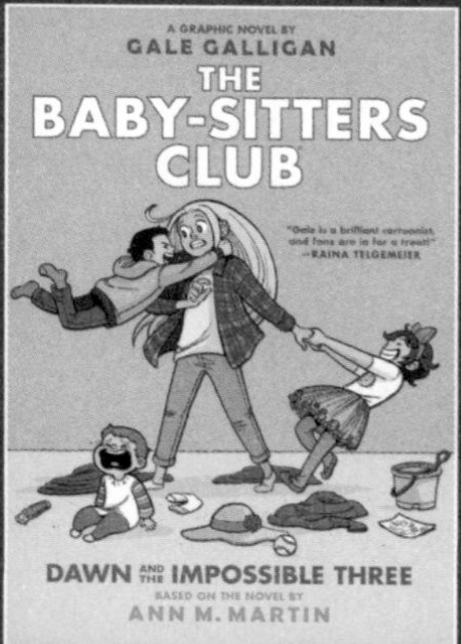
A GRAPHIC NOVEL BY
GALE GALLIGAN
THE BABY-SITTERS CLUB
"Gale is a brilliant cartoonist, and fans are in for a treat!"
—RAINA TELGEMEIER
DAWN AND THE IMPOSSIBLE THREE
BASED ON THE NOVEL BY
ANN M. MARTIN

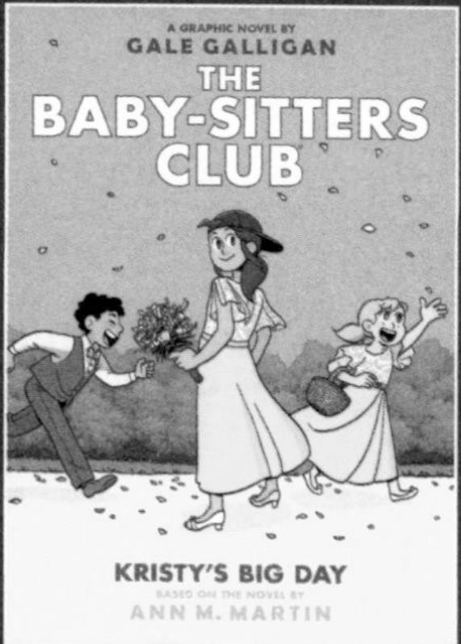
A GRAPHIC NOVEL BY
GALE GALLIGAN
THE BABY-SITTERS CLUB
KRISTY'S BIG DAY
BASED ON THE NOVEL BY
ANN M. MARTIN

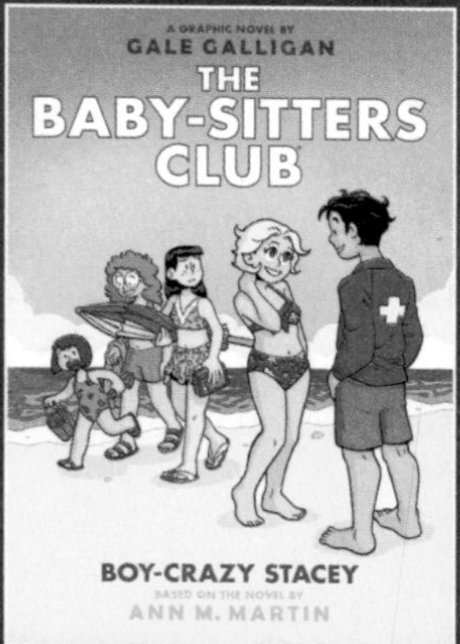
A GRAPHIC NOVEL BY
GALE GALLIGAN
THE BABY-SITTERS CLUB
BOY-CRAZY STACEY
BASED ON THE NOVEL BY
ANN M. MARTIN